MONUMENTAL PROPAGANDA

MONUMENTAL PROPAGANDA

Vladimir Voinovich

Translated by Andrew Bromfield

Alfred A. Knopf   *New York*   2004

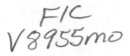

THIS IS A BORZOI BOOK
PUBLISHED BY ALFRED A. KNOPF

Translation copyright © 2004 Alfred A. Knopf

Originally published in Russia as *Monymehtajibhar Nponarahia* by Izographus Eksmo,
Moscow, in 2002. Copyright © 2002 by V. Voinovich. Copyright © 2002 by Izographus.

Library of Congress Cataloging-in-Publication Data
Voinovich, Vladimir, [date]
[Monumental'naia propaganda. English]
Monumental propaganda / Vladimir Voinovich ;
translated by Andrew Bromfield. —1st ed.
p.   cm.
ISBN 0-375-41235-2
I. Bromfield, Andrew. II. Title.
PG3489.4.I53M6313   2004
891.73'44—dc22   2003060476

Manufactured in the United States of America
First American Edition

In loving memory of my wife, Irina

MONUMENTAL PROPAGANDA

PROLOGUE

When I opened the envelope, out fell a newspaper clipping about the size of a matchbox. On it, in a black border of mourning, a group of comrades from the city of Dolgov informed the reader with profound regret of the tragic death of the pensioner Aglaya Stepanovna Revkina, member of the Communist Party of the Soviet Union since 1933, veteran of the Great Patriotic War and outstanding social activist.

I was surprised, thinking that someone must have sent me a text from days long gone. But when I turned over the piece of paper and read "New in the Internet," "Paging Services" and "Tax Inspec" (the end of the word was cut off), I was even more surprised. Who on earth would want to mention membership in the CPSU nowadays?

The anonymous individual who forwarded the notice had evidently expected it would strike a chord with me, and he was right. It was a long time since I had been in Dolgov; I was not aware that Aglaya had attained such an advanced age and found it hard even to imagine her alive in these times. I set out for Dolgov immediately and took up residence in the former Collective Farmers' House, now the Hotel Continental, where I stayed for about two weeks, interviewing various people who knew anything at all about the final years of Aglaya, or Oglashennaya ("the woman possessed") or Ogloedka ("the bone gnawer")—people used to modify her name in various ways, adapting it to suit her character. Her previous biography was well known to me. I had recounted part of it in my past novels *Chonkin* and *The Scheme*. Allow me, without repeating myself unduly, to remind you briefly: When she was a Komsomol member, youthful and

3

ardent, she altered her documents to add five years or more to her age and plunged headlong into the class war. In her leather jacket and with her revolver at her side, she galloped around the local district on her horse, dekulakizing the rich and herding the poor into collective farms. After that she became the manager of the orphanage and married the district Party secretary, Andrei Revkin, whom she was later forced to sacrifice for the sublime cause. When German forces entered Dolgov in the fall of '41, Aglaya blew up the local power station while her husband, who had laid the charges, was still inside. "The motherland will not forget you!" she shouted to him down the phone as she touched the ends of the wires together.

During the war Aglaya Stepanovna commanded a partisan unit, which was awarded two decorations for distinguished service in action. After the war she herself was the district Party secretary until she was "gobbled up" by more predatory comrades. She returned to her prewar place of employment and worked once again as director of the Felix Dzerzhinsky Children's Home, where in February 1956 she was taken unawares by the historical event which provides the starting point of our narrative.

PART ONE

CONSOLIDATION

1

In February 1956, on the day the Twentieth Congress of the CPSU ended, in the Dolgov District House of the Railroad Worker, Khrushchev's secret speech about Stalin's personality cult was read to the local Party core of activists. The reader was the second secretary of the district Party committee, Pyotr Klimovich Porosyaninov, a plump, well-nourished, red-cheeked, bald man with thick, moist ears covered in whitish bristles — his surname, with its obvious resemblance to the Russian word for "piglet," suited him very well. In fact, in Dolgov there were many people with names that had meanings. There was even a period when the town possessed simultaneously a head of police called Tiuryagin (an obvious hint at the word "tiuryaga," or jail), a public prosecutor called Strogii (meaning "strict") with a deputy who rejoiced in the name of Vorovaty ("light-fingered"!), a judge called Shemyakin (reminiscent of the seventeenth-century hanging judge Shemyaka) and a head of the department of public education called Bogdan Filippovich Nechitailo (a surname which could be interpreted to mean "illiterate").

Porosyaninov read slowly, smacking his lips together loudly as though he were eating cherries and spitting out the pits. At the same time, he lisped and stammered over every word, especially if it was a foreign one.

As Porosyaninov read, the core of Party activists listened in silence, their faces tense, their thick necks and the backs of their skulls shorn in semi–crew cuts.

Then they asked the speaker questions: Would there be a purge of the Party? And what should they do with the portraits of Stalin, take them off the walls and rip them out of the books as they had done many times before with former leaders of the Revolution and heroes of the Civil War? Porosyaninov involuntarily turned his head and squinted sidelong at the portrait of Lenin, then shivered and said that no purge was expected and there was no need to go overboard with the portraits. Although a certain number of individual actions taken by Stalin had been incorrect, he was and remained a distinguished member (that was the phrase the speaker used) of our Party and the world communist movement, and no one intended to deny him due recognition for his services.

Aglaya Revkina, who had been through so much in her life, proved to be unprepared for a blow like this. As they were leaving the club, several people heard her declare loudly, without addressing anyone in particular: "Such filth! Such terrible filth!"

Since on that particular evening the street was not covered in filth — in fact, it was cold and there was a blizzard swirling the snow about, so that everything could more accurately have been described as pure white — no one took Aglaya's words literally.

"Yes, yes," said Valentina Semenovna Bochkareva, the planner from the Collective Farm Technical Unit, backing her up. "What people we put our faith in!"

Elena Muravyova (secret-agent alias "Mura") reported this fleeting dialogue to the local department of the Ministry of State Security, and her report was confirmed by Bochkareva herself during an interview of a pro-phylactic nature that was conducted with her.

But Bochkareva had misunderstood Aglaya. Her words about filth had indeed been intended in a figurative sense, and not the one in which Bochkareva had taken them.

When she got home, Aglaya was absolutely beside herself. No, it was not Stalin's crimes but the criticism of him that was what had astounded her most of all. How dare they? How dare they? She walked around all three rooms of her flat, beating her tough little fists against her tough little hips and repeating aloud the same words, addressed to her invisible oppo-nents, over and over again: "How did you dare? Who do you think you are? Who are you to raise your hand against him?"

"And you, disdainful descendants . . ." — Lermontov's line, which she thought she had forgotten long ago, came drifting out from some dark corner of her memory . . .

She had never believed in God, but she would not have been surprised in the least if Porosyaninov's tongue had withered or his nose had fallen off or he had been paralyzed by a stroke in the middle of giving his speech. The words he had uttered in the House of the Railroad Worker had been too absolutely blasphemous.

She had never believed in a God in heaven, but her earthly god was Stalin. His portrait, the famous one with him lighting up his pipe, holding a lighted match close to the slightly singed mustache, had hung over her writing desk since the times before the war, and during the war it had traveled the partisan forest trails with her and then returned to its place. A modest portrait in a simple limewood frame. In moments of doubt over her most startlingly dramatic actions, Aglaya would raise her eyes to the portrait, and Comrade Stalin seemed to screw up his own eyes slightly and urge her on with his kind and wise smile: Yes, Aglaya, you can do that, you must do it, and I believe that you will do it. Yes, she had been forced to make some difficult decisions in her life—harsh, even cruel, decisions concerning various people—but she had done it for the sake of the Party, the country, the people and the future generations. Stalin had taught her that for the sake of the sublime idea it was worth sacrificing everything, and no one could be pitied.

Of course, she respected the other leaders as well, the members of the Politburo and the secretaries of the Central Committee, but nonetheless she thought of them as just people. Very clever and bold, utterly devoted to our ideals, but people. They could make mistakes in their thoughts, words and actions, but only he was ineffably great and infallible, and his every word and every action expressed such transcendent genius that his contemporaries and the generations to come should accept them as unconditionally correct and absolutely binding.

2

A large statue of Stalin stood in the center of Dolgov on Stalin Square, formerly Cathedral Square, formerly the Square of the Fallen. It had been erected in 1949 in honor of Stalin's seventieth birthday, on her—that is, Aglaya's—initiative. At that time Aglaya was the first secretary of the district Party committee, but even she had been forced to overcome opposition. Everyone understood what great educational importance the monument could have, and no one dared oppose it directly, but secret enemies of the people and demagogues had raised their heads to object, citing the present state of postwar devastation. They incessantly reminded everyone that the district suffered delays and irregularities in deliveries of foodstuffs, that the people were destitute and swollen-bellied from hunger and the time was not yet right for grandiose projects that were too great a burden on the local budget.

One of the monument's main opponents had been Wilhelm Leopoldovich Livshits, editor-in-chief of the newspaper *Bolshevik Tempos.* He wrote an article called "Bronze Before Bread" and published it in his newspaper. In it he stated that monumental propaganda was, of course, a matter of great importance—Lenin himself had emphasized that it was a matter of great importance—but did we have the moral right today to spend so much money on a monument when our people were suffering? "Just whose 'ours' and 'yours' are these?" Aglaya inquired in a letter to the editor, in which she also explained that our Russian people are long-suffering, they would tighten their belts still further, they would suffer in the short term, but the monument erected by them would endure forever. In his reply Livshits informed her that all of us have only one people, the Soviet people, and that the monument was indeed essential, but it could be erected later, when the economic situation in the district and the country as a whole improved. He even had the effrontery to enlist Stalin himself as one of his allies. According to Livshits, Stalin, being wise and modest, would not have approved such prodigal expenditure at an hour of such great difficulty for the Motherland.

Of course, that was demagoguery. Livshits undoubtedly knew, as everyone knew—only one did not say it out loud—that the economic situation would only be easy under communism. Well then, were we supposed to just sit back and not build anything, neither saw nor sew nor plane nor forge nor sculpt until the advent of communism? Perhaps that was what the rootless and tribeless cosmopolitan Livshits was counting on? But he had miscalculated. Soon thereafter he had been exposed as involved with the international organization of Zionists and spies known as Joint and suffered the well-deserved penalty. In the quiet hour before dawn one of the automobiles popularly known as a "black raven" or "black Marusya" had pulled up at the Livshits' house and removed the self-appointed representative of the people to a place far distant from the city of Dolgov.

Livshits was not alone. Others may have expressed their opinions less openly, but they had also dropped hints.

Having overcome the resistance, Aglaya had her way and erected the monument—although it wasn't actually bronze, as had been anticipated at the beginning, but cast iron. Because the railway wagon with the bronze, having left the city of Yuzhnouralsk one fine day, never arrived at the city of Dolgov. (Where it did arrive remains a mystery even now.) This delighted certain spiteful faultfinders. Perhaps it also delighted Wilhelm Leopoldovich Livshits as he squatted on his prison toilet, but his delight was premature. Aglaya's enemies knew her well, but not well enough. They had underestimated her will to victory and failed to appreciate that she never retreated from her chosen goal. She went to Moscow, consulted the sculptor Max Ogorodov and commissioned him to forge the statue out of cast iron.

3

Stalin was seventy years old on Wednesday, December 21, 1949.

Aglaya remembered for the rest of her life that dark, frosty, misty morning, the granite pedestal and the figure swathed in white canvas wrapped around with string.

A gusty wind flapped the edges of the canvas in the air and swirled the dry gray snow across the square in a low, thin, shifting layer. Although it was a workday, the entire district leadership had turned up—men in identical dark coats and deerskin caps—and Aglaya had covered her own head with a light Orenburg shawl. And in addition, the regional Party secretary, Gennadii Kuzhelnikov, had arrived, wearing a woolen cloth coat with a padded lining and an astrakhan collar, and boots with galoshes from the Red Triangle factory. The head of the district Ministry of State Security office, Ivan Kuzmich Dyrokhvost, stood out in his fur-lined leather coat and peaked leather cap. The chairmen of the collective farms were all to a man rosy-cheeked and red-nosed, wearing sheepskin coats, sheepskin caps and felt boots. Also present, naturally, was the monument's creator, the sculptor Ogorodov, who had delivered himself from Moscow to the venue for the occasion in a thin autumn coat and a red scarf, with a dark blue velvet beret set on his head at a jaunty angle and patent-leather shoes entirely unsuited to the prevailing weather conditions. Ogorodov had also brought his wife Zinaida with him.

Zinaida is unlikely to play too important a part in our narrative, but since she has found her way into these pages, let us note that she was a plump, domineering woman four years older than Ogorodov, that she possessed a voice rendered hoarse by smoking and was foul-mouthed to a degree encountered less frequently in those chaste times than nowadays.

She had found Ogorodov on a garbage heap before the war. That was what she said herself. In actual fact, it was not a garbage heap, but a hall of residence in Malakhovka, where he was living in absolute obscurity as a student, having arrived in Moscow from Kostroma or Kaluga. The appearance he presented was downtrodden, to say the least. He was barely surviving on bread and water from one student grant payment to the next, his only property being what he stood up in, what was in his suitcase, and the suitcase itself, made of plywood covered with glossy green paint, something like an ammunition box with a handle made of bent wire five millimeters thick.

Zinaida had taken the future sculptor home to the communal flat where she lived with her ancient and querulous mother, washed him off, cleaned him up and begun to live with him. They had survived the poverty of his student years together. At that time Ogorodov used to fashion clay whistles in the shape of cocks, wolves, bears and hares and bake them in the oven, and she used to sell them at the Tishinsky market. There was no question of any other kind of sculpture—what would he have made? Where, from what and for whom? But then when he came back from the war with four medals, with a red stripe on his sleeve for having been slightly wounded and a "Guards" badge, Zinaida began promoting him everywhere as a combat veteran, a hero and a genius. By dexterously exploiting his services to the country, she opened doors and made essential contacts but never overstepped the mark (or if she did, it was only in exceptional circumstances, for the good of the cause). She managed to get Ogorodov membership in the Union of Artists, with a separate studio and an apartment in a wooden house. Heated by a woodstove, but with no one else sharing it. She did everything for him, and he himself would confess, especially when he was a bit under the influence: "Zinka, my precious, I'd never have made it without you."

Zinaida made sure that her husband was always neatly dressed, but with that certain license appropriate for an artist. She herself sewed him the wide flannelette shirts and trousers and the velvet berets in which, as she thought, he resembled Rembrandt. She cooked fish dishes, believing fish contained a lot of phosphorous, which helped to enhance the intellect, talent and male potency. Eventually, Max acquired more or less tolerable working conditions, and in these conditions he was intending to fashion cocks and bears on an even grander scale, but that was when Zinaida had directed his efforts toward new goals and told him that now he must fashion leaders.

Naturally enough, of all the leaders, Max chose Stalin, and soon he became very successful at manufacturing statues of the great man.

4

The group of people who were gathered, stamping their feet, below the pedestal were at one and the same time participants in the ceremony and its audience. Because of the inclement weather there were no other onlookers, and those who had turned out looked as though they were waiting impatiently to rush through the burial of a poor relative rather than engaging in a solemn political ceremony of state importance.

The monument was unveiled by Aglaya Stepanovna in person. The small number of witnesses later recalled her speech as being precise and firm, without the slightest sign of nervousness, although, of course, she was nervous.

"Comrades," she began in a voice made hoarse by a cold and the effects of smoking, and rubbed her frozen nose, "today the entire Soviet people and the whole of progressive mankind is celebrating the glorious jubilee of our very greatest contemporary, the wise leader, the teacher of the peoples, the luminary of all the sciences, the outstanding military leader, our own dearest beloved Comrade Stalin."

As she spoke, the gathered public applauded in a habitual manner, reacting to the key words. She briefly explained to her listeners what they already knew, having learned it in their weekly political study sessions. She retold the life of the great leader, recalling the facts of his difficult childhood, his early participation in the revolutionary movement, his role in the Civil War, collectivization, industrialization, the liquidation of the kulaks, the crushing of the opposition and, finally, the historic victory over German fascism.

She managed to convey in a few words the idea of the exceptional usefulness and necessity, especially in our days, of all forms of propaganda, and in particular of large-scale, monumental visual propaganda designed to endure through the ages. This monument, she said, which had been erected despite the opposition of our enemies, would stand here for thousands of years, inspiring future builders of communism to new feats of heroism.

Gennadii Kuzhelnikov took note of this phrase. What does she mean by that? he thought. That the Soviet people will be building communism for another thousand years? A stupid slip of the tongue or an act of sabotage? He had not even finished thinking his thought when Aglaya declared the monument open and handed him a large pair of shears like the ones used for clipping sheep. Kuzhelnikov took the shears without removing his gloves, brought the blades together and the ends of the string flew apart, fluttering in the wind. The cover was pulled off with great difficulty, because it had inflated like a parachute and kept tearing itself out of their hands. But when they did finally manage to subdue it, the participants in the event took a few short steps backward, looked up at the monument, gasped in a single breath and froze on the spot.

None of these people, except for Ogorodov and Zinaida, had the slightest idea about any kind of art, especially about sculpture, but even they could see that they had before them not simply a statue but something quite extraordinary. Stalin was sculpted in full dress uniform with the shoulder straps of a generalissimo, his uniform coat parted slightly to reveal his military jacket and decorations, with his right hand quite obviously raised in greeting to the masses of the people as they passed by, and his left hand lowered, clutching his gloves.

Stalin looked at the people gathered there as though he were alive. He gazed down on them, grinning mysteriously into his mustache, and everyone thought they saw him actually wave his right hand and move his left, smacking the gloves against his knee.

At first Max Ogorodov couldn't believe his own eyes, and when he did, he opened his mouth wide and froze with an expression on his face that can only be called idiotic, as if he himself had been instantly transformed into cast iron.

In recent years he had sculpted Stalin, only Stalin and nobody but Stalin, but he had sculpted every possible aspect of him: Stalin's head, Stalin's bust, Stalin full length, Stalin standing and sitting (lying was the only position he hadn't sculpted), in a field jacket, in a high-collared tunic, in a long-skirted cavalry greatcoat and in the uniform of a generalissimo. He had eventually grown so skillful at his work that he could fashion Iosif Vissarionovich with his own eyes closed.

The authorities had given him their seal of approval as a truly fine artist who had completely mastered the method of socialist realism. They valued him and held him up as an example to others, encouraging and supporting him by moral, material and combined means, rewarding him with positions, decorations, bonuses, adulatory articles in the newspapers, the inclusion of his name in the encyclopedia, in the lists of the great modern masters and the lists of recipients of various food products that were in short supply. But his colleagues regarded him as a confirmed second-rater, a cold mechanical artisan, even a hack, and in general whenever his name came up, they said, "Oh him!" And they would gesture dismissively, never suspecting that he had any divine spark in him and thinking that he knew his own worth well enough, and was only concerned to tend his own petty affairs without hankering after an exalted position in art. And that was their big mistake. In actual fact, while well aware that he produced rubbish, the sculptor Ogorodov did hanker after an exalted position, perhaps even one on Mount Olympus itself, and every time he fashioned yet another Stalin he didn't just churn it out, he strove to create, weaving spells and performing entire religious rites. Each time, he made slight changes to the bearing, the inclination of the head, the narrowing of the eyes and the pressure of the closed lips. As he added the final touches, he would run a long way back, then run up close, sometimes shutting his eyes and making a dent somewhere on a sudden intuition, squeezing up, drawing in and retouching with his fingernail in the insane hope that a miracle would occur through some chance accident. Then he would run away and back again and breathe on his creation through his hands folded into a tube—perhaps it might have seemed funny to an outsider, but he was trying to breathe a soul into his creation! But yet again the creation would turn out lifeless—it had no mystery, no wonder. Ogorodov suffered, sometimes he even wept, tugging at his sparse hair, hammering his fists against his head and calling himself a talentless hack, but he was wrong: a talentless hack is a man who is unaware of his own lack of talent.

While this sculpture was in the studio, Ogorodov had thought that it too was ordinary, but now, elevated on its pedestal (so that was what had been lacking!), it had come to life and gazed down in mocking triumph on all of them and its own creator with an expression that seemed somehow insolent, even suggesting that it had created itself.

"My God! My God!" muttered the astounded creator, his eyes fixed on the statue. But it's alive, really alive, isn't it? he asked himself, amazed that he hadn't noticed it before.

"Calm down!" Zinaida told her husband quietly but firmly, sticking a coarse cigarette with an icicle dangling from its frozen cardboard tube into her mouth.

"No," said Ogorodov, without making it clear what he was rejecting, then he reached out his arms to his creation and shouted: "Hey!" And then again: "Hey! Hey!"

"Who are you yelling at?" Kuzhelnikov asked in arrogant amazement.

"Not you," said Ogorodov, dismissing the other's elevated rank out of hand. And he called out again: "Hey! Hey! Hey!"

Astounded, the people standing beside Ogorodov drew away from him just in case he might be crazy, and he stepped toward the monument with his arms raised aloft in passion and shouted to it: "Hey, say something!"

Of course, he was not the first sculptor to address such a request to his own work. Long before his time the great Michelangelo had asked the same thing of the Moses he had created. But the people gathered in the square, unsuspecting of any plagiarism, exchanged glances, some of them in fact suspecting—respectfully, of course—that perhaps the sculptor was not quite all there: after all, he was an artist. However, the poet Serafim Butylko approached his brother in art, clapped him on the shoulder and, breathing out fumes of stale alcohol, garlic and rotten teeth, said in a respectful tone: "That's right, he is almost alive."

"Nonsense!" the sculptor protested in a whisper. "What do you mean, 'almost'? He isn't almost alive—he is alive. Just look, he's watching, he's breathing and there's steam coming out of his mouth!"

This was a quite absurd assertion. The iron lips of the sculpture were clamped firmly shut; there was no steam emerging from between them. And there could not be. Perhaps there might just have been a chance eddy of snow in some surface irregularities. But be that as it may, not only the sculptor but everyone else thought they really did see something swirling in the air beneath the iron mustache.

While Ogorodov shouted incoherently, his wife Zinaida was once again chewing on her extinguished cigarette as she contemplated her immediate future. She had doggedly promoted Ogorodov's career, foreseeing even as she did so that if he should really become famous and fashionable, he would be swamped by predatory young female admirers and in the subsequent havoc the position of the faded wife would immediately become untenable. But Ogorodov failed to notice his wife's emotional turmoil: he tugged off his beret, threw it under his feet and with a cry of "I have vindicated my life!" began trampling the poor rag as furiously as if it were to blame for his not having vindicated his life sooner. "Vindicated, vindicated, vindicated my life!" he carried on bellowing, not understanding that life is given to us just as it is, without any obligations attached, and there is no necessity to vindicate it in any particularly cumbersome fashion.

He carried on trampling his beret until the wind, taking pity on the miserable rag, snatched it away from Ogorodov and bore it off into the frosty gloom, and Ogorodov, his balding head exposed to the elements, once again raised his hands toward the monument and implored it: "Tell me you're alive! Prove it, move, give me a sign. Can you hear me or can't you?"

And then something happened that is very rare during the winter season: somewhere in the distance there was a low rumble of thunder, as though a cart had rolled along a cobbled street.

The comrades standing behind Ogorodov were all without exception dyed-in-the-wool materialists and none of them officially believed in either the Supreme Providence or the powers of darkness, but the stronger their official nonbelief, the more they suspected that both of the aforementioned did exist. And so they all flinched instinctively at the sound of thunder, and those at the front stepped back, treading on those behind them, and the lightning that then flashed across the winter sky without any sound of thunder at all left the gathered company absolutely dumbstruck. When the lightning flashed, the eyes of the cast-iron generalissimo lit up with a greedy orange flame that lingered in his eyeballs and faded slowly, as though it were being drawn inward. At this point several participants in the ceremony were overcome by an inexplicable fear, and they involuntarily recalled their transgressions against their wives, their motherland, their Party and Comrade Stalin in person. Remembering the embezzlements, the bribes and the unpaid Party membership dues, they found themselves frozen to the spot, mesmerized by the thought of possible retribution. When this stupefaction began to release its grip, Serafim Butylko spoke up again. In an attempt to raise his own spirits and everyone else's, he remarked that things still occasionally happened in nature that science was unable to explain.

"Yes," regional Party committee secretary Kuzhelnikov replied significantly, "certain inexplicable things do happen in certain districts." And he shuffled off in his galoshes in the direction of his waiting Pobeda automobile, leaving the participants in the event to ponder what his remark might have meant and what he had been hinting at. That the district was not among the most exemplary? But what had natural phenomena to do with that? A natural phenomenon decides for itself where to manifest itself, without applying to the district Party organs to stamp its papers. Nonetheless, their top Party boss had expressed dissatisfaction, and his subordinates realized there would be personnel changes in prospect, a thought that troubled some of those gathered there and inspired hope in others. And a struggle began, as they used to say in those days, between the good and the better, as a result of which Aglaya was replaced in her responsible post by a certain Vasilii Sidorovich Nechaev, who had previously worked as the Party organizer at the creamery. And Aglaya was transferred, as we have already mentioned, to the children's home, to nurture the coming generation.

5

An abundance of poets is a sign of a people's savagery.

At least that was the opinion of my oldest friend, Alexei Mikhailovich Makarov, nicknamed the Admiral, concerning whom we shall speak later. When he said it the first time, his assertion seemed ridiculous to me, but then he listed the countries and the regions of the world where people were wallowing in poverty and ignorance, some not even knowing what electricity or toilet paper were, and yet they had among them an immense number of bards, minstrels and other varieties of folk or court poets. The authorities there regard the state of the poetic word with anxious concern and good poets (who write good words about the authorities) are generously rewarded with all sorts of good things, whereas bad poets (who write bad words about the authorities) have their heads cut off. The risk of being left without a head can act as such a powerful stimulus to the mind that on occasion bad poets write much better poetry than good poets and people copy the poems of bad poets into notebooks, learn them by heart and transmit them from one generation to the next.

Although in Dolgov the education of poets was conducted in accordance with a less extreme system (their heads were not cut off, but their lives were made a misery), the number of versifiers per head of the local population was clearly in excess of essential requirements. In the late forties the most famous and prominent among them was, of course, our past master and local sage Serafim Butylko, but he was already growing old and antiquated in every sense. He had lost his six upper front teeth and turned gray, he dragged his feet and stooped, his control of metaphor was weak, he was unable to sustain a regular meter and he used weary, banal rhymes: "love—dove," "folk—awoke," "desire—perspire," "hurry—flurry." And this at a time when the young generation was boldly mastering word-root rhymes—assonant, dissonant, complex and God knows what other kinds of rhymes—such as "empower—yell louder," "birchtree—lurching free," "attributes—hard rebukes," "forest thickets—foreign critics," as well as quite mind-boggling images and metaphors. Our most sophisticated and versatile writer was Vlad Raspadov—poet, art historian, essayist, journalist and generally multitalented artist of the word. In 1949, when he was still an eighth-grade schoolboy, he wrote a composition dedicated to the monument. The piece was written as a school essay, but it was so interesting that it was published in the *Dolgov Pravda*. This essay was called . . . Actually, I can't quite recall just at the moment . . . Either "A Melody Frozen in Metal," or "Music Congealed in Cast Iron." Something of that sort. It was a very vivid and graphic article, with a profound subtext. In speaking of the sculptor Ogorodov's creation, it said that it could not have been what it was were it not for the miraculous combination of the artist's talent and his genuine love for the prototype, which had fused into a single unity. "Gazing upon this marvel," Raspadov wrote, "it is hard to imagine that it was molded or carved or manufactured in any physical fashion at all. No, this is simply a song that has broken free, that has been breathed out from the sculptor's soul and frozen in human form to our wonder and amazement."

Raspadov's article, although it was not entirely correct from the viewpoint of socialist realism, impressed the readers and pleased the ideological authorities, and after reading it Pyotr Klimovich Porosyaninov said of Raspadov: "Yes, he's one of us!" Then he thought for a moment and repeated it: "One of us!"

As for Max Ogorodov, having created such an absolute masterpiece, he became extremely famous, won many state commissions and a Stalin Prize, Third Class, then Second Class, and then First Class, and soon changed his wife Zinaida, just as she had feared, for a new wife, First Class, who was eighteen years younger. And of course, he became very conceited. In his newfound conceit he claimed that he had surpassed all of his contemporaries in sculpture, even Tomsky and Konyonkov. And the only sculptors of the past he acknowledged as his equals were Myron, Praxiteles, Michelangelo and to some extent Rodin.

We will not attempt to deny that the miracle created by Ogorodov was a genuine miracle. It inspired awe and amazement in even the most worldly, distrustful and jealous connoisseurs of art. Scholars of art history made the journey to Dolgov especially, not only in eager anticipation of the twenty-six rubles a day travel allowance, but out of a genuine desire to be convinced by seeing it with their own eyes. One of them, having been convinced, took a handkerchief out of his pocket, dabbed his eyes with it and said: "That's it! Now I can die." And no one felt this response was oversentimental. Everyone could see that the monument really did radiate a mysterious power that distinguished it from other similar works. It stood in the middle of the square, on which streets large and small converged from every side. But previously they had simply met here as the accidental consequence of centuries of chaotic town planning. Whereas now every individual could sense physically that these streets and side streets were drawn here by the exceptionally powerful magnetism emanating from the monument, which was itself the natural focus of the town and, more than that, the center without which the town could not function, like a wheel without an axle. It was impossible for anyone who visited Dolgov in those days to imagine how the town could possibly have existed for all those hundreds of years without this statue.

Crowds of people, both locals and people passing through, came to look at the statue and noted the fact that, whichever side of the statue a person stood on—right or left—the cast-iron chief was looking at him, and even a person approaching the statue from behind had the feeling that it could actually see him with its back. Moreover, the iron man's direct gaze instilled in all comers an incomprehensible fear that expanded into icy terror. And this applied not only to humans but also to animals of a lower order. Even the pigeons did not sit on the iron peaked cap, although its upper surface was round and flat, most convenient for taking off, landing and performing other functions natural to birds. And in addition (though this is a mere detail) the statue was never attacked by rust.

The fame of the sculptor Ogorodov's exceptional creation spread far and wide, and one day an influential member of the Politburo came to Dolgov specially to see whether it would be worth transferring the monumental masterpiece to Moscow. Upon arriving in the square accompanied by Kuzhelnikov and looking at the statue, he also experienced quite evident agitation, and when he recovered, he said: "We don't want any of that!" And once again the matter went no further than a review of personnel: Kuzhelnikov was removed from his position and sent off as an ambassador to somewhere in Africa. But a short while later this Politburo member himself disappeared mysteriously, and precisely because of that phrase "We don't want any of that!" The phrase was reported to Stalin, and Stalin took the words "We don't want any of that!" as a reference to himself, not the sculpture, following which the Politburo member vanished and his name was dropped from various lists, textbooks, reference works and encyclopedias, so that now not even the historians are able to say for certain whether he ever really existed or not.

When the monument was erected, there were few people who had regarded as too bold Aglaya's assertion that it would stand for thousands of years. And it would have been quite impossible then to imagine that children born in that year would not even have entered first grade at school before the very ground would be shaken beneath the monument, and also beneath the great leader's entire cause.

6

When she got home from the Party activists' meeting, Aglaya didn't know what to do with herself. She drank some vodka, then some valerian drops, then more vodka. She lay down, jumped up, ran around the room thinking, but she couldn't understand how it could all have happened. After such words had been spoken, it was impossible to carry on living in the same old way—or perhaps at all. Khrushchev had said it; Mikoyan had supported him; Molotov, Malenkov, Voroshilov and Kaganovich had kept silent. All of them had been faithful disciples and brothers-in-arms of Comrade Stalin. They had all sworn they were prepared to give their lives for him. What had happened to them? Had they gone insane? Had they turned out to be traitors? So wise and perspicacious, how could he have seen through everyone and failed to spot them?

Now she recalled that there had been certain hints at a change in the attitude to Stalin even earlier. At the end of the previous year Porosyaninov had come to the children's home and advised her, seemingly in passing and yet insistently, to take down the long banner hanging in the entrance hall with the words THANKS TO COMRADE STALIN FOR OUR HAPPY CHILDHOOD! "The slogan's out of date," he had commented, and gave Aglaya a meaningful look. But when she had asked what slogan to put up instead of the old one, Pyotr Klimovich had told her she could put up the same one, but with the words COMRADE STALIN replaced by THE COMMUNIST PARTY, so that the entire text read THANKS TO THE COMMUNIST PARTY FOR OUR HAPPY CHILDHOOD!

"It'll be too long," Aglaya said doubtfully.

"Never mind if it's long, so long as it's politically correct." Then he had looked at her and added that you had to take life realistically—or, as he said, "reelsickly."

Aglaya had done as she often did in such cases: she had promised to take the banner down, but in reality she had no intention of doing so. She had thought Porosyaninov would forget, but the next day he phoned and asked whether she had done as they agreed, and when he heard she hadn't got around to it yet, he insisted firmly: "Get around to it!"

And she had obeyed. For her Party instructions were law. Moreover, the situation had not been clarified yet, and two loves still dwelt in her heart in perfect harmony: love for Stalin and love for the Party. But now she was being urged to commit an act that she absolutely could not justify with any theories. Now everything had been said clearly and unambiguously and she faced a stark choice: to stick with the Party or stick with Stalin. An impossible, unnatural choice. For her, Stalin was the Party, and the Party was Stalin. For her, Stalin and the Party together were the people, the honor and the conscience of the entire country, and her own conscience as well. Harsh and uncompromising, a woman possessed, as—we repeat—she was called in those days, she was used to brushing all obstacles aside, but so far she had always forced her march in the direction indicated by Stalin, and that had been an easy and joyful thing to do. But now her guiding star had split into two halves, into two separate luminaries, and each was calling her to follow it.

That very night she fell ill, as she herself said afterward, with her nerves, although the doctor called in by her neighbor said it was simply flu. A rather nasty flu, certainly, brought to us either from Asiatic parts or—which was more likely—from America. Where, as everyone knew, they deliberately cultivated all sorts of viruses and microbes in scientific laboratories, as well as insects and rats, in order to infect the trusting and defenseless Soviet people and make them suffer.

By the evening of the following day her temperature had risen above forty degrees Celsius. Aglaya tossed and turned, burning up; she shuddered in her fever, sweated, lost consciousness, raved. But in her raving she experienced a joyful sense of anticipation, of something exceptional about to happen, and she was not deceived. During the first and second nights, Comrade Stalin came to see her alive and in person, dropped in just like a member of the family, genial and good-natured in his prewar-style field jacket and soft box calf boots. He opened the door silently, walked silently across to her bed, sat down at her feet, sucked on his smokeless pipe and looked at Aglaya affectionately. The first time, she failed to appreciate the situation and tried to talk to him, but scarcely had she parted her lips when he instantly disappeared, vanished into thin air. During his subsequent appearances she made no attempt to speak. She remained silent, and he remained silent, but she could feel that they were communicating with each other without words, and it was far better than with words.

Afterward, when she recovered, she retained in her memory the feeling that an extremely important conversation had taken place between them and although she could not recall its content, she realized that an absolute truth had been revealed to her, a truth beside which all words and all human knowledge paled into insignificance.

7

In itself Dolgov was just an average town. A bit too big for a district center, but not big enough for a regional center. It had a few factories, agroindustrial trusts and combines, shops, an oil tank farm, a service station, a poultry farm, a district Party committee, a district Soviet executive committee, a public prosecutor's office, a police station, a sobering-up station and a branch of the KGB. In the very center, on the opposite side of the square from the district committee of the CPSU, before you reached the collective farm market, there were even the remains of some structure that people referred to either as the kremlin or the arcade. At the time here described, it contained the district public utilities office, a dressmaking and tailoring establishment, an automobile repair shop and the "Hardware" shop. Standing nearby was the Church of SS. Kozma and Damian, which was repeatedly being closed as part of the campaign against religion and opened again out of economic considerations—while religion might have been regarded as opium for the people, it nonetheless contributed a lot of money to the budget. But then genuine opium generates a pretty decent income too.

The house in which Aglaya lived was built in 1946 on her instructions for the district Party's ruling class, or nomenklatura, as it was known. After the war they were more in need of housing than were simple Soviet people. Of course, they were always more in need. The further things went, the greater their need, and the less there was, the greater their need of it. However, after the war they were particularly needy, because the Germans had destroyed the nomenklatura apartment houses (since they were the best in the town) as they withdrew. Only the mansion in which the children's home was located had survived, thanks to an oversight on the part of the Germans.

There were no other decent houses in the town, and it would have been genuinely indecent for the Party's nomenklatura workers to live in poor-quality houses, but even more indecent for them to live in communal flats. And not just because the Party's nomenklatura workers did not know how to coexist in crowded conditions, but because then the details of their lives would have become known to simple Soviet people and that must never happen. Living apart from other citizens, the nomenklatura of those times (just like its counterpart in these times) had to appear and did appear to be a special breed of people, superior, mysterious and possessed of the entire body of human knowledge. Our fears and weaknesses were foreign to them. They understood the secrets of our being, what was and what would be, but they had no interests apart from constant concern for the good of the motherland and our well-being. And if they needed living conditions a little better than ours, then it was exclusively in order that they might think about us without being distracted by anything irrelevant. And we, who thought only of ourselves and our own petty affairs, could do that in any conditions.

The house where Aglaya lived had been intended to be a good one. It was quite unique in the town, with comforts hitherto unheard of in these parts, like gas, hot water and even a sewerage system, which in those days no one in Dolgov had ever even seen before.

On the outskirts of town people still simply relieved themselves in the open air, but nearer the center the public was a little more civilized and made use of communal facilities designed for this purpose—in the form of little planking sheds with two separate entrances and two doors that were often torn off their hinges, one of which bore the letter M and the other the letter W. Naturally, in these little sheds (the younger generations perhaps cannot even picture this) on both the M side and the W side the wooden floor was embellished with a dozen or so large holes in a long row and soft heaps deposited haphazardly around them, as though the bombardment had not been conducted point-blank, but from long-range guns, and shots had fallen short or overshot the target.

The author appreciates that the picture he paints of these facilities is none too appetizing, but we really should bear witness to such an essential aspect of our life. Otherwise the people of centuries to come will not even be able to imagine these holes and these heaps sluiced down with carbolic and sprinkled with lime, which in summer gave off such a strong smell that it made your nose smart and your eyes water as if somebody had tossed a handful of snuff into them. This smell could only be tolerated by Soviet people and large green flies about half the size of a sparrow. In hot weather it was too hot here, and in frosty weather it was too cold, and it was always slippery.

The visitors squatted in a row, like sheaves of wheat standing in the field, and I recall with particular sympathy the old men suffering from arthritic joints, constipation and hemorrhoids, who strained until they turned blue, wheezing and moaning and groaning as if they were in a nativity home.

Alexei Mikhailovich Makarov, also known as the Admiral, used to say that if it was up to him to decide what monument to erect to our Soviet era, he would not have commemorated Stalin or Lenin or anyone else, but the Unknown Soviet Man squatting like an eagle on the peak of a tall mountain (Mount Communism) deposited by himself.

However, let us return to Aglaya's apartment building. It was built in an unsuitable season—in autumn and winter—and in a rush. Using poor building technique. On a very weak foundation—that is, almost without any. In the semibasement they installed a gas collector consisting of twelve interconnected cylinders. The collector was constructed by local technology rationalizers, and it aroused serious doubts in the mind of the head of the fire safety office. But Aglaya had smacked him down and the fire safety chief had signed the certificate of approval, keeping his doubts to himself.

The building's walls were brick, but the internal cladding was wooden, and the wood (later it was suspected that this was sabotage) was of poor quality, infected by mold. Aglaya was asked at the time what to do about it, and she had encouraged them to continue: build, build; once we get on our feet and provide for the people, then we'll get around to thinking about ourselves last of all. In her modesty she had taken only a three-room apartment for herself and her son, although she was offered four rooms. But she only took three. With fifty-seven and a half square meters of useful floor space. She accepted it temporarily, until the end of the housing crisis. But the housing crisis proved to resemble the unattainable horizon that merely recedes as you advance toward it. The crisis had never come to an end, although in time some detached houses had been built. However, a place in one of them was not found for Aglaya—by that time she had been dropped from the nomenklatura. And in addition, after her son went away to study at college, she was effectively left alone. She had remained alone in her three rooms on the second floor. The first room was regarded as the sitting room; it had a big, round, extending table (no one ever extended it) and eight oak chairs around the table and a sofa bed for potential guests (she never had any). Lying in the middle of the room was a brown bearskin with glass eyes and bared fangs—a present from local huntsmen. Of the two other rooms one was the study to which she had been entitled by rank during her time as Party secretary and the other was her bedroom. These were fitted out with massive, cumbersome furniture: in the bedroom a large metal-frame bed with badly sagging spring mesh, in the study a heavy oak desk with two columns of drawers, its top covered in cloth that had originally been green and then turned gray with dust (no one ever worked at it), an oak armchair, a table lamp with a green shade made of glass, a heavy writing set with a bronze bird and two stone inkwells with desiccated entrails.

Aglaya's colleagues, who had not been dropped from the nomenklatura listings, gradually left this house, and their apartments, immediately transformed into communal facilities, began to be filled up with people from the lower orders, including two professors—one of agricultural science and one of Marxism-Leninism—who were biding their time here until they were rehabilitated. At one time there was even a certain Shakespeare scholar registered here, and a lady violinist with an international reputation, and the assassin-doctor Ivan Ivanovich Rabinovich. That was what they used to call him, although he had not killed anybody and he was not even a doctor, but a medical assistant, and not even in human medicine, but in veterinary practice. Nonetheless, he too had found himself in that category of people whom the Soviet authorities first wore down in the camps and then scattered into places of exile, not allowing them to settle in the big cities. They even picked smaller towns that were at least a hundred kilometers from the capital. Dolgov was just such a town. Which clearly worked to its advantage as far as its average intellectual and cultural level was concerned. That had risen here, while in the capital cities, by contrast, it had fallen. It would appear that the law of communicating vessels holds good not just for liquids.

In this same house there also lived the teacher of German Ida Samoilovna Bauman and her aged mother and Father Yegor, the priest of the Church of SS. Kozma and Damian, with his wife, Vasilisa, and his son, Deniska, the worst hooligan of all the courtyard kids. Also resident was the family of the public bath attendant Renat Tukhvatullin, all six of them—himself, his wife and four children aged from fourteen to four; the lame, deaf, one-eyed cat-lover Shurochka, nicknamed Shurochka the Idiot; and in the room next to Aglaya's bedroom there dwelt in solitude the quiet, smiling Savelii Artyomovich Telushkin, who had once served in the NKVD, the secret police, carrying out death sentences. He had served there for a long time and in the course of his service he had personally shot 249 people (he recalled the precise figure) on his own and many more in open battle, so to speak (for instance, he had taken part in the execution of the Polish officers), but he had not gone insane, had not suffered any pangs of conscience or been tormented by any doubts and his dreams were calm and idyllic: meadows, daisies, cows and May Day demonstrations.

Clearly, in the course of the house's existence there had always been movements taking place within it: people moved in and moved out, swapped one apartment for another, died, went away to the army or to jail, and it is impossible to mention everyone who ever lived at this address.

Among them, however, special mention should be made of the yard-keeper Valentina Zhukova and her son. Valentina was a large woman with a broad face and a broad, sloping back. She walked clumsily with her feet turned inward, holding her arms out slightly ahead of her, as though she were about to fight someone. Despite her apparently unalluring appearance, in her young days she had been very popular with the men, and from among them she had chosen as her husband, Seryoga Zhukov, an accordion player, joker and general troublemaker. At the very beginning of the war, without waiting to be called up, Seryoga had gone to the front as a volunteer. Valentina had spent part of the war as a member of Aglaya's partisan detachment, in which she had distinguished herself with her exceptional physical strength and bravery. One day in hand-to-hand combat she had first felled two Germans with a knockout blow from her fist and then tied them together and brought them back to the detachment as prisoners. After the war Valentina had worked for a while as district Party secretary Aglaya Revkina's driver. And after that, for the sake of a room in the semibasement, she had become a yard-keeper. She no longer had a husband. Seryoga had not come back from the war and he was listed as missing. Since there was no proof that he had not surrendered to the enemy alive, with his rifle in his hand, the missing man was regarded as a traitor, and Valentina as the wife of a traitor. Not only, therefore, did she not receive any pension for her husband; she was not even awarded any partisan medals for her own feats of courage.

She raised her son alone as well as she could. For old times' sake Aglaya sometimes hired Valentina to clean her apartment, do her washing or run errands to the shop, which the yard-keeper did for a small payment. Valentina's son, by the way, was called Georgii Zhukov, exactly like the famous general. This Georgii Zhukov (or simply Zhorka) also served in the army, but he didn't climb as high as the rank of marshal; in fact, he only reached junior sergeant. Despite his father's offense against the motherland, because of an oversight by his superiors he had served in a tank crew in Hungary, from where he brought home an accordion, and on Sundays he would perform the waltzes "The Blue Danube" and "On the Hills of Manchuria" and a tango about the exhausted sun. At first he would play his accordion in the yard, but later he was invited to weddings and birthday parties.

It goes without saying that sometimes furious rows would break out among the residents concerning a broken window, noise after eleven o'clock at night, the queue for the toilet, washing the floors and clearing out the garbage. But all that did not affect Aglaya; she lived separately, she had her own toilet and kitchen, and she didn't get into arguments with anyone. Her neighbors were afraid of her, with the possible exception of Shurochka the Idiot, who possessed (or so it was believed) the gift of foresight, and every time she met Aglaya, she would predict with a nasal twang that fire would flare up, iron birds would fly, iron horses would gallop, the earth would tremble and a dead person would fall on a living one.

8

On March 5, Aglaya Stepanovna was woken by unbearably bright sunshine. Her head was clear and she felt well and so she decided it was time to get up, live and work. "That's it," she said out loud, addressing herself strictly in her habitual manner, "enough of this lying around in bed and malingering." As she pulled on her stockings, she remembered that today was the anniversary of Iosif Vissarionovich Stalin's death—and she called herself an idiot for almost missing the important date. On this day last year and the year before, she had visited the monument with a small bouquet of geraniums specially cultivated on her windowsill.

When she came out into the street bearing the same gift today, she saw that it was spring. The freshly fallen powdery snow was glinting in the sun, melting and settling, slipping down from off the hummocks, laying bare the earth with its sparse covering of grass. The roads had turned dark, and there was melt water flowing along their edges. Icicles were falling from under the edges of roofs and shattering noisily. On the garbage lot in front of the building, black jackdaws or crows (Aglaya could see no difference between them, but she hated them both) were hopping and strutting about, and sitting on the bench by the building were identically black old women (also rather repulsive), their heads huddled in like the birds. The number of old women in front of the house changed, but there were two who sat there constantly, one of them called Old Nadya and the other known by the nickname of Greta the Greek because of her family origins. They had been sitting on the bench in front of the building constantly for many years, perhaps even since time began. It seemed as though they had never been born and would never die, had never been young, but always the way they were now, and they sat there now the way they always had sat and would go on sitting forever. They sat and watched life flowing past in front of their eyes like some eternal soap opera, to use a modern term. Without listening to the radio or reading the newspapers, they knew everything about everybody who lived in the town of Dolgov and even something about the inhabitants of the surrounding area: who'd won money on the government bonds, who'd been jailed for embezzlement, whose husband had been taken off to the sobering-up station, who'd had twins, whose mother-in-law had fallen under a train, where there'd been a fire and who'd been stabbed. They acquired this information by constantly asking all passersby "who?-what?-where?" but they were also able to deduce a great many things by using their own heads. If a stranger entered their field of view, the old women would engage their intellects and in some mysterious manner determine fairly closely to the truth who he was, where he was coming from and going to, what he did for a living and what his intentions were. Sometimes they would simply note that last Monday before lunch a man in a hat had walked by. They were sitting on the bench now too, looking straight ahead at the snow, the sun and the children playing their noisy games. They saw a man and a woman walking by, perfect strangers and quite unremarkable, looked them over carefully, and when they had moved off, Old Nadya asked Greta the Greek: "What d'you think, is he living with her?"

"Who can tell?" said Greta the Greek. "I think he is."

"He must be," Old Nadya agreed with a sigh, evidently not approving of this cohabitation.

"Cossacks," old Granny Bauman mumbled toothlessly, shaking her head shrouded in a fluffy shawl, "those people, my-oh-my! They had no pity for anyone. My sister Mira was pregnant, and they said to her, we'll arrange the birth for you, and they began danshing on her belly and she had a mishcarriage, but she shurvived, only she went totally inshane."

Old Nadya and Greta the Greek listened, extending the storyteller temporary forgiveness for the crucifixion of Christ and the matzos made with the blood of Christian infants. The story about the Cossacks was interrupted by the appearance of Aglaya, who halted as she emerged from the hallway, blinded by the sun. She was wearing a black coat, black boots and a black beret with a little tail, pulled down to one side of her head, her face black like a gypsy woman's, black like these old women and the jackdaws and crows on the waste lot. She gave the old women a disdainful glance, for she had never liked people who sat around doing nothing, and without even saying "Morning" to them, she strode out of the courtyard quickly and lightly, as though she had not been ill at all. At her appearance the old women had become silent and subdued, but when she moved off, Old Nadya said, "Ooh, what a shnoot!"

"She is, right enough," Greta the Greek agreed, although if they had been asked, neither one of them would have been able to say what a shnoot was.

Aglaya left the courtyard and set off across the waste lot along the still firm and icy path that was beginning to thaw in the sun. Her steps were rapid and light; she rejoiced in the sunlight and the colors and the smell of spring, without actually understanding the reasons for such keen feelings. But her body understood. Her body knew the illness had been serious and Aglaya's recovery was a miracle, and now every cell in her body was rejoicing at its good fortune in still being alive.

9

At its non-dead-end, Komsomol Cul-de-Sac emerged into Rosenblum Street, which ran out onto Stalin Prospect not far from Stalin Square.

The monument stood facing the building of the district committee of the CPSU, her very own old territory. In her time Aglaya had made her way here (actually, she had been driven; her position did not allow her to walk) as if she was coming home. The policeman at the door had stood to attention and saluted her, the secretary in the waiting room had jumped to her feet and tidied her hairdo and the fat local bigwigs she came across in the corridor had pressed back against the walls, exuding a smell of garlic and raw vodka as they opened mouths crammed full of gold or more base metal. They smiled or even laughed, with their bellies shaking, showing how happy they were to see her, and some even performed something like a curtsey.

In her time Aglaya had occupied the very largest office here, with walls paneled in walnut and numerous telephones. Here, enveloped in dove-gray cigarette smoke, she had sat behind the broad desk under the portraits of Lenin and Stalin, looking like some frenzied Pasionaria. To this office she had summoned those who distinguished themselves by their labor efforts, but there had always been fewer of them than those who had committed an offense of some kind, and at these she had hammered her fist on the desk, bellowed and cursed obscenely. Here men with high positions and large physiques used to tremble before her, sweating and stammering, clutching at their hearts and losing consciousness. There was even one occasion when one of them had quite simply messed his pants, and another—the director of a state farm who was unable to explain how he had managed to drink the farm's entire six-month budget—had collapsed on the spot, felled by a stroke.

Parting with great power is as hard as parting with great wealth. It is unpleasant and even humiliating to walk where you used to be driven in an automobile, with all that speed and commotion and blaring of the horn: Stop, make way, can't you see—it's Revkina's car? It is hard to grow used to the fact that you can't give out orders left and right: serve, bring, take away, show, report. It was strange not to see flattering smiles on approaching faces or an obsequious question in other eyes. But gradually Aglaya had become accustomed to her lowly position, comforting herself with the thought that she had done a lot of good in her life. She had introduced the collective farm system, and participated in the rout of the opposition, and fought as a partisan, and rebuilt the district from ruins, but she believed the very greatest service she had rendered, the crowning achievement of all her efforts, was the erection of the monument, without which the town would quite simply not have been what it was.

As for the district committee—what of it? It had been her home; now it was someone else's. There was nothing for her to do in there. And she wasn't going there now, she was going to see Stalin. But she paused at the Avenue of Glory, which was located in front of the district Party committee building. The first object worthy of note on the alley was the Board of Honor, on which the portraits of labor heroes and industrial shock workers were displayed in two rows: the faces, well known to Aglaya, of progressive collective farm chairmen, agronomists, doctors, teachers, milkmaids, tractor drivers, ammunition-factory workers, cardboard men and thread women (that is, workers from the cardboard and sewing thread plants). Hanging here among the others was Aglaya Stepanovna's own portrait, since last year the children's home where she was the director had been awarded the Red Challenge Banner. And behind the board was the site for which the avenue had been named—the graves of the glorious warriors who had fought for our future and our present day. Beginning with the Red Commissar Matvei Rosenblum, who had arrived on the armored train Decisive and announced to the people the final establishment of the new power in these parts, following which he had immediately been shot by the socialist revolutionary Abram Tsirkes, the incident providing the pretext for the temporary immortalization of Rosenblum's name in the title of one of the central streets. When it later became possible to joke, some people had actually suggested it was Tsirkes who should have been immortalized—after all, he was the one who hit the target. After Rosenblum came the tin obelisks with stars and the gravestones of the heroes of the Civil War, the Finnish campaign and the grueling battles of times of peace, arranged in two neat rows like the Board of Honor. In the very center of the row, under the name of Afanasii Miliagi, lay the bones of the gelding Osoaviakhim, who became almost human (those who have read *Chonkin* know about him). Under a thick covering of moss and mildew, a stone standing nearby bore the deceptive inscription ANDREI EREMEEVICH REVKIN. 1900–1941. HE SACRIFICED HIS OWN LIFE. AS THE GERMAN INVADERS APPROACHED, HE BLEW UP AN IMPORTANT INDUS- TRIAL SITE AND PERISHED IN THE EXPLOSION.

People who came here by chance bowed their heads over the stone, or perhaps they didn't, but simply stood here in meditation, believing that this was truly the resting place of a hero who had performed a feat of out- standing courage. In actual fact, there was no one resting here. Because it had not been possible to find Revkin's body after the explosion, especially as no one had searched for it, and especially as there had been nothing to search for, since the explosion had blown the entire power station into lit- tle pieces, and what was not blasted apart had burned away, and if it had not burned away, then in the conditions of German occupation, who could possibly have searched for bodies on the site of the power station and buried them with full honors? It was nothing but plain nonsense. Aglaya, of course, knew there was no one lying there, or she should have known it, but the brains of ideologically oriented individuals are arranged in such a way that while knowing one thing, they believe in something else. And Aglaya knew that Revkin was not lying there, but she believed that he was.

The snow had melted a little and slipped downward, revealing the humps of the graves covered in withered grass. Aglaya stood by the grave, mentally promising the man who was not lying there that she would come back in early summer, dig up the old grass and sow new.

The remainder of her route was straight and short.

On reaching the monument, she first laid her flowers against the pedestal and then stepped back, raising her head, and only then noticed that something was wrong. Stalin was standing in his former place, in his former pose with his habitually raised right hand, but his glance was sad, his stance had shifted, as though somehow (but it was impossible!) he had begun to stoop. And on his cap—this was really incredible—two fat, disgusting gray pigeons were billing and cooing. It might seem there was nothing unusual in that; what else could be expected from these brainless creatures—after all, they never missed a single monument. But this monument was different from all the others, and they themselves had differentiated it. In all this time not a single bird had dared to lay either foot or wing on the statue. There had been only one solitary occasion when a crow with a crust of bread had tried to land on the cap, but it had barely even touched the surface before it dropped its food, flew up with a wild cry and came crashing down like a stone onto the asphalt of the square. Since that time it was quite certain that not a single winged creature had even attempted to use the statue as a landing ground. And now here were these stupid birds! How had they realized that now it was possible to land here and defile the monument? They had already covered the top of the cap with white excrement, streaks of which were visible on the peak and on the left shoulder and the flap of the greatcoat.

"Shoo!" Aglaya called out in a weak voice. "Shoo, you cursed brutes!"

But the cursed brutes responded to her call with absolute disdain. The fatter of the two, evidently the male, cocked his head to one side and squinted at Aglaya with one eye, then turned to the female and cooed something to her, and she gurgled something to him in reply. Aglaya had the feeling that they were simply laughing at her. She looked around to see if there was a stone near her feet, found a gray pebble the size of an egg and flung it. The stone hit the top of the left boot and fell in front of the pedestal, and as she followed its fall, Aglaya only now noticed a poor, miserable, solitary spray of yellow mimosa lying in the snow beside her geraniums. Her heart beat faster in joy. So she was not the only one in this town who remembered and honored the dear and beloved, the unique and irreplaceable.

"Yes," she heard a thin, ingratiating little voice say behind her, "not everybody's forgotten everything. People love iron, birdth love iron, but when the iron fallth, the birdth will fly away, but people can't fly. They're heavy, they haven't got wingth and they're heavy, they can't fly, and iron will fall on iron."

Aglaya turned around. Shurochka the Idiot, dressed in a plush jacket wrapped around with sackcloth, was watching Aglaya with a crazy, mysterious glimmer in her eye.

"Now what are you driveling about?" Aglaya cried indignantly. "What iron? Where is it going to fall?"

"People can't fly," Shurochka repeated with conviction. "And iron fallth down from above."

"Buzz off!" said Aglaya, and stalked away with a rapid, unwavering stride.

10

The children's home was located in an old mansion fronted by six columns. It had once belonged to the marshal of the local nobility. Judging from the general decrepitude of the façade and the peeling paint of the columns, the building had not been repaired even once since those times. But it was one of the few valuable structures that had not been damaged in the war.

After forcing her way through two heavy doors, Aglaya entered the front hall, and the first thing that caught her eye was the wall newspaper "Happy Childhood." Sveta Zhurkina, a pupil from Class Seven B, was standing in front of the newspaper with her tongue sticking out in the general direction of her left ear and copying something into a notebook. Catching sight of Aglaya, she said hello, closed her notebook with an embarrassed gesture and left.

The pupil's behavior seemed suspicious to Aglaya. She walked over to the wall newspaper and froze as she looked at it. The verse text that Zhurkina had not actually finished copying out was in the third column, after a leading article devoted to the education of young people through labor.

The poem, bearing no signature, was called "And We Believed in You So Much." It contained reproaches addressed to a certain military commander (who was not named, but it was clear to everyone that Stalin was meant). It said the commander had led us from victory to victory, but at the same time abused our boundless trust by committing deeds of great wickedness. The final stanza contained an expression of the author's profound disenchantment with his former devotion to the commander, but also the optimistic hope that in the future everything would be different. The verse concluded with a polemical question: "The ascent does not always go smoothly when storming a peak that is new. I believe in collective reason, I believe in the Party. Do you?"

The strip of paper with the poem was poorly glued on — evidently with mashed potato. Or starch. Or simply spit. Aglaya grabbed hold of the paper by a corner that had come away and tore it off, crumpling it up like a snake, and strode off quickly toward her office. The secretary, Rita, was squinting into a little mirror and plucking her eyebrows with tweezers. Seeing Aglaya Stepanovna come in, she leapt to her feet.

"Good morning, Aglaya Stepanovna. Have you recovered?"

"I have," Aglaya said grumpily. "Where's Shubkin?"

"He was fussing around here just a moment ago. I think he went to the dormitory to check that the girls have made up their beds properly."

"Tell him to come and see me," she ordered, and disappeared into her office.

She tossed the piece of paper onto the floor. Picked it up. Put it on the table. Tossed it down again and picked it up again. She took off her coat and began striding rapidly from one corner of the office to the other. But she immediately felt tired, began panting for breath and sweating. She was still weak, after all. Hearing voices in the outer office, she sat down at her desk and assumed a stony expression.

Mark Semyonovich Shubkin was a man of about fifty with a large physique, growing plump and balding, with the fresh complexion that is shared by rural residents and convicts. He also just happened to look like Lenin. He was a lot taller, but just like Lenin he had an absolutely massive head that was, so he claimed, a size ten.

He worked as class teacher with the preschool children's group and edited the wall newspaper by way of community service. This work had been entrusted to him without due caution. No one else would volunteer to run the newspaper, and ever since Shubkin got his hands on it, he had constantly published his own poems and comments. Which could in fact have been regarded as a considerable honor for the newspaper. Dolgov had its own poets—Butylko, Raspadov and so forth—but they had never risen any higher than the regional press, whereas Shubkin at the age of thirty had been printed (would you believe it!) in *Izvestiya*, *Komsomolskaya Pravda* and *Ogonyok*.

"Come over to the desk," Aglaya ordered without replying to Shubkin's greeting. "Who wrote this trash?" Her lips twisted in a grimace of disgust and she gestured with her eyes to the strip of paper curled into a spiral.

Shubkin reached out a hand, but thought better of it before picking up the paper.

"I don't catch your meaning," he said, giving Aglaya a meek look.

"I'm asking you," she repeated, tapping her fingers on the table, "who wrote this trash?"

"Do you mean this poem?" he asked, inviting her to correct her terminology.

"I mean this trash," said Aglaya Stepanovna, standing her ground.

"This po-po-poem," said Shubkin, beginning to stammer in his agitation, "was written by me."

"And who gave you permission to write this trash?" she repeated with uncompromising hostility.

"I was per-permitted to write this tra-trash by the Pa-Pa-Party," said Shubkin, turning pale and thrusting out his chest.

"Oh, the Pa-Pa-Party," Aglaya mocked him. "The Party gave you permission. No, my dear friend, the Party does not yet permit you to write all sorts of garbage and exploit an important theme for your own ends. See what I'm going to do with this garbage, look." The tiny scraps of paper went flying to the floor. "If you think the Twentieth Congress abolished the general line, you are mistaken. The Party has been obliged to introduce a few corrections, but we will not allow anyone to doubt the fundamentals. Stalin was and still is the mind, honor and conscience of our epoch. Was and is. That's all there is to it. And if someone up there happens to say something about him, it doesn't mean that everyone will be allowed to do it. What are things coming to!" She was gradually calming down. "Everyone writing whatever comes into his head. 'I believe in collective reason.' What a true believer! If you're such a great satirist, why don't you write about the trash bins. They're standing out there without any lids, giving off a stink; it's unsanitary, there are flies. How many times do I have to tell them to make lids? I've already slapped two reprimands on the building manager and I'll hit him with a third one soon, a severe reprimand with a caution, but he couldn't care less. If you're such a talented satirist, why don't you turn the force of your satire against the trash bins?"

Shubkin turned even paler and drew himself up, offended. "I don't wish to turn my satire against the bi-bi-bins. I wa-wa-want to turn its force against Sta-sta-sta . . ."

"I understand," said Aglaya, putting an end to the interview. "You're sacked. Collect your pay at the accounts office tomorrow."

11

As a matter of fact, she'd seen right through this character long ago. Back when he'd come looking for a job. She'd had no teacher of literature at the time, and then he'd turned up out of the blue. With a first-class diploma from IPLI—the Institute of Philosophy and Literature—the very place where many of our outstanding personalities had studied before the war, including the poet Tvardovsky and the first secretary of the Komsomol central committee, Shelepin.

"Well I never!" Aglaya said in amazement, eyeing the diploma. "What distinguished people we have honoring this backwater of ours!"

For the reasons explained above, people with college-level education were to be found in Dolgov, but someone like this was a rare find.

"And where did you work after the institute?"

"In a logging camp," Shubkin said simply.

"Why?" she asked, then immediately realized she had said something stupid; there was no need to ask.

And while he was spinning her some complicated yarn about unjustified repression and things being carried to extremes, she had already made up her mind.

"I see," she interrupted him, "and why exactly have you come to us?"

"Well, in the first place because I saw the announcement, in the second place I have the right qualifications and in the third place"—he paused deliberately and turned his eyes up slightly—"I am very fond of children."

"Everybody's fond of children," Aglaya remarked. "Especially," she said with emphasis, "our Soviet children"—meaning "ours, not yours." "Do you have any children of your own, by the way?"

"No," said Shubkin, as if he was apologizing for something. "I never had any. Because . . . you understand."

"Of course," she said charitably. "That's quite understandable. But"—she shrugged and spread her arms—"unfortunately we don't have a job for you."

39

And making it clear that the conversation was at an end, she had begun reaching into the pack for her next Belomor.

But he had been in no hurry to leave.

"But you just said that you do have a job."

"I did say so, but I can see that you have insufficient teaching experience. Your educational qualifications, of course, are very high. Perhaps even too high for us. But we have a specific context here. We have difficult children, without parents. It would be better for you to try an ordinary school for a start."

Clearly, the words about his lack of teaching experience were merely an excuse. In actual fact, she had refused Shubkin because she did not like people like him. She knew for certain that nobody ended up "there"—the camps—for nothing. Her logic followed a well-known line of reasoning: I've lived my life honestly and no one put me in prison. And they didn't put this person or that person away either. But if someone was put away, there's no smoke without fire, it was for something. Granted, times are different now. The socialist order is firmly established and the Party is strong; it can be a little more indulgent with its enemies. It can shorten their sentences and give them jobs. But to trust characters like that with the education of future generations is something that can never be allowed under any circumstances.

However, she had been corrected.

It had been yet another sign of the changes that were brewing. Shubkin had complained to the DDPE—the District Department of Public Education—and from there the order had come down: Give him a job. Aglaya had obeyed, only instead of appointing the new staff member to teach the senior classes, as he had requested, she had assigned him to the oldest preschool group.

But she had continued to regard him with suspicion. She did not like the fact that he told his little wards stories about all sorts of flitty-flies, ugly ducklings, little goats, little pigs and wolves.

"If you have to tell them about these little pigs," she lectured him, "then at least set them on an ideological foundation. Explain that the little pigs are the developing countries of Africa, Asia and Latin America, and the gray wolf is who?"

"Who is he?" asked Shubkin, who had his own ideas on that point.

"The gray wolf," Aglaya explained, "is American imperialism."

"But the children are still too young to understand things like that," Shubkin had protested.

"It's good they're still so young. Little children assimilate things quicker."

Shubkin had kept silent, but she could see in his eyes that he disagreed. She suspected Shubkin was deliberately smuggling in alien ideology under the guise of those little pigs of his. And strangely enough—we shall come back to this later—she was more or less right.

Now Shubkin's behavior and his poem had convinced Aglaya that his past record was no accident. He'd been lying low before, but now look, he'd crept out from his crevice, like a cockroach—forgotten about his little goats and pigs and launched a direct attack against the holy of holies.

12

She soon discovered that Shubkin was not alone in his endeavors. In the District Department of Public Education, to which he complained once again, they refused to confirm her order. She decided to visit the director herself.

When she entered the office, Bogdan Filippovich Nechitailo was sitting there under the portraits of Lenin and Krupskaya. He was late middle-aged, a sad-looking man dressed in a cotton jacket and a dark shirt with the top button unfastened. At the time described here many district-level bosses lived poorly and dressed badly because their pay was not very high and they immediately squandered all their bribes on drink—and anyway, how many bribes does a deputy head of a district department of public education get?

Unshaven and inebriated, Nechitailo was folding the newspaper *Pravda* into something resembling a little book with fingers stained yellow by tobacco smoke.

"I've come to see you," said Aglaya, lingering in the doorway as she suddenly felt her courage fail her.

"I can see you've come to see me," said Nechitailo with a nod.

"There's no one in here," he said, turning his head this way and that, "apart from myself. So tell me, Aglaya Stepanovna, in what way can I, for instance, be of assistance to yourself?"

While Aglaya presented the essential facts, he finished folding up his little book, tore one page out of it, curved it into a little trough and reached out for a silk tobacco pouch lying in front of him with an intricately embroidered, faded inscription: SMOKE AND DON'T COUGH. This pouch of his contained homegrown tobacco—in other words, the kind that people used to grow, dry and shred themselves. If they shredded it with the roots, they got relatively weak shag or makhorka, but if only the leaves went into the mix, it could be so strong that it made the most inveterate smokers cough and choke, with tears spurting from their eyes as if they were clowns in the circus. This tobacco was popularly known as "samson," and there was a widespread belief that in young men it stimulated sexual activity and in old men, sleep, although it is hard to imagine that any regular smoker of such poison had even the slightest chance of living to be an old man. Nechitailo took a generous pinch of samson out of the pouch, scattered it evenly along his curved trough, moistened the edge of the paper with spittle and chewed it with his front teeth to make it stick better, twisted together a tightly packed roll-up as thick as his thumb and took out of his pocket a cigarette lighter made from a rifle cartridge with a little wheel at the side.

"Frontline souvenir," he said to Aglaya, and struck the flame. There was a smell of bad tobacco and burning paper. Nechitailo struggled to light his roll-up, his eyes popping out of his head and his cheeks flapping in and out, making sounds like a steam engine: "Chuff-choo, chuff-choo, chuff-choo."

As Nechitailo puffed away, the tobacco crackled and snapped, scattering sparks in every direction. When the roll-up eventually lit, Bogdan Filippovich inhaled with relish and began to cough, wheezing as if he were in his death agony, and disappeared for a while in a swirling, dark gray mass.

"And so," Aglaya concluded her story, "I'm asking you, is it really possible to allow a man like Shubkin to be involved in educating our Soviet children?"

"Yes, I think it is," she heard a voice say out of the smoke, which by this time had begun to disperse, and Nechitailo emerged from it like an airplane out of a cloud. "I think it is possible," he repeated, holding the roll-up in his left hand and waving away the smoke with his right, "and in general let me tell you, Comrade Revkina, approximately the following. As you know, the Party's new policy emphasizes a considerate attitude toward personnel. Not the way things used to be—the slightest thing and off with his head. People have to be treated what I'd call humanely. Especially people like Shubkin. You could call him a man of unique intellect. He has two college-level educations, speaks twelve languages fluently and can use all the rest with a dictionary. And his memory is simply phenomenal. I can tell you he rattles off by heart the *Odyssey*"—Nechitailo bent down his little finger—"the *Iliad*"—he bent down his ring finger and went on bending down the rest of his fingers and thumbs as he ran through his list—"*Eugene Onegin*, Mendeleev's periodic table, the 'evergreen' chess game, the 'Song of the Stormy Petrel,' the fourth chapter of the *History of the CPSU*(B.) and Lenin's work 'What the "Friends of the People" Are and How They Fight the Social-Democrats.' I didn't believe it myself, Aglaya Stepanovna, but I followed him with the text and he just reeled it all off, word for word straight out of his head. You see! Not just a head, you might say, more like an entire Council of Ministers."

"But Comrade Stalin," said Aglaya, "taught us that the cleverer the enemy is, the more dangerous he is."

"Why are you talking to me about Comrade Stalin?" Bogdan Filippovich sighed and took another drag, started coughing again and leaned toward the desk, clutching at his chest. "Comrade Stalin"—he coughed again—"as we know now, made a few mistakes of his own. During the war he even used a globe to command our forces. He used to spin the globe and say, Take this town here for the October anniversary, and this one, he'd say, for Red Army Day. And how to take it, which side to approach it from, where to move up the reserves, all that, he says, is no concern of mine, I'm the Supreme Commander, he says, and I command supremely. Understand? And let Zhukov or Tolbukhin think about the details."

"Nonsense!" said Aglaya angrily. "Comrade Stalin was a genius and he had a close personal grasp of all the details."

"Aha," said Nechitailo, sounding bored. "Aglaya Stepanovna, I'm not going to get involved in an ideological debate with you. Especially since the leadership of our Party has a different opinion."

"What about you?" Aglaya asked in a less formal tone. "Do you have an opinion of your own?"

"I do," Nechitailo assured her. "But like the opinion of every honest communist, it's no different from the opinion of our supreme leadership. And therefore I declare your order dismissing Shubkin—how shall I put it—null and void. That means," he concluded decisively, stubbing out his butt in the ashtray, "that tomorrow morning he can turn up for work."

Aglaya realized there was nothing more to be said and she got up from her chair.

"Very well!" she said in a threatening tone, although any threat was quite pointless. "Very well!"

And as she left the room, she tried to slam the door as loudly as possible.

Nechitailo sat there for a while until she had gone, said "Idiot," shook his head and began manufacturing another roll-up.

13

This time around, Aglaya defied superior authority and refused to allow the sacked man back to work. That was when things began to get unpleasant. Porosyaninov called her in to see him, sat her down in a soft leather armchair and ordered in tea with hard crackers and lemon.

He began the conversation with a sigh: "Ah, Aglaya Stepanovna, you hot-blooded partisan! Just what position do you think you're storming now? So you don't like this Shubkin, but who does like him? I don't like him, and I confess I can't stand their entire nation. And what's going on at the top isn't to my liking either. Stalin stood at the head of the state for thirty years, we lauded him to the skies. A genius, a universal luminary, a generalissimo. And now they tell us he had Kirov killed, he devastated the peasantry, uprooted the intelligentsia, decapitated the army, exterminated the Party. And who are you and me, if we're not the Party?"

"Right!" said Aglaya, delighted. "That's exactly what I'm talking about."

"Everybody's talking about it. Only between themselves, in a whisper. But out loud we must support the Party line. Whatever it might be, whichever way it might turn, we're communists and we vote in favor."

"Without principles?" asked Aglaya.

"Without conditions," said Porosyaninov.

Aglaya was incensed, she was about to object, and rather sharply, but just then the door of the office opened and first secretary of the district Party committee Nechaev came in without making a sound, as though he weren't even moving his feet. He shook hands with Porosyaninov, who leapt to his feet, and with Aglaya, laying a hand on her shoulder to prevent her getting up, and asked, "I won't be in your way, will I?" Then he sat on the couch and froze in the position of a passenger waiting for a train that he doesn't expect to arrive very soon. And with an expression suggesting that what was going on here had nothing to do with him.

"Well then, Comrade Revkina," Porosyaninov continued. "It's not a matter of Shubkin, but of the Party line. Our Party's new policy is directed toward overcoming Stalin's personality cult. You know as well as I do that he committed many serious political errors. He ruled the country individually, devastated the peasantry, decapitated the army, led the persecutions of the intelligentsia, effectively annihilated the cream of our Party and encouraged his own glorification. And now the Party is courageously telling the people the entire truth, and what do you do? Are you," Porosyaninov went on, looking Aglaya honestly in the eye, "opposed to the truth?"

"Who are you saying all this to?" Aglaya asked in amazement, recalling that a minute earlier Porosyaninov had been saying something entirely different.

"I'm saying it to you," said Porosyaninov, casting a quick glance at Nechaev. "I'm telling you that we have the principle of democratic centralism, according to which if the Party has taken a decision, then the rank and file communists carry it out. That's all."

At this point Nechaev stood up and left the room as quietly as he had entered. Aglaya followed him out with her eyes and then turned to look at Porosyaninov. Obviously highly agitated, he took a cracker from the dish and snapped it apart, took another one and snapped it, took a third and looked at Aglaya.

"Well then, Aglaya Stepanovna?"

"Well what?" she asked.

"Are you going to recant?"

"Me?" she asked, amazed.

"Take a sheet of paper and write: 'I, Aglaya Stepanovna Revkina, being slightly crazy, have failed to understand the new policy of the Party and failed to appreciate the wisdom of Party decisions, of which I do thoroughly repent and solemnly declare that I will never do it again.' "

"You can't be serious!"

"Comrade Revkina!" said Pyotr Klimovich, getting up. "Here in these offices, as you yourself know, we are always serious. I advise you seriously to think about it."

"You chameleon!" said Aglaya, and left the room without even noticing his outstretched hand.

Shortly after that Aglaya received a severe reprimand for opposing Party decisions, and her status was reduced to that of an ordinary class teacher, like Shubkin. Which she took as a terrible insult.

14

Aglaya complained about her misadventures to her son, Marat, who was studying in Moscow at the Institute of International Relations. From her letter he learned that his mother was less distressed by her own personal misfortunes than by the general direction in which events were moving. "You know," she wrote, "that neither I nor your father who perished so heroically ever spared ourselves, and I am not sparing myself now, but it makes me ashamed, so ashamed that I could cry to look at people who pour scorn on what they were glorifying yesterday. When Stalin was alive, I can't remember anyone ever saying there was anything about Stalin they didn't like. Everyone said the same thing: A genius, a great commander. Our father and teacher. The luminary of all the sciences. Did they really not believe what they were saying? Were they all really lying? I don't understand—when were these people being sincere, now or then? And how can they be so indifferent when they see that faith in the most sacred thing of all, in the truth of our cause, is being undermined among young people your age!"

Not once in her long letter did she ask her son how he was getting on, where he was living and in what conditions, whether he was well, what he ate or drank, or how he spent his free time. But she did express her opinion that no one has a right to judge and condemn a genius who stood at the head of the state for thirty years, carried through the collectivization of agriculture, crushed the opposition, transformed a backward country into an industrial power and won a victory of universal historical importance over the enemy.

In the same letter she expressed her dissatisfaction at the release from the camps of all the enemies of the people, who instead of saying thank you were now demanding all sorts of rights and privileges and shouting from every corner that they had suffered for nothing. Perhaps by some accident there had been isolated innocent victims among them, but you can't make an omelette without breaking eggs, and you couldn't just let them all out indiscriminately. "And didn't we suffer?" Aglaya wrote. "Didn't we go short of food and sleep, wasn't it us the kulaks' sawn-off shotguns were pointed at? Those who spent a few years sitting in jail were fed in there for free, but your father gave his life without hesitation for the motherland and for Stalin. Then why aren't we complaining to anyone? See what great heroes they are! They suffered. Suffered so badly that now they want to weep for themselves. But I think that if anyone was wrongly punished, then now, when he has been corrupted in the camps and infected with anti-Soviet sentiment, there's no point in letting him out. He's an enemy now anyway, and he ought to be treated like an enemy."

To her surprise her son responded coldly. He wrote to her that none of these problems concerned him and repeated almost word for word what Porosyaninov had said, remarking that you had to take a realistic view of life.

At the age of twenty-two Marat himself had already mastered the practice of taking a realistic view and was managing rather successfully in arranging his own affairs. Since according to Soviet notions he was of noble origin (Party workers were regarded as the advance detachment of the working class), he was studying in one of the most prestigious and exclusive institutes. He did not possess any brilliant talents, but he was quick-witted and observant. And he was very quick to note that while the general privileges he possessed as the son of Party members allowed him access to the academic subjects taught in the institute, there was among the students of the institute a narrow inner circle that was completely closed to him.

The children of the big bosses, generals, ministers and Central Committee members lived an entirely different life and could get away with a great deal more than their classmates. They skipped classes, held drinking sessions, cruised around in their parents' cars, arranged orgies with girls from their own circle (or not, as the case might be), sometimes even raped them, and in one instance they actually threw a girl off a balcony. It looked like there was bound to be a major scandal, but there was hardly even a murmur. The incident was very deftly hushed up by announcing that the girl student who was thrown had been depressed and threw herself off the balcony in question. And when it came to relatively minor pranks, these guys were absolutely home free. Marat knew he could never do what they were allowed to do and would never be forgiven for doing the things that they did. On the other hand, he could reach their level or even overtake them, but for that he had to prosper in other areas, pick up points where these boobies couldn't because they took no care for the future and relied on their dads and didn't realize that today your dad was everything, but tomorrow he would be nothing, and you would become nothing with him.

Marat drew the correct conclusions and behaved accordingly. He lived modestly, frequented the student research club and gave boring papers, took an active part in Komsomol life and prepared himself to join the Party. He absorbed the academic subjects with some difficulty, but he made a real effort, realizing that for his future career it was not achievement but effort that really mattered—the bosses had to see you were making an effort, listening with your mouth wide open and taking notes. And his notes could have been exhibited in a museum. Neat, tidy exercise books covered with pages from *Pravda*; upright, clear handwriting; important ideas underlined in red pencil to prove that after writing the study notes he had also read them. Marat had also learned that active involvement in social life was encouraged more than zeal in the acquisition of knowledge. He knew you had to be able to get along with people and be guided by sober calculation, not the heated impulses of passion, remembering that in real life it was not the written laws that mattered but the unwritten rules of behavior.

He had not formulated this thought for himself; it had come from the deputy minister of foreign trade, Salkov, the father of Zoya, the girl he was courting. And in his courtship of Zoya he was guided in the first instance by the rules. He was making a career, and he had observed that the age of the fanatics was finished. It was not just anti-Soviet types or malcontents who did not like them, but Party people as well. Party people no longer wanted to work in the old way, sitting up all night long waiting in case the Father of the Peoples might suddenly require some piece of information or something else; they were tired of living in constant fear and remembering that Party workers were still being shot. Now was a less dangerous but more complicated time to make a career; you had to be flexible and not be too hasty in adopting one position or another before it had taken clear shape.

Marat also realized that the time of excessively modest dressing— Russian collarless shirts, military tunics, semimilitary field jackets, coarse-fabric greatcoats and tall boots—was over too. He dressed as well and as neatly as he could, had his hair cut before it got long by an expensive hairdresser, and even used a little perfume. He avoided speaking to Zoya in the customary overfamiliar manner of the youths in her circle and actually demonstrated a certain old-fashioned gallantry. Which eventually won her heart.

15

What can we say of the others, if even Aglaya's own son did not understand? She took offense and began writing to him less often and less warmly.

Her relations with her fellow staff members in the children's home were strained or openly hostile. Nobody smiled as they used to do or went rushing to carry out her requests, and even the secretary, Rita, greeted her through clenched teeth. Meanwhile, Shubkin had been elevated even higher. He was appointed teacher of literature for the senior classes, and he now entered the children's home with a triumphant air that suited his position perfectly.

The new director of the children's home, Vasilii Ivanovich Chikurin, had no interest in anything except drink, and he allowed Shubkin very extensive leeway, of which Shubkin took full advantage. He not only taught literature in the senior classes; he set up a literary club called the Brigantine, ran the Meyerhold Drama Club and was still editor of the wall newspaper "Happy Childhood."

Aglaya had never been a snitch and she didn't like snitches, but in accordance with her Party duty she pointed out to the new director on numerous occasions that Shubkin was exploiting his position to instill "ideas that aren't ours" in the heads of the pupils. During literature classes and literary club activities he made ironic remarks about the creative method of socialist realism, promoted writers of dubious reputation from nonrealist tendencies and praised writers condemned by the Party such as Zoshchenko, Akhmatova and Pasternak. He expressed a high opinion of Vladimir Dudintsev's flawed novel *Not by Bread Alone*, which had been rejected by the Soviet public, and he distributed this novel among the wards of the children's home; he also paid too much attention to western literature. Chikurin took no notice of these warnings; he merely shrugged, as if to say, Let him do as he wants. Especially since interest in literature among the pupils had clearly increased, they were studying better and their discipline had improved.

For the October festivities Shubkin and his pupils organized a large amateur concert which was attended by the bosses from the tannery and the Victory collective farm and also, naturally, the entire staff of the children's home.

Aglaya also came to the concert. She ended up in the middle seat in the third row, next to the chairman of the Victory collective farm, Stepan Kharitonovich Shaleiko, a thick-set, shaven-headed man about forty years old, whom she knew from the time when she was the Party secretary. She thought he was from the same district as Nechitailo; in any case, they spoke the same way, in a language that wasn't really either Russian or Ukrainian. At one time it used to be called the Little Russian dialect. In Ukraine this language is known as surzhik, and surzhik is a hybrid of wheat and rye. Shaleiko himself was like a hybrid of a man and some plant, perhaps some kind of baobab tree—bulky and gnarled, with coarse facial features and a drooping nose like an immature eggplant. He was dressed in the already almost outmoded fashion of the rural bosses of those times: a diagonal-weave Stalin field jacket with external pockets and box calf boots. He smelled of Chipre eau de cologne, shoe polish, sweat and agricultural activity.

Shaleiko greeted Aglaya pleasantly, almost even rising from his seat.

"I haven't seen you in a long time," he said with a good-natured smile. "How are things?"

"So-so," Aglaya shrugged.

"I heard about your spot of trouble," he said in a low voice and sighed. "You're a woman of principle, inflexible. But it's the time of the flexible people now, the ones who know how to bend at the right moment. Especially since everything's changing now. Changing down here, changing up there."

He pointed upward with his eyes. She followed his glance and saw two portraits of Soviet leaders above the stage. There had always been two portraits hanging there. But before, they had been portraits of Lenin and Stalin, and now . . . what incredible impudence . . . Lenin and Khrushchev! Or "that Baldie," as she referred to Nikita Sergeevich. Aglaya was outraged to the very depths of her soul. She had managed to come to terms with Baldie's attacks on Stalin, but she hadn't expected him to take his insolence this far and set himself in Stalin's place. Beside Lenin. Who, by the way, was also bald and whom, without really admitting it to herself, she also did not like very much.

Sometimes Aglaya was overwhelmed by such paroxysms of fury that she quite literally began to shake. She clenched her fingers into tight fists, pressed her elbows against her sides and shuddered, feeling her heart pounding with incredible force. Once she had even tried to explain her condition to a neuropathologist. She had been afraid he would laugh at her, but he listened to her attentively and advised her to be wary of such occasions of extreme stress and shun them.

"Forgive me," he said, "but I am a doctor and I must speak frankly. Your problem is that you're an angry person. And the first person the feeling of anger destroys is the one in whom it arises. You're the one who experiences this feeling inside yourself, it's your heart and nobody else's that pounds so furiously, and entirely without any point. And the person you're so angry with might not even notice. I advise you very strongly, try not to be so angry, be kinder to people, not for their sake, but for your own."

She had taken the doctor's advice seriously and more or less tried to stick to it, but at the sight of Baldie's portrait she was unable to control herself, and once again she began shaking as though she was having a fit, although she realized that she was only harming herself. If only at least a part of her feelings had actually reached Baldie, he would probably have been incinerated, reduced to ashes on the spot, but there was no chance of that. She felt upset and wanted to leave. But at the very moment she started to get up, the lights in the hall went out, the stage was lit up by the beam of a spotlight and Shubkin appeared wearing crumpled trousers and a gray wool cardigan. He stood in the center of the stage looking out into the hall and squinting against the beam of the spotlight, then after a long pause he said quietly, "I have been around almost all the world . . ." And fell silent.

"He's lying," Shaleiko whispered to Aglaya. "He went around the camps, not the world."

"And life is good," Shubkin continued thoughtfully, "and it is good to live."

"It's a poem," said Aglaya.

"He's lying all the same," said Shaleiko.

Shubkin said nothing for a moment, then suddenly began speaking abruptly, sawing the air with his right hand.

"But in our combatant exuberant commotion, it is better still."

Aglaya began to feel bored. Stalin had said that Mayakovsky had been and still was the best, the most talented, poet of our Soviet era. She didn't dare to argue with Stalin, but she didn't like Mayakovsky. She was much fonder of Demyan Bedny and Mikhail Isakovsky, whom she knew from his songs. She listened to Shubkin with only half an ear, gazing straight past him.

And Shubkin said: "The snake-street twists and turns, the houses in a row along the snake."

At these words the boys and girls of the preschool group came running out from the wings, lined up in single file and began to run around the stage in a sinuous winding line, representing the snake-street.

"My street!" cried Shubkin. "My houses!"

The children surrounded Shubkin, and he flung out his arms, as though gathering them all in to protect them, and all of them together began shouting out triumphantly:

> "The shops stand with their windows open wide,
> Showing off the foodstuffs, tasty fruits and wine . . ."

Aglaya felt something touch her and looked down to see Shaleiko's knee rubbing against her own. At another time she might have enjoyed it. But now she wasn't in the mood. Onstage, Shubkin was behaving as though he was celebrating his victory over her. She looked into Shaleiko's face and said: "No."

He asked her in a whisper: "Why?"

She answered him: "Because."

He snorted in offense and began watching the stage, where the junior schoolchildren were performing a Red Navy sailors' dance. After that the intermediate-age schoolchildren performed the songs "Grenada" and "The Brigantine," and the senior pupils performed extracts from some play about Lenin, which Shubkin had apparently written himself and in which he had given himself the leading role. When he came back out on stage wearing makeup and a beard, everybody simply gasped at how much he looked the part! He ran quickly around the stage, gesticulating wildly, screwed up his eyes cunningly, burred his *r*'s French-style, slapped Stalin on the shoulder (he was played by Sveta Zhurkina in a false mustache) and called him "old chap," pointed out his mistakes and shook a finger under his nose: "Wemember, old chap, legality is one of the sup-wemely important features of socialism."

Aglaya watched the stage, clenched her fists and, forgetting the doctor's advice, she thought, I hate him!

Shubkin took over the second part of the concert completely, once again with poems by Mayakovsky and other poets. She heard "Verses About a Soviet Passport," clenched her fists and thought, I hate him! He recited "Anna Snegina" and she thought, I hate him! He read extracts from "Vasilii Tyorkin," and even then she thought, I hate him! But then he went on to some unprincipled modernist rubbish. Some Leonid Martynov or other:

> *What's this that's happened to me now?*
> *I talk to you and yet somehow,*
> *Although it's you my words are for,*
> *They're echoed in the room next door.*
> *And there's an echo I can hear*
> *In woods and forests far and near,*
> *In ruins right across the land*
> *And people's houses close at hand.*
> *I think it's no bad thing at all*
> *If every sigh and every call*
> *Travels so easily so far.*

An echo that resounds and chimes.
Must be the kind of times these are.
Must be the echo of the times.

I hate him, thought Aglaya, pressing her fists hard against her knees.

However, most of the audience enjoyed the concert. There was a lot of applause and, of course, the loudest was for Shubkin.

16

After the concert the celebrations continued in the director's office, at two long desks set end to end. Aglaya found herself sitting between Shaleiko and Shubkin. She didn't speak to Shubkin at all and even pretended not to notice him. Turning her back, she began asking Shaleiko loudly about collective farm business: how had the spring harvest gone and had they sowed a lot of winter crops? As he informed her in a low voice of the main figures, Shaleiko touched her knee with his hand under the tablecloth. She shook his hand off and asked about the livestock—had the cattle sheds been coldproofed for the winter?

"But of course," said Shaleiko, thrusting his hand back into place. "The roofs have been re-covered, the walls have been plastered, there are heaters everywhere."

She forced him off again and carried on sitting there as if she were alone, pouring her own port.

Bogdan Filippovich Nechitailo proposed a toast to the October Revolution, to the Party that had successfully overcome the consequences of the cult of personality and to our own dear Nikita Sergeevich Khrushchev, who was leading the country along the path of renewal. He made special mention of Nikita Sergeevich's efforts in the area of reinstating Leninist norms of socialist legality.

Continuing the toast, Chikurin asked people to raise their glasses for one particular example of reinstated legality—in other words, for Mark Semyonovich Shubkin. Who, as Chikurin put it, had not taken offense at the Party. "People don't take offense at the Party," Shaleiko put in.

"That's just what I'm saying," Chikurin agreed happily. "People don't take offense at the Party. Soviet people have their pride, they might take offense at their neighbor, their fellow worker, their wife, brother, mother and father, but not the Party . . ." he paused for a long moment, thrust out his lower lip and held up his forefinger, wagging it from side to side. "Uh—uh! And Mark Semyonovich hasn't taken offense . . . You haven't taken offense, have you, Mark Semyonovich?"

"Not in the slightest," responded Mark Semyonovich. "I haven't taken offense. And what's more, I've acquired some quite invaluable experience of life."

"You should have acquired a bit more," Aglaya joked unexpectedly.

"What?" asked Shubkin, turning toward her.

"Nothing," she said, and turned away.

"Yes," said Chikurin, continuing his speech. "Mark Semyonovich hasn't taken offense, he hasn't become embittered, he hasn't withdrawn into his own shell. He has launched himself energetically into work and social activity. He educates children and produces a newspaper, and he organized our amateur performance. Soon we're going to the district festival, where I have no doubt we'll take first prize."

Naturally, Aglaya took the praise of Shubkin as a reproach to herself, but she didn't meddle in the conversation again. All the toasts proposed were alien to her, but she felt like drinking and she did, only without clinking glasses with anyone. And the more she drank, the more she became aware of a strange attraction to Shubkin. Even though Shaleiko was still occasionally pestering her from her left side and annoying her with his hands. After two glasses of port and half of a third, she began feeling boisterous and, leaning across to Shubkin, asked, "Are you glad you won?"

"No, it wasn't you I was fighting against," Shubkin replied in a respectful tone, although he was three years older than she was. "I was defending principles. And I wish you no harm."

"Oh, of course not!" she said in disbelief. "Sure you do! I think if it was in your power," she said, surrendering to an agitation she was not even aware of, "you'd crack down pretty hard on me."

"Only in one way," said Shubkin. "I'd move you as far away as possible from children. But that's all."

Meanwhile, the merriment continued. After supper they moved the tables aside and began dancing to an accordion. The musician was

Aglaya's neighbor Zhorka Zhukov, a shock-haired, wild young guy who had been specially invited to perform for the gathering. He sat on a chair by the window with his glass of vodka set on the windowsill, and in the breaks between dances he took up the glass and sipped from it, then went on playing again with his eyes closed, as if he were asleep. Shaleiko persisted in his attentions, inviting Aglaya to dance. She danced one waltz with him but didn't really enjoy it.

Afterward, Shaleiko and Nechitailo sang a duet—"Boys, unharness the horses"—and Nechitailo's wife, Rada (which would translate from the Ukrainian as "Soviet"), performed an aria from the opera A *Zaporozhian Beyond the Danube*—"I'm a maiden from Poltava and my name it is Natalka."

When it was all over and the group of colleagues went tumbling out into the cold, rainy evening, Aglaya caught up with Shubkin outside the gates and tugged on his sleeve: "Listen you . . . if I had my way, if I'd come across you during the war . . . you mangy cur . . . my pistol . . . I'd have emptied the entire clip into you . . ."

Then she suddenly grabbed hold of him and pulled him hard against herself so that he thought she was trying to strangle him, not realizing that what she was feeling was a simultaneous upsurge of hatred and of passion. She wanted to kill him and at the same time she was consumed by the desire to be crushed beneath him, for him to trample her, smash her, flatten her out like dough on a board.

He was bigger than she was, the stronger sex, with muscles that had been pretty well developed in the logging camps. But coping with this frenzied woman proved anything but easy. He tried to break away but couldn't. She pulled his head down toward her and in her contradictory desire forced her mouth against him as though in a passionate kiss, but then pressed her teeth together and bit through his lower lip. The taste of blood made her want to keep on biting him, in anticipation of the onset of some exceptional state, but he cut short her passionate impulse with a rough shove and threw her off him so that she fell, bruising her knee and tearing her stocking, while he fled in horror, pressing his hand against his lip, spattering blood as he went and looking back over his shoulder.

Such behavior on her part may perhaps seem strange to some people. It seemed strange to this author. He even thought it might perhaps contain some key to the riddle of Aglaya's character and consulted a highly prestigious leading psychologist of the Freudian persuasion on the matter.

The psychological luminary thought long and hard before delivering judgment: "Your heroine evidently belongs to the type of woman who suffers from constant sexual frustration. Some endure it relatively calmly. But she's from a different category. She can't accept anything at all calmly, and especially this. Under certain circumstances her desire is so passionately aroused that she cannot control it and becomes irrational. This desire arises suddenly, like a fit, and it is capable, even without any sexual act, of driving her to the point of orgasm, but at the very last moment the fit passes, the peak of desire and passion remains unattained and the result is a powerful and painful emotional devastation that renders her harsh, vicious and cruel."

"All right," I said, "let us assume all that is true, but what has it all got to do with Shubkin? What desire can he provoke, if she hates him so much she could shoot him?"

"Well that," said the luminary, "is a fairly common psychological derangement. Insane hatred arouses the same kind of attraction as insane love. In a person like your Aglaya the most powerful manifestations of love and hate are quite indistinguishable from each other."

17

I feel sorry for those future generations who will not even be able to imagine that there was a time when the broad extensive lands of the Union of Soviet Socialist Republics (broad extensive lands, not expensive foreign brands) were all under the sway of a general system of sociopolitical views that were progressive in every respect and compulsory for every one of the three hundred million representatives of the peoples, nations and tribes (some of them still pretty wild) who occupied those extensive lands, and which went by the name of the Sole Correct Scientific World Outlook.

This world outlook was uniquely correct, and it was promulgated by the only political party (there was no need for any others). But while all the members of the Party accepted the Sole Correct Scientific World Outlook, they were divided among themselves into two hostile tendencies. One tendency was Marxist-Leninist and the other was Stalinist. The

Marxist-Leninists were good Marxists, kind people. They wanted to estab-
lish a good life on earth for good people and a bad life for bad people, but
it had to be done in accordance with the World Outlook. And therefore
they killed bad people, but whenever they could, they left the good people alive. The Stalinists, however, were essentially democrats—they killed
everybody without distinction, and they regarded the World Outlook not
as a dogma but as a guide to action. Consequently, the Marxist-Leninists
were regarded as humanists and devotees of the Sole Correct Scientific
World Outlook, while the Stalinists were devoted to Stalin and were prepared to follow him in any direction, wherever he might lead them.

And so the difference between Mark Semyonovich Shubkin and
Aglaya Stepanovna Revkina was that he was a Marxist-Leninist and she was
a Stalinist. But they both, each in their way, preached the Sole Correct
Scientific World Outlook, which our Admiral referred to by the acronym
SCOSWO, pronouncing it rather like a Japanese word—Scuswu.

By the way, about the Admiral. It's about time he was introduced in a
little greater detail.

Alexei Mikhailovich Makarov did not bear this sobriquet because he
had an admiral's surname. And it was not derived from his chosen profession, for by qualification he was a linguist and literary scholar. Nor was it
the result of his actual labor activity, for he spent his working hours as a
night watchman at a lumberyard. He was called Admiral because of his
infatuation with the sea, which he had never seen, but about which he
knew everything—from books. As a matter of fact, he knew everything
about everything from books. Even more than Shubkin. When they asked
him how he had acquired such extensive knowledge, he used to say it was
simply good luck. In his childhood he had been confined to bed by
poliomyelitis, so he had never played soccer or tag or chased the girls.
And in those days he had never seen a television or computers, or computer games or the Internet. And it was yet another stroke of luck that
he hadn't been born in America, where they would have invented some
kind of electromechanical gadget to help him get about that would have
distracted him from the acquisition of knowledge. Here in Russia he
had been provided with absolutely ideal conditions, in which there was
absolutely nothing else he could do but read an absolutely huge number
of books and learn an absolutely huge amount about everything.

Like many other people condemned to immobility, in his childhood
Alyosha Makarov had been fascinated by tales of sea voyages and adven-

tures. He began, of course, with Jules Verne and Robert Louis Stevenson and then delved deeper into the subject, studying the biography of every seafarer who was even slightly famous and the history of the discovery of various lands, and descriptions of sea battles, and he knew the different types of ships from ancient Greek galleys to modern atomic-powered vessels. In addition, he had an entire collection of navigational charts and nautical almanacs, but most important of all, he had a ship's wheel attached to the head of his bed, and it helped him plow his furrow through imaginary seas and oceans. By the age of eighteen Alyosha Makarov had made a partial recovery from his illness, had learned to walk with the support of two sticks, graduated from college (although largely by correspondence) and had even written a postgraduate dissertation on problems of linguistics. It was so brilliant that at first they wanted to award him a doctorate for it, but then they gave him five years in exile instead. That was how he had ended up in Dolgov from Moscow. At first he had lived here with his mother and then on his own. He couldn't work as a literary critic or perform any physical labor, and he wouldn't have been able to survive on his pension. Kind people fixed him up with a job at the lumberyard opposite his house, and he used to struggle across there on his sticks and spend every second night on watch.

And so our Admiral, being a man of immense learning and absolutely independent views, who always had his own original opinion on everything, regarded SCOSWO disrespectfully even in those times when very few people could even conceive of such a possibility. Under his influence I also began to ponder and to doubt things that had seemed incontrovertible to me only recently. I began to wonder why SCOSWO was regarded as exclusively true and scientific and why the cause of the people's future happiness required so many of the people to be killed, hounded, ruined, starved and frozen. And whether it might not have been better to invent some Uniquely Incorrect SCOSWO that would be a bit less hard on people. To this very day, however, the devotees of SCOSWO claim that the theory was good but the practice was bad. Lenin devised it correctly, but Stalin applied it wrongly. But who, where, in what country, has ever applied it correctly? Khrushchev? Brezhnev? Mao Tse-tung? Kim Il Sung? Ho Chi Minh? Pol Pot? Castro? Honecker? Who? Where? When? What is so good about this theory if it can never be confirmed in practice anywhere under any conditions?

Nowadays, of course, the number of people selflessly devoted to

SCOSWO has fallen a bit. But in the times we are describing here the broad expanses of our homeland were home to quite large numbers of them, one of whom was Mark Semyonovich Shubkin, a faithful adherent of SCOSWO, a disciple first of Lenin-Stalin and then of Lenin alone. But he held on to Lenin for a long time, with firm, total commitment. Shubkin remained faithful to SCOSWO and to Lenin before and after his arrest, during his nocturnal interrogations, even during the years he spent engaged in public works. Despite the cold and hunger, never, not once, not for a single moment (until a certain time came) did he doubt. Major and minor devils frequently tempted him, trying to sow doubt in his mind, but he endured like Jesus Christ, in whom he did not believe.

The investigator Tikhonravov beat Mark Semyonovich very painfully with a towel twisted into a heavy rope while abusing him in the vilest possible terms, blinded him with the table lamp, prevented him from sleeping and wouldn't let him sit down, but when Mark Semyonovich, enduring all of this stoically, pointed to the portrait of Lenin hanging above the investigator's head and rebuked him with quotations from the leader, Tikhonravov replied simply, "I couldn't give a shit for your Lenin." To which Shubkin was unable to find sufficiently convincing counterarguments. But he continued to display his previous fortitude. And he left the camp unbroken, undefeated, with his views unchanged. That is, in the words of the Admiral, he left it the same fool he was when he entered it. A sealed and certified fool, the Admiral called him, meaning a fool with certificates with big seals on them.

I must confess there were times when the Admiral's judgments seemed too harsh to me. And in Shubkin's case undeservedly harsh. After all, if a man had been through the camps and not changed his convictions in spite of everything, surely that was worthy of respect?

"Sheer stupidity, no matter what," the Admiral used to reply mercilessly, "and not even stupidity—absolute idiocy."

The Admiral regarded Shubkin with mild contempt, although at first he himself had attempted to shatter his faith in SCOSWO and its supreme idol. He used to tell Shubkin about the German money and the German railroad carriage (which also happened to have seals on it), about the priests and prostitutes executed on the personal orders of "the most humane man ever to walk the earth," about his progressive paralysis as a result of syphilis, and many other things which at that time were known to only a few. None of these stories produced even the slightest effect on

Shubkin. Especially since he knew many of them already. But he explained the actions of his idol by objective circumstances, harsh necessity and the fact that revolutions are not made wearing kid gloves. He advised the Admiral to undertake a close rereading of Lenin's full collected works. "And then," he said, "it will become clear even to you that Lenin is a genius." "If he's a genius," the Admiral used to argue, "then why is this prison camp socialism of ours so badly constructed?" Shubkin would object, "Lenin didn't intend to build what exists now, but something better." "But a genius," the Admiral used to say, "builds what he wants to build, not something else." "Lenin," Shubkin would explain, "could not foresee the inertness of the peasant masses, which would not appreciate the advantages of socialism, and he could not foresee that the petit-bourgeois element would work its way up to the leadership of the country, that the leadership would turn aside from the road he had chosen, reject the New Economic Policy and advance too fast into collectivization." "But a genius," the Admiral would persist, "is only a genius if he does foresee things. It doesn't take a genius not to foresee things. We can all do that." "Vladimir Ilich," Shubkin would sigh, "was born a hundred years ahead of his time." "Well there I agree with you," the Admiral would say, nodding his head in confirmation, "but at your age you should know that premature children are often retarded."

Shubkin withstood all the Admiral's onslaughts and for a long time, throughout the sixties and halfway through the seventies, he remained faithful to SCOSWO, and moreover, in doing so he behaved almost entirely in accordance with the behest of Christ, who had told his apostles: Go forth and preach. Shubkin preached to the old and the young, even to children of preschool age, hammering SCOSWO into childish heads in a form accessible to them.

For instance, in the form of folktales. Aglaya Stepanovna Revkina had been right when she suspected Shubkin of investing the apparently innocent tales that he told to children with far-from-innocent meaning. That was precisely it. When he told them about the wolf and the three little pigs, Shubkin did not make the gray wolf into the embodiment of American imperialism, as Aglaya wanted, or even a simple predator of the forest, but Stalin and the little pigs represented a trio whom he now regarded as faithful Leninists—Trotsky, Bukharin and Zinoviev.

18

The first person in Dolgov to make the acquaintance of Mark Semyonovich Shubkin had been the girl behind the counter at the railroad station
buffet, Antonina Uglazova, usually known by her diminutive "Tonka," a
short, plump woman of thirty-five with sad eyes who had been treated
badly by life. On that calm, cobweb-tangled summer day she had been
feeling bored, standing there with her fulsome breasts propped up on the
counter, when a passenger who had got off a train suddenly appeared in
front of her, dressed in an old army greatcoat and a cap with long earflaps
made out of the same material. He took off the cap and wiped his extensive bald patch with it (even at this stage Tonka noticed that his head was
unusually large), then asked how much the cabbage pies cost.

Tonka was about to reply out of force of habit, "Look for yourself, can't
you, you blind or something?" and nod at the price list standing there in
front of his eyes. But she took a look at him and changed her mind,
snatched up the price list and said, "Four a roople," although they cost
twice that much. He was surprised: "Why so cheap?" She shrugged her
shoulders: "That's what they are."

"Give me four pies and a glass of tea."

"With lemon?" she asked genially.

He fumbled in his pocket and said, "Lemon would be good."

"We're out of lemons," she sighed, spreading her hands.

He took the four pies and the tea and installed himself at a little table
by the window that looked out onto the dusty station square. In the middle of a flowerbed in the square, he could see a monument to Lenin representing the days spent by the original hiding from the Razliv police in
the forest near St. Petersburg on the eve of the revolution. The plaster
Ilich, perched on a plaster tree stump, was writing his "April Theses" in a
plaster notebook, while a drunk clutching a bottle lay slumped in a doze
against the foot of the pedestal with two goats grazing beside him. The
new arrival looked out of the window, Antonina looked at the new arrival,
and although he was eating his pies carefully without chomping, and
drinking his tea in little sips, she realized that he was from that place. How

could she not realize, when she herself lived in the world that people left to go to that place and to which they returned, or failed to return, from that place? One of those who had left and not yet returned was her husband Fedya, who had first beaten Antonina half to death, then taken a mistress and beaten her as well and finally hacked her to pieces with an ax. At the time, her women friends had been delighted for her: "Ooh, Tonka, what a stroke of luck! If he hadn't had Lizka, he'd have hacked you to bits."

This newcomer was not one of those men who resolve their relationships with the help of an ax, but Antonina had met men like him as well: they had been called "politicals," "contras" or "fascists," but all in all they were pretty civilized.

The newcomer ate his pies, washing them down with tea. She looked at him and for some reason felt like crying. Once she even bent down under the counter and brushed away a tear.

Encouraged by the cheap prices, the newcomer took another four pies, this time with jam, and another glass of tea and asked her if she knew anyone who could offer him temporary lodgings around here. And since she had a room in the station residential block, she said she could. Without giving it a second thought, he lugged his suitcase over to her place and they began living together.

She addressed him formally, using his first name and patronymic — Mark Semyonovich.

"You've got a big head, Mark Semyonovich," she used to say sometimes, pressing his head against her equally big chest.

"Big and bald," Mark Semyonovich would elaborate jokingly.

"It's good that it's bald, there's nowhere for the lice to breed. And if anything does try to live there, it'll slip off, because you're as steep around here as . . . well as I don't know what." And she would fall silent, unable to find an appropriate comparison.

She looked after him like a little child. From the time he moved in with her, the shirts he wore were always clean, his socks were darned and his trousers ironed. In less than three months his cheeks had filled out and he was beginning to develop a belly. Mark Semyonovich, once reduced to skin and bone in the prison camp, frequently glanced at his own belly and stroked it respectfully. Everything Antonina did to take care of Shubkin, she did unselfishly, without demanding either love or a visit to the church or a wedding certificate or faithfulness in return. She just looked at him often, happy that he was there and sad because she realized he probably wouldn't be staying for long.

Antonina understood that she was no match for her roommate. What she didn't know was that this suited him very well. He had a match once. She was called Lyalya. She called Mark Semyonovich "Markel" and had no regard for his talent, but she loved glad rags, restaurants, operatic tenors and generally putting on the style. It was impossible to imagine her standing at the stove, darning or even sewing on a button. Fortunately for Shubkin, Lyalya had proved unable to withstand the test of a lengthy separation, concerning which he had been informed by the arrival in the Khanty-Mansiisk taiga of a telegram:

SORRY STOP IN LOVE SOMEONE ELSE STOP VERY BEST WISHES STOP FIRM HAND SHAKE STOP LYALYA STOP

And so Antonina's position was actually far more promising than she could have imagined.

Having spent many years of his life building socialism in particularly difficult conditions, Mark Semyonovich Shubkin now attempted to make up for lost time. He bought himself a secondhand German typewriter, a Triumph-Adler with a large carriage and several missing letters (the Russian letters had been welded over the German ones, like on like, but the Russian alphabet had more of them). With his own hands, which he admitted were incapable of drawing a straight line, he put together a shaky table without a single straight line in it from badly planed planks and plywood, on which he stood a table lamp constructed to his own design from aluminum wire, with a shade made from the newspaper *Izvestiya*, and under this lamp he spent the greater part of his free time. But he didn't have very much free time. He worked from morning till late in the children's home, where he also held rehearsals with the Meyerhold Drama Club (he had chosen that name for the club himself) and classes with the Brigantine Literary Club and edited the wall newspaper "Happy Childhood," and when he came home, he dashed straight over to his Record valve radio and listened to "the voice of the enemy" as he lit up a High Tide cigarette and immediately, wasting no time, loaded four sheets of paper with carbon paper into his typewriter and beginning to hammer out the lines or columns of his next text with furious speed. He was working simultaneously on his lyrical verse and the allegorical poem "Dawn in

Norilsk" (about the sun rising after the long winter), and the novel *The Timber Camp* (about the work of convicts in the Khanty-Mansiisk taiga), and his memoirs under the title "Years of My Life Remembered," and articles on questions of morality and pedagogy, which he submitted in large numbers to the central newspapers, and letters to the Central Committee of the CPSU and to Khrushchev in person, which always began with the words "Dear and Respected Nikita Sergeevich!" Antonina sat on the divan beside the table, knitting her cohabitant a cap, since not a single piece of headgear available in the shops would fit on his head. Our Soviet industry was oriented toward the head size of the average Soviet man and gross output figures, and mass production could not cater to Mark Semyonovich's size ten.

Antonina worked away with her needles, from time to time glancing curiously at Shubkin. Sometimes, when he fell into deep thought about something, his eyes would glaze over and his mouth would fall open and he would stay like that for many minutes, so that Tonka, frightened that Shubkin had departed for a place from which there is no return, would call out to him: "Mark Semyonovich!"

But there were times when his trance was so deep that he was deaf to all her calls. She would repeat his name again and again, go over and shake him, shout right in his ear: "Mark Semyonovich!"

He would shudder violently, stare at her with crazy eyes and call out: "Ah? What?" Then as he came around, he would ask: "What is it, Antonina?"

"Nothing," she would reply in embarrassment and explain with a blissful smile, "it's just that I'd like to know, Mark Semyonovich, what it is you keep thinking about all the time, racking your brains so hard."

"Ah, my dear Tonka," Mark Semyonovich would reply with a sigh. "It seems to me that our Party is overshadowed by the threat of a new Thermidor and petit-bourgeois degeneration."

Since she didn't know the word "Thermidor," he would begin to enlighten her, telling her about the Great French Revolution, and then about something else, so that everything became jumbled up together: literature, history and philosophy. He recited by heart to her Pushkin's *Poltava* and *Eugene Onegin* and Mayakovsky's poem *Vladimir Ilich Lenin*, related the contents of Chernyshevsky's novel *What Is to Be Done?* or Tommaso Campanella's *City of the Sun*. At one time he had attempted to expose Lyalya to enlightenment in a similar fashion, but while he was telling her something, she would be putting on her lipstick or trying on a new dress in front of the mirror, or she would interrupt him with remarks about some new show or snatch up the phone when it rang and generally give the impression that she knew all this stuff herself anyway. Antonina was a far more grateful listener. She gazed unblinkingly at Mark Semyonovich with her mouth wide open as he strode about the room gesturing wildly and introducing her to the myths of Ancient Greece, telling her about distant countries, about journeys and travelers, revolutionaries, dreamers and fighters for the people's cause, about seas, stars and future flights into outer space. Unfortunately, as she said herself, she had a head like a sieve, and everything flew straight out through its holes and on out into space—not a thing was retained. Thanks to those holes, he could tell Antonina one and the same story an infinite number of times, and she always listened just as attentively.

But educational activity wasn't the only way Shubkin and his Antonina passed the time. In the morning she would arrive at work weary and exhausted, with dark rings under her eyes. The station cashier Zina Trushina would ask her enviously: "Well, how was it?"

Tonka didn't reply by reciting poems or retelling the story of Campanella's utopia, or even by talking about potential flights through space to other worlds. She shook her head, screwed up her eyes and reported in a low voice: "Never took it out once all night."

"Does he beat you?" Zina once asked her.

"What do you mean!" Tonka was outraged. Then she glanced around before explaining in a whisper, with a certain degree of pride, "He's a Jew-boy!"

19

In the summer of 1957, Aglaya's unassuming neighbor Savelii Artyomovich Telushkin passed away. The room of the deceased proved to contain no furniture and no valuables apart from a simple iron bed, a pine kitchen table with a single set of drawers and a stool. But when they opened up the mattress, they discovered an entire hoard of treasure:

watches, bracelets, earrings, wedding rings, rings with stones, a silver cigarette case, a pouch crammed full of gold crowns from teeth and a Gold
Star medal which was real gold, but a false medal, without a number. Not
even the agents of the Ministry of State Security knew where the dead
man had come by these valuables. When the supreme measure was
implemented, the belongings of the people who were shot were confiscated, and if they were stolen, then naturally it was not by the execution-
ers but by somewhat higher-placed individuals. They did say that after
Telushkin's death the secret services made an attempt to investigate the
source of the dead man's riches. For this purpose an employee of the
investigative agencies, who introduced himself by the fictional name of
Vasilii Vasilievich, would turn up from time to time in the house on Komsomol Cul-de-Sac and go around to the neighbors asking what they
remembered about the deceased's way of life, but they didn't remember
anything, apart from the fact that Telushkin was quiet and inoffensive and
used to say "Good health to you" or "Keep well" whenever he met anyone. We have already mentioned that the scene he left behind him was
squalid. But in addition, the walls were covered all over with various
words of wisdom from world-famous great people and the thoughts of the
author himself, who employed nonstandard grammar and orthography in
his writings, either omitting vowels completely or using the wrong ones.
For instance, he had written: "In Strovskys stry 'Hw the stil was tmpred'
the lif lin is corrct." "The Rusn will alwys achive hs gol," "Childrn are our
fture." "18 Agust is the day of our brav pilts." "Mn trnsfrms nautre." "The
lov of a man for a wman is an illnss and suffring of the orgnsm." "Ther is
no lif on Mars" and "The dearst thng for mn is lif."

Many people joined in the contest for Telushkin's room, but as a victim of unjustified political repression, Mark Semyonovich Shubkin was
awarded it ahead of the line.

20

Of course, Aglaya was not pleased by Shubkin's prospective move to
become one of her neighbors. But this was partly eclipsed by another,

even more unpleasant event—the June 1957 Plenum of the Central Committee of the CPSU and the hastily convened district Party conference, to which Aglaya was one of the invited delegates. The regional Party representative, Shurygin, who came down for the occasion, brought the comrades alarming news. In Moscow they had discovered an anti-Party faction including not just anybody, but members of the Presidium of the Central Committee of the CPSU—Coms. Malenkov, Molotov and Kaganovich. And in addition, according to the formulation of the official announcement, their close collaborator Shepilov. In the bureaucratic Party grammar of that time the abbreviation "coms." signified "comrades"—but not simply comrades: it meant "bad comrades." If it was necessary to say that good comrades had spoken, for instance Comrade Khrushchev or Mikoyan or someone like that, then they wrote the full word—"comrades"— but if they were bad comrades, then they weren't "comrades" but "coms." As for their collaborator Shepilov, he immediately became the butt of numerous jokes and anecdotes and a legendary figure of fun to the alcoholics of the Soviet Union, in particular in the town of Dolgov, where individuals of that particular category magnanimously identified this character as one of their own, and when two of them were standing in line for vodka, they would address a presumptive third drinking partner as follows: "Fancy being Shepilov?" Meaning: Fancy a bit of collaboration? No doubt in time this joke reached Shepilov's own ears, and he must surely have been offended that every alcoholic who had a ruble to spare could become Shepilov, if only for a short while.

The essence of the conflict that took place in the leadership of the CPSU (no one remembers it nowadays) was that the bad coms. had disagreed with the ideas of the good "comrades" and the decisions of the Twentieth Congress of the CPSU. They had not accepted the Party's policy directed at overcoming the consequences of the cult of personality and had even entered into a conspiracy to seize power.

After this announcement the floor had been taken by district Party committee secretary Nechaev, a flabby man with cheeks that were round and pink from premature arteriosclerosis and thick ears that looked as though they were molded out of dough.

"The communists of the district," he said, "wholeheartedly and absolutely approve the principled line of our Leninist Central Committee and pour scorn on the pitiful band of turncoats and factionalists."

The resolution to be voted on was written and presented in the same spirit.

"Who is in favor?" Nechaev asked.

Everyone immediately threw their hands up in the air and Stepan Kharitonovich Shaleiko, sitting in the front row, threw up both hands and cried out: "We approve! We approve! We wholeheartedly and absolutely approve!"

"Whosagainstabstained?" Nechaev asked quickly, running the words together without waiting for any answer. He had already opened his mouth to utter the customary "Carried unanimously" when suddenly Porosyaninov nudged him in the side with an elbow, and in any case he had already noticed a slim arm raised in the back row like a solitary blade of grass swaying in the breeze. "Comrade Revkina?" Nechaev couldn't believe his eyes. "You?" He glanced around at Shurygin and shrugged, indicating that he was not to blame, that for him this was a very great and unpleasant surprise. "You? Aglaya Stepanovna? How is this possible? Are you abst—are . . . you abstaining?"

He was bewildered, but Aglaya was not entirely in control of herself either. She recalled afterward that it had been easier to advance into the attack against a withering barrage of fire than publicly oppose a Party decision. But even so . . .

"Yes," she confirmed in a quiet voice. "I mean, that is . . ." And she fell silent, unable to pronounce another single word.

The hall froze, and the silence that fell was so complete you could hear the drops of sweat rustling as they dripped from Nechaev's soft ears. Aglaya's action had taken everyone by surprise. These questions about who was in favor, who was opposed and who abstained had never been more than mere ritual, and in every single case, important or unimportant, according to the ritual, people voted only in favor. Always in favor and never against. And they never abstained. There was no difference between "abstained" and "opposed" because, as Mark Semyonovich Shubkin's favorite poet had put it: "Whoever does not sing with us today, he is against us."

Everyone sitting in the hall was overwhelmed by contradictory feelings. On the one hand, they were terribly curious to see where all this would lead. None of them would have minded a scandal that would introduce a little excitement into their uneventful, boring, stagnant provincial life. But on the other hand, they were afraid. If it could have been simply a scandal and no more: somebody stole something from somebody, or took a bribe from somebody, or gave somebody a poke in the face or even was unfaithful to his wife, or something of the sort. Such things did happen in the district Party organization and they were condemned, but they were regarded with sympathetic understanding. In such cases the culprit was reproached, shamed and threatened with exclusion from the Party. The culprit repented, wept, pounded his fist against his chest, and that was the end of the matter. But this time the scandal that had erupted was so serious it was bound to extend beyond the district and on up to some higher level, where they would consider it and take note that in the district concerned something was amiss with the communist consciousness of the masses, propaganda and agitation, that there was ideological vacillation and deviation afoot, and in general the whole business smacked of nothing less (how terrible even to utter the words!) than ideological sabotage. And all sorts of checks and purges would begin in the district. Involving the elucidation of who had stolen how much from where. Or taken a bribe from somebody. Or given somebody a poke in the face. Or taken and given. And although the delegates at the Dolgov conference were all to a man absolutely devoted to SCOSWO and the latest instructions from the highest levels of the Party, to claim that none of them had ever stolen anything, or given anybody a bribe, or taken a bribe from anybody or entered a fake item in the accounts, or written off an item and pocketed the money, would have been excessive. But the more a man stole, the more intransigent he was in the area of ideology. The reaction of the assembly to what had happened was therefore sincere and decisive, although it only followed after a slight delay. At first the silence was absolute. Not a single voice. Then it began—flowing, sweeping, rolling forward from the back rows to the front. Rustling, rippling, rumbling, roaring like the pounding of ocean waves on the shore, and the closer to the presidium, the more powerful it became. The rumbling and coughing and clattering of chairs and individual cries fused into a single sound, and suddenly there came a piercing squeal from someone—"Shame! Shame!"—and everyone there was caught up in the mounting wave of passion—yelling, howling, whistling, clapping their hands and stamping their feet. Like dogs loosed from the leash, they were excited by the chance to bite and tear the victim who had been thrown to them without fear of punishment. The director of the meat combine, Botviniev, suddenly leapt up onto the stage in front of the presidium, waving his fist in the air as though he were twirling a rope above his head, and began shouting: "Glory to the Communist Party! Glory to the Communist Party! Glory to the Communist Party!" with an expression that suggested he was passionately eager to give his life for the Party without delay, right there and then. Only a few days earlier, in fact, criminal proceedings had been instigated against him for the theft of meat products on an exceptionally large scale, but his response had been to demonstrate his devotion to the Party and rely confidently on the indulgence of the forces of law and order. The audience in the hall seemed so wild that it could no longer restrain itself, but Nechaev raised his hand and the delegates who only the moment before were out of control suddenly became calm and docile, and only a few of them went on squealing for a while, but even they gradually grew quieter.

"Aglaya Stepanovna," said Nechaev, speaking quietly in the silence that had fallen, "if I understand you correctly, you disagree with the Party line. Perhaps you would approach the podium and explain your position."

"Yes, let her tell us," Porosyaninov said loudly.

"Let her tell us." The head of the district hospital, Muravyova, leapt to her feet and began shouting, to make sure that the presidium would note her zeal: "Who are you working for, Revkina?"

"Not for you," said Aglaya, setting out for the podium. But the closer she got to it, the less determined she felt. And when she reached the podium, her courage had deserted her completely. Her knees were so weak she wanted to sit or even lie down. She leaned against the top of the lectern and began mumbling something about Russian Ivans who had forgotten their origins, and something else equally unintelligible.

In the hall the tension mounted again and shouts rang out: "Stop that!" "That's enough." "No more!" "Get her off!"

Botviniev, back up on the stage again, shouted: "Long live our dear beloved Nikita Sergeevich!" Then he pointed at Aglaya and began asking questions. "Comrades, can anyone tell me what's going on here? Why is this woman here? What makes her think she can oppose our Party, the people, the state, you and me and our children . . ."

"Shame on her!" a bass voice boomed from the back.

"Shame!" another voice squeaked.

And it started again, rolling around the hall: "Shame! Shame! Shame!"

Aglaya had not expected this kind of reaction. Partisan and war hero that she was, she was genuinely frightened, and she covered her face with her hands and ran out of the hall in tears. Nechaev and Porosyaninov tried to stop her: "Aglaya Stepanovna! Comrade Revkina!"

She didn't stop.

Yes, Aglaya had never believed in what came to be called errors of the cult of personality, deviations from the Leninist norms or transgressions of socialist legality. She had been irritated by discussions of illegal repression and innocent victims. She had always said that in our country (after all, it was ours!) no one would ever be imprisoned unjustly. But on that day her sense of justice underwent a sudden and drastic transformation. When she got home, she locked all the bolts on her door, then stood the table against it, and she wanted to put the wardrobe there as well, but she wasn't strong enough. She moved the bed across and lay down on it fully dressed, only taking off her boots.

Since her partisan days she had kept a captured eight-shot Walther pistol hidden in an old felt boot in the closet. Now she took it out and put it on a chair beside her, promising herself she would never be taken alive.

She didn't sleep at all until four in the morning, and even then her sleep was troubled. She dreamed of tall boots squeaking as they walked up the stairs on their own, holding big revolvers in their hands. Afterward, she herself was astonished: how could boots have hands? But the difference between a dream and reality is that in a dream anything is possible. The boots with the revolvers climbed up the stairs, something hairy tried to climb in through the window and the steely voice of Chief Prosecutor Vyshinsky echoed down an iron pipe, pronouncing sentence: "In the name of the Union of Soviet Socialist Republics . . . " In her dream Aglaya tried to call out, but although her mouth opened, it produced no sound. Twice in her dream she grabbed hold of her pistol, but it wasn't her pistol, it was only a rubber toy.

As morning approached, she finally fell into a sound sleep and slept for what seemed like a long time, but she was woken by the sun in her eyes and the sound of an automobile driving into the yard. The automobile drove in, the engine was switched off, she heard several voices and a man's voice asked: "Where is it then?"

Greta the Greek's voice answered: "On the second floor, dearie. When you get up there, it's the first door."

And straightaway there was the squeaking of footsteps on the stairs—several people were walking up in step. She leapt up, looked out of the window and froze at the sight of the black raven standing in the yard and the driver with the shoulder straps of a sergeant in the forces of the Ministry of the Interior who was lighting up a cigarette as he leaned back against the radiator.

The people walking up the stairs had reached the second floor, and now they were shuffling about on the landing in apparent indecision.

Aglaya dashed back to the bed, grabbed the pistol and unlocked the safety catch. She began thinking quickly: Should she shoot herself immediately or . . . after all, her Walther had eight shots, and she only needed one cartridge—the last.

21

As far as the author has been able to observe in the course of his life, most people, even the most educated, have neither any awareness nor any understanding of the fact that they exist in history. The majority think that everything will always be the way it is today. And if a historical event happens to have taken place before their very eyes, they see the reason for its occurrence in a temporal coincidence of misunderstandings. And it seems to them that everything can be put back the way it was. Some of them hope for this and others fear it. Aglaya hoped and Shubkin feared, but neither of them understood that history does not make any reverse moves. For better or for worse, a process was under way, and the further it proceeded, the more illusory Aglaya's hopes appeared and the more pointless Shubkin's fears became. Of course, things did not actually go so far that Aglaya was punished for ruining the peasantry and Shubkin was glorified for the injuries he had suffered, but by and large there was a definite movement in a certain direction, and one of the more petty outcomes of these great changes was that Mark Semyonovich was offered a room of his own in a two-room flat in house no. 1 on Komsomol Cul-de-Sac. This room was twice as big as the barracks-block room that Mark Semyonovich and Antonina had occupied previously. It had a kitchen, a bathroom and a water closet, and all with only one other person sharing—Shurochka the Idiot.

Mark Semyonovich had received his certificate of entitlement on Saturday, and on Sunday, after packing his own things and Tonka's into bundles and tying together with string a bundle of books from his still-small library, he went out onto Poperechno-Pochtamtskaya Street hoping to catch some means of transport. He hadn't figured on it being a Sunday, when most of the state's trucks would be standing idle. And ordinary automobiles were no good to him. He stood there waving his hand for a long time. Two trucks went by without stopping. The third, a dump truck, did stop, but it had just been carrying coal and was so dirty that after glancing into the back Shubkin said no thank you. He had already given up hope when a black raven pulled to a sharp halt beside him.

You can easily imagine what feelings Mark Semyonovich experienced at the sight of such a familiar form of transport. He shuddered, expecting a squad of Ministry of the Interior agents to come tumbling out of the vehicle and grab him by his lily-white arms. But there was no squad in the van; there was only the driver, Senior Sergeant Opryzhkin, with a cheerful expression on his face.

"In you get, Pops, I'll take you," he said, swinging open the right-side door.

"Where will you take me?" Shubkin asked cautiously.

"Where you need to go, that's where."

As anyone who has read *Chonkin* will remember—and anyone who has not will know anyway—in popular speech the phrase "where you need to go" was used to refer to places where no one really wanted to go. In other words, the public prosecutor's office, the police and other agencies of violent coercion. So it is quite easy to appreciate how Shubkin felt and to understand why he began assuring Opryzhkin that he didn't need to go anywhere.

"If you don't need to go anywhere," said Opryzhkin, getting angry, "then why are you standing here waving your hand about?"

Recovering his wits and realizing the driver was alone and the situation in general didn't really look much like an arrest, Mark Semyonovich told the senior sergeant that he did need a vehicle, only not this kind, but one in which he could move furniture.

"So what's wrong with this one?" Opryzhkin asked, almost offended. "It's no different from a bus, it's just got bars on the windows."

He proved to be quite talkative, and on the way he explained that his job was very hard work, his family was big and his paycheck was small, and the boss of the prison, Major Bugrov, was a good guy and allowed him to earn a bit on the side when he wasn't busy transporting prisoners.

"Naturally, I split the proceeds with him, how else? If you want to live, give the other guy a break. Isn't that right, Pops?"

"Perhaps," Shubkin answered evasively.

Opryzhkin began pondering some thought and then he asked: "Generally speaking, Pops, what d'you reckon, is life better now than under Stalin, or worse?"

Of course, if Shubkin had been more cautious, he might have suspected that this question was a deliberate provocation, but Mark Semyonovich had never been cautious and even the camp had failed to teach him much in this regard. He believed there was some good in every man, and so he answered Opryzhkin ingenuously that in his view life was much better without Stalin than with him.

"That's what I think too," Opryzhkin agreed readily. "Although, of course, under him there was order. But then again people were scared all the time. For instance, under Stalin, would I have been earning a bit on the side? Not on your life."

22

We parted company with Aglaya Stepanovna Revkina at that dramatic moment when, after spotting the black raven, she had prepared herself for the worst. She was expecting the people who had come up to the second floor landing to start hammering on her door with their fists and demanding that she open it in the name of the Union of Soviet Socialist Republics. And then, without waiting for a reply, they would start breaking the door in or shooting through it with all sorts of firearms. But none of this happened. The people stomped about a bit on the landing, then began quietly walking back downstairs. Aglaya waited a little longer before peeping around the edge of the net curtain and only then realized the banal purpose for which the black vehicle was being used.

This picture was perhaps more effective than the Twentieth Party

Congress, the current Plenum of the Central Committee of the CPSU and any other events in convincing Aglaya that the era of Stalin had retreated irretrievably into the past.

Aglaya was actually rather disappointed to discover that no one was planning to arrest her. Her willingness to die a heroic death had been wasted, and now she would have to live an ordinary, everyday, boring life once again. As soon as she realized this, she immediately felt hungry. She stuck her Walther back in the felt boot and stuck her head into the refrigerator — it was empty.

The grocery store was closed since it was Sunday, so Aglaya decided to visit the tearoom and take breakfast there, settle her nerves a bit and listen to what the people were saying.

In the yard the unloading of the black raven was proceeding under the gaze of the inhabitants of house no. 1-a, who had nothing better to do. They all had nothing better to do because it wasn't a working day and it wasn't raining. The grannies had lined themselves up on the bench to observe the proceedings and pass comment.

"All them books, look at them all!" Greta the Greek said in amazement. "What does he need all those for? They collect heaps of dust!"

"And bedbugs!" put in Old Nadya.

"Nah, bedbugs don't live in books," Greta the Greek said doubtfully.

"Why can't they live in books? They live everywhere else, so why not in books?"

"Well they don't live in books," Greta the Greek insisted. "They live in the wall, in the bed, close to your body. But why would they live in books, what would they feed on? Eat the letters, would they?" She even laughed at the very idea.

"The point is, what's the good of so many of them?" said Old Nadya, giving way. "Just to show people how smart you are, reading all those books. But no one's going to believe it anyway."

"Why wouldn't they believe it?" Greta the Greek objected. "My grandson Iliukha's always reading too, all the time. Even in bed and at the table. And sometimes he gets so carried away reading it's like he's blind and deaf. He laughs and he cries. I tell him: 'Iliukha! What is it? What do you want with these books, if they only make you suffer like that? Why don't you run outside and play with the boys, kick a ball about and get a breath of fresh air?' But oh no! He just goes on reading and reading . . ."

Old Nadya was about to express some opinion of her own on this matter, but the grannies were suddenly distracted by the appearance in the yard of Aglaya, who, as the grannies observed, was not in a good mood following the previous day.

The process of unloading the black raven was approaching its completion. Antonina and the driver were placing bundles of books and belongings on the nickel-plated bedstead with four knobs on its corner posts that had been taken out beforehand. Shubkin was walking toward Aglaya, carrying his Record radio in front of him. He seemed to be embarrassed, or perhaps even scared, at the sight of his future neighbor and stepped aside so she couldn't bite him, but he said hello. Aglaya surprised even herself by mumbling "Morning" and walked on, accompanied on her way by the glances of the neighbors sitting on the bench.

The tearoom was located in a single-story wooden building with a high porch and a planking veranda. Sitting on the veranda was a bearded beggar with a pack of dirty little dogs huddling close against each other and a piece of cardboard lying in front of him with the words WE WANT TO EAT TOO. Beside it lay a cap for donations. Aglaya had encountered this beggar in many different parts of town. She had never given him anything and never seen anyone else give him anything, but this time in some mysterious fit of generosity she tipped out all the change in her purse into the cap. The tearoom was dim and smoky, damp and stuffy. The floor was not covered with carpet but with a thick layer of sawdust that couldn't possibly have been changed since the First World War, and walking on it was like walking on powdery snow. There were sticky flypapers dangling in yellow spirals above the tables, and hanging along the wall that divided the kitchen from the dining area, there were two lengths of canvas bearing aphorisms. The first (which they hadn't got around to taking down yet) said:

NUTRITION IS ONE OF THE FUNDAMENTAL CONDITIONS OF HUMAN EXISTENCE AND ONE OF THE FUNDAMENTAL PROBLEMS OF HUMAN CULTURE.

I. Stalin

And the second said:

GOOD, WHOLESOME FOOD MUST BE EATEN WITH
APPETITE AND EXPERIENCED AS A PLEASURE.

Acad. I. Pavlov

There was a wide variety of people gathered in the tearoom. Chairmen of local collective farms, engineers on working visits, land surveyors, agricultural machinery operators, drivers, public prosecutors and other folk either more or less important, some wearing jackets, others in shirts with short sleeves and some simply in their undershirts.

The place was never empty on Sundays, but today the number of visitors had been sharply increased by the arrival of the Harvest soccer team from the nearby town of Zatyopinsk. The final of the district cup was being played at the Dolgov stadium, and the visiting team had turned up complete with two trainers, six reserves and the medical assistant Tamara, who was holding a large traveling bag near her feet containing bandages and lotions for dealing with the various kinds of trouble that might occur during the forthcoming game and especially after it. The point being that the Harvest team and Dolgov's own Avant-Garde were constant rivals. Both teams had their own supporters who beat up visiting sportsmen after the game if the visitors won, and very severely too, regarding it as their patriotic duty. Harvest had defeated the Dolgov team for several years in a row in every game, both at home and away, and so their players had been beaten up regularly. There had been times when they were willing to cut a deal with their rivals to draw or even lose a game, but the next time they played, they were carried away by their sporting enthusiasm, forgot all about the inevitable punishment in prospect and, unfortunately for them, won yet again. The footballers had moved several tables together by a window and were drinking compote made from dried fruits with macaroni and ground beef and keeping quiet, trying not to attract any special attention.

The tearoom smelled of sour cabbage soup, damp sawdust, machine oil and sweat.

Aglaya's feet sank into the sawdust as she advanced into the hall, screwing up her eyes and trying to spot a free place through the thick tobacco smoke. She spotted Stepan Kharitonovich Shaleiko by the window, redfaced and jolly in a Ukrainian shirt and suspenders, gabardine riding breeches and white canvas boots cleaned with tooth powder. His canvas jacket was hanging on the back of the chair beside him, his canvas briefcase was lying on the chair and his wide-brimmed straw hat was lying on the briefcase. Aglaya thought Shaleiko would turn away and pretend he hadn't noticed her, but in fact, when he caught sight of her in the distance, he began smiling broadly and waving his arms around, inviting her to join him at his table.

"Siddown," he said when she got closer. He moved the jacket to the back of his own chair, stood the briefcase by his feet and, since he could find no other place for it, placed the hat on his head. There was a plate in front of him, smeared with the remains of macaroni and ground beef, with an aluminum fork, an empty spirits glass and a half-drunk glass of beer. The combined beverage with which Shaleiko was regaling himself on this day off work went by the name of "one fifty with a chaser," since it consisted of 150 cubic centimeters of vodka and a glass of beer. How many "chasers" Shaleiko had consumed remained uncertain, and his tongue managed the conversation clumsily.

Shaleiko sat Aglaya down beside him and clapped his hands, and immediately the waitress, Anyuta, appeared—fat and square with short legs and extremely popular with heavy truck drivers who happened to be passing through.

"Right," Shaleiko said to her, "for the lady a hundred grams of Moldavian cognac and as for the food—everything that Aglaya Stepanovna desires."

The number of dishes in the tearoom that could be defined as desirable and appropriate in terms of Academician Pavlov's definition was restricted to two: macaroni and ground beef, and goulash with stewed cabbage. Aglaya ordered the goulash and in the meantime sipped at her cognac without any food.

Shaleiko watched her closely and good-naturedly with his small eyes under ginger eyelashes.

"Yesterday at the conference," he said, swigging from his beer mug, "I was listening to you, Stepanovna, and I was delighted that we still have communists like you. Honest, principled, courageous. Especially among the female sex. To tell the truth, our menfolk are a bit short on gumption. But you gave it to them—smack between the horns!" He even swung his fist through the air in imitation of the blow struck by Aglaya against some horned creature. "That was really something. So here's to you. Well done!" He took another swig. "But you know, yesterday I was so upset, really upset I was! After I heard the way you spoke and the way they all shouted at you, I was so upset I just wanted to drive straight back home. And I was going to, but on the way out of town—bang, the clutch went. We've just pulled out on the highway and my driver's fiddling with something. I ask him what's up; he says, 'The clutch.' So, of course, we turn back again." Shaleiko took a pack of Northern Palmyra papyrosas out of his side pocket, offered Aglaya one and lit up himself. "Went all over the place, begging around the motor depots, the Agricultural Technical Station—not a clutch to be had anywhere. Spent the night in the Collective Farm Workers' House. They promised me one in the district Party committee garage, only not till Monday morning, they said. No sooner, just no way. Spent the night in the Collective Farm Workers' House. Lying there alone, smoking, thinking. What's happening to us, I'm thinking, why are we all like, you know what. I'm a Cossack. I went into attack at the front without any helmet—and I wasn't afraid. And now at this conference I sit there with my head pulled into my shoulders, sit there without breathing, thinking, Lord let it pass me by, don't let them call me up. My whatsit . . . my clutch has gone, and there I am lying in the hotel thinking what's going on here—you know? Only yesterday everyone was for Comrade Stalin, every single one, but today every single one's against? They've already made up this ditty about it. You haven't heard it, I suppose?"

"No, I haven't."

"I'll tell it to you." He leaned down toward her ear and recited: "Europe thinks we're really crass, thinks our gray cells must have gone. Thirty years licking one . . . backside—begging your pardon—turns out it was the wrong one."

"Rotten filth," was Aglaya's reaction.

"That's right, it's filth," Shaleiko agreed readily. "My driver told me. You know, he's not politically aware, just comes out with anything he hears. But if the people are putting that kind of thing around, it's significant. So here's what I think. Yesterday everyone was in favor of being in favor, and today everyone's in favor of being against, and hands up, everyone! Some communists—just a bunch of backsides. I was so upset I would have gone back home, but my clutch went, and I put it in that garage there. And I'm lying in the hotel, thinking. If they touch Aglaya Revkina, I think, I'm going too. Myself, voluntarily. Party card down on the table. And that's it. I'm Shaleiko, I'm a Cossack. Anyuta," he managed to grab hold of the edge of the waitress's apron as she went running by. "Why do you just keep running past us all the time, ignoring your customers like that? Bring me the same again."

"With a chaser?" Anyuta asked.

"With a chaser. A hundred fifty. And another hundred grams of cognac for Aglaya Stepanovna. You know yesterday my clutch went . . ."

Anyuta left without waiting to hear what came next.

"Backsides, that's all they are," Shaleiko went on. "But you gave it to them smack between the eyes. And when you left, that ugly pig Porosyaninov said we had to address the question of your continued membership immediately. But Nechaev stood up for you. He's a straight guy. Said we're not going to ruin anyone for no reason. Comrade Revkina, he says, is basically a good comrade, and we can work on this misunderstanding of hers with her. That's what he said: we'll work on it. So it's not all been decided for certain yet. No need for you to be bothered, Stepanovna, so let's drink to you. And I . . . I got stuck here, my clutch bust . . ."

They drank and ate and drank some more. Shaleiko mellowed, unfastened another button, gave Aglaya an attentive glance. He'd liked the look of her before anyway, and now he'd seen more than just a Party comrade in her, and under the influence of the cognac and gratifying words, she began feeling better disposed to Shaleiko herself.

"You know what, Stepanovna, I could tell you, in general, you're a pretty likable kind of woman. Attractive. Meaning good-looking. And what I was thinking was . . ." He looked around and began whispering. "After all, you and me, we're sort of . . . kind of . . . So, maybe you could invite me around?" he asked, emphasizing the first syllable of "invite."

"When?" asked Aglaya.

"Right now if you like," Shaleiko said, perking up.

Aglaya hesitated. She didn't really fancy Shaleiko that much, but it was a long time since anyone had courted her, although she was only forty-two and all her vital cycles still functioned as regularly as the rising and the setting of the moon. At night she still dreamed of the delights of carnal love—not often, but sometimes so tangibly she felt the next moment her longings would be satisfied, but the moment never arrived and she woke feeling disappointed and irritable.

"Not right now," said Aglaya, not wishing to be too easy a conquest for Shaleiko. "If you don't go away or change your mind, then drop by this evening."

23

While Aglaya was having lunch, her neighbor Shubkin was making himself comfortable in his new apartment. For an extra charge Opryzhkin had put up some bookshelves for him, and they now displayed the works of Lenin, Gorky, Mayakovsky, Korolenko, Kuprin and the coming fashionable writer Saint-Exupéry. The shelves with Shubkin's library occupied all four walls with the exception, naturally, of the door and window apertures, and in front of the books Shubkin had hung portraits of his idols, which included Lenin, Dzerzhinsky, Gorky, Mayakovsky and the hero he had especially revered in his youth, Giuseppe Garibaldi. When he was finished with the library, Mark Semyonovich installed his so-called writing desk at the window with his homemade table lamp, then put his Record radio on it and threw the wire antenna out of the window. He could scarcely wait to listen to one of the foreign radio stations and check how good the reception was here, but for some reason in this area he couldn't pick up the Voice of America at all, Radio Liberty was jammed very powerfully and the BBC only worked in the evenings.

24

Aglaya spent the whole day busy around the apartment: doing the laundry, washing the floors and windows, changing the sheets. All the while realizing that Shaleiko might sober up, change his mind and not come. But shortly after seven o'clock in the evening, there was a knock at the door. When she opened it, she saw Stepan Kharitonovich beaming brightly with a bottle of cognac in one hand and a paper bag in the other.

"Did anyone see you?" Aglaya asked

"I don't know," said Shaleiko with a shrug. "I think there were a couple of old women sitting on the bench, but what's that to you? You're not married."

"I wasn't thinking about me," said Aglaya, "but about you. Aren't I supposed to be in disgrace right now?"

"Oh, forget it. In disgrace!" her guest replied casually, standing the bottle on the table and tipping two lemons and some Mishka in the North candies out of the paper bag. "What do I care if you're in disgrace? Do you think I'm going to avoid you now? I'm Shaleiko. A Cossack! I went into the attack without any helmet." He slapped his bald patch to show how he fought without a helmet. "I wasn't afraid of the bullets, I didn't cringe at the shrapnel, so now what? I wouldn't want my wife to catch me, but as for the Party committees, what can I say, I couldn't give a hoot for the damn lot of them. Now show me how you live," Shaleiko asked her.

He went around the entire apartment, knocked on the walls, tugged at the window frames, flushed the toilet and pronounced judgment: "Good apartment. Bad that it hasn't got any real foundation at all. But all the conveniences are good. The bath, and this thing, just pull the chain and it goes glug-glug. We still do everything the old-fashioned way out in the village. Water from the well, conveniences out in the yard, wash yourself in the bathhouse. But where d'you get the gas from?"

"From the collector," said Aglaya.

"And what's that?"

"It's in the basement. Twelve cylinders of gas. Propane and butane."

"Gases for the masses," Shaleiko said with a laugh, and then gave his approval. "Gas is good. I lived in Kiev with relatives, and they have gas too. You can put on a pan that size and it boils in five minutes. I think maybe we'll live to see electricity in every house, and gas and sewers. They ask me, 'Are you crazy or something?' But I say I'm not crazy, I have a dream. Lenin dreamed about it and so do I. No, I'm not comparing myself. Lenin is, you know, oho, and I'm something different altogether. Lenin had a dream maybe a kilometer long, and mine's only fifty centimeters, but everyone has a right to dream. But it's bad your house has almost no foundation. What if there's an earthquake?"

"How could we have an earthquake?" Aglaya objected. "That's for places in Central Asia. Or in Italy. Or in Turkey. We've never had anything of that sort."

"That's true enough," said Shaleiko, "we haven't. But we will now."

And he swept Aglaya up in his arms and dragged her into the bedroom. "Oh, what an earthquake there's going to be now!"

She didn't resist. She just asked: "But what about the cognac?"

"It'll keep," Shaleiko assured her.

I can clearly picture my pampered modern-day reader frozen in anticipation of the details of what actually happened in Aglaya Stepanovna Revkina's bedroom, what positions our characters assumed, which of their body parts were conjoined and how, what words they whispered to each other while they were doing it, and how exactly they climaxed. But the author is not going to relate any of this. And not even primarily out of his own innate modesty (which goes without saying), but because there is nothing particular to talk about. Our characters came from a workers' and peasants' background and upbringing, they never had any sex education, they hadn't seen our modern television programs "about that," they hadn't read any Indian, Chinese or other books about the refinements of erotic pleasure. For the most part they read the newspaper *Pravda*, *The Agitator's Notebook* and *The Short Course in the History of the All-Russian Communist Party (Bolsheviks)*. Aglaya had never even heard the word "sex," and although Shaleiko had heard it, he thought it meant "six" in German. So it all went off without any particularly spicy bits, although it should be noted that the persistent Stepan Kharitonovich did succeed in rousing some kind of feeling in Aglaya because, although he lacked education, he was physically strong and he tried hard, he snorted and chomped on her hair and told her: "You're my pussycat."

And just when she was approaching the station her train had never reached in all her life, and he was riding the same track and they were both ready to go tumbling down the mountainside, plunging headlong into Nirvana, somewhere very close by (but not inside them, somewhere outside) music began to play and a low woman's voice announced simply:

"This is the BBC broadcasting from London. Western correspondents in Moscow inform us that according to rumors circulating there the policy of de-Stalinization is encountering significant resistance from the more orthodox members of the CPSU. In this connection the Presidium of the Central Committee of the CPSU is considering the possibility of purging the ranks of the party of those who secretly or openly oppose the new general line as defined at the Twentieth Congress . . . As one party representative put it, the party will expose and punish not only those who openly oppose the new line, but also those who do not ostracize them with adequate vigor."

That means me! Shaleiko thought with a sudden unpleasant feeling in his chest.

"What's that?" he asked without abandoning his efforts, but feeling himself beginning to sober up.

"Take no notice," Aglaya whispered, panting and trying not to lose her grip on her mounting excitement. "It's my new neighbor. Shubkin. You know him."

"Shubkin," Shaleiko repeated with disappointment. "But if we can hear him, that means he can . . ."

"I don't know. I don't care," Aglaya said rapidly, annoyed, but she told a lie because in fact it excited her a lot that perhaps Shubkin could hear, and if Shaleiko had only had the wits or the tact to stay silent for a second or two . . .

"But I do care," Shaleiko whispered in her ear, carrying on moving. "You heard, they say there's going to be a purge. For those who oppose and those who don't ostracize them. But I don't oppose and I wholeheartedly and absolutely"—he began moving even more energetically— "condemn your position!"

"Ah, so you condemn it, do you?" she cried in outrage, trying at the same time to stay hot and to reach that final point. But by this time he was going through the reverse process, and although out of politeness he was still slithering up and down on top of her, his energy was declining. She sensed this, her mood turned sour, she lost patience and pushed him off herself rather roughly. Muttering unintelligible apologies, he slid down on to the floor and began to get dressed.

She didn't reproach him, but she glared at him spitefully. She threw on her silk Chinese dressing gown with the peacocks and waited impatiently for him to fasten up all his buttons. He had already put on his hat and set off toward the door when she snatched his briefcase out of his hands and started stuffing the cognac and lemons into it.

"Don't do that, Stepanovna!" he said, trying to reason with her, but she handed him the briefcase and said: "Get lost, sissy!"

Shaleiko thought this label was very insulting, and it was all the more insulting because he had actually been called "a sissy" in his childhood.

He went out onto the landing with a heavy sigh, hoping that he could make an inconspicuous exit from the house. Of course, he remembered, there were some old women sitting out in front of the house. They were always ready to stick their noses into everything, but they were so blind, deaf and stupid they probably wouldn't realize who he was and where he'd been.

But before he met the old women again, right there on the landing he ran into Shubkin. After listening to the latest broadcast from the BBC, Mark Semyonovich had decided to take out the garbage pail and on the way to think over current events. He also had various ideas concerning a possible purge in the CPSU, and as he walked along, he was already composing yet another letter to Khrushchev with a demand not to limit the action to the expulsion of high-placed factionalists, but to purge the Party of the most extreme Stalinists ensconced in Party structures at the regional and district levels.

Shubkin emerged onto the landing with the pail and came face-to-face with Shaleiko. Seeing Shubkin there, Shaleiko decided he must have heard the bed squeaking and the words "You're my pussycat" and wanted to see who had spoken them, not realizing that a creative individual (such as Mark Semyonovich Shubkin undoubtedly was), being entirely absorbed in his own thoughts (and he was always absorbed in them), became so cut off from everything going on around him that he didn't hear any conversations or other extraneous sounds, and if he did hear occasional oohs and aahs and spoken words, then it was only as unintelligible noise, like the distant pounding of the surf on the shore. But Shaleiko, who did not understand the subtle spiritual constitution of the creative individual, was convinced that this snake had been listening and perhaps even eavesdropping, and so there was no point in trying to hide anything from him.

"Aha," he said, donning an expression of sincere joy at seeing Shubkin. "Hi there!"

"Hello," said Shubkin absentmindedly or, as it seemed to Shaleiko, evasively.

"I was just, you know . . . Well, I had a couple of drinks. And the clutch went. I spent the night in the Collective Farm Workers' House . . ."

"Ah, good," said Shubkin abstractedly, without meaning anything by it, but it seemed to Shaleiko that the word "good" concealed Shubkin's suspicions concerning what he had heard.

"Look, I'm trying to explain to you," said Shaleiko, taking offense at something or other. "Well, I was a bit tipsy. I confess it happens to me sometimes. And I met her. I lead a dog's life, always traveling on business. Either Party conferences or leading workers' seminars, or a course, or an exhibition. My wife's got women's problems. She says to me herself: 'You can do what you like, Styopa, just don't leave me.' And I'm not a weak man, after all. At the front I went into the attack without any helmet, with bullets whistling between my head and my ear, but I didn't cringe for them. I'm Shaleiko, I am! I'm a Cossack. But when I see a good-looking woman, especially if . . . And so . . ." He sighed and assumed a dignified air. "But on the ideological level I accept no compromises. Shaleiko's hard as flint when it comes to that." He held up a clenched fist, no doubt intending it to illustrate the hardness of the aforementioned mineral. But he decided to try a different approach. "Listen, fancy a glass of cognac? Look, it's good stuff, Moldavian, four stars. No? Suit yourself. So what are they saying about us now on the BBC? Some kind of twisted slander, eh?"

He pronounced the final phrase as though in passing and without any emphasis, but as if he was hinting that if you should happen to inform on us, then we've got something we can pass on to the right place as well.

"Not really," Shubkin replied absentmindedly, "nothing special." He wanted to get rid of Shaleiko as quickly as possible and be alone with his own thoughts. So he pretended he'd forgotten something and went back into his room, without taking the garbage out after all.

Shaleiko stood there on the landing for a little while, shrugged and set off reluctantly down the stairs.

25

It was already getting dark, but since it was a Sunday and a warm evening, the courtyard was full of people. There were children playing soccer, hide-and-seek, forfeits and mumbly peg. The policeman Tolya Saraev was pumping up the tire on his Kovrovets motorbike. Shurochka the Idiot was boiling up some kind of slop for the cats on a Primus stove. The full complement of old grannies was seated on the bench. Zhora Zhukov was playing the "Weary Sun" tango on his accordion. His mother, Valentina, was

dancing with Renat Tukhvatullin, and Tukhvatullin's wife Raya was taking the washing down from the line, casting jealous glances at the dancing couple.

In short, when Shaleiko emerged after seeing Aglaya, there was such a
large throng of people with a keen eye for others' lives already gathered
outside that even an ant could not have crawled past unnoticed. And
Shaleiko was by no means an ant, but a large man who was conspicuous
from every angle. And, moreover, he was wearing a straw hat. So he hoped
in vain that the people in the yard, being exclusively absorbed in their
own affairs, would not pay any attention to him. Of course, they did. They
paid attention when he went in. And when he came out, they paid even
more. And when, in an attempt to avoid being recognized, he lowered his
head and pulled his hat down over his eyes, they paid attention to the fact
that he lowered his head and covered his eyes with his hat. Shaleiko
moved off in the direction of Rosenblum Street. The grannies watched
him go, and Greta the Greek asked, employing the conditional interroga-
tory intonation pattern: "Would he have just come out from the shnoot's
then?"

To which she received the reply: "From the shnoot's, sure as sure,
where else?"

Being an individual of a relatively sober cast of mind, Shaleiko did not
suppose that the people he met as he left Aglaya's place were following instructions from anybody; experience of the world had taught him
that since their minds were not overburdened with matters of practical
necessity, old grannies who whiled away the time on benches were keen
observers with retentive memories, and if anyone were to ask them
whether they had been sitting on a bench on such and such an evening
and whether they might have noticed a man of a particular appearance
walking by in a straw hat, then naturally they would say, "Why certainly,
of course we noticed him," and immediately recall in detail how he was
dressed, what he looked like, when he arrived and at what time he left.

26

Of all the leisure-time amusements available to a Party man of substantial resources, the regional Party committee secretary Nikolai Ivanovich Gryzlov had three favorites: hunting, fishing and the bathhouse. On Saturday he set out for the Aspens hunting enterprise and spent the night there. In the evening he steamed himself for a while. Two Komsomol girls gave him a good lashing with bundles of twigs, lathered him with soap, rinsed him off, wrapped him in a sheet, brought him beer and gave him other kinds of satisfaction, and then afterward sang a few songs with him. In the morning there was hunting. And it went well. Gryzlov bagged two ducks and a wild boar. The same Komsomol girls prepared a splendid lunch. "Capital" salad made with fresh vegetables, solyanka soup with mushrooms and olives, Peking-style duck with cranberry jelly, and there was vodka in a carafe straight from the fridge. Ooh! Aah! Eeh! said Gryzlov, staring at all this abundance, but he said it in his head, because a leading Party comrade could not have human emotions, and if he still had them, he would take good care not to display them in front of subordinates. Even in the bathhouse, when the girls were giving Gryzlov various kinds of satisfaction, he had accepted their exertions with a face of stone and the same expression he wore when he was sitting fully dressed in the presidium. While they were attending to him, the girls could never tell whether he had recourse to their services for the sake of pleasure or because he thought it was expected of him. He was a secretive comrade, nailed as tight shut as a coffin.

But after he downed his first glass of vodka, he gave way and grunted out loud, and he'd just sunk his fork into the Capital salad when there was a sudden rumbling and clattering outside—a special courier had turned up on a motorbike with the minutes and resolutions from the district Party conferences in the region. Nikolai Ivanovich signed for receipt of the papers and began leafing through them as he sipped his solyanka. He leafed through them lazily, peeping at the end of each one, knowing in advance what he would find. The communists of the district had been uplifted and inspired by the news of the Plenum of the Central Commit-

tee of the CPSU; they had condemned the pitiful anti-Party group consisting of the coms. and their collaborator. Everywhere at the end were the
words "Passed unanimously." The text after the resolution that had arrived
from Dolgov also said it had been passed unanimously. But the wording
was slightly different: "Passed unanimously with a single abstention on
the part of Com. Revkina." When he read this phrase, Gryzlov's jaw
dropped so far that his solyanka ran back into his plate. He lost his
appetite. Without even touching his Peking-style duck, Gryzlov went
straight to the director of the enterprise and called Nechaev at home from
the phone in the director's office. Nechaev was also just sitting down to his
lunch and had already tucked his napkin into his collar when his wife
called him to the telephone with a fearful whisper: "Gryzlov."

Nechaev took the receiver, and realizing that Gryzlov would not call
on Sunday without good reason, he said in a formal voice: "Nechaev
speaking."

Expecting the response to be a greeting or an inquiry into how things
were going, but without asking any questions, Gryzlov said immediately:
"It seems you have your own opposition in the district."

Meaning, of course, Aglaya Revkina. And when Nechaev began talking about Aglaya's merits and the need to work things out with her, Gryzlov remarked sharply: "In our Party, my dear friend, we don't work things
out with the opposition, we exterminate them."

And without waiting for a response, he put down the phone.

That was when it all started. Nechaev sent his wife to fetch Porosyaninov, who was soon located at the hairdresser's. Believing that he had been
invited to lunch, Porosyaninov promptly turned up with a bottle of
Ambassador vodka and a stock of fresh jokes to amuse his boss.

As he wiped his feet thoroughly in the doorway, he said: "Yesterday I
heard this joke about a goat and a magpie. This magpie was flying . . ."

"Don't bother wiping your feet, just turn around and go," Nechaev
interrupted him grimly. "Tomorrow we're excluding Revkina. I'm
instructing you to convene the Party bureau, and make sure there's a full
quorum.

"Why, what's happened?" Porosyaninov asked in amazement.

"A full quorum," Nechaev repeated.

"How can there be a quorum? How can I get them together for tomorrow?" asked Pyotr Klimovich.

"Use the phone, use your legs. Use whatever you like, just make sure there's a quorum," Nechaev said, and turned away.

27

After leaving the courtyard of Aglaya's house, Stepan Kharitonovich set off back to his room in the Collective Farm Workers' House, which was on the other side of the railroad track. Walking along with his bouncy stride in the direction of the railroad station, Shaleiko had the feeling that someone was creeping along behind him, hiding behind the trees, or watching him from behind the dark windows.

Shaleiko walked fast, but the evening advanced even faster, as though the very darkness were stealing along after Shaleiko on soft paws. And gradually, lightbulbs began to light up in the windows and on the lampposts along the road, or rather, not on all the lampposts, just one of them on the approach to the station. The lightbulbs on the other lampposts had either burned out or been broken by last year's heavy hail, and some had been shot out by the local urchins with their slingshots. And since then there had either been no bulbs or there had been no one to screw them in, and at night the street had dwelt in total darkness. In contrast, the station, through which Stepan Kharitonovich's path lay, was lit up like an electric paradise on every side.

In Dolgov, as in many similar towns, the railroad station fulfilled a distinctive cultural function. Lacking a more suitable venue for their evening promenades, the local populace converged here on Saturday and Sunday to greet the arrival of the long-distance trains.

There were four trains of this kind, all of them on the Moscow line. Two of them—one from Moscow and the other to Moscow—passed through during the day. And the other two that followed the same routes halted here in the evening, with a gap of about half an hour between them. Each halted for four minutes. And the minutes which preceded the arrival of the first train, followed the departure of the second and filled the gap between them, and especially the minutes while each train stood at the platform, were regarded by Dolgovites as a thrilling experience. The sight was indeed both beautiful and impressive, for the smooth platform of well-rolled crushed brick contrasted sharply with the dark, crooked streets of the town, paved at best with cobblestones.

The two-story station building, erected at the beginning of the century, was built of undressed gray stone. It had everything a station should have: a waiting room, ticket offices, two buffets and a restaurant. On the pediment of the façade, on either side of the round clock and the illuminated sign with the name of the station, there were portraits of the founders of communism: Marx, Engels, Lenin, Stalin.

And as it happened, in that very same year of 1957 the International Festival of Youth was due to take place in Moscow. Dolgov was also preparing for this great event, and in anticipation of the foreign visitors passing through on their way to the festival, the Dolgov station had been cleaned and tidied and an important announcement had been hung over the main entrance, with the Russian rendered in foreign letters so that foreigners would understand it:

TUALET NAKHODITSYA ZA UGLOM
[i.e., The toilet is around the corner.]

And by the flowerbed in front of the station, the following message had been painted on special plywood for the same class of passengers:

ZVETY NE RVAT! PO TRAVE NE HODIT'!
[i.e., Do not pick the flowers! Do not walk on the grass!]

As yet, foreigners had been a rare sight in Dolgov, but even without them there was frequently a lively, jovial crowd on the local railroad platform in the evenings.

The first to appear, long before the arrival of the next train, were the girls. They walked about in twos and threes, exuding the odor of a strong perfume of local manufacture. Immediately after them the local lads appeared in their velvet shirt jackets and wide bell-bottoms. Married couples, dressed up in their Sunday best, proceeded unhurriedly along the platform, greeting each other with a respectful inclination of the head and an elevation of the cap or hat. Bagels with poppy seeds, fizzy water with Fruit Punch syrup and ice cream in wafer cups were sold at the entrance to the station, and sometimes even balloons for the children. And so everyone strolled back and forth in patient anticipation of the fleeting festival that was approaching right on schedule. The girls rustled along in their crepe de Chine, and the boys trailed after them, sweeping the platform with their bell-bottoms and attempting to strike up a conversation: "Hey darling, something's dropped out of you and it's steaming."

The girl would either maintain a haughty silence or else reply: "Idiot!" And in this way she would offer the pretext for further socializing.

About fifteen minutes before the arrival of the train, the public on the platform was swollen by the members of the Harvest soccer team. Today they had managed to tie the home team 1 to 1, and after the match they had switched from drinking compote to vodka. Now they were augmenting their consumption from stocks bought for the journey, all of them taking turns to use a single glass. Their mood was one of boisterous merriment and hope that this time they would manage to leave Dolgov without a beating. But their hopes were vain: a section of the local fans had already infiltrated the platform and was waiting for the rest, in the meanwhile strolling around in ones and twos and observing the soccer players with a gaze that was far from indifferent.

The train made its appearance in the distance, emerging from the darkness. First they heard the distant but powerful call of the locomotive, then springing out from around a distant bend and advancing rapidly toward them came three glowing eyes, the three headlamps, with their light running along the tracks in narrow threads and becoming ever brighter and more blinding until, panting and whistling, enveloped in clouds of steam, working its gleaming levers and crankshafts as it erupted into the station, there was the Iosif Stalin, the pride of Soviet locomotive-building, with a five-pointed star on its mighty breast. It drew in a long string of carriages smelling of soot, all the doors of which swung open simultaneously, so that there was even more light as the passengers in pajamas and slippers jumped down from the steps and some carrying teapots hurried off to get hot water, others went for bagels and ice cream and others mingled with the locals. The platform was filled temporarily with the bustling atmosphere of a populous city, almost a capital. There was the sound of pure Muscovite speech—"Just look at this charming little town!" "How much are your cucumbers?"—and suddenly it felt as though this wasn't the wretched platform of a godforsaken little railroad stop, but somewhere like Gorky Park or Gorky Street, or even Broadway.

This time there was even more merriment than usual on the platform, because as soon as the lights of the locomotive appeared in the distance the local soccer fans, taking the light approaching from afar as a signal for action, immediately threw themselves on the soccer players and a brawl commenced, which nonetheless failed to disrupt the general flow of events.

At this very moment Stepan Shaleiko arrived on the platform. Here he encountered many and various acquaintances, spoke to them about his broken clutch, the weather and the prospects for the harvest and, having furnished himself with a perfect alibi, was about to leave the platform when he suddenly came nose-to-nose with Pyotr Klimovich Porosyaninov, who was running somewhere with an anxious look on his face but, on catching sight of Shaleiko, prodded him in the belly with a finger and said: "Oho! You're the very man I need." And at the same time inquired: "And by the way, why aren't you at home on a Sunday?"

Suspecting that the question was not posed idly, Shaleiko hastily began explaining for the thousandth time that yesterday on the way out of town his clutch had broken and they'd promised to fix it at the district Party garage, but the more he explained, the more he himself felt as though his explanation was a pack of lies, although he was telling the simple truth.

Porosyaninov certainly didn't believe him and thought he'd simply gone on the sauce. But he didn't carp. He had no time for that.

"You know what, my bosom buddy," he said amicably. "You'll have to stay on a bit longer, don't you even think of leaving tomorrow morning."

"What's the problem?" Shaleiko enquired.

"You'll know soon enough," Porosyaninov promised. "How do you feel about Aglaya Revkina?"

Unaware of the background to this question, Shaleiko became even more frightened. How could they have reported me already? he thought. Then he quickly tried to imagine what exactly could have been reported. If it was that they'd sat together in the tearoom, that didn't mean anything. She was still a communist, after all, she hadn't been excluded yet. She was behaving incorrectly, of course, but she wasn't a goner yet. Nechaev said we were going to work things out with her. And you could say he had been working with her, attempting as a communist and senior comrade to persuade her to refute her errors. He had appealed to her to judge for herself, not to go against the Party, not to look to the past, but to look only forward. He even began to feel that he really had been associating with Aglaya for educational purposes. And as for what happened afterward, who knew about it? Would Shubkin tell? He wouldn't. He was in deep too—he listened to the BBC. And those old women . . . Well, what did they know? He'd no sooner got in than he was out again . . ."

"What's wrong?" he heard Porosyaninov's voice asking from somewhere very far away. "Do you understand me? I asked you how you feel about Revkina."

"Why do you ask?" Shaleiko inquired, hoping the answer would allow him to determine how much Porosyaninov knew.

"Because tomorrow you've got to turn up without fail at a district Party committee bureau extraordinary meeting. We're going to hear a personal case."

"A personal case!" Shaleiko gasped. "But what for?"

"For making a hostile sortie," Porosyaninov explained. "You didn't think we'd forgive that sort of thing, did you?"

Naturally, Stepan Kharitonovich thought that the hostile sortie intended was his own hostile sortie. Or more precisely, perhaps, his sortie into the bed of a certain enemy of the people.

"What sortie do you mean? What are you talking about?" Shaleiko said nervously. "What sortie? What is it I'm supposed to have done? I just dropped into the tearoom and had a drink or two, treated a woman to lunch and saw her home, what kind of sortie's that? I never told her I agreed with her about a thing."

"Listen," said Porosyaninov, "I can't be bothered who you treated to what. Although you're a communist and you shouldn't go with other women, especially in public, but I'm not talking about women, I'm talking about the communist Aglaya Revkina. Tomorrow we're going to exclude her from the Party."

"Aglaya?" Shaleiko queried. "Revkina?"

"Aglaya," Porosyaninov confirmed. "Revkina."

"Aha. Well yes, yes," said Shaleiko, nodding readily with a feeling of relief, trying to pretend that was what he'd thought all along. And in order to clear himself of the slightest suspicion, he promptly informed Porosyaninov of his own profound indignation at the anti-Party behavior of the aforementioned female individual. But at the same time, he felt he wanted to say something positive about her.

"I simply don't understand," he lamented almost sincerely. "After all, she was our comrade. Honest and principled. She took part in collectivization; during the war she commanded a partisan detachment . . . They say she fought very bravely."

"But now," Porosyaninov interrupted brusquely, "she's fighting against her own people. And against the Party. So anyway, tomorrow you're going to give a speech of resolute condemnation. Understand?"

"I understand," Shaleiko agreed sourly.

"I don't hear any conviction in your voice," remarked Porosyaninov. "Tell me straight, will you speak or not?"

Just then the platform attendant's whistle shrilled. The locomotive responded with a joyous, impatient hoot. It had been standing here too long; the seething steam was bursting open its breast, summoning it to journey onward into the darkness. The locomotive shrieked loudly enough to shatter eardrums and set off, discharging a dense cloud which temporarily engulfed Porosyaninov. A crazy idea flashed through Shaleiko's mind: what if he was to disappear right now? But before he was even fully conscious of the idea, Porosyaninov was reincarnated before his eyes and repeated his question: "So will you speak or won't you?"

Shaleiko didn't answer, watching the railroad carriages as they rolled past in front of him. The Harvest sportsmen hanging on to the handrails twitched convulsively, shaking off the most tenacious local sports-lovers on the move, the same way Stepan Kharitonovich would have liked to shake off Porosyaninov, but Porosyaninov had taken a tighter grip on him than the Dolgov fans had on their quarry: "Stop avoiding the issue and give me a straight answer—will you speak or not?"

"We-ell," said Shaleiko, prevaricating, "if necessary, then of course I will. After all, I'm . . . you know . . . a communist. So it's understood." He paused. "As long as I don't fall ill. I've got a bit of a sore throat, you know. There's a draught in that hotel like you wouldn't believe . . . I'm afraid it's my tonsils or something of the sort." He touched his Adam's apple and gave a little cough, like a singer before his stage entrance. "Heh-heh! What I need is some hot milk with honey, put on some cupping glasses, rest up a bit . . ."

"I get you," Porosyaninov interrupted him. "You want to run out on us."

"Me? Run out on you? What d'you mean?" Shaleiko asked with a start. "At the front I went into the attack without a helmet. I had bullets whistling between my temple and my ear . . . The number of times company commanders said to me, 'Shaleiko, are you tired of having a head,' or . . ."

"So you'll speak then?" Porosyaninov asked again.

"Well of course," Shaleiko sighed. "If it's necessary, I'll do it. I'm Shaleiko, I am. I'm a Cossack. I can be weak in some things, like any man. But when it comes to ideology, then the communist Shaleiko is as unshakable as . . . as the fortress of Brest."

"That's all right then. But the Brest fortress was a defensive action, and we're going to take the Reichstag. Tomorrow. Meanwhile, you go to your room and forget about milk with honey and cupping glasses — have a glass of vodka with pepper and you'll be right as rain."

28

That summer was an uncomfortable one in Dolgov. Thanks to high pressure that remained stuck over the region for a long period, the heat was extreme and interminable. During the afternoon the temperature in the shade reached thirty-four degrees, and at night it never sank below twenty-five. The heat withered cereal crops in the field, the local streams ran shallow, the peat bogs ignited spontaneously and in town a constant smoky haze became an unvarying feature of the weather, even rating a mention in the meteorological reports. This kind of weather was hard for people with cardiovascular problems to tolerate; several of them actually found it intolerable and died. And soon after that the toll of cattle and people was sharply increased by the appearance in the diminished local waters of the bacilli of either plague or cholera — the bacteriologists failed to identify which.

But Stepan Kharitonovich was as strong as a horse — no cholera ever got a hold on him, his circulatory system was sound, his heart functioned rhythmically and that tickle in the throat was, as we recall, something he had simply invented. Realizing there was no way he could wriggle out of speaking at the bureau meeting, he drank until three in the morning, then slept, and though no one thing on its own could have overpowered him — neither the vodka, nor the heat, nor the bedbugs — all of them together took their toll even on him, and he turned up at the bureau session wretched, pale and crumpled. He turned up after everyone else in the hope of somehow concealing himself behind their backs, but Porosyaninov, his elbows already propped on the presidium table, directed him with his eyes to a seat in the second row behind the public prosecutor, Strogii, a man of limited size in all three dimensions, behind whom there was no way you could hide.

As he squeezed his way between the chairs and the knees to reach this place, Shaleiko noticed that Aglaya Revkina was sitting directly behind him, dressed for the front line in boots, a dark woolen skirt and military tunic caught in with a commander's belt, wearing two orders, four medals and some other badges. Not knowing how to reply to her unspoken question, he nodded to her almost imperceptibly, with nothing but his chin, and sat down, his shoulder blades squirming under her physically palpable gaze.

They started the session without any procrastination. The case was presented by Porosyaninov. Even reading from a sheet of paper, he confused his noun cases and prepositions, like a foreigner who had begun studying Russian at an advanced age. Shaleiko listened without hearing him. He only took in fragments of individual phrases. Comrade Revkina, a communist of long standing with great services to her credit, had recently been showing signs of failing to understand certain things. She had demonstrated a tendency toward conceit and arrogance. At a time when the Party, together with the entire Soviet people, had set itself new goals, Comrade Revkina was clinging to the old. Bearing in mind her former services, they had taken a humane line with Comrade Revkina, they had conversed patiently with Comrade Revkina on numerous occasions, they had explained to Comrade Revkina the essential significance of the policy of the Party and the government at the present stage, but comrade Revkina had failed to heed the opinion of her Comrades and had become obstinate in her errors. She had supported the anti-Party group and thereby set herself outside the ranks of the Party.

This time Aglaya had prepared herself for the occasion.

She walked out with her thumbs thrust into her belt, straightened her tunic and shook herself so that the medals on her chest jangled.

"Have you," she began, addressing the auditorium, "thought about what you are doing? If you don't like Comrade Stalin, then why didn't you say so while he was alive? You should have told him back then: 'We're sorry, Comrade Stalin, but we don't like you. And we don't like Molotov, or Kaganovich.' If you'd said that back then, then I'd respect your position now. But back then you said that you loved Comrade Stalin very much and you were prepared to go through hell and high water for his sake . . ."

The hall was filled with a timid silence. Sensing that she had the audience in her grasp, Aglaya raised her voice: "Stalin and his comrades-in-arms made the revolution. And without the revolution, who would you be? You'd be nobody. Stalin raised every one of you from beggars to kings . . ."

The first to come to his senses was Nechaev, who banged on a carafe with its stopper. Porosyaninov also shook himself awake: "Comrade Revkina, we don't need an elementary course in politics. Speak about yourself."

"I am speaking about myself," Aglaya countered. "Like all of you, I grew up with the name of Stalin. Under his leadership we carried through collectivization, industrialization . . ."

Nechaev tapped on his carafe again and Porosyaninov began lisping again: "Comrade Revkina, there's no need to tell us the history of the Party—we already know it."

"If you already know it, then I'd advise you to recall how Stalin fought against opposition and opportunists. Essentially, against the likes of you . . ."

"Comrade Revkina!" said Nechaev, raising his voice.

"You don't like that?" said Aglaya, turning toward him with a smirk. "Well, I think Comrade Stalin wouldn't have liked you either. He wasn't fond of people like you. Comrade Stalin loved honest, principled communists. But when it came to traitors—"

"No more! No more!" Nechaev shouted. "You no longer have the floor. Leave the podium! Leave the podium immediately!"

"No," she resisted. "I haven't finished speaking. I'm sure all of you sitting here agree with what I'm saying. You have your convictions too."

She was half-right. These people did have convictions, but all they amounted to was that you should never, under any circumstances, go against the bosses. And they didn't like Aglaya's speech because they could sense opposition and reproach in it: I'm good, principled and brave, but you are cowards, toadies and puppets.

Refusing to accept that they were pitiful nonentities, the delegates were indignant; they stamped their feet and yelled out single words, such as "Shame!"; "Out!"; "Enough!"; "Cheek!"

"Recant!" Muravyova called from her seat.

The boss of the meat-processing combine, Botviniev leapt to the front once again, yelling: "Rip the bad grass out of the field!" And he began jerking his arms, as though he was pulling up weeds.

The author of these lines once had occasion to observe a dramatic incident from the life of chickens. One unfortunate crested hen happened to fall into water. Strangely enough, she didn't drown, but she was so thoroughly soaked that every last feather on her body fell out. Encountering her in such a miserable condition, the other chickens threw themselves on the unfortunate fowl like natural-born predators. It turned out that great passions rage even in the breasts of these insignificant creatures and they harbor the urge to hound and henpeck anyone weaker than they are no less than we do ourselves. They flung themselves on their denuded sister with the screams of an eagle, and they really would have pecked her to death if not for the intervention of their owner. The chicken was separated from the others, and after a while, having grown new feathers, she was once again accepted as a full-fledged member of the family of chickens.

For a long time the members of the bureau shouted, shrieked, whistled, foamed at the mouth and suffered collective convulsions, like members at a meeting of the Russian Holy Rollers sect. In vain, Secretary Nechaev leapt up and down, banged on the carafe and shouted, "Comrades! Comrades!" The comrades did not hear him, and they did not listen to him, realizing perfectly well that this insubordination would be recorded as a point in their favor. In a certain place it would be noted as an ideologically justified psychopathic response.

When they finally did settle down, individual orators began to take the floor: the head livestock specialist, Obertochkin; the director of the reinforced concrete combine, Syrtsov; the head of bathhouses, Kolganov, and yet again, Muravyova. They all condemned Revkina, saying that she had lost her way, had become obstinate in her errors, demonstrated signs of complacency, conceit and arrogance, that she was providing grist to the mill of the enemies and was perhaps herself an enemy. A schism in Soviet society was the very thing on which our enemies had always counted. At this moment Revkina was being applauded, at least mentally, by the international imperialists; the Pentagon had its eye on her as it finalized its plans of aggression, and the CIA had added her to the rolls of its voluntary agents and paid thirty pieces of silver into her account.

I do feel a certain apprehension that the modern-day reader might regard this description as an ill-judged grotesque and, reasoning logically, think: dozens of people gathered together couldn't possibly say things like that! You can think what you like, but in those days that is exactly what people did when they gathered together in dozens and hundreds in enclosed premises and in thousands upon thousands on squares under the open sky. And was there really not a single normal person among them who would have said: Fellow citizens, what kind of gibberish is this? You should all be consigned to the madhouse immediately? People like that did turn up sometimes. But they were the really mad ones. Because a normal person understands that it's dangerous and pointless to oppose universal insanity, and rational to participate in it. It should also be noted that people are all actors, and many of them easily adapt to the role written for them out of fear or in hopes of a worthwhile reward. The enlightened modern-day reader thinks that half-wits such as those we have described no longer exist. The author is unfortunately unable to agree. The sum total of viciousness and stupidity in humanity neither increases nor decreases, but fortunately the times do not always deploy it in full.

29

The session of the bureau of the district committee of the CPSU was drawing to a close. Everyone, naturally, was agreed that Revkina had to be excluded from the Party and isolated from society, and someone even had the idea of suggesting (and this at the local level and long before the case of Boris Pasternak) that if Revkina didn't like our Soviet society in its renovated form, she could run off to her transoceanic masters. An essentially absurd proposal, because Revkina's ideas would scarcely have been to the liking of the transoceanic masters either.

Shaleiko sat there listening to the speakers and hoping that the words spoken by others would be enough and he would be left in the position of the local Pilate, able to wash his hands of the business and then wash them really clean when he got back to the hotel. But just when he was sure that the danger had passed, Porosyaninov fixed him with a keen stare and asked with undisguised malice: "And why does our communist Shaleiko have nothing to say?"

Shaleiko leapt to his feet as though he had been scalded. As he made his way out of the row, stepping on someone's feet, Aglaya watched him, assuming that he would make some kind of attempt to defend her. What could have given rise to such an impossible hope in her mind? Why did she hope to discover in someone else a virtue that she herself did not possess? In the past, when taking part in dozens of similar tribunals, had she ever defended anyone? Even though she was a brave woman, a partisan. Capable, in an attempt to save a comrade, of hurling herself into a raging torrent, an inferno or a hail of machine-gun bullets, of risking her life anywhere at all, except in a closed Party meeting.

Shaleiko walked slowly toward the podium. Perhaps hoping there would be an earthquake or that the Americans would drop a hydrogen bomb on Dolgov and the need to speak would be averted. But neither one thing nor the other happened. He arrived at the podium without mishap, loitered while he gathered himself and said: "Right then, I won't wander on overmuch, I'll just say that our Party, led by the faithful Leninist Nikita Sergeevich Khrushchev, is waging—now what's the simplest way of putting it?—a gigantic, a titanic, struggle for the affirmation, strictly speaking, of Leninist norms, and we won't allow anybody to crap in our kitchen garden."

Having expressed this opinion, he left the stage and, instead of going back to his place, set off toward the exit, but he was stopped.

"Comrade Shaleiko," Nechaev called to him.

"What?" Shaleiko stopped and looked at Nechaev in bewilderment. He'd said the most important thing, hadn't he, so now what?

"You spoke somehow too briefly and reluctantly," said Nechaev.

"I spoke reluctantly?" Shaleiko asked dejectedly.

"Yes indeed. Reluctantly and briefly, as though you were simply taking the easy way out. Perhaps you might offer some arguments in support of your idea?"

"All right then." Shaleiko went back to the podium. "If you want arguments," he said, putting the emphasis on the *u*, "I personally don't have any and I don't need any. The arguments are given to us by Aglaya Stepanovna herself, who has moved on way ahead of us and informs us by her own behavior that she's a great swell and we're collective farm yokels and don't understand a thing. And at a time when our Party is steering a grandiose and universally historical course to overcoming. Which provokes a natural rumpus and dismay in the camp of our enemies. Aglaya Stepanovna has . . . no of course, I won't say that . . . in the past she had definite, so to speak . . . But that's no justification, and that's not what . . ." He thought for a moment and turned to face Aglaya, realizing he had nothing more to lose: "I stand here looking at you, Aglaya Stepanovna, and wonder why you sit there so proud and stubborn, like you were some kind of queen or something? What happened to you? Maybe you've fallen under someone's influence? I know there's some people who might listen to some—pardon the expression—BBC, flap their ears and start—well, you know what. But don't you go listening to those there voices, look here with your own eyes. Come to our collective farm at least and I'll show you personally how our rank-and-file, so to speak, farmers, live. Every one, literally every one of them, has a cow in the barn, a calf, and some even have a heifer. Our collective farm workers have four motorcycles and one Moskvich automobile. They've bought a new Radiola for the club. And we have a dream for the future—well, maybe not for us, but for our grandchildren—of putting in water pipes and one of those toilets so when you pull on a chain the water runs down. That's where our dreams are leading us, but you, Aglaya Stepanovna, are an old woman. Take a look at yourself, come to your senses and stop. If you don't stop, you know, then we'll trample you underfoot, sweep you aside and that . . ."

Shaleiko left the podium to applause, which was later described in the newspaper as "tumultuous." Whether it was really tumultuous or not is not so very important; what is important is that the resolution to exclude Com. Revkina from the ranks of the CPSU was approved unanimously. As was only to be expected.

Aglaya sat upright without her face showing the slightest sign of any feeling whatsoever. But her thoughts were somewhere else completely, and she didn't immediately understand the question that she was asked.

"What?" she queried.

"I asked you," said Nechaev, "if you have your Party card with you."

"I always carry my Party card and my Party conscience with me," Aglaya said distinctly.

"As for your conscience," said Nechaev, "you can take that to church, but I must ask you to hand your card in here."

"Well, there's your answer!" said Aglaya, giving him the finger, which the members of the Party bureau did not like at all. As they went their separate ways afterward, they were still discussing what an outrageous gesture it was. Pah! How crude!

"Revkina!" Porosyaninov growled menacingly. "Remember where you are!"

"Comrade Revkina," Nechaev said politely, "you must surrender your Party card."

"I didn't get it from you."

"Hand it in quietly," said Porosyaninov, "or else we'll take it by force."

"Take it then," Aglaya suggested, shifting the card from her pocket to her bosom.

The members of the presidium exchanged glances, and Nechaev settled on a compromise.

"All right," he said, "everyone's tired and we'll postpone the handing in of the card for the time being. But you, Aglaya Stepanovna, will not be needing it anytime in the near future. Not until you reflect on your behavior and draw the appropriate conclusions. And if you do and you come to us and recant, then perhaps we'll give you a chance to rejoin the Party, with a severe reprimand."

Aglaya did not accept her exclusion, but she did not bother to appeal. She decided that now she was her own communist, and her own Party too. The day after her exclusion she opened a special account in the savings bank and began paying her Party membership dues into it every month. She herself deposited the money, and she herself noted in her Party card that the dues for such and such a month had been paid.

30

It was only now that Aglaya was able to appreciate what a good neighbor the deceased Telushkin had been. Never the slightest noise. But that Shubkin? A monster! If the radio wasn't blaring through the wall, or the typewriter clattering, then the bed started creaking. And sometimes the radio was blaring and the typewriter was clattering and the bed was creaking and something else was either panting or squealing or sobbing. Although she tried, Aglaya was unable to imagine how such heterogeneous actions—the possible causes of all these sounds—could be carried out simultaneously.

In such cases people normally express their dissatisfaction by banging on the wall. Aglaya didn't bang on the wall, thereby indicating to Shubkin that she didn't even notice his existence. When she ran into him by chance in the yard or on the stairs, she walked past him just as if he weren't there.

She wasn't the one who informed the local agencies that Shubkin listened to the foreign radio, but she was his closest neighbor and suspicion fell on her. From the agencies referred to by the people simply as "the organs," the letter was forwarded to the Party agencies—that is, to the district committee—following which Porosyaninov called in Shubkin for a talk. Shubkin thought it was because of the poem by Bunin that he'd read at the district amateur concert on Teacher's Day. But his concern proved unfounded. Porosyaninov didn't give Shubkin a dressing down for Bunin, because he didn't know who Bunin was. He sat Shubkin down in a soft armchair, offered him tea with hard crackers and lemon, asked him how things were going in the children's home, about his personal problems and then hemmed and hawed a bit and went on to the main point, at the same time switching to a more intimate tone of voice: "You know, we've received a tip-off that you listen to hostile radio stations in the evenings."

"Who was the tip-off from?" asked Shubkin.

"I don't know. It's anonymous. Our people," Porosyaninov said with a smile, "like to write. Some people find it easier to tip us off than to tap on the wall."

Shubkin understood the hint and began assuring Porosyaninov that he listened to the radio exclusively for purposes of counterpropaganda. He was a socially active individual, a propagandist of communist ideology. In order to struggle effectively against bourgeois ideology, he had to know the enemy's arguments.

"That's right," Porosyaninov agreed. "But I think that the enemy's arguments will be just as clear to you if you place your radio by a different wall. And turn it down a bit."

Shubkin took the advice and moved the table with the radio on it farther away from Aglaya and closer to Shurochka the Idiot, especially since the latter was a bit deaf and didn't hear anything she didn't want to hear. But even so, sometimes when something extraordinary happened, he would put the radio against Aglaya's wall in order to enlighten her too. And strange as it may seem, she didn't object, since she had also begun to feel a need for information from sources apart from the newspaper *Pravda*.

31

Although events in general were developing in a direction that Shubkin found to his liking, certain isolated details put him on his guard, concerning which he anxiously informed the Central Committee of the CPSU. After writing one of his letters to the leaders of the Party, he would read it for a start to his Antonina to see how it was received by the simple people. He would strike a pose close to the window, the letter in his left hand and his right hand extended forward, and begin:

"Dear and highly respected Nikita Sergeevich!

"Are you aware. . ." That was the way he almost always began: "Are you aware . . ." An introduction like that sounded like a challenge. What did "Are you aware" mean? The very post that Khrushchev held assumed that he was aware of everything . . . Of course it was a rude way to begin, but if only he had continued a bit more softly. What came next, however, was even worse: "Are you aware that the Party which you lead is in the process of degeneration? . . ."

As he was reading, Antonina stopped knitting and frowned.

He asked in surprise: "Don't you like it?"

"Na-ah," she objected quickly.

"You don't like it?" he repeated, even more surprised.

"Na-ah." She paused before explaining, "I like it. But why strain your poor head like that? You know, Mark Semyonovich, for that they could . . ."

"What? Do you think they'll put me in jail again?"

"They could," said Antonina, nodding. "Oho, they could."

"No, surely not," said Mark Semyonovich, dismissing the possibility, "the decisions of the Twenty-first Party Congress can no longer be revoked. But precisely in order to prevent that from happening, we, the rank-and-file communists, must not keep quiet—we have no right to keep quiet."

"And do you think we'll live to see communism?" Antonina asked, pulling her legs up under her.

"Oh, Antonina!" Shubkin exclaimed, throwing his hands in the air. "What does that mean, do I think or not think? I know for certain that communism will come. Sooner or later, but without fail. You must understand that Marxism is not some religion made up of a load of cock-and-bull stories, but a science. Foreknowledge based on precise analysis. It's not very likely that I'll live to see communism, but you're young, you will. Do you know what communism is? Communism is . . ." And Mark Semyonovich would begin to walk around the room, telling Tonka the dreams of Vera Pavlovna from Chernyshevsky's *What Is to Be Done*, and he related them as colorfully as though he had just dreamed them himself the night before. She would listen in a trance, smiling gently, and when he finished she would inform him: "And last night in our buffet someone crapped another big heap right there on the table. But how it happened, who did it and when, no one saw, even with the station guard on duty and the police there. Just like real partisans, they are."

32

They say that an individual's mental capabilities are determined by the weight of his brain. But a big brain can only be contained in a big head. Turgenev had a big head. And his brain, accordingly, weighed as much as two loaves of bread. Lenin had an even bigger head, and naturally no one in the world had a bigger brain than him, and in Soviet times it was dangerous even to doubt it. You could lose your own head, whatever size it was. But since Soviet power has run its course, I can share with you my observation, admittedly made by eye, that Mark Semyonovich Shubkin's head was perhaps even bigger than Lenin's. But then, how can you judge? I only ever saw Lenin from a distance and in his coffin, while I saw Shubkin alive and close up. No one, as far as I am aware, ever weighed Mark Semyonovich's brain (not even later, when it became a real possibility), but it was obviously also not small—and with an astounding processing capacity (that much I know for certain), thanks to which Shubkin did not read books the way we do, line by line, but entire pages at a time, as though soaking them up whole. One look at a page and he'd read it— he just looked and it was read. At first I thought he was just . . . how can I put it . . . sliding his eyes from the first line to the last, but he only laughed at me for that. "What you mean," he said, "is speed reading; even you could master that method if you tried. But my way of reading is photographic. I look at a page, and I take in all of it from top to bottom in a single moment. One glance at a page and I've read it and remembered it completely. Do you want to check?" So of course I used to check. I took any book from the shelf and opened it at any page, allowed Shubkin just to glance at it, and then he would recite the entire text with his eyes closed. What an exceptional talent!

As we have already heard, Shubkin knew practically all languages, having learned the majority of them in the camp. Foreigners were not often encountered in Dolgov, but during the period of reduced tension they would sometimes arrive to familiarize themselves with our agricultural achievements. Then the bosses would immediately call in Shubkin. And he would explain the advantages of our collective farm system to these foreigners in any language, from English to some obscure dialect of the Finno-Ugrian group. Many people, astounded by the extent of his knowledge and memory, assumed it to be a sign of great intellect and preferred to remain modestly silent in his presence. And those who ventured to argue with him always lost. I used to lose too. Because he would crush me with his erudition, beat me down with quotations from the classic works of Marxism-Leninism. He simply laughed at my doubts concerning scientific and applied communism, regarding them as the product of ignorance.

"First, my dear fellow," he used to tell me ironically, "you try reading Marx, Engels and Lenin, make an effort to grasp the essence of their thinking, and then you can argue. How can you judge the ideas generated by the finest minds of humanity if you're not even acquainted with those ideas?"

"I am acquainted with them," I would sometimes be bold enough to argue. "I am acquainted with the effect of these ideas on my own hide, and in great detail."

"You are acquainted with their deformations," Shubkin would object, "but I appeal to you to acquaint yourself with the ideas themselves. To begin with, try reading *Das Kapital, Anti-Dühring* and at least half of the collected works of Lenin, about fifty volumes."

I tried to follow this advice. I used to take the works specified out of the library, but every time reading them made me feel sleepy and I got nasty buzzing noises in my head.

And so I stopped reading these books and tried not to argue with Shubkin anymore because—well, what was the point, with my level of learning?

But one night I happened to visit the Admiral in his watchman's hut at the lumberyard. The hut was cobbled together from stripped timbers and faced with fresh planks of pine that still had a lingering scent. The Admiral had managed to transform even his watchman's hut into a ship's cabin. There were maps pinned to the walls; standing on the table there was a model of a seventeenth-century sailing ship; and lying on a stool by the trestle bed there was an old nautical almanac for the ports of the Azov Sea. The trestle bed itself was like a cross between a sailor's bunk and a hobo's doss: the Admiral was half-lying on a bundle of rags, covered with an old gray traveling rug with tassels and drinking tea brewed thick and strong in his aluminum mug. And for me he located among his household reserves a glass tumbler in a tea-glass holder. I also tipped some tea into it and then poured on some hot water.

It was wintertime. There was a hard frost outside, but here inside the blocks of birch wood blazed cheerfully in the little iron stove with its door standing open. It was hot, the Admiral was sweating and resin was oozing out of the pine planks of the walls.

We drank tea with Tula spice cakes and I told the Admiral about my conversations with Shubkin. I told him honestly that when I argued with Shubkin I sometimes felt that I was right, but I couldn't prove it because he crushed me with his authority. And the fact that he was older, and that he'd been in the camps for so long, and he knew everything. I'd express some thought, and he'd come back with a quotation from Lenin or from Marx, or even from Hegel or Descartes.

"Tell me," the Admiral asked, breaking a spice cake, "does it not seem to you that this Shubkin of yours is an absolute fool?"

"But how," I objected in confusion, "how can I consider him a fool when he's so learned?"

"Why, do you think learning and intelligence are the same thing?"

"Well . . ." I thought about it. "Of course, if a man is learned, he has a lot of learning in his head—when he's thinking something over, he can operate with a large quantity of data—"

"There you go!" the Admiral broke in cheerfully. "He can operate! But what if he can't? You talk about quotations. But has he ever told you a single idea of his own that he personally devised?"

"Why would he?" I asked. "If he has so many good ideas invented by other people in his head, why would he need to think up his own?"

"Ah, I see, you're also . . . how can I put it . . ."

"You're trying to tell me I'm a fool as well?" I put in, offended.

"No, no," said the Admiral. "I'm a polite person and I wouldn't express myself so harshly in the present case, but you think it over for yourself. The human race has already expressed so many extremely clever ideas, but does that mean we don't need anything else? Why are you and I sitting here thinking, and not just firing quotations at each other? Although, believe me, I've got plenty of them in my head too. And some of them are quite brilliant. I can use some of them to corroborate my line of thought. But it's not possible to replace original thought with quotations."

"Why?" I asked.

"Because no thought is worth a damn unless it's born in the head of a concrete person in concrete circumstances on the basis of his own experience as a result of his own thinking. Perhaps," he said with a condescending chuckle, "you should note that down as a quotation and then use it in an argument with Shubkin. But meanwhile, throw a bit of firewood in the stove."

I rearranged the almost burnt-out embers with the poker, put on some fresh blocks of wood and took the kettle to the standpipe. I got chilled to the bone while I collected the dribble of water, then went back to the Admiral and said in Shubkin's defense: "You tell me that he's a fool, but he's got such a huge head, it must be full of something."

"Yes, it's full of foolishness," the Admiral said ruthlessly. "Let me tell you something. You've probably been out in the country. You may have noticed that every village has one idiot and one wise man. Some simple peasant. With a head the size of your fist and a brain that's probably not very big. But he thinks simply, clearly and soundly on the basis of his own knowledge of life and personal experience. So what I'd advise you to learn is this. The human brain is distinguished not only by its dimensions, but by its ability to assimilate input. The brain, crudely speaking, can be a warehouse, a mill or a chemical laboratory. A warehouse can be really vast and stocked with various kinds of items, but the more items there are, the harder it is to make sense of them. A mill can only grind up whatever is poured into it. It may be small and primitive, but it will still grind good grain into pretty good flour. But even if you take a big, modern mill, the very finest, with good grindstones and ideal sieves and load it up with bad grain, it won't turn out anything that's any good. The creative brain is the highest type, a chemical laboratory—load anything you like into it and it produces something fundamentally new, a synthesis. Everything in it works: knowledge, memory, the capacity for independent thought. That kind of brain is very rare, even among people with big heads."

"I suppose Lenin must have had that kind of brain?" I suggested.

"Lenin?" the Admiral repeated in amazement. "Oh, come on! Lenin had an ideological brain. Yet another type that's not very common. Not a warehouse, not a mill, not a laboratory, but a kind of stomach in the head. Put in all sorts of high-quality foodstuffs and they're all digested and transformed into shit."

"Well then," I exclaimed, delighted to have discovered this definition, "that means Shubkin has a stomach-brain too."

"No, no," the Admiral protested. "What Shubkin has is a mill-brain. If you poured good grain into it, you might get good flour. But he's loaded up his mill with Lenin's shit, so what comes out is shit too."

I scraped the used tea leaves out of my glass, threw them into the flames and brewed myself a new batch of tea.

"Shall I make you some too?" I asked the Admiral.

"Yes, please."

"I'd still like to finish off our conversation though. So you believe a man can be very learned, know a great deal, possess a phenomenal memory and an exceptional talent for languages, and still be no more than a fool?"

"Why yes," said the Admiral with a nod. "Your Shubkin's an example."

"And Lenin?"

"Lenin's a fool too," the Admiral said calmly.

I couldn't restrain myself at that.

"Look here," I said, "of course, you're an original character and a paradoxical thinker, and I regard Lenin critically myself, but calling him a fool is going too far. He turned the whole world upside down."

"For what purpose?"

"The purpose is a different matter."

"No," said the Admiral, finally growing heated. "It's not a different matter. I've already explained that to your Shubkin. An intelligent man is a man who sets himself a goal and achieves it. But a man who sets himself an unachievable goal and doesn't understand that it's unachievable cannot be regarded as intelligent."

"Well, let's assume that in terms of everyday life you're right. But Lenin didn't just set himself a simple goal; he set himself a grandiose one."

"Because he's not just a simple fool," said the Admiral. "He's a grandiose fool. Put that down in your notebook too: Lenin is a grandiose fool."

The Admiral paused for a moment; then he must have decided that he ought to offer some arguments for his idea after all.

"I . . ." he began, ". . . unlike you, I have had the time . . . I've read him from cover to cover. And he, begging your pardon, made a total asshole of himself. In every sense. He made a revolution and seized power and turned Russia upside down, but what for? Where are the things that he predicted? Where is communism? Why is capitalism still alive today if it had reached its final stage in his lifetime? Shubkin tried to prove Lenin's intelligence by saying that after the revolution he realized they'd gone too far and decided to make a partial return to capitalism and declared the New Economic Policy. But isn't it stupid to destroy something that existed in complete form in order to go back to it in partial form? In general, I repeat, your Lenin was a grandiose fool, or a brilliant fool if you prefer me to put it that way. But it seems so obvious to me that he was a fool, I can't even be bothered to argue about it."

It was already late, but I took the risk of missing the last bus and asked the Admiral what he thought about Stalin. Was he a fool too?

"No," said the Admiral, bundling himself up in the blanket. "Stalin was by no means a fool. He set goals that were quite clear to him and achieved them very precisely."

"But in doing that he said—"

"What difference does it make what he said?" the Admiral asked with a tired yawn. "What matters is what he did. And he always did exactly what he wanted."

33

In October 1961 at the 22nd Congress of the CPSU, the old Bolshevik Lora Lazurkina accused Stalin of numerous violations of socialist legality and proposed the removal of the violator from Lenin's Mausoleum. It was clear to everyone that the proposal was made with the approval and on the instructions of more highly placed comrades. Therefore, the more lowly placed comrades (those whose seats were quite literally lower) supported the proposal and approved it (while censuring it in their hearts) with tumultuous applause, and later other comrades separated Com. I. V. Stalin from Comrade Vladimir Ilich Lenin and buried him in a cowardly manner under cover of inclement weather and in secret from the people, by the Kremlin wall. Naturally, mass disturbances had been anticipated. Additional KGB and MVD (Ministry of Internal Affairs) forces had been moved up to Moscow to deal with them. Police patrols were intensified, and a state of high alert was declared in the Kantemir and Taman army divisions. But all these efforts proved entirely unnecessary. The people, who only recently had one and all adored Comrade Stalin, responded to the action that had been taken with absolute, indifferent silence. As the people themselves say, they couldn't give a hoot. But what could you expect from the people if even the Party leaders, from the very highest ranks to the very lowest, who only recently had been lauding Stalin to the skies, swearing eternal love and devotion to him and promising to give their lives for him just as soon as the slightest need or opportunity arose, had immediately begun hastily taking down their darling's portraits and removing the volumes of his collected works from the bookshelves and dumping them out with the trash, freeing up the space for the already swelling collected works of "our dear and beloved" Nikita Sergeevich Khrushchev?

On October 31, the day the congress finished, Aglaya received a letter from the distant Isle of Freedom, as Cuba was then known. Having graduated from the Institute of International Relations, Marat had been posted there as an assistant press attaché in the Soviet embassy. In his first letter he described his new life without any superfluous detail, mentioning the unbearable heat, the local customs, the cigars, drinks, dances and music. The letter concluded with the announcement that Zoya had given birth to a son in a Havana hospital, and the young parents had named the child Andrei in honor of Marat's deceased father. "Our boy," wrote Marat, "was a big baby, four and a half kilograms, but he's restless. He doesn't sleep at night and he cries. The doctor advises us not to leave him in a nursery. We have had to hire a housekeeper, whose wages are only partly covered by the embassy." But despite his modest salary and large outgoings, Marat was hoping to save up for a Volga automobile and a house in the country, and therefore he would have to deny himself absolutely all indulgences.

The envelope also contained a photograph of the naked tot with his thumb in his mouth. Having glanced at the photograph, Aglaya put it away in the drawer of her writing desk and wrote in reply that she cursed Lora Lazurkina and her audience. By which, of course, she meant Khrushchev and all the delegates to the Communist Party Congress, but anticipating the likelihood of correspondence being opened and read, she limited herself to the single word "audience." The audience that had failed to demonstrate its devotion to principle and had unanimously approved decisions imposed from above, including, as she hinted, "the destruction of things that were not built by them." Attempting to conceal her central ideas in the subtext, Aglaya gave vent to her indignation toward the modern-day vandals and destroyers of sacred values, to whom nothing was precious: neither homeland, nor people, nor history, nor the individuals who had made that history. At the same time, she stated her conviction that the gravediggers had miscalculated. You could bury the body of a great man anywhere you liked, but his memory could not be buried. Armed with historical optimism, Aglaya promised her son that he would live to see the total and unconditional restoration of justice, to see the day when, as the great leader had once foreseen, "there'll be dancing on our street."

After sealing the envelope, Aglaya decided to send the letter by registered mail, and so she set out for the post office.

As usual in Dolgov, this time of year was dreary and rainy. The rain had been falling cheerlessly for a week and a half or two weeks and the entire natural landscape had turned faded, gray and turbid and spread out through the streets in a liquid goo. The mud squelched underfoot with excruciating relish, sucking in Aglaya's rubber boots. In order not to be left barefoot, she had to pull up the tops of her boots with her hands at every step as she tugged her foot free.

And so Aglaya was making her way along the walls and fences, wresting every step by force from the sodden ground, when suddenly she saw a Chelyabinsk Factory tractor wallowing radiator-deep in the mud and grunting with the strain as it cruised toward her, hauling along on a cable a large, elongated object that Aglaya took for a log. But on looking more closely, she made out the toe of a boot at one end of the log and a nose, mustache and the peak of a cap protruding in a highly absurd fashion at the other end.

It was absolutely impossible to run through mud like that but, impelled by the strength of her feeling, Aglaya managed to overtake the tractor, then leap out into the middle of the street and, ignoring the slop that had flowed into the top of her left boot, she spread her arms picturesquely and cried: "Stop! Stop!"

The tractor carried on grunting and advancing on Aglaya. Unfortunately, at that moment there was no sculptor or painter beside her who could have recorded this unforgettable scene: the tractor pressing on stupidly regardless and the frail woman with her outspread arms in the hood that had slipped down to the back of her head to reveal her hair (already streaked with gray), her eyes filled with the determination to die rather than give ground. No, there was no sculptor or painter at the scene, but just a little distance away there was the poet Serafim Butylko with a string shopping bag full of empty bottles. By this time he had long ago abandoned his plans for achieving fame and glory but had still not lost all hope of a bit of successful speculation. To be precise: that he would manage to return all six Zhigulevskoe beer bottles and the woman checking them would not notice that the mouth of one was slightly chipped. Then he would add the money recovered in this way to the two rubles he already had, and he would have just enough for a bottle of Kubanskaya vodka, a pack of Pamir cigarettes and box of matches to go with it. A modest plan, but it had been calculated down to the last kopeck and it was realizable. In his baggy coat with the darned elbows, the poet was clinging to the fencing slats as he made his way toward the reception point for empty jars and bottles, when he caught sight of Aglaya standing there in the middle of the road with her arms outstretched. However, he failed to discern any heroic gesture in her impulsive action, deciding that the woman must have made up her mind to hire a vehicle for carrying firewood, which was something he needed to think about too. Or perhaps he did discern a heroic gesture, but being in a state of creative crisis, he failed to convert his observation into verse. In any case, no mention at all of this event was subsequently discovered either in his verse or among the entries in his diaries. Especially since he never kept any diaries.

The tractor advanced on Aglaya; she stood her ground, gritting her teeth and clenching her fists. The tractor stopped. Its driver, Slava Sirotkin, stuck his head out of the cabin and, sheltering his tousled head of hair against the rain with an oilskin mitten, he inquired of Aglaya whether she might by any chance have escaped from the madhouse. Aglaya sidled up to him, and nodding at the object being towed by the tractor, she asked: "Where are you towing that?"

"What?" asked Sirotkin.

"Do you know who it is you're towing?" she shouted above the noise of the engine.

"Who?" Sirotkin eased back into the cabin and took out the coarse cigarette he'd been holding in reserve behind his ear.

"Do you realize that's Stalin?"

"Who else could it be? Obviously it's him."

"So where are you towing him then?"

"They told me to drag him down to the station," said Sirotkin, lighting up. "They must be sending him on from there for melting down. The country needs metal awful bad for the space program."

"Metal?" Aglaya cried indignantly. "You call this metal? It's a monument to Comrade Stalin. We all erected it together, all the people. We put it up when folks had no bread to eat and nothing to feed their children with. We denied ourselves everything to put it up here. And you're dragging it through the mud like some lump of pig-iron. You ought to be ashamed of yourself!"

"What have I got to be ashamed of, Ma? There's no shame if you keep it hid, as they say, but I'm just . . . you know . . . just the tractor driver. They tell me to tow it, and I tow it. If they don't tell me, I'll go for a smoke, that's what I'll do, see," and he showed her how he would smoke, "and no questions asked."

"And what if they hook Lenin on—will you drag him along too?"

Sirotkin gave her a reproachful look.

"Listen, Ma, let's not get into politics. That's all right for the folks up there with the big heads. But I'm a tractor driver. Sixty-six rubles a month, and I can earn a bit on the side if someone needs a kitchen garden plowed or something. But who gets hooked on and towed, that's for the foreman, Dubinin, to decide. Let's say he says, 'Sirotkin, you've got to take that there.' What am I supposed to say? If he says take it there, should I take it somewhere else? Am I crazy or something? So you just shift yourself, Ma, and let's get moving again."

Sirotkin went back to his levers, but Aglaya stood in front of the tractor again. Sirotkin let go of his levers, leaned back and relaxed.

"Listen, son," Aglaya said to him sweetly, "what if . . ."

Serafim Butylko saw Aglaya get into the cabin beside the tractor driver, who shuffled his levers and the tractor moved forward, made a wide circle and hauled its iron billet off in the direction it had come from.

To the uninvolved observer the tractor's subsequent route would have seemed strange. After following a long and winding path, dragging the work of art along behind it, the tractor ended up on the northern outskirts of the town by the gates of the Collective Farm Building Trust's transport depot. There Sirotkin left Aglaya in the tractor with the engine running and ran off to find his friend, the motorized crane driver Sashka Lykov. Sashka wasn't there, but they said he was at the station helping to rehang the portraits for the imminent anniversary of the October Revolution. Marx, Engels, Lenin and Stalin had been hanging on the pediment of the façade, but now only Marx and Lenin were left. Engels had been removed for the sake of symmetry.

They found Sashka in the buffet, where, having rehung the portraits, he was drinking beer and chatting about this and that with the counter girl Antonina. They tore him away from the counter girl and took him along with them, this time to the house where Aglaya lived. The tractor went first, with the statue dragging behind it, and the motorized crane came behind that. They hauled the statue up to the window and dumped it. Of course, the residents came running up to see what would happen next. It seemed the idea was to introduce the monument into Aglaya's apartment. The dimensions fitted. The statue was two and a half meters high, and Aglaya's ceilings were three meters and ten centimeters. Sashka, being the most quick-witted, examined the work site and said: "We'll go in through the window."

"How?" asked Aglaya.

"We'll lever it in. Archimedes, Ma, said, 'Give me a lever, I'll turn anything you like upside down.' So that's the way we'll go. We'll lash some rope on it, hoist it up, give it a heave and shove it in. If we work clever, Ma, I can get you an elephant in there."

How they carried out this unusual commission is hard even to imagine now, but on that afternoon the iron generalissimo, with the help of a motorized crane, four hands and four bottles of vodka, was raised, dragged in through the window and installed in Aglaya Revkina's drawing room, in the corner between the two windows—one of which overlooked the yard and the other faced east, toward the motor depot on Rosenblum Street. Of course, the generalissimo himself was not able to stand on his own two feet, some kind of pedestal was required. Sashka Lykov brought around a piece of five-millimeter iron sheeting and a welding kit and welded the statue to it. Moreover, he did it entirely free of charge.

In the old days, when someone who had no living space was moved in with someone who had an excess of it, it was known as consolidation.

PART TWO

WE SING AS WE FIGHT AS WE CONQUER

34

On the sixth of November, as evening was drawing in, there was a stealthy knock on Aglaya Stepanovna Revkina's door. She came out into the corridor, holding a towel in her wet hands, but before she had time to ask who it was, the door began creaking open in a sinister fashion worthy of a horror movie, revealing a shoulder tautly clad in threadbare military fabric, which gradually evolved into the familiar crumpled profile of the house manager, Dmitrii Ivanovich Kashlyaev, nicknamed Divanich, a red-cheeked and red-nosed former colonel of the meteorological service who had been discharged from the army for drunkenness. Well, not simply for drunkenness—for drunkenness, the entire officer corps of the Soviet army could have been dismissed—but specifically because Colonel Kashlyaev, while the head of the meteorological service of the Ministry of Defense in northern latitudes, had permitted his subordinates (even, apparently, collaborating with them) to drink the alcohol out of various sensitive instruments and replace it with water. Things had gone so far that the main thermometer at the main meteorological station in the military district used to freeze at precisely zero degrees Celsius. But even so, the service continued to operate, compiling weather reports and forecasts that were used by the ships of the Soviet navy and units of the strategic air arm. Divanich, it is true, was a very experienced meteorologist. He could easily determine the current temperature and wind direction simply by holding up a finger moistened with saliva, and he compiled the short-term forecast on the basis of general weather signs and the aching in his knee that had been injured at the front during the war. Certainly, he made mistakes—he was bound to—but no more than the All-Union Hydrometeorological Center. But then, perhaps the Hydrometeorological Center made its mistakes for the same reason. Divanich had been discharged from the army, and now he worked as a house manager, receiving a colonel's pension in addition to his modest pay.

The door creaked as Divanich forced his way in past it with stubborn determination, holding it back with his hand in order to leave himself only a crack to squeeze through, thereby zealously emphasizing the insignificance of his own person, as though it were not deserving of full and free access. At the same time, however, he demonstrated a distinct effrontery, his expression indicating that he might have opened only a modest crack for himself, but he was going to creep in through it come whatever. Eventually, he materialized completely, dressed in an officer's uniform with dark, unfaded patches where the shoulder straps and collar tabs had been ripped off and with two buttons, one of which was a military button, but the other was from a trade-college uniform.

"Good health to you, so to speak, Aglastepna" (the form of address into which he unvaryingly conflated her first name and patronymic), "and best wishes, so to speak, for the coming holiday." The colonel tugged off his cap with the red band and cracked peak and shook his head, sending flakes of dull white dandruff swarming into the air, where they hovered above Divanich's head in a wan halo before settling back onto his shoulders.

Aglaya looked at the new arrival inquiringly, saying nothing. He looked back at her, clearly having forgotten what he'd come for.

"Here I am then, so to speak," said the colonel, and shook his head again.

"Well, since you're here, come through, only take your shoes off, I'm not swabbing the floors after you."

"Whatever you say," Kashlyaev readily agreed. "The mud outside's pretty much knee-deep, and trailing it into the house . . ."

Without bothering to finish the phrase, he kicked off his shoes, with their lingering vestiges of light brown coloration, and set off, slipping and sliding on the painted floor in his gray woolen socks with holes in the big toes. The colonel skidded into the drawing room after his hostess and stopped, dumbfounded, as though he had suddenly been confronted by an elephant or the Empire State Building.

Standing there before him full-length in his cast-iron full-dress uniform was the Supreme Commander-in-Chief, his left hand clutching his gloves and his right hand thrust up almost against the ceiling. Newly cleaned and washed by Aglaya, he stared Divanich straight in the eye, his entire left side glinting dully in the light of the five-branched chandelier.

Divanich had known the statue was standing here, it was the reason he'd come, but the visual impact of the monument reduced him to total stupefaction.

"Fu-aa-oo!" moaned Divanich, after which there wasn't enough air left in his chest for any more intelligible interjection.

He carried on standing there with his mouth open until his hostess brought him back to reality with a question concerning the purpose of his visit.

"Well, you see . . ." Divanich began, embarrassed, then fell silent, leaving his thought unspoken, his gaze riveted once again to the statue.

"What do you want?" Aglaya repeated her question.

"Well, you see . . ." Divanich twitched one shoulder in an attempt to progress further with his deliberations. "Well you see," he said, pointing to the statue, "it's like this, the residents have written collectively that it's a pretty heavy, so to speak, load. The floors here are pretty much made of wood, and the Tukhvatullins have got cracks in their ceiling."

"And what of it?" asked Aglaya.

Kashlyaev indicated with a simultaneous parting of the hands, shrugging of the shoulders and pursing of the lips that he possessed no satisfactory answer to the question he had been asked. But he made an effort to express his opinion more intelligibly: "Look, he says, a crack. And I say, so it's a crack, what of it, what harm's it doing you? Not in your head, is it, that crack? And he says, it's not right, I'm sitting here eating my soup and I feel, he says, something hard, I think, he says, my tooth's fallen out, but I look and I see it's not a tooth, it's a bit of plaster. It's not really meant, so to speak, for indoor conditions. Out on the square's a different matter, he can stand there and even if he keels over, it's not like it's any of our business. He's in the right spot there, and people can go up and leave flowers or come around with the tour guide, but this here is pretty much a residential, so to speak, building and the beams are wood and it's got rot. Anything goes wrong, let's say, and it's the jailhouse, so to speak, for me and pretty much a death sentence for the Tukhvatullins, and the other residents, they're worried about it too."

Aglaya listened to all of this with her arms crossed on her skinny chest.

She sighed: "So what are you trying to tell me? That I should throw him out? Throw Stalin out—where to? The dump? Out with the garbage? Eh?"

Kashlyaev gave a deep, sad sigh.

"What can I say, if only he was just alive, for him I could, pretty much, so to speak . . . how can I put it . . . off the fifth floor." Kashlyaev left his thought unfinished and gave the statue a respectful glance, as though hoping for its understanding. But when he met the statue's eyes, he felt uneasy. And the statue was regarding him with such hostility that he began feeling positively apprehensive. He even staggered backward a few steps toward the exit and didn't immediately hear the question his hostess asked him. "What?" he asked her.

"I asked if you want a drink."

"A drink?" Kashlyaev froze and licked his lips. The colonel badly wanted to say: No, never, not for anything—and proudly withdraw. Or before he withdrew, click his worn-down heels together and express some exalted sentiment concerning the honor of a Soviet soldier which—or so it sometimes seemed to him—he had never completely drowned in drink. But he had never done anything of the kind, and never said anything of the kind. Although there had been plenty of occasions to say it. For whenever it was needed, or just in case it might be, the residents would slip him a five-ruble or three-ruble note (although some, seeing his shabby appearance, restricted their offering to a single crumpled ruble), and he took everything they handed him. This time too the offer of a drink provoked only a second's hesitation in him before, turning his gaze away from the statue, he said "Uh-huh" and was duly invited into the kitchen and seated at the round table covered with oilcloth with pictures of the Kremlin towers on it.

Aglaya always had vodka in the house. Since the partisan days she had regularly drunk a glass or two with supper, but never went beyond that, having heard that inveterate alcoholism inevitably resulted in petrification of the liver.

She took a bottle of Moskovskaya vodka with a picture of lots of medals drawn on its label out of the Saratov refrigerator, took out two cold meat rissoles, cold potatoes, some sauerkraut and a tin of Atlantic skippers. Aglaya used her teeth to tear off the bottle's thin metal cap with the lug that you could pull with your fingers.

"Oh!" said Divanich admiringly. "That's the way to do it! But I can't.

My teeth are all loose thanks to not getting enough calcium and vitamins."

"Right then, here's to him," Aglaya proposed, raising her glass.

"Without clinking glasses, then," said the house manager.

"We'll clink!" she protested. "For us he's eternally alive."

"Eternally alive!" Kashlyaev agreed and stood up, quite reasonably assuming that you should stand to drink for the eternally living. His hostess stood up with him.

Long after midnight, when Divanich was already standing with his coat on in the hall, he went back to the statue, stood in front of it respectfully and said quietly: "He was a great man. A commander!"

"There aren't any more like him," Aglaya responded.

"And never will be." Beginning to cry, the colonel hastily brushed away a tear and went out.

35

The next day there was another stealthy knock at the door. Aglaya thought it was Kashlyaev again, but when she opened it, she saw a little old man who looked like Kalinin, with a goatee and thin mustache, wearing steel-rimmed glasses, a blue cloth coat trimmed with ancient rabbit fur that was moth-eaten even though it smelled strongly of naphthalene and button-up felt boots with galoshes. The little old man showed her the official identity card of an inspector of the Directorate for the Exploitation of Civil Structures, asked permission to come in and removed his galoshes.

He halted in front of the statue, peered at it over the top of his glasses, clucked his tongue and shook his head from side to side.

"Oi, madam, what a big, heavy thing it is! Pardon me, but I have to take some measurements."

Removing his coat, he laid it on a chair and dragged another chair over to the statue.

"With your permission . . ." And without waiting for her permission, he clambered up on the chair, took a tailor's tape measure out of his pocket and set about measuring the statue.

"What are you doing that for?" asked Aglaya.

"That ought to be clear enough, my dear. It seems quite obvious to me that before expressing an opinion about an object, you need to measure it. When I was young, by the way, I worked as an assistant to a tailor's cutter, so I have been familiar with this procedure ever since. The cutter was a fine man, but very strict. The slightest mistake and he gave you the finest smack around the ear you can imagine. We were raised strictly, but it did us a lot of good."

He jumped down onto the floor like a young man, took a notepad and an indelible pencil out of his pocket, and added and multiplied the dimensions he had taken. Then he groaned: "Oh no, that's quite impossible."

"What's impossible?" asked Aglaya.

"The whole thing's impossible. As my immediate superior says, the dimensions exceed the limits. The floors here won't support such a heavy load. The hardware will have to go."

"It's not hardware," Aglaya protested angrily, "it's Comrade Stalin."

"Oh no, my deary!" The little old man waggled his beard. "It's not Comrade Stalin, it's an alloy of iron and carbon, with a specific weight of — about eight grams per cubic centimeter. Let me give it to you straight — this thingy has to be removed."

Aglaya rushed into her study and emerged with a red ten-ruble note, which she proffered to her guest without the slightest embarrassment.

"There, take it."

"What's that?" the old man asked, squinting at the offering.

"Can't you see for yourself?" Aglaya asked sarcastically.

She had always been a convinced communist, with a firm belief in Soviet power and the Soviet people. Always believed in the people's devotion to the ideals of communism, its moral rectitude and incorruptibility. And at the same time, she had never had any doubt that each individual member of that people would sell outright his body, his soul, his country, his people and his communist ideals for five rubles, let alone for ten. If she had read in some novel or story that an imaginary official invented by the author had accepted a bribe from some imaginary suppliant, she would immediately have written an irate refutation to the editors. Libelous defamation of our social reality. Our Soviet officials do not take bribes and the author of such malicious fabrications should be punished with all possible severity. But in real life she could not even imagine that any

Soviet functionary, great or small, would scorn the opportunity to take what was offered, or not to grant what was requested. And yet such people did exist. Not, of course, in every region and not in every district, but here and there they were to be found, as relics of the past. One such person was the inspector we are describing here, who said firmly: "Absolutely not, thank you."

"Not enough, is it?" Aglaya asked, descending to sarcasm.

"It's enough," said the little old man. "For my rank it's quite enough. Except, my dear, that I don't take bribes at all. I prefer to live on my salary. It makes things a bit tight, but at least my soul's at peace. I don't have dreams at night about the black raven and bolts clanking shut on prison doors."

Embarrassed, Aglaya began mumbling something about it not being a bribe but a friendly gift, but even then the old man stood firm.

"No, I'm sorry, but I don't take friendly bribes either. But don't you worry. Other people will come to see you, perhaps even tomorrow, more important people than me. They'll take it. Of course, this ten rubles of yours won't be enough for them. But then, my precious, they'll allow you and your statue to go crashing down onto the heads of your neighbors. But that's none of my business. I'll go now and write my report."

The old man was a true prophet.

One after another Aglaya was visited by a whole pack of agents from all sorts of monitoring and inspecting and absolutely irrelevant organizations, and unlike the little old man, all of them took five or ten rubles. Some even extorted twenty-five. The resulting situation was described by Aglaya's neighbor Georgii Zhukov as follows: "That lodger of hers doesn't drink and he doesn't smoke, but he still demands money."

According to local standards, Aglaya was not poor. Her modest hard-earned savings, as she herself called them, had lain untouched in her post-office savings account for years. There had been a time when a Party special courier dressed in paramilitary uniform with a revolver in a tarpaulin holster would mysteriously appear every month and hand her an envelope that she signed for. It contained her second salary, the one that nomenklatura Party workers received for bearing on their shoulders such a great burden of responsibility. She had two salaries, but with her style of life one was enough. She put the entire second salary in the savings bank, and even to her, let alone to the envious glance of a stranger, the accumulated sum appeared a great, inexhaustible fortune. But this fortune proved insufficient to feed all the local inspectors. Her modest savings melted away before her eyes, and the inspectors became more and more insolent and insatiable.

36

The Admiral believed that in dethroning Stalin, Khrushchev had made a fatal error. He had transgressed the fundamental unwritten law of SCOSWO, according to which nothing should be subjected to doubt. If it was permitted to berate Stalin, that meant it was also possible to have doubts about Lenin. And if faith in Lenin's infallibility faltered, the temptation arose to start wondering just how correct SCOSWO was.

"Scoswu," the Admiral stated, "is like an automobile tire. You can ride on it with confidence as long as it has no leaks. Prick one little hole in it and it has to be changed."

"Or patched," I said.

"Or patched," the Admiral agreed. "But then you have a patched-up tire. And unlike a tire, ideal Scuswu must have the reputation of being unpuncturable in any circumstances."

Beginning in the fall of 1961 many inhabitants of Dolgov—or more precisely, all of them—began to get the feeling that some irreparable dislocation had occurred in the life of the town and the district. When they removed the monument, it was like taking the axle out of a wheel. The center everything had revolved around was gone. As long as Stalin had stood in his place, he had served as an invariable reference point in both the literal topographical sense and another, metaphysical one. When a chance visitor to the town asked a local resident how to get to some place or other, he used to be told: Go straight on till you reach the monument, then turn right. Or left. Or carry straight on. But now there was no monument, only an empty pedestal with an inscription that someone had attempted to erase, but had not erased completely: I. V. STALIN. This granite cube affected people's imaginations in a strange way. When they looked at it, they felt very powerfully that there ought to be someone standing on it. And if no one was standing on it, then the whole of life lacked an essential core, in the absence of which many things became possible that had previously been impossible.

They say that was the precise time from which children became less obedient to their parents, discipline in industry deteriorated and the revenue from sales of alcoholic beverages to the public increased, along with the number of abortions and the frequency of violent crimes threatening the lives, honor and property of citizens. Of course, even before then for domestic reasons and on public holidays, the residents of Dolgov had stuck knives in each other, run each other through with pitchforks and beaten each other to death with fence poles, but all that had merely been the observance of old local customs. With the dethroning of the statue, however, the phenomenon began to emerge that was later christened "free-for-all." The public prosecutor, Strogii, was caught molesting his own underage daughter. At about the same time, the first serial killer in the entire history of those parts made his appearance in the district, and he turned out to be a lecturer in Marxism-Leninism in the cultural-vocational school, an individual who had published regular articles in the *Dolgov Pravda* on aspects of Soviet morality. On the Avenue of Glory vandals desecrated several graves, overturning the headstones and defacing them with villainous graffiti, paying special attention to the grave of Rosenblum—the stone on his resting place was shattered with a sledgehammer.

And as for the statue of Stalin, the rumors concerning it circulating in the town were each more absurd than the last. Aglaya's downstairs neighbors had definitely heard someone heavy walking around on the second floor at night. They could hear the footsteps and the beams creaking; they saw their chandelier swaying and plaster flaking off the ceiling. Then someone saw a figure wandering around the waste lot in the twilight. Late one night after a heavy drinking session, when Georgii Zhukov went outside for a smoke, he saw an old man in a military greatcoat sitting on the bench. Sitting there hunched over and smoking his pipe. Zhukov went up to him and asked: "Can you give me a light, Pops?"

Pops turned his face toward him, and Zhukov saw that the old man had a face made of iron, and he had big eyes with holes instead of pupils, but he was still looking straight at Zhukov.

"Excuse me," said Zhukov, and quietly withdrew. After climbing the stairs to his apartment, he lay down in bed with his back to his wife and slept for exactly four days, which was officially certified in his sick note.

Nothing happened after that in Zhukov's life except that he gave up smoking. He drank even more than before, but he dropped smoking entirely and for good. And not at all out of any concern for his health — he just gave it up, and that was it. The morning after his lethargy he got up, grabbed a cigarette without having anything to eat first, went off to the toilet, made himself comfortable and lifted the match to the cigarette — but suddenly, at the memory of those iron eyes with holes in them, he didn't feel like having a smoke.

Zhukov didn't tell anyone about his nocturnal vision, but he listened attentively to other conversations about the mysterious old man of iron. And the conversations continued, more and more of them as time went by. People said that someone had met Him somewhere (people tried not to mention the name of the person who was met) in either his iron or ordinary form, and supposedly he had questioned them about the lives of the simple people in the district and whether the leadership was oppressing them and doing too well by itself. There were also reports that every full moon the statue mounted the pedestal and stood there with its hand raised, but immediately disappeared, dissolving into thin air as soon as a living human being approached. But then, all of this was no more than rumors, which should be regarded with great caution. The populace of the town of Dolgov and its environs had always had its fair share of wild and credulous people who believed in witch doctors, psychics, spies, the global Jewish conspiracy and Colorado beetles. I myself was acquainted there with fantasists who claimed that they had personally encountered devils, ghosts, house spirits, forest spirits, water spirits, witches and aliens, and had even journeyed to other galaxies in their flying saucers.

Naturally, an enlightened individual is not obliged to believe in all of this, but the fact that for many years after Stalin's death his spirit hovered over the Dolgov district and the entire territory of the Soviet Union, and over an even more extensive territory, is historically indisputable.

37

Aglaya paid no attention to rumors of the statue's unauthorized perambulations, knowing perfectly well that her iron lodger never went anywhere.

But it sometimes seemed to her that even without going anywhere he nonetheless responded to events of All-Union or local significance, and even had premonitions of some of them. She noticed that as soon as some development that she found gratifying was imminent in the country, he began, if not exactly glowing, then at least brightening up just a little from the inside. Such a very little that it was unlikely any commission of experts would have been able to detect it with even the most sensitive of instruments. Or detect the imperceptible change that occurred in the expression of his face. In fact, Aglaya didn't even trust herself completely and wondered whether she was just imagining it. But somehow her imaginings were always opportune. What she imagined today happened tomorrow.

One day when she woke up later than usual to bright sunshine, she glanced at her iron lodger and saw that he was covered in a layer of dust. Feeling suddenly ashamed, she filled a basin with warm water and took a sponge and some toilet soap. She put the table beside the statue, set a stool on the table with the basin on it, risked life and limb by clambering up onto a second stool and set to work.

The sculptor Ogorodov had made a thorough job of everything: he'd drilled out the nostrils and scraped out the intricate indentations of the ears, and now all of this was clogged with dust. She wound some cotton wool onto a hairpin and cleaned out the holes with it. As she washed, she spoke words that her own son had never heard from her.

"Now," she intoned, "we'll wash your nice hair, wash your lovely eyes and nose, and then your ears, then your shoulders and your chest and back and tummy . . ." Until she reached the place where the flaps of the greatcoat were parted to reveal the lower edge of the jacket and immediately below it the spot from which the legs began. Aglaya suddenly felt embarrassed. The spot, as a matter of fact, was smooth, the way it could only have been in a being that was either female or entirely sexless. And for some reason Aglaya felt strangely perplexed by this. She suddenly wondered—and felt angry with herself for doing it, but her doubts still remained—what had the living Comrade Stalin had at this spot? She was unable to think of him as having something at that spot, but to imagine that there hadn't been anything proved even harder. She abused herself, calling herself a fool and an old fool for having any such thoughts at all. She tried to drive the thoughts out of her head, but they came back and embarrassed her again. She knew that Stalin was a man, but she was unable to imagine him going to the toilet or fathering children. Quite impossibly stupid as they were, these notions kept on visiting her, and she began noticing that when she wiped down the statue she tried to avoid the spot that was causing her embarrassment. After a while she noticed that although he was clean everywhere else, that spot wasn't really clean at all. She began washing him equally well all over, but she was unable to rid herself of a distinct feeling of embarrassment.

Naturally, she didn't share her doubts with anyone. And she didn't give anyone any excuse for the rumors that soon began to spread through the town about her cohabiting with the statue as if it were a man. This surely had to be nonsense. How could a live human being cohabit with an iron statue? It should have been impossible even to imagine it, but as we have already noted, the people of Dolgov were quite remarkably gullible.

Aglaya's experience as a woman had been relatively modest and not very successful. Of course, she had had her husband, Andrei Revkin. And there had been (just a couple of times in her life) other brief attachments. But intimacy with a man had never had the effect on her that she had heard about from others. Her younger sister Natalya used to tell her that intimacy with a man excited her so much she went absolutely wild and experienced a quite incomparable sensation of heavenly bliss. She called this feeling an orgasm. When asked to describe it more precisely, Natalya rolled her eyes and giggled: "Do you think it can be described in words? It's, you know . . . It's, well it's just something else altogether."

Natalya had been unable to come up with a more intelligible explanation, but Aglaya had understood it after a fashion. There had been times with some men, even that time with Shaleiko, when that "something else altogether" had almost happened to her. But it hadn't happened—either that time or before it or after it.

Apart, that is, from one occasion . . .

In the fall of '39 she had gone to Moscow to visit the All-Union Agricultural Exhibition. She had been sent there as a leading worker of agricultural production, which was a way of showing appreciation for her Party activity. At the exhibition, it goes without saying, it was all meetings, speeches and banquets, and afterward there was a rally of shock workers of socialist labor in the Hall of Columns in Trade Union House. The guests included people famous throughout the entire country: five-year-plan heroes, collective farmers, steelmakers, miners, participants in all sorts of polar winter camps and record flights, and sports champions too.

There was the miner Alexei Stakhanov, the woman tractor driver Pasha Angelina, the flyer Mikhail Vodopyanov and the actor Mikhail Zharov. Sitting beside Aglaya in the fourth row was the famous steam locomotive driver Pyotr Fyodorovich Krivonos. He drove very heavy trains and was as famous as though he, and not his locomotive, were the one who pulled them. Everyone took a long time finding their seats, then they waited for something, looking at the dimly lit stage, at the table covered with red cloth and the rows of carafes standing on it. Suddenly, the stage was lit up brightly and the members of the Politburo emerged from the wings on the right and walked toward the table in single file. Krivonos began whispering in Aglaya's ear the names of the leaders and the order in which they appeared. She knew them all herself, but she just couldn't believe that they were right there, alive, not just in their portraits: Voroshilov, Budyonny, Kalinin, Mikoyan, Kaganovich, Shvernik. The delegates to the rally greeted the leaders with a tumultuous standing ovation, and the leaders applauded the delegates in return. The leaders began taking their seats, and Kalinin gestured with both hands to show that the audience could also be seated.

"I wonder why Comrade Stalin's not here," Krivonos whispered to Aglaya.

"He must be very busy," she suggested.

"Comrade Stalin's always very busy," said Krivonos. "But he always finds time for the workers."

Before he had finished speaking, a figure emerged from the wings on the left and walked unhurriedly toward the presidium—a short man with a mustache wearing a modest, semimilitary cloth field jacket.

"Glory to Comrade Stalin!" Krivonos roared like a steam locomotive, leaping to his feet.

The entire hall had stood on a single impulse and Aglaya had jumped to her feet with the rest of them, and then that "something else altogether" had suddenly and completely taken possession of her. It was as though lightning had pierced her body through and through; there was an incredible surge of heat in her chest that sank down to the bottom of her belly. Out of control, she clutched the back of the seat in front of her, shouted out, and felt herself burst apart. When she recovered her wits, she was afraid her neighbor might have noticed and guessed what had happened to her. But her neighbor hadn't guessed—he'd been howling and yelling in an incoherent frenzy himself—and afterward Aglaya thought it probably hadn't happened just to her, but to everyone else who had been thrashing about in hysterics.

38

Aglaya had once altered her documents, adding seven years to her age so that she could join the struggle for the establishment of Soviet power sooner. In 1962, even according to her documents, she still hadn't reached retirement age, but she was put out on a pension on account of the time she had served at the front during the war. The pension she was given, however, was not the personal merit pension to which she was entitled by her entire life of devotion to the Party and the government, but an ordinary pension that amounted, with a supplementary service bonus, to eighty-two rubles and sixty kopecks. On an income like that, you'd think twice before buying a bar of soap. Especially since it wasn't the ordinary kind she bought, but perfumed toilet soap at thirty kopecks a bar. Her expenditure on inspectors had finally come to an end though. Stalin hadn't fallen through the floor, the other residents had got used to him and stopped complaining, and no one bothered Aglaya anymore.

Freed from the responsibilities of a daily job, she had absolutely no idea what to do with herself or how to occupy her time. She wasn't going to sit out on the bench with the old grannies and listen to their complaints about rheumatism and indigestion. Or their dream-readings, stories about grandchildren's pranks and recipes for pickling cucumbers. She made up her mind to try to learn English and even picked up a self-instruction manual for beginners from somewhere, but after a week of self-torment she gave up. What good was English to her anyway, even if she did manage to learn it?

But one day she glanced at her bookshelves, where the works of Stalin occupied the place of honor, took down Volume 6, chosen at random, opened it at the work *On the Foundations of Leninism* and realized what her goal was for the immediate future. She would learn this work by heart. Day by day. One page at a time. A hundred and twenty pages—that was only four months of work.

Late that afternoon she organized the spot for her daily study session. She dragged the bearskin over to the statue (what an incredible amount of dust there was!), then dropped two cushions, a copybook and a fountain pen from the Union factory onto it. She brought the table lamp from her study and stood it beside her, drank a shot of vodka, took a sip of tea from a mug and set to work, beginning with the foreword.

"The foundations of Leninism," she read aloud to herself, "are a big subject." And she thought to herself: I should say so! Very big. "To exhaust this subject," the text continued, "would require an entire book." One book wouldn't be enough, thought Aglaya, and found to her delight that her thought coincided perfectly with the author's. "More than that, it would require an entire series of books," was what he said. Encouraged, she began reading loudly, with expression, taking pleasure in her own hoarse, smoke-roughened voice: "To expound the foundations of Leninism does not mean to expound the foundations of Lenin's world outlook . . ."

She imagined Stalin, not the statue, but the living man she had seen that time in the Hall of Columns. She imagined him walking slowly from corner to corner of the room smoking his pipe as he dictated pensively in a mild Georgian accent: "Lenin's world outlook and the foundations of Leninism are not identical in volume. Lenin is a Marxist and the basis of his world outlook is, of course, Marxism. But from that it does not at all follow that an exposition of Leninism must be begun with an exposition of the foundations of Marxism . . ."

"It doesn't follow," Aglaya agreed, and, closing her eyes, she decided to repeat the entire paragraph. "To expound the foundations of a world outlook means . . ." She stumbled to a halt. "It means . . ." What did it mean? She couldn't remember, she glanced at the book . . . Does not mean . . . Ah, it does not mean! "To expound the foundations of Leninism does not mean to expound the foundations of Lenin's world outlook . . ."

Eventually, she memorized this sentence, but when she reached the end of the paragraph, she had retained the final words in her memory but forgotten the first ones. She decided not to give in, and each evening, arranging herself at the foot of the monument, she read, repeated, wrote notes and repeated again. Her head, unused to such intense exertion, felt as if it were splitting open, but positive progress was achieved. It was slow though. It took her two weeks to reach the question: "And so, what is Leninism?" She struggled to master this page for three weeks, but still didn't understand what Leninism was, and the author himself didn't seem to have understood, because he concluded his lengthy critique of Lenin's ideas with the same question: "What then, after all, is Leninism?"

39

Meanwhile, in Aglaya's opinion the events that were taking place in the country were simply disgraceful. Baldie took a trip to America and spent some time in the state of Iowa. He saw how vigorously the maize grows there and decided that the shortcomings of the collective farm system could be counterbalanced if the expanses from Kushka to the tundra were sown with this magical cereal. One word was all it took, and the entire country was planted with maize. It didn't grow. They divided the party into agricultural and municipal regional committees. It didn't grow. They transformed the ministries into national economic councils—NECs— and the maize still didn't grow; it refused. They gave up on the maize and set about introducing a reform of the Russian language that would have meant a hare was called a "her" and instead of "cucumber" people would have written "queucamber."

In '62 the Caribbean crisis erupted. Baldie sent ships to Cuba with rockets so they could be installed and pointed at America. The Americans said they would never allow it. They dispatched their aircraft carriers and submarines to Cuba. Baldie wouldn't withdraw, the American president Kennedy wouldn't give way. The war of nerves lasted two days, with the gap between the fleets of the two superpowers narrowing all the time. The most sensitive Americans gulped down nitroglycerine and jumped out of windows on top stories. Soviet people, not being sufficiently well informed, were not alarmed and remained inside their windows. But some more knowledgeable individuals were concerned.

During those days Marat wrote to Aglaya that the clouds were gathering over the island and the weather forecasters were predicting a typhoon, so he had sent his wife and child home to Russia. But since the typhoon might possibly even reach Moscow, wouldn't it be better for Zoya and little Andrei Maratovich to pay a visit to his granny? Granny replied that in her view society was degenerating still further. The central press was publishing more and more pseudohistorical material about Stalin and his comrades-in-arms. Abominable jokes were circulating among the people; some people openly listened to foreign radio stations, wrote anti-Soviet works and circulated them. And as time went on, the Party was becoming more and more polluted by an alien element, by people who only joined it for the sake of their careers, in order to exploit their position for their own grubby purposes. While her letter was on its way from Dolgov to Havana, the crisis was successfully resolved, and the need for the grandson to visit his granny was averted.

In that same year of '62, rumors spread of an uprising in Novocherkassk having been ruthlessly suppressed by the armed forces with the use of tanks. Aglaya's reaction to this event was ambivalent. She sympathized with the workers who had risen in opposition to the antipopular regime and Baldie, but at the same time she was in no doubt that such uprisings had to be suppressed as antipopular themselves, and in the harshest manner possible. On learning that the instigators of the uprising had been shot, she was incensed both by the fact that they had been shot at all and the fact that not enough of them had been shot.

The echoes of this event had still not died away when something else happened that was really obnoxious, something that she took to heart far more than the Caribbean crisis. The literary journal *New World*, long famous for its critical stance, published a novella by a totally unknown political prisoner, who was immediately declared a great writer. And the characters in this novella were unlike any that there had ever been in Soviet literature. Not collective-farm workers, not factory workers and not the labor intelligentsia, but convicts. And not convicts who had gone astray by chance and were now on the road to correction, but politicals. Enemies of the people. And they were depicted as good people who had suffered for nothing. And the author described the soldiers of the interior forces in the blackest possible light and called them mindless parrots. And the worst thing of all was that the readers turned out to be so politically immature that they flung themselves on this work, passed it from hand to hand and when they met each other they glanced around over their shoulders and asked in low voices: "Have you read it?"

Aglaya read the beginning. Six or seven pages. And promised herself she would never touch that journal again. But unfortunately this novella proved not to be the only one of its kind. First one journal then another, thick ones and thin ones, and then the newspapers published novellas, stories, poems, articles and exposés in which the authors besmirched Soviet history, and what they wrote about Stalin was simply too disgusting to repeat. He deceived Lenin and wiped out the Leninist old guard, he murdered Kirov, annihilated the intelligentsia, ruined the peasantry, decapitated the army, failed to prepare for the war, hid in a bunker, and he couldn't tolerate criticism.

40

After its initial publication by *New World*, the work that had shaken Aglaya so badly by the unknown political prisoner (who immediately became very well known) was published in a popular mass edition by the periodical *Novel Newspaper*, in a separate hardback edition and another edition in paperback, immediately achieving total coverage of the entire country, like the Hong Kong flu. In Dolgov, too, people forgot about absolutely everything else and talked of nothing but this book, read it as soon as they could and, after they'd read it, expressed their enthusiasm in the loftiest possible terms. And the general opinion was that anyone who wasn't absolutely ecstatic was either stupid or—even worse—acting on instructions from "the organs."

Of course, the first person to own the novella was Mark Semyonovich. He brought the journal from Moscow, where he had received it from the author himself, with whom he had been personally acquainted in the Khanty-Mansiisk taiga. Having brought the journal back to Dolgov, Mark Semyonovich gave it to various people to read, of whom I was one. Which was a status I achieved only with great difficulty. Shubkin said there was a queue for the journal, so he would only give it to me for two hours.

"Are you being funny?" I said. "How can anyone read an entire novella in such a short time?"

"What's the problem?" Mark Semyonovich asked in surprise. "It's only a hundred and twenty pages long. Can't you read at a speed of a page a minute?" And then he remembered: "Ah yes, my dear fellow, I forgot. You haven't even mastered speed reading."

Eventually, I managed to borrow the journal from him until the following morning, and I kept it until lunchtime, because I felt I had to share the joy of my discovery with the Admiral, who had mastered speed reading. The Admiral asked me to go for a walk, and while I went to the shop, the post office and the house manager's office, he read the whole thing. He liked the novella. "Not too bad," he said, and that was high praise coming from him. For him Tolstoy's *Anna Karenina*, Turgenev's *Fathers and Sons*, Dostoevsky's *Brothers Karamazov* and the stories of the Serapion Brothers were all "not too bad." True, there was an even higher category—"not at all bad"—but that applied to Tolstoy's *War and Peace*, Gogol's *Dead Souls*, Pushkin's *Eugene Onegin*, Homer's *Iliad*, Dante's *Divine Comedy*, and I think that was all. As a matter of fact, he had only four categories for things that could be read: "not at all bad," "not too bad," "all right" and "tolerable"—and a fifth for things that weren't worth reading in any weather—"rock bottom." The fifth category included the whole of Soviet literature except Sholokhov's *And Quiet Flows the Don*, a large part of modern Western literature and Gabriel García Márquez. I usually took an ironical view of the Admiral's assessments, but this time I was in no mood for joking. I didn't regard him as stupid, and I didn't want to suspect him of being connected with "the organs." I started to argue with him, claiming the novella was "not at all bad." He said it was "not too bad." I said "not at all bad." He said "not too bad." I said: "I don't agree with your opinion." And he said: "You can't agree or disagree with my opinion because you haven't got any opinion of your own." "What have I got then?" "You have the idea that in keeping with the moods of a certain circle of people at a certain time you ought to have opinion such-and-such about item such-and-such. And in your circle, having generated an idea, which you believe to be your opinion, you wage a campaign of terror against those who disagree. And if I tell you that I think so-and-so or so-and-so about a certain item, but not what I ought to think about it in your opinion and the opinion of your circle, you cannot even imagine that it is my own honest opinion, you find it easier to imagine that I'm saying it because I have some complexes or other, or even worse, at someone else's prompting, in order to please someone, or"—he gave me a piercing look—"even on someone's instructions. That's what you're thinking, isn't it?"

Of course, I didn't dare to suspect the Admiral of such things, and I listened patiently as he told me that I and others like me had renounced the primary SCOSWO, but in our heart of hearts we were still SCOSWOites. And we attempted to find a uniquely correct and scientific explanation for each individual case, allowing for no other interpretations.

I don't think I had ever seen the Admiral so worked up.

"Well then," I said to him, "I see that for you no authorities exist."

"Absolutely right, for me no authorities exist."

"But come on," I said, confused. "I don't understand. There has to be someone whose opinion you can trust."

"I don't see why I should trust anyone more than myself. And as for your idol, I assure you, a little time will pass and you'll lose interest in him and find yourself another."

"Never as long as I live," I said.

The Admiral proposed a wager and I accepted.

"We'll write down the terms on paper," said the Admiral, "or you'll only renege later."

I agreed, and I composed something like a promissory note to the effect that I, so-and-so, affirm that the writer so-and-so is one of the greatest writers of all times and all peoples and I doubt whether this firm opinion of mine will ever change.

I hate having to admit this, but after maybe fifteen or twenty years had gone by, I happened to call in to visit the Admiral, already an old man by that time, and found him reading a book. I asked him, "What's that you're reading?" "I'm not reading it, I'm rereading it," he said, and showed me the cover. I said, "Why would you want to waste your time on that kind of nonsense?" He shot me a glance laden with irony: "You don't think much of the author, then?" "I don't think anything at all about him," I said with a shrug of my shoulders. And then the Admiral—what a rancorous man he was!—asked me to push an old cracked trunk across to him, opened it with a gloating smile, took out a piece of paper, held it out to me and asked, "Do you know that handwriting?"

The blood, as they say, rushed to my face. I couldn't believe my memory had played me such a vicious trick. I'd completely forgotten that I once sincerely worshiped that writer and had classed him in the top flight of world literary classics.

For me this is probably one of the most unpalatable confessions possible, but as an absolutely honest man, I cannot refuse to make it. Especially since I deduced a certain principle from it. When we promote a living person to the rank of idol, we only recognize him in that capacity.

The moment we begin to doubt his divine qualities, we immediately cast him down into the abyss, no longer noticing even his genuine virtues.

As I took my leave of the Admiral in great embarrassment, I said to him: "Well, yes, of course back then, in specific circumstances, perhaps I exaggerated a bit. I'm ashamed, but what are you reading it for now?"

"Well now," said the Admiral with a gentle smile, "I'm reading it because in places the writing's really not too bad."

41

While I accept, at least retrospectively, that the Admiral's opinion was honest and unbiased, I can't say the same thing about Shubkin. At first he distributed his former camp comrade's work on every side, praising him to the heavens, and then he began to feel envious of him. He became jealous of his success and began saying he'd seen more interesting things and he could write about them just as well. Only he didn't have the time. And he even discovered several faults in the novella, saying that it gave a one-sided picture of camp life. The author had depicted the camp as though there were nobody in it but so-called ordinary people. He hadn't noticed the genuine intellectuals, the people with high aspirations, the warriors of principle who, despite everything, had remained faithful to their convictions and ideals.

By that time our circle had already arrived at the definite conclusion that Shubkin was a good man, socially active and gifted; he could write a decent story or essay, a poem or a letter to the Central Committee of the CPSU, but he was hardly capable of a great literary work. Then suddenly one day I ran into Shubkin in the barber's, where he was having the borders of his bald patch trimmed behind his ears. He asked me: "What are you doing this evening?" "Why?" "Nothing special, but if you're not doing anything, drop in around sevenish." I asked him why, but he said mysteriously: "You'll find out when you get there." Of course, I went. And there was a crowd of people there. His pupils Vlad Raspadov, Sveta Zhurkina, Alesha Konovalov and someone else, I can't remember who. There weren't enough chairs—after all, there were only two of them. Some of us sat on the bed, some on the floor or the windowsill. Shubkin installed himself in a collapsed armchair under a standard lamp with a straw shade. Antonina served the guests tea. Some in glasses, some in teacups, some in half-liter jars. I got a mayonnaise jar. Shubkin himself was not drinking tea, but kefir. Gulping it straight from the broad mouth of the milk bottle. He gulped a bit and set the bottle down beside his left foot. Lying on the low table was a heap of jam pies, which we rapidly polished off.

And so our host sat in his armchair, holding a light-brown cardboard file with badly soiled silk ribbons bearing an inscription in large letters—LECTURE NOTES—and a greasy ring from the frying pan.

It was unlike him, but he was obviously feeling nervous and irritable, and everything annoyed him. He untied the tapes with trembling fingers, took out the first sheet of paper, adjusted his glasses on his nose and began reading: " 'Have you ever seen a spar pine fall, sawn off at the root? . . .' "

I thought this must be an imitation of Gogol and the next phrase would be "No, you haven't seen a spar pine fall, sawn off at the root . . ."

At this point Shurochka the Idiot's black cat walked in through the door, crossed the room and jumped up on my knees. I stroked her to calm her down, but she began purring. Shubkin stopped reading and fixed me with a gaze of silent reproach, as though I were the one purring. Embarrassed, I threw the cat out into the corridor.

" 'Have you ever seen . . .' " Shubkin began again, but then the cat began scratching at the door.

Raspadov went out into the corridor and kicked the cat away.

" 'Have you ever seen . . .' " Shubkin read again, but then a wasp flew into the room and began buzzing and banging against the window. All of us together tried to drive it out through the small upper window, but it didn't understand what we wanted to do and carried on stubbornly and stupidly pounding against the window until Antonina swatted it with a towel. We closed the small window to be on the safe side and everyone froze and sat there quietly without moving a muscle, so that neither of the chairs or the bed would creak, but as soon as Shubkin opened his mouth, we clearly heard a voice speaking on the other side of the wall.

"Lenin's world outlook and the foundations of Leninism are not identical in volume. Lenin is a Marxist and the basis of his world outlook is, of course, Marxism. But from that it does not at all follow that an exposition of Leninism must be begun with an exposition of the foundations of Marxism . . ."

"Oh my God!" said Antonina, throwing up her arms, and the others burst into laughter. At which Raspadov remarked: "It seems to me we're dealing with related themes here."

But Sveta Zhurkina didn't understand, and nodding toward the wall, she asked what the next-door neighbor was reading and to whom.

"It's Stalin's work *The Foundations of Leninism*," said Shubkin, who had recognized it.

"But who's she reading it to?"

"Stalin," said Raspadov.

And everyone burst into laughter again.

"Lenin's world outlook . . ." Aglaya repeated beyond the wall.

"Okay," Shubkin said quietly. "I'll continue, and you just ignore her."

" 'Have you ever seen a spar pine fall, sawn off at the root? . . .' "

What came next wasn't Gogol, but something rather different: " 'A pine falls straight without bending, like a guardsman struck down by an enemy bullet.' " An image that was, of course, both affected and inaccurate. What kind of guardsman? From whose guards? In what situation is he struck down, and why does he fall without bending? I've never seen guardsmen struck down, but it seems to me that when they are struck down by bullets, they probably fall in all sorts of ways, just like other people.

But I didn't cavil, not even to myself, especially since the narrative gradually took a grip on me. Shubkin performed his task with artistry. Using intonation to emphasize certain phrases or words. Reading the dialogues in different voices, rising from a deep bass to a falsetto, somehow managing even to imitate the crunching of snow underfoot, the roar of a Friendship chain saw and the crash of a falling tree.

The first chapter, as the author later explained, set the tone for the entire work. It was about a brigade of convicts in a timber camp. The best brigade in that particular prison camp zone. It was led by Alexei Konstantin Navarov, a Bolshevik, a hero of the Revolution and the Civil War who had escaped shooting by chance. Even though he was actually a very experienced lumberjack, Navarov made a mistake and was crushed by a pine that he felled. I must say that Shubkin gave a really vivid description of the handsome pine tree, the way it was sawn off at the root and still carried on standing there without wavering. They sawed right through its trunk and still it stood. And then Navarov undercut it with an ax. It began revolving around its own axis and its crown spun around against the background of the clear sky as though moving to some accelerating dance rhythm, and then the entire tree began heeling over as it spun and finally came tumbling down with a deafening crash, breaking branches off the pines standing beside it and crushing the bushes beneath it. The convicts working nearby didn't hear the faint moan at first, but when they came running up, they saw the Bolshevik Navarov lying under the pine, crushed. He was lying there pressed down into the snow, with the pine across his chest. It was so huge it was impossible to shift it or to pull the crushed man out from under it, and cutting the tree into sections would have taken too long. The hero of the story, apparently Shubkin himself (the narrative was in the first person), ran over to the crushed man while he was still alive. " 'He was lying,' " Shubkin read, lowering his voice, " 'with his head thrown back. Blood was bubbling out of the corner of his mouth. There was blood pouring from his nose and his left ear. I moved close to him, thinking that he was unconscious, and I was about to leave, when suddenly I noticed that one of his eyes had opened and was watching me, and his lips were moving, whispering something that was obviously very important to him. Overcoming my fear, I put my ear to his lips and heard words so astounding that I will never forget them as long as I live.

" 'Read Lenin,' Navarov wheezed. 'Always read Lenin. Read him in good times, read him in bad times, when you fall ill, when you are going to die, read Lenin and you will understand everything, surmount all difficulties. Read Le——' "

I won't describe in detail how deeply all of us who heard the first reading of *The Timber Camp* were affected by this scene and with what great interest we followed the subsequent history of a man who passed through the hell of Stalin's camps without losing faith in his "shining ideals." This faith helped him to survive quite inhuman suffering, and when he was freed, his devotion to these ideals was as unshaken as when he lost his freedom.

By that time, of course, I was already a badly damaged individual. Talk of shining ideals irritated me, but in this case . . . Although the novel was about a Leninist communist, what was described were Stalin's camps, the solitary interrogation cells, transit prisons, punishment cells, investigators, armed escorts, secret service agents, guard dogs . . . In short, the time for such works had not yet come, and it wasn't clear that it would come very soon. But while the novel's time had not yet come, the time of Article 70 of the Criminal Code (anti-Soviet agitation and propaganda—from three to seven years in the camps) was not yet gone. So this was more than what is usually called an artistic achievement; it was a demonstration of civic courage. And after all, the author had already had a bellyful of all this. Naturally, this situation affected the way the entire work was received, and I was conquered by it. And although, of course, I had certain doubts, I took Shubkin's *Timber Camp* to the Admiral in his lumberyard.

"Well then?" I asked when I dashed around to his place the next morning. "What do you say about that? Not at all bad, eh?"

The Admiral put on his spectacles and gave me a lingering look over the top of the lenses (if he was looking over the top, why did he put them on?).

"Are you trying to tell me it's not too bad?" I asked in embarrassment.

"No," the Admiral answered. "What I can say about your Shubkin is that as a writer he's weak and as a thinker he's stupid, but in every other respect I kneel before him in admiration."

42

"This is the BBC. Western correspondents in Moscow inform us that Nikita Khrushchev has been removed from the post of first secretary and excluded from the Presidium of the Central Committee of the Communist Party of the Soviet Un——"

And then came the crackling and howling of the jamming stations that had not been switched on for a long time.

Aglaya jerked her head off the pillow and began wondering whether she had dreamed the words or they had really been spoken. Western correspondents inform us . . . When she'd gathered her wits, she went dashing over to the television.

Although it was still early morning, on Channel One they were already showing the children's cartoon film *The Little Girl and the Bear,* but Channel Two wasn't working yet. Aglaya had an old single-channel radio-speaker shaped like a plate, so she switched it on and listened to the broadcasts for a whole hour without a break: *Rise and Shine for Exercise!*; *For the Laborers of the Village*; *Pioneer Dawn*; *At Home with the Composer Tulikov*. Finally, the news came on, but there was nothing in it except the flight of the three cosmonauts, the battle for the harvest, the blowing-in of a blast furnace somewhere and the launching of a new diesel-electric ship. With her long experience as a consumer of the Soviet media, Aglaya also derived certain information from what she didn't hear. The presenters said not a single word about Khrushchev, but this total failure to make any mention of an individual whom it was absolutely compulsory to mention was a sign that the BBC had not been indulging in idle speculation.

After first making herself decent she went out of her flat and knocked on Shubkin's door. He came out looking yellow and unshaven, wearing flannel pajamas.

"You?" he said in surprise when he saw Aglaya. "To see me?"

"To see you," said Aglaya.

"Come in," he said, stepping aside, putting his hand over his chin and shuddering. "Only please don't bite — I'm infectious, I've got the flu."

"Don't worry," Aglaya said meekly, "I just wanted to ask you something. That whats-its-name of yours" — she wanted to ask and at the same time express her contempt for the subject of her inquiry — "that BBC of yours . . . does it tell the truth?"

"It tells lies!" the sick man cried joyfully, suddenly animated. "They always tell lies, but all the lies they tell actually come true."

Without answering her neighbor, Aglaya went back to her flat and was immediately overcome by an elation so tumultuous that she surrendered to it and went dashing to her iron idol, embraced him, kissed him (bruising her nose aganst him), laughed, cried and called out incoherently: "They've thrown him out, they've thrown Baldie out. A knee up the backside. Thrown him out like a dog." She jumped up and down, taunting her invisible enemy, curled her lips and stuck out her tongue, chanting: Our beloved . . . dear . . . most dear . . . precious . . . maize man, NEC man, manure man . . ."

That evening Divanich turned up at her place uninvited and unannounced in his colonel's dress uniform, cleaned up a bit, darned a bit (and with all the buttons in place), in a glitter of metal teeth, orders and medals. He didn't come empty-handed—he had a red carnation and two bottles of Moldavian cognac at four rubles twenty kopecks each.

"Permit me, Aglastepna," Divanich said in an unexpectedly ceremonious fashion, "on the occasion of this portentous event, to kiss you fraternally and, pretty much, as a frontline comrade."

And he followed this preface by kissing Aglaya on the left cheek and the right cheek and then fastening his mouth on her lips like a vampire, even attempting to insinuate his tongue as a hint, but she pushed him away rather roughly.

"What are you doing?" she asked angrily.

"What's wrong with it?" Kashlyaev asked simplemindedly.

"There's no point," she said. "I'm a pensioner—in the bazaar they call me a granny already."

"And I'm a grandfather," said Divanich. "My daughter's gone and produced a granddaughter for me."

"All the more reason," said Aglaya. "You a granddad, and letting your hands wander."

"Within moderation," said Divanich. "I'm a military man. If they tell me I can, I advance, if they say I have to, I get up and charge into the attack, and if they say I mustn't, I retreat, but I never surrender."

Even so, she felt flattered. No one had attempted to court her since Shaleiko.

To mark this festive day, which Aglaya wanted to celebrate "together with Him," she covered the table in "His" room with a tablecloth. They drank the first glass for Him. He glowed with intangible good nature.

"It feels like May 9, 1945," said Aglaya.

"To be quite honest, I'd stopped believing it would ever happen."

"You were wrong then," said Aglaya. "Stalin taught us that you should never lose faith. Remember his parable about those . . . you know . . . those men in the boat. There was a storm, they got frightened and gave up, a wave swamped them and . . . goodbye, Mama. But the others don't give up, they just keep on and on rowing"—she began swaying to and fro on her chair, in a rough imitation of a rowing action—"they row straight into the waves and the wind, they don't give way to doubt and . . . Listen," she said, interrupting herself, "what do you think they'll do with Baldie now?"

"Put him in jail is what I think," said Divanich, biting the head off a sprat.

"I think they'll shoot him," Aglaya said dreamily.

"Na-ah," the house manager objected, "those times are gone. It's all reinstatement of Leninist norms and socialist legality nowadays."

"Oh come on, Colonel, come on! What socialist legality? When they shoot Baldie, that'll be socialist legality. What they had was nothing but lousy corruption, not legality. The state they reduced the country to! Take him over there"—she nodded toward the wall behind which Shubkin lived—"he writes whatever he likes. He writes about the camps. Nowadays everybody writes about the camps. As if there weren't any other subjects. They let everybody do whatever they want. People listen to the foreign radio, they tell anti-Soviet jokes, Party people have their children christened in church and they're not afraid of anyone. No, I'd have Baldie executed on Red Square in front of all the people . . . And I wouldn't shoot him, I'd hang him."

"But all the people wouldn't fit in Red Square," Divanich observed. "Although more than enough would turn up to trample quite a few to death. But they wouldn't all fit in the square."

"Then we'd show the people who couldn't fit in the whole thing on television, with all the details. Have you seen what it's like?"

"Nah," said Kashlyaev, "God has, so to speak, spared me that. I've seen plenty of things, but not that."

He topped up his own cognac and hers and set two round slices of salami sausage on a piece of bread.

"You've missed something. When we retook Dolgov from the Germans, we hanged the mayor, the head of police and a prostitute for sleeping with Germans. Would you believe it, the prostitute held up to the very last and spat in the face of the partisan who was hanging her. The mayor was shaking with fear, but he didn't beg and plead. But it makes me sick to remember the *Polizei*, he crawled on his knees, 'Forgive me,' he said, 'have mercy.' But I said to him: 'You vermin, what mercy did you show to our lads?' And then when the trio of them were hanged, some people with weak nerves fainted, but I watched."

"Was it interesting?" Divanich asked cautiously.

"Very! You know, when they hang a man, first he starts trembling all over, trembling like he's having convulsions, and then his eyes start bulging, he sticks his tongue right out and . . ."

"Oi, oi, oi, don't, don't!" cried the house manager, stopping up his ears.

"Why not?" Aglaya asked in surprise. "You're a military man. A front-line veteran."

"I was on the frontline," Kashlyaev confirmed proudly. "Pretty much the whole war, so to speak, from Brest all the way there and back again. I apologize sincerely, Aglastepna. I may be a frontline veteran, but I've never . . . never . . . I've never hanged anyone, that's what." And as he spoke, his expression was sad and guilty, as though he was aware of the full extent of his evident inferiority.

"Because you served in regular units, but I was in the partisans. And in the partisans you're commander and mother and father and court-martial all in one. We caught them ourselves, sentenced them ourselves and executed them ourselves." She sipped from her glass and nibbled on a slice of sausage. "Do you think it was easy? Do you think I'm not a human being?"

"Don't say that, Aglastepna!" said Divanich, frightened. "How can you, about yourself! Even though you are, pretty much, a human being of the female, so to speak, variety, I think we should all learn a lesson from your great Party qualities and courage."

"Learn it, then," said Aglaya. "I'm a woman, a mother. I have a son who's in the diplomatic line . . . But when I face the enemy, I've no mercy for him, I'll put the noose around his neck . . ."

"Aglastepna, my dear," said the colonel, waving his arms in the air, "no more! Don't, I'll be sick."

"Damn you then," said Aglaya with a wave of her hand. The drink had already gone to her head and she was in a good humor. "If you don't want to listen, then let's sing something."

"That's a different matter," said the house manager. He drew himself up and straightened his jacket, touched his Adam's apple, coughed and began in a low voice: "His orders were to go west . . ."—but he was interrupted.

"Why that old stuff?" Aglaya asked. "Let's sing this." And with a broad, smooth sweep of her right hand from left to right and upward, she began in her hoarse, smoky voice:

> *In our wondrous homeland's wide expanses,*
> *Striving in war and laboring in peace,*
> *We have composed a bright and joyous anthem*
> *Of our dear friend and our most mighty chief.*

She gestured with her left hand for Kashlyaev to join in and he coughed again and picked up the refrain:

"Sta-lin, our glo-ry in the batt-le . . ."

"Stalin, the free flight of our youth," she sang, drowning him out.

"We sing as we fight as we conquer"—their two voices fused into one—"our people following in Stalin's steps."

It must be hard for the modern reader to imagine that in those times people sang such songs not only on the stage or lined up in ranks, but for themselves, personally, and actually derived pleasure from doing it.

At midnight there was a knock on the door. Aglaya opened it. Ida Samoilovna Bauman was standing on the doorstep in a washed-out flannel dressing gown with newspaper curlers in her still-damp hair.

"I'm sorry to bother you," she said, "but could you be a bit quieter? My mother's not well and she can't get to sleep."

"She will if she wants to," said Aglaya. "At the front we slept through artillery fire and bombing raids."

And she slammed the door shut.

"Who was that?" asked Divanich.

"Nobody," said Aglaya. "Let's try this one." And she began swaying from side to side:

From land to land, where mountain peaks do rise . . .

There was another knock at the door. Thinking her neighbor had come back again, Aglaya opened the door feeling annoyed, but it was Georgii Zhukov she saw standing there with his accordion around his neck and two bottles of vodka in his hands.

"What do you want?" she asked in surprise.

"What are you celebrating?" he asked.

"What difference does it make to you?"

"It makes no difference to me, but I've got something to celebrate too. I've had a son, and I've got no one to drink with. Four and a half kilograms. That big!" He spread the hands holding the bottles to demonstrate the approximate size of his progeny, and later, the more he drank, the wider he spread his hands, like a fisherman showing the size of the catfish he caught.

"Come in," said Aglaya.

43

Meanwhile, Rebecca Moiseevna was developing another of her attacks of angina pectoris. Her daughter had measured her out a triple dose of Valocordin drops and was now sitting on the bed beside her, uncertain what to do. They had no telephone, of course, and it was a long way to go to fetch an ambulance, and pointless in any case. The last time they'd asked her: "How old is your mother? Eighty-two? We don't go out to people that old."

Ida Samoilovna held her mother's hand. The attack seemed to have passed, the Valocordin seemed to have taken effect and the old woman began falling asleep. But no sooner had she begun than there was the sound of singing from the other side of the wall, only now accompanied by an accordion and much louder than before. They struck up "In the wide spaces of our glorious homeland" and without a break launched into "From land to land, where mountain peaks do rise, where mountain eagles soar on outspread wings, of our beloved Stalin dear and wise, in beauteous songs the grateful people sing."

Ida Samoilovna picked up an old shoe and banged on the wall with the heel.

At that moment Mark Semyonovich Shubkin was sitting at his typewriter, writing one of his missives to the Central Committee of the CPSU. First of all, he congratulated Comrades Brezhnev and Kosygin on the occasion of their election to the high posts of first secretary of the Central Committee and chairman of the Council of Ministers of the USSR, and wrote that he entirely supported the Party's courageous and timely decision intended to avert a new personality cult, this time not of Stalin but of Khrushchev. He condemned Khrushchev's dictatorial decisions in foreign and domestic policy, but at the same time expressed the hope that the Party would not permit a return to Stalinism, would not seek to excuse Stalin's heinous misdeeds and would completely abolish the censorship.

His typewriter clattered loudly, but this time its clatter was inaudible because the music and singing were even louder.

Some time after two in the morning Ida Samoilovna, with her coat thrown over her dressing gown, ran to the police station. There she happened to find Precinct Captain Anatolii Sergeevich Saraev, who until recently had also lived at 1-a Komsomol Cul-de-Sac until he was moved to a new building to improve his living conditions. Saraev's presence at the station at such a late hour was explained by the fact that he and the senior lieutenant on duty, Zhikharev, were celebrating the latter's birthday, in honor of which they were sitting behind the glass partition, pouring confiscated moonshine from an aluminum teapot into mugs of the same metal and drinking it, while snacking on bread, liver sausage and onions sliced in thick rings. They were conversing on a range of substantial themes, such as: is there life on other planets, what the difference is between a zebra and a horse and whether a new police uniform would be introduced some time soon.

The night had been relatively calm. The holding cells contained only three arrestees: a collective farmer who had killed his wife with a rake in a drunken fit and two sharp dressers from the group of students who had come to help with the harvest. The boy had been arrested because he'd grown his hair too long and the girl because she'd come to a dance wearing jeans, but even worse than that—with an image of the American flag on her backside. When the man was installed in his cell, he clambered onto the bunk and immediately lapsed into a deep sleep. The female student cried a bit and went to sleep too, but the male student banged on the door and kicked up a racket, shouting about his rights and demanding to be released immediately.

"In the morning we'll shave both your heads and let you go," Zhikharev promised.

"You've no right!" the student shouted from behind the door. "Where does the law say anything about the length of people's hair? In the Constitution? In the Criminal Code? In the Program of the CPSU?"

"Stop yelling, or we'll work you over good," Saraev said good-naturedly.

"What!" the student shouted. "You've no right! Just you try it! I'll take you to court!"

"Hang on," Zhikharev said to Saraev, and went into the cell, and immediately there was the sound of shouting and screaming.

"What are you doing? Bandit! Fascist! Gestapo pig! I'm going to comp——"

At that point the shouting ceased and Zhikharev came back to the table, licking blood from his fist.

"Scratched it on his glasses," he explained to Saraev. Then he complained: "Some people, eh! Can't get on quietly with their own lives, just have to get on other people's nerves."

He poured himself and his friend yet another shot. They drank, snacked, talked about their wives and mothers-in-law, about the advantages of Izhevsk motorbikes over Kovrov motorbikes, and naturally they didn't fail to comment on the main political event of the day.

"They've given Khrushchev the shove," said Zhikharev.

"Yeah," agreed Saraev, after which they were both silent for a long time, trying to think of something to say.

"Yeah, given him the shove," Zhikharev finally repeated.

"Yeah," agreed Saraev.

And they sat through another long silence.

"And now," surmised Zhikharev, "Stalin will sort them all out his own way."

"How can he sort them all out, when he's dead?" Saraev asked doubtfully.

"That's the whole point, he isn't dead," said Zhikharev.

"In what sense?" asked Saraev.

"In the sense that he's not dead, but alive," said Zhikharev, and related to his colleague a story he'd heard from his brother-in-law, who worked in the Kremlin as a waiter, that in '53 Stalin hadn't died, he'd just pretended to die. And he'd gone into hiding, shaved off his mustache, dressed himself in rags, and like Tsar Alexander I before him, he was wandering around Russia begging for alms and looking to see how the people lived and whether they were carrying on building communism.

"Bullshit!" was Saraev's opinion of the story, and just as he said it, his former neighbor Ida Samoilovna appeared in front of him with her complaint about Aglaya Stepanovna Revkina and her noisy guests.

"Tolya," Ida Samoilovna said to Saraev. "I'm begging you, please. You know my mother. You know how ill she is. And these people are yelling at the top of their voices in the middle of the night."

Saraev wiped his mouth with his sleeve, looked at the clock and promised he would come and get to the bottom of things.

"Will you come soon?" asked Ida Samoilovna.

"Soon, soon," the policeman answered impatiently, and as soon as she was gone, he expressed to Zhikharev his opinion that Zhikharev's information was nothing but a load of hot air, to which fact Saraev could testify in person. In March of '53, when he was a cadet at the police school, he'd been sent to Moscow and had personally taken part in the cordon on Pushkin Street by Hunter's Row station on the Lazar Kaganovich Metro, and at night the policemen had been allowed to approach the coffin.

"And I saw him there dead, just like yourself."

"What d'you mean, just like me?" objected Zhikharev, ready to take offense. "I'm not dead."

"Not in the sense that you're dead, but I was standing right beside him. Only a meter or half a meter away from him. I'm standing here, and he's lying here." Saraev even tipped his chair back to represent the recumbent corpse, but being not entirely sober, he lost his balance and would have fallen if Zhikharev hadn't caught him in time. "So," continued Saraev, setting the back of his chair upright, "I could see his face as well as I can see yours. And he was quite dead. He wasn't breathing, he didn't blink, he was made up and the color was like a live person all right, but he was dead as a doornail."

"I'm not saying the corpse wasn't dead. Only the corpse wasn't Stalin, but People's Artist Gelovani. They buried him instead."

"Alive?" Saraev asked in horror.

"Why alive?" Zhikharev asked with a shrug. "Don't be stupid—alive! Are they brutes or something, to put a live man in a coffin? They put him down first and then buried him."

"Well, if they put him down, that's all right. Got money for it, I suppose?"

"Heaps," Zhikharev said confidently. "He's a People's Artist of the whole USSR. D'you know how much they get paid?"

"How much?" asked Saraev.

"Lots," said Zhikharev with a sigh.

Saraev inclined the teapot and topped up his own moonshine and his comrade's. They clinked mugs without speaking, drank, grunted and took a bite to eat.

"All right then," said Saraev, after thinking hard for a moment, "they put this guy in the coffin. But where did Stalin get to?"

"Hey, I told you already! He went away. Didn't say anything to anybody. The only one he left a note for was Molotov."

Captain Saraev didn't believe a single word Zhikharev said, especially since all the drink was finished and the hour was rather late. But on the way home he suddenly remembered that not long ago he'd arrested an indigent old beggar at the railway station and was going to bring him in to the cells, but the old man had bought him off with twenty-five rubles. Which hadn't surprised Saraev in the least—he'd known for a long time that the bulk of beggars were rich. Now, recalling the beggar, he also recalled that there'd been something unusual about his face, that he reminded him of someone, and now he thought that the beggar had reminded him of . . . But then that was all nonsense, Saraev told himself, nonsense and nothing more, and at that very moment he heard loud singing coming from an open window.

44

As always, there was no light in the entrance, but there was a glimmer somewhere upstairs. It was the lighted candle that Ida Bauman was holding where she was standing on the landing in her dressing gown and slippers.

"Oh, at last! Thank you for coming," she said, touched. "It's really quite impossible. Mother's had an attack, and just listen to the way they're carrying on. All right, it's allowed until eleven. And we put up with it until twelve. But it's just too much!"

Realizing that references to doctors, laws and the late hour might prove to be an insufficient argument, Ida Samoilovna thrust into the policeman's hand a three-ruble note which he took by touch to be a fiver and immediately stuck in his pocket. And then he knocked resolutely on the door of Aglaya's apartment. At first tactfully, with the knuckle of his middle finger. Then with his fist. Then with the handle of his revolver. No one answered, and he went in on his own.

The spree was in full swing. Wafting away the cigarette smoke with his hands, the policeman finally made out the lady of the house, sitting sideways to him in a dark blue jacket, and her guests Divanich and Georgii Zhukov. Behind them in the thick cigarette smoke, his hand pressed against the ceiling, stood the cast-iron generalissimo.

Divanich, his face red and sweaty from effort, was in his green uniform shirt and suspenders. His colonel's jacket was hanging on the back of his chair. Zhukov, leaning slightly backward on his stool with his eyes narrowed, was expanding his accordion bellows. Aglaya was conducting. She did this with true inspiration, feeling that perhaps she had never been as happy as she was today.

If on the holiday we should encounter . . .

And at that very moment Saraev appeared. The singers completed the next line about "a few old friends" and fell silent, turning to face him. But Saraev was looking at them and at the iron man standing behind them. Under that iron gaze Saraev somehow wilted, and instead of addressing Aglaya firmly, as he had been planning, he said very timidly: "I beg your pardon . . ."

But Divanich waved a finger at him to tell him he must be quiet and returned to the couplet they'd left unfinished.

". . . a few old friends . . ."

". . . all we hold dear comes back to mind," Aglaya picked up the refrain, "and our song sounds the sweeter."

"I beg your pardon, Aglaya Stepanovna," the captain repeated, "but you'll have to cut short your fun . . ."

The accordion gave one last pitiful squeal; Zhukov squeezed the bellows shut and reached into his pocket for a handkerchief. Divanich said nothing and looked at the captain attentively, and Aglaya took out a new cigarette, softened it between her fingers, tapped the cardboard mouthpiece on the table and lit up, sensing that her mood was about to be spoiled.

"I beg your pardon," Saraev said for the third time, "but after twelve o'clock it's not allowed."

"Not allowed?" Aglaya asked.

"Not allowed," Saraev repeated.

"And what if people have something to celebrate? If people, so to speak, have had a baby?" asked Divanich. "Isn't it allowed then?"

"Who's had a baby?" the policeman asked.

"I have," Zhukov owned up. "Four and a half kilos. That big," he said, holding his hands up. "Howls like a steam engine."

"Like a steam engine." Divanich echoed. "And he howls after eleven o'clock? Arrest him and give him fifteen days. Isn't that right, Captain?"

"But he'd howl even more in there," said Aglaya. Even she was in the mood for jokes today.

"Well anyway, I've warned you," said the policeman with all the severity that he could muster. "So just you be careful. If you break the law, then . . . I personally . . . I could do without this . . . but I'll have to . . . I beg your pardon . . . take appropriate measures . . ."

Divanich was suddenly enraged. "Appropriate measures? Against whom? Her?" he said, prodding Aglaya with his finger. "Our heroine? Our legendary heroine? Or him? He's a soldier, he fought against counter-revolution in Hungary. Or me, a colonel, a veteran of two wars? An honored, so to speak, that is . . . Or him?"

Divanich stretched out his arm toward Stalin and then, frightened at his own audacity, he switched into a whisper. "I tell you what, my dear friend, why don't you just drop it? Sit down with us and we'll celebrate. Since such important events have taken place. On the one hand a man has been born, and on the other, as they say, you know . . . Do you get my meaning, Captain?"

"Certainly, Comrade Colonel," Saraev agreed.

"Right then, sit down. If our hostess has no objections . . ."

The hostess had none, and for a start she suggested the policeman should drink to the health of Stalin. And although the captain doubted whether you could drink to the health of someone who was dead, he figured that if it was their treat, then that was all right. And anyway, dead people could be regarded as healthy because they never got sick.

45

"Now you see," Ida Bauman said to her aged mother. "Everything's fine. The policeman came and put those hooligans in their place."

She dripped forty drops of Valocordin into a glass, adjusted the pillow, put a hot-water bottle against the old woman's feet, tucked in the blanket on all sides and went to her place on the couch, and just then behind the partition wall they started roaring out a song about artillerymen, as loud as a cannonade.

Ida Samoilovna couldn't take any more. She threw her dressing gown back on, ran out and went tearing into her neighbor's flat without knocking, just as the four of them were singing in total abandonment:

> *"Gunners, Stalin's order has been given!*
> *Gunners, our homeland calls to us . . ."*

Ida Samoilovna froze in the doorway, staring at the singers with emphatic reproach.

> *"A hundred thousand batteries*
> *For all our mothers' tears,*
> *For our motherland—*
> *Fire! Fire!"*

"You ought to be ashamed of yourselves!" Ida Samoilovna said, but she couldn't hear her own voice. The singers took absolutely no notice of her, unless you count the fact that when they reached the refrain again, especially for Ida Samoilovna, Captain Saraev replaced the canonical words with ones more appropriate to the occasion:

> *". . . A hundred thousand batteries*
> *The Jew called on the radio—*
> *For our motherland:*
> *Fire! Fire!"*

It is only possible to reconstruct a partial picture of what happened next, based entirely on the contradictory testimonies of the actual participants in the event, since there were no other witnesses. It seems that Ida Samoilovna, incensed by the behavior of the nocturnal hooligans, began shouting at them and stamping her feet. Then Captain Saraev got up and started stamping his feet at her, simply mimicking her, as he explained later, as a joke. She didn't understand his joke and spat in his face. He couldn't tolerate an insult like that, especially since he was in uniform and armed, with his holster hanging on his chair. He grabbed the revolver out of the holster and pointed it at the long-suffering Ida Bauman.

"I'll shoot you, you bitch!" he shouted, but immediately remembering his hostess, he turned to her and said: "Pardon my language."

With a cry that cannot be conveyed in words, the victim rushed away. Saraev, obeying (as he subsequently testified) the hunting instinct that had been aroused in him, dashed after her, and the two of them together burst into the room where a crazy-looking old woman with skinny, naked legs was sitting on a bed in a linen nightshirt with her feet lowered onto the floor. Seeing a man burst into her home with a gun, the old woman collapsed onto the floor with a cry of "Cossacks!" and tried to crawl under the bed. A maneuver that she failed to complete, her heart giving out as she kneeled there on all fours with her head stuck under the bed. The neighbors who had come running at the noise were in time to see it happen. They said that, realizing what had happened, Captain Saraev sobered up completely, put his revolver away, felt the old woman's pulse and, getting up from his knees, said to no one in particular: "What kind of Cossack am I? We don't have any Cossacks here, but we do have legitimate Soviet power." And with that he left the room.

Of course, the celebrations were spoiled. Whatever our heroes might have been like, they hadn't wanted to kill the old woman. But having a joke and giving someone a fright—now that was a different matter altogether.

The affair didn't blow up into any great scandal. Although Ida Bauman tried to get all four of them brought to trial, it was eventually explained to her that citizens Revkina, Kashlyaev and Zhukov were only guilty of a minor infringement of public order and they had been cautioned. And as for the policeman Saraev, although he had exceeded his authority, he had not fired and citizeness Rebecca Bauman had had no business trying to climb under the bed and perform such complicated movements at her age, especially in the middle of a heart attack. And anyway, many people reasoned that the old woman's time was up and she would have died anyway, one way or another. In short, Captain Saraev was given a reprimand and his next promotion to the rank of major was put back a year. Everything else carried on as normal.

PART THREE

VAIN EXPECTATIONS

46

With the accession to power of a new leadership, many rumors that were to Aglaya's liking appeared. Either Brezhnev or Kosygin had called Baldie's period of rule a shameful decade. One of these two, or perhaps it was some third person, had said that in the near future the rotten liberalism of the last decade would be done away with. And all the signs were that these words had been spoken in earnest. At Party meetings, plenums and conferences, Stalin's name was mentioned, at first timidly and then more confidently, with positive connotations. These allusions were invariably greeted with applause. In the local cinema, Victory, the old familiar image began to appear, at first in old documentaries and then in feature movies. At first there was just his portrait, glimpsed for a second somewhere in some office. That same one with the pipe that Aglaya had above her desk. Then they showed the man himself at the meeting of the Big Three in Teheran. Then for the anniversary of the Battle of Moscow, he was where he ought to be, on the platform on top of Lenin's Mausoleum. Divanich regularly informed Aglaya of Stalin's latest appearance in the cinema, and she immediately went hurrying off to the matinee show, eager to catch at least a fleeting glimpse of the face she loved. And what's more, she noticed she was not the only one waiting eagerly. Every time the face appeared on the screen, there was timid applause, sometimes quite solitary, from somewhere in the back rows. Aglaya applauded too, feeling that she was making a heroic gesture, although hers was a heroism thoroughly approved by the newly installed authorities. But anyway, she clapped her hands and turned her head this way and that as she tried to guess where he or they—her invisible fellow thinkers—might be. Only she couldn't make them out in the darkness, and people's faces as they left the cinema afterward were inscrutable. As though they hadn't been applauding themselves and hadn't heard anyone else doing so. Then one day she noticed a man wearing a gray rabbit-fur cap. He was sitting three rows away from Aglaya, directly behind her. Hearing the sound of applause, she quickly swung around and caught him in the act: he hadn't lowered his hands yet. When the movie was over, she ran after him. He turned a corner, she followed and, finding she couldn't keep up, called out: "Young man!"

He turned around in mute inquiry, unsure whether it was him that was meant.

"Wait," she said, "wait." She ran up, puffing and panting, and started gasping out the words: "Thank you so much. Thank you, thank you."

"Thank you for what?" he asked, peering sideways at her suspiciously.

"For your courage," she replied hastily. "For your loyalty. I saw you clapping."

"Who was clapping? Where?" he asked abruptly, nervously.

"You were clapping in the cinema, I saw you," said Aglaya, letting him know she was on his side and shared his feelings completely.

But he didn't understand; he suspected she was an agent provocateur, and he began twitching as he yelled at her: "What did you see? What?"

"Young man!" she exclaimed, perplexed. "I mean no harm . . . I was just saying that I saw—"

"You didn't see anything! You fool! You old fool!" the young man shouted and took to his heels.

Aglaya watched him as he ran off, uncertain which insult was the more offensive—"fool" or "old fool."

He, by the way, was Mitya Lyamikhov, an individual well known to the staff of our capital city's Serbsky Institute of Forensic Psychiatry. When Stalin was alive, Mitya had been subjected to treatment for criticizing Stalin, to whom he had written in person that he was a tyrant, a bandit and an enemy of the people. If he had written in gentler terms, he would have found himself in a camp or facing a firing squad. But what he wrote was so unbridled and extreme, so clearly lacking in the slightest concern for the preservation of his own life, that all the doctors genuinely concurred in declaring him insane. His insanity manifested itself, among other things, in always being opposed to all decisions and actions taken by the current regime. If for some historical reasons the authorities began to agree with his opinion, he immediately changed that opinion to its opposite. When Stalin was in charge, he was against Stalin; under Khrushchev he was for Stalin; now he remained for Stalin by inertia, but if Stalin had been fully rehabilitated, he would have been against him again.

47

Aglaya also greeted with hope other signs of change following the 1964 Plenum of the Central Committee of the CPSU. Khrushchev was condemned. The national economic councils were disbanded. The division of regional committees into rural and urban was abolished. The expression "personality cult" disappeared from the pages of the press. Hardly anybody anywhere mentioned cases of illegal repression, and incidental references were qualified by claims that they had not been so very numerous and the matter should not be exaggerated. They stopped calling maize "the queen of the fields." And they stopped planting it. Instead, they put writers in jail. Only two of them at first, it was true. But there was hope that they would put away the rest of them as well. They shut one mathematician away in a madhouse. Then they put a historian in there with him. The Czechoslovakian revisionists declared that their goal was socialism with a human face. Soviet tanks arrived and put the revisionists right. Aglaya was delighted by all these events, although it still seemed to her that the leadership of the CPSU was behaving indecisively. They showed Stalin in films, but only occasionally and tentatively. Her own situation remained the same as it had been. No one was in any hurry to apologize to her and reinstate her in the Party.

48

But while Aglaya was dissatisfied with the slow pace of events, her neighbor Mark Semyonovich Shubkin was dissatisfied by the direction in which they were moving. And as a Leninist communist, he couldn't simply overlook it. He wrote the Central Committee a letter demanding freedom for the writers, the withdrawal of troops from Czechoslovakia, a return to the Leninist norms of Party life, the erection of a monument to the victims of Stalinism, the abolition of censorship and the printing of his novel *The Timber Camp* in one of the leading Soviet literary journals. The reply to this latest letter of his came very quickly, and from its tone Mark Semyonovich realized that times had changed more radically than it had seemed at first. He was informed that his suggestions were overtly provocative in nature, that they reeked of political immaturity and perhaps, even, of something worse. He was notified that if he did not desist from disseminating his absurd fabrications, he would be obliged to quit the ranks of the CPSU and further consequences could not be ruled out. With his rich experience of life and highly developed artistic imagination, Shubkin immediately pictured further consequences in the form of the dense forest of the Khanty-Mansiisk taiga with chest-high snowdrifts, frost at fifty degrees Celsius below zero, the whining of the Friendship chain saw and a frostbitten nose. For a short while he stopped writing letters and lay low, and he might well have gone on lying low for a long time if one day when he switched on the radio he had not learned from a program on the BBC that his novel *The Timber Camp* had been published in Munich by the famous émigré publishing house Globus. How this had come about, Shubkin had no idea. Evidently, the manuscript had been passed from hand to hand until eventually it had passed into hands that had carried it off to the West.

In this way the local district acquired its own dissident. Which initially delighted the local organs greatly. In the absence of dissidents the central leadership could have got the idea that there was no need for any organs in this area. But if there were dissidents, then they had work to do. They could enlarge their permanent staff and demand a larger budget, the volume of work would increase and so would their chances of distinguishing themselves in their heroic field of professional activity without the slightest risk to their own lives because a dissident is dangerous ideologically but not physically; he is unarmed and inept; he doesn't know how to hide and avoid being shadowed. And so if there had been no Shubkin in Dolgov, it would have been worth inventing him. They knew how to invent as well, but in this case there was no need. They had the real Shubkin and they had the entire circle of his pupils and admirers, who also had to be shadowed, and this all required personnel, salaries, cars and so on.

And so once Shubkin popped up and was identified, the organs set to work and sent him a subpoena. Just in case, Shubkin collected together the most essential items for prison life in a sack: warm socks and long drawers, a mug, a spoon and a volume of poetry by Edward Bagritsky.

And he took this sack with him to that place. Antonina, naturally, went to see him off. On the threshold they said goodbye in earnest.

Shubkin had come prepared for long, exhausting hours of interrogation with shouting, abuse and a blinding light in his eyes, but was delighted to discover that reality failed to live up to his expectations. The investigating officer, Korotyshkin, was a man of medium height, middle age and nondescript appearance, with rounded shoulders, soft, pudgy hands and soft, pudgy cheeks. His hair was lightish, his eyebrows sunbleached, his eyes colorless and his teeth uneven—but without fangs. He did not resemble a vampire; he was not even much like an old-time Cheka agent with eyes inflamed by devotion to the workers' and peasants' cause, hatred of enemies of the revolution, vodka, tobacco smoke and lack of sleep. Dressed in a cheap suit the color of dust, he met Shubkin at the entrance and was greatly surprised by the sack: "Well really, what are you thinking of? What's that for? Do you really have such a low opinion of the organs? Do you really believe all we ever do is stick people straight in jail? Is this lady with you? Leave that with her. If necessary—of course things could turn out that way—she can bring it later."

Shubkin left the sack with Antonina, and that was a good sign. Another hopeful indication that things would turn out well was that the pass they wrote out for Shubkin was temporary. After that Korotyshkin led Mark Semyonovich down a long corridor, along the way discussing the paradoxes of the current weather conditions and the possible influence on them of human advances in the areas of chemistry and atomic energy. Eventually, Shubkin found himself in a spacious office where the desk on the right, beneath a portrait of Dzerzhinsky, was occupied by a man with the name of Mukhodav, a sullen, skinny, peevish individual who looked very much indeed like a Cheka agent from the twenties. The desk on the left, under a second portrait of Dzerzhinsky, belonged to Korotyshkin. He offered his visitor a chair, an ordinary one with a thin leatherette-covered cushion and a leatherette-covered back, seated himself at the desk and linked the fingers of both hands together, leaving his thumbs free so that he could twirl them as though he was pondering deep thoughts.

"Well then," he said, twirling his thumbs and smiling at Mark Semyonovich, "before we start our little talk, please tell me your forename, patronymic and surname."

"Is this an interrogation?" Shubkin asked.

"Why, of course not!" Korotyshkin protested. "It's just a conversation."

"So far!" Mukhodav muttered from his corner, but Korotyshkin appeared not to hear this muttering and explained in a perfectly friendly manner that the requirement to state one's forename, patronymic and surname was purely a formality, and one that was probably superfluous and could be ignored, but essentially what he would like to talk about was the following: "I read your little story *The Timber Plantation.*"

"It's not a story, it's a novel," Shubkin corrected him.

"A libelous anti-Soviet lampoon," said the voice in the other corner.

Mukhodav was apparently not taking any direct part in the conversation. He sat there at his desk, studying some papers or other—read something, wrote something, underlined something—and his remarks were not directed at anyone, as if he were talking to himself.

"I don't know about anyone else," Korotyshkin continued, casting a glance at his colleague, "but there was a lot in it I liked. Of course, I'm not a specialist, my professional area's architecture. Apartment houses and public buildings, palaces of culture—so . . . But they called me in to the regional Party committee . . . You're a communist too, aren't you?"

"Communists like that ought to be shot," Mukhodav said loudly to himself.

"They called me in to the regional Party committee, and they said to me, 'It has to be done, Sergei Sergeyich,' the international situation requires it. Well, if the Party asks, who am I to refuse? There's no way I could, Mark Semyonovich, because first and foremost I'm a soldier of the

Party and a patriot. So here I am sitting here. Although my heart"—he sighed wearily and pensively—"is yearning for my drawing board. But that's just me waxing lyrical . . . Well then, you could say I actually liked this *Forest Steppe* of yours. Parts of it. The style's very good, the descriptions of nature work well, especially the Khanty-Mansiisk taiga . . . You've been there, haven't you?"

"Yes, I have," said Shubkin with a nod.

"Another trip could be arranged," said Mukhodav without lifting his head from his papers.

"But generally speaking," Korotyshkin continued, "the impression created by the scenes you describe is rather oppressive. It seems to me that you—how can I put it?—you pile the colors on a bit too thick . . ."

"I write about phenomena which the Party condemned at its Twentieth Congress," Shubkin reminded him.

"That's just the point, that the Party has condemned them. It has condemned them, and that's enough. Enough," Korotyshkin repeated, looking imploringly at Shubkin. "Why should we keep on remembering the bad things all the time, reopening old wounds, wallowing in the past? We have to move forward, Mark Semyonovich. Look at the events taking place all around you. The construction of the Bratsk Hydroelectric Station goes on, a new blast furnace has been blown in in Sterlitamak, our cows produce up to three hundred liters of milk a year, our Party is waging a titanic struggle for peace all around the world, and you just harp on about your forest belt. It would be all right if you'd written your *Logging Zone* just for yourself or your friends, but you sent it to the West."

"I didn't send it," Shubkin said quickly.

"It just flew across on its own," Mukhodav mused.

"I don't know whether it got there on its own or not," said Shubkin, turning toward him, "but as you know, I don't travel abroad. Or perhaps I did go and you didn't notice?" he asked sarcastically.

Mukhodav went on leafing through his papers, paying no attention to Shubkin, but Korotyshkin agreed with him: "Well of course, of course you didn't go. No one's saying you did. But to forward a manuscript, you don't have to travel yourself. Foreign diplomats and correspondents travel back and forth, don't they? And not always with the purest of motives."

"CIA agents, every one of them," Mukhodav remarked.

"Exactly," Korotyshkin agreed. "We have information that the CIA has stepped up its activity, and it's gambling on the politically immature section of our intelligentsia. Trying to find the weak link in our chain. It's no accident that your satirical article was published by an anti-Soviet publishing house where the employees are all White Guards, Vlasovites and former *Polizei*, who used to hang Soviet citizens and send people of Jewish nationality to the gas chambers. And of course, it's no accident that they happened to seize on your so-called work. They must have liked it."

"If they liked my work, that means it's good," Shubkin said smugly.

"It's anti-Soviet," Mukhodav pronounced.

"If only it was simply anti-Soviet," Korotyshkin sighed. "Unfortunately, Mark Semyonovich, the book is also antipopular, directed against the people. But no," he said, although clearly in doubt, "we won't take any punitive measures against you at this stage . . ."

"We ought to though," sighed Mukhodav.

"This isn't 'thirty-seven and we're not those people. We're not at all those people, Mark Semyonovich," he assured Shubkin earnestly. "The most important thing for us is to save the man, to protect him from acting incorrectly. There's an uncompromising ideological war going on nowadays. Only one side can win. And in these conditions . . . It would be a good thing if you sent a statement to our press, and we'll help you do it, yes, we'll help . . ." He rolled his eyes up and began muttering a strange sequence of words as if he'd fallen into a trance: "We prompt you, you help us, you write, we print, a public declaration of your attitude . . ."

"Or things will go badly," said Mukhodav, as if to himself.

"Is that a threat?" asked Shubkin.

"By no means," Korotyshkin hastened to assure him. "No threats. But you do understand that if you don't draw the correct conclusions, then we . . . well, what can we do? Mark Semyonovich, you understand, don't you, that we're humanists, but . . ."

"If the enemy doesn't surrender, he's exterminated," Mukhodav concluded.

"And I have one important request. Very, very important. Not a word to anyone about our conversation."

And that was all. Korotyshkin didn't even take a written agreement of confidentiality from Shubkin.

Some people in Dolgov, such as Aglaya or even Divanich, couldn't understand the humane approach taken by the organs. This Shubkin had written an appalling anti-Soviet work and published it in an émigré journal—how could he not be put in jail for that? But there were many things they didn't understand. For instance, that Shubkin, as we have already noted, was the only one of his kind in the district. If there'd been ten of them, one or two could have been put away. But if you put away the only one, then who would you wage a struggle against?

49

Korotyshkin, of course, was hoping that Shubkin would realize the fatal nature of his errors and take fright. And he was right. Shubkin believed in socialist legality, but with very substantial reservations. He decided not to write any more letters to the Central Committee, not to circulate his literary opuses, not to travel to Moscow and not to associate with dissidents and foreigners. And he began behaving in such an exemplary fashion that our organs should have been delighted and displayed his portrait on their walls as the most dutiful and deserving citizen-imitator. But since they needed Shubkin precisely in his capacity as a dissident, they tried to think up a way of inciting him to show his hand again, and think one up they did.

The *Dolgov Pravda* published an article entitled "The Deeper You Go in the Forest, the More Firewood You Find." In summarizing Shubkin's biography, it either noted openly or hinted that he was a Jew, that he had broken Soviet laws, had been convicted of anti-Soviet activity and released early on humanitarian grounds. Not a single word about his having been rehabilitated, although it was noted that Mark Semyonovich had failed to learn the lessons of his past, had backslid into anti-Soviet activity and was presently the Western security services' most highly prized lickspittle and purveyor of slander against his homeland, which had raised him, fed him, clothed him, put shoes on his feet, provided him with an education and given him the hope of happiness.

Shubkin took this article as a signal that he was going to be jailed again and he decided to follow the advice of a certain experienced Moscow dissident, who explained to him that his salvation lay in maximum publicity.

"If you keep quiet, they're bound to put you away. But you start kicking up a rumpus, and you'll attract serious attention from the West, then instead of your being afraid of them, they'll be afraid of you."

Shubkin believed him. He started to take action. And far more audaciously than before. Previously, he had written letters to the Central Committee of the CPSU. Then he'd sent copies of his letters to *Pravda* and *Izvestiya*. Then to the international communist newspapers: *L'Humanité*, the *Morning Star*, *L'Unità*. But now every letter went direct to the *Times* (London), the *New York Times*, *Le Figaro*, *Die Welt* and *Aftonbladet*. And it was instantly clear to Shubkin how these newspapers differed from the communist ones. His letters were printed immediately, and in the most conspicuous positions on the page. People began talking about Shubkin. His texts began to be broadcast regularly. The Voice of America, Deutsche Welle, Radio Liberty and the BBC broadcast them with numerous repeats, while showering Shubkin with flattering compliments. The longer it went on, the more imposing the compliments became. A leading dissident. A major writer. An outstanding advocate of human rights.

The Dolgov organs were thrown into consternation. They themselves had pushed Shubkin into acting so decisively, and now they didn't know what to do. He had become too famous, and now they weren't sure from which angle to approach him. Just recently, he could quite easily have been jailed without any particular fuss. But now . . . Korotyshkin himself could be sacked and jailed at any moment, even shot if it was really necessary, and nobody would notice. But Shubkin? Lay a finger on him and all these voices would set up a deafening howl all around the planet. The case would come to the notice of all sorts of human rights organizations, they would appeal to their presidents, the presidents would tell Brezhnev about Shubkin, Brezhnev would get angry and summon Andropov, Andropov would summon the head of the fifth section, the head of the fifth section would summon the head of the Dolgov office, and how it would all end for Korotyshkin no one could tell.

Not knowing what to do, Korotyshkin decided not to do anything and pretend that Shubkin simply didn't exist. Which, of course, played into Shubkin's hands. Seeing that no one did anything to him, he cast caution to the winds and in addition to newspapers he appealed to presidents and prime ministers and to international public opinion in general, in other words effectively to the whole human race. He wrote about everything. About the official authorities' retreat from communism. About bureaucracy and bribe-taking. About universal drunkenness. About people being persecuted for their religious beliefs. About the authorities' failure to preserve cultural values.

One way or another he sent all these materials to Moscow, from where everything found its way to the West, and in the evenings when Shubkin searched for his name on the airwaves, he almost always found it.

"Come here!" he would shout to Antonina. "Listen to what they're saying!"

He was delighted, but Antonina was distraught.

"Oh, they'll put you away, Mark Semyonovich, oh, they will, they will," and she would shake her head in misery.

"Don't be afraid, Tonechka, they won't put me away," Mark Semyonovich would comfort her. "How can they put me away now, when the whole world knows who I am?"

Of course, he was sacked from his job, and excluded from the Party.

But this was the very time when he himself began to deviate from Marxism and Leninism. A crisis began to develop even in his view of the world around him. But being the kind of man who simply can't live without a SCOSWO, he began seeking one in the very world outlook which he himself had only recently called opium for the people.

50

There was a knock at Aglaya's door; she opened it without asking who was there and started in surprise. Standing on the doorstep holding a large watermelon was a sporty-looking young man wearing jeans and a leather jacket.

"Marat!" Aglaya gasped, suddenly overcome by a joy she hadn't expected to feel. She was surprised and delighted both by Marat's appearance and her own maternal feelings, by the fact that she actually had any.

"Hello, Mom!" said Marat, clutching the melon to his belly and smiling, while a young blond woman in jeans and an unbuttoned denim jacket stood smiling behind his back.

"Hello, son," said Aglaya, skirting around the melon and kissing Marat somewhere close to his ear. She held out her hand to the blonde: "Aglaya Stepanovna. And you are . . ."

"Mom, this is Zoya, my wife," Marat said reproachfully. "I wrote you lots of times."

"Yes, of course you did," Aglaya agreed. "But what does marriage mean nowadays? Not a thing. It used to be different . . . When your father and I got married . . ." She faltered, recollecting that her union with Andrei Revkin could hardly be represented as ideal. "Never mind," she said, interrupting herself. "But you're a bolt out of the blue. You could at least have sent a telegram." She led them through to the room. "Come in. How could you come without a telegram? The place is a mess and the refrigerator's empty."

She entered the room first, shrugging her shoulders as she carried on talking, turned around and saw they had barely stepped over the threshold. The two of them were just standing there, he wearing an expression of amazement and she one of horror.

"Ah yes," said Aglaya. "Didn't I write you about it? I'm keeping it. Have been for almost eight years." A sudden thought struck her. "Have we really not seen each other for eight years? Or even longer? Will you put that watermelon down!" she shouted at her son, and he lowered the fruit onto a chair and rocked it to and fro to make sure it wouldn't roll off.

Then they sat in the kitchen at the round table covered with the Kremlin towers oilcloth and waited for the water to boil in the big battered aluminum kettle. The kitchen was grubby and untidy, with cobwebs in the corners. Aglaya set a half-kilogram jar of sugar and half a packet of Greetings biscuits on the table, gave Marat the glass in a glass-holder, gave Zoya the porcelain cup with no handle and the inscription WPRA— 20 YEARS and for herself she took the enamel mug, after first wiping it with a towel.

Marat observed that his mother had aged since they had last seen each other. There were bags under her eyes, and bags under the bags, and her entire face had somehow turned knobbly, with deep, open pores. As she poured the tea, he noticed that her hands were trembling and her fingers were dark and crooked, like twigs. But why, he thought, after all, she's not that old. Fifty-four. Zoya's mother was two years older, but she looked a lot younger. Perhaps because she went to a beautician and dyed her hair. He's got older, thought Aglaya, looking at her son. How old is he now?

About thirty-five and already bald, with a paunch and a double chin and going gray at the temples.

"What's the WPRA?" Zoya asked, examining her cup. Aglaya looked at her in surprise, unable to believe it was possible not to know that, and Marat explained: "The Workers' and Peasants' Red Army."

"When did you arrive?" Aglaya asked.

"We've only just got here," said Marat.

"Only just got here." She looked at her watch. "What train were you on?"

"We didn't come by train," Marat said with a smile. "We came by car. I collected coupons in Cuba—and there you are . . ." He led her over to the window. "You see the light blue Volga?"

"Is it yours?"

"My very own. Yes, by the way, I forgot to take off the windshield-wiper blades. How are things around here? Do they steal them?"

"Where don't they steal them?" asked Aglaya.

"I just thought that maybe here . . . This used to be a quiet kind of place."

"There used to be order," she said. "It was quiet everywhere then. Now some people gasp and say: 'Oh, under Stalin they gave you ten years for a single ear of wheat.' And they did right. Nowadays they thieve it by the wagonload, not the ear. By the trainload. Never mind, what am I talking about that for? Tell me how you are, how both of you are."

She was entirely unprepared to receive guests, with nothing in the house for supper except some potatoes, half a bottle of kefir and the same amount of vodka. But it turned out that in a cooler bag in their car her guests had two roast chickens, boiled eggs and salami sausage, and Marat went to the delicatessen and bought a pack of butter, a bottle of sunflower oil, three cans of Bulgarian stuffed cabbage leaves, two bottles of Algerian dry wine and a Capital torte.

When Marat was on his way to the delicatessen, the wiper blades were still there and he thought he'd remove them on the way back, but when he returned, they were already gone. This event cast a pall of gloom over their supper. However, Aglaya had an acquaintance who was the boss of the motor depot, and she hoped to get hold of some wipers in the morning.

During supper Marat sat facing the half-open door of the room, glancing from time to time in the direction of the darkness out of which the statue was observing him curiously. This iron gaze played on Marat's nerves. He turned away, shifted his chair, sat sideways to the door, but the mysterious force emanating from the statue lured him, making him twist his neck to meet the incomprehensible question projected in that gaze.

Aglaya knew that Marat had a son, but not being certain whether there was anyone else, she asked cautiously: "How's the younger generation?"

Marat was delighted she'd remembered about her grandson and told her that Andrei was staying with Zoya's parents. The boy was in first grade at school, but he was a poor student because he got into too many fights.

"He's a lot like you," said Marat.

"Because he gets into too many fights?"

"I mean he looks a lot like you."

"That means he's a lot like me on the inside too. I was a real little scrapper when I was a kid," she recalled with satisfaction. "All the boys were afraid of me. And you," she said, turning to Zoya, "what do you do? Are you a housewife?"

"Certainly not," Zoya objected. "While the baby was small, I stayed at home with him, but now I work at Intourist."

At Intourist she worked as a guide in the department of individual services for especially important foreign political figures, artists and writers. She happily related how she had traveled all over the country with Howard Fast, James Oldridge, Rockwell Kent and some other people whose names meant nothing to Aglaya. But from the enthusiasm with which the names were pronounced, she could guess that these were famous people and the services provided to them were fuller and more comprehensive than those required by the formal responsibilities of the job.

Usually the foreigners were taken on the customary routes: "Moscow—Leningrad—Kiev—Zagorsk," but the moment you turned aside from the well-trodden path, unforeseen and amusing incidents occurred. For some reason the Indian prime minister, Jawaharlal Nehru, whom Zoya accompanied on one trip, had wanted to visit the city of Tselinograd. At first they attempted to dissuade him, but while they were dissuading him, the order was given for the double-quick completion of building work on the city's central hotel, a building that had been under construction for several years. The local construction brigades were reinforced with crack workers from the Moscow construction trust, Mosstroi, who did their damnedest, and by the time the foreign guest arrived, they had managed to complete the second floor, the staircase leading to it (the unfinished sections were covered with a red carpet runner) and the hall, where all the pompous uniformed attendants standing around with simpleminded expressions on their faces held the rank of at least major. The walls were decorated with a motley selection of lamps and animal horns, and that day the bar sold all sorts of drinks never seen before by the locals, while the newspaper kiosk offered all sorts of newspapers and magazines, local and foreign, including, of course, Indian ones. In order to create the impression that publications and beverages could be freely purchased, KGB agents approached the counters and bought both kinds of items, but everything was taken away from them at the exit to prevent them from trying Coca-Cola and becoming infected with the spirit of consumerism, or being subjected to ideological pressure by the newspapers, which, not knowing foreign languages, they would have been unable to read in any case.

The deluxe room for the exalted guest was equipped by the secretary of the regional Party committee with his own furniture, very luxurious and with no bedbugs. Everything was going well, or even better than well, but there was still no plumbing in the hotel and the sewerage system had not been linked up yet. And since the guest was an important individual who couldn't just relieve himself out in the street, they rigged up two barrels on the third floor and brought in water through the back entrance, pouring cold water into one barrel and hot water into the other. As for the sewage system, they dealt with that very simply: the discharge pipe broke off short in the deluxe room on the first floor with a bucket standing under it, and Aunty Sima, the cleaning lady, kept guard by the bucket. In the morning Granddad Java (as Zoya called the honored Indian guest) did his business, then pulled the handle, sending the load crashing down into the bucket, which Aunty Sima then grabbed, setting another in its place. Zoya gesticulated energetically and constantly repeated the expressions "great" and "a gas." "When the water runs, Aunty Sima runs," she said (she thought that was funny). And she deliberately mangled some words to make them sound folksy. When Marat asked if he should pour her more wine, she said: "Nacherly."

Aglaya drank her wine with a frown—she liked vodka better, but she concealed her weakness from her son. She hardly touched the food at all, smoked her coarse Belomor cigarette and leaned forward over the table in fits of hollow coughing. Marat offered her his foreign Marlboro cigarettes, she tried one, began coughing even more and said: "Rubbish, like straw, our Belomors are far better." She listened to Zoya's stories politely but with great impatience, and she interrupted an attempt to tell her about the trip Marat and Zoya had made to Kizhi with a question.

"What interests me is . . . your father has an important job—I suppose he rubs shoulders with the big shots?"

"Sometimes," Zoya agreed, not without a certain pride.

"So are they going to do anything up there about restoring justice?"

"What for?" Zoya asked with a frown. "It seems to me justice has been restored already. All the politicals were released ages ago, they get higher pensions, and there's enough talk about them already."

"Perhaps even too much," said Marat, with an involuntary sideways glance at the statue.

"That's what I mean," said Aglaya, "that there's too much. But I didn't really mean them, but him." She pointed to the statue. "He did so much for the country, and then they dumped him like so much garbage!"

She hadn't drunk a lot, but a little was enough for her. She flushed bright red and tears sprang to her eyes.

"Yes," Zoya agreed, "I think the same. Papa said the top leadership had plans to rehabilitate him, but international public opinion and the Western communist parties—"

"Damn the Western communist parties," Aglaya said coarsely, and lit her next cigarette from the last. "Don't we have a mind of our own?"

"In principle you're right," Zoya agreed again, "but in the present world situation . . . Of course, the time's ripe, but . . . I think the same, and papa thinks the same, and lots of people do, so perhaps there'll be a resolution for the ninetieth anniversary."

"There won't," said Marat. "There won't be any resolution."

Zoya looked at him in surprise and Aglaya asked: "Why not?"

"Because, dear Mama," Marat said with a laugh, "after the Stalin personality cult there was the Khrushchev personality cult, and after that there'll be the personality cult of our present living general secretary, and it will go on like that, and no one needs a dead rival. One dead Lenin is quite enough."

Aglaya looked closely at her son. Marat caught her glance and read the condemnation in it.

"I'm sorry, perhaps you think I'm too cynical. But every cynic is a disenchanted romantic. First he believes in ideals, then he sees that they don't correspond to the realities of life and he starts to trust nothing but his own eyes."

"That's not cynicism, that's called realism," objected Zoya.

"Clever girl," Marat agreed. "You could put it like that."

"But I still don't understand," said Aglaya. "It seems to me the present leadership regards Stalin with respect, then why—"

"Because, Mama dear," Marat interrupted her, "there's a lot more pleasure in licking a live ass than an iron one."

That night she opened out the sofa in the sitting room for the young couple. It was a long time since it had seen active service as a bed. She went off to her own bedroom. She lay there smoking and thinking that Marat was obviously right. The present leadership had their merits, but they also had quite obvious failings. They weren't rehabilitating Stalin; they were fudging the job with the dissidents. They were afraid of the Western communist parties and international public opinion . . . And the result was a load of nonsense. The bigger the dissident and the more damage he did, the more they pampered him. They didn't put him in jail but polemicized against him in the newspapers, and that was just what he wanted. Who would fight seriously against these dissidents anyway, if politics at the top was nothing but toadying and time-serving? Brezhnev was lauded and decorated at the slightest excuse, or even without one. Only recently, he'd been honored with the title of Hero of the Soviet Union. For what? Length of service? And they talked about Stalin. Yes, Stalin . . .

She took a long time to get to sleep, and so did her guests. Hearing noises outside, Marat leapt out of bed three times to check that no one was stealing the car. Then he lay down again. He lay there, looking at the statue, and it looked at him. He closed his eyes, and then he thought the statue had begun to move and was coming toward him. He had no time for mysticism, he knew it couldn't happen, but he couldn't resist opening his eyes. The statue was standing in its original position, but Marat had the feeling (which he didn't believe) that it had only just got back there. He closed his eyes again, and there were times when he almost fell asleep completely, but as soon as that happened, the statue immediately came across and leaned over to gaze at him. In his dream he assessed his own state critically, asking himself: Am I asleep or not? And he answered himself: No, I'm not asleep, because I can see and feel everything that's going on around me, I'm lying here and Zoya is lying beside me, here's my nose, here I am twitching it, no I'm not asleep. An automobile went roaring past the window, the glare of its headlights burst into the room and skidded along the wall and Stalin dashed quickly back into his corner, but as soon as the light disappeared, the statue crept silently over to the sofa bed. Marat tried to ask Stalin what he wanted, but when he opened his mouth, he couldn't say anything and his fear woke him. When he woke, he noticed that Zoya wasn't sleeping either.

"What's wrong?" he asked.

"I'm afraid of him," Zoya whispered.

"Nonsense!" he growled irritably, trying to reassure himself as much as her. "It's nothing but an inanimate object, cast iron, a piece of monumental propaganda, that's all."

He thought he would distract her, and himself, in the way people usually distract themselves, especially since they were in a new place, and a new place always excited him precisely because it was new. And the process of distraction had already proceeded very far when Zoya objected in a whisper: "No! No!" And she pushed him out of her.

"What's wrong?" he asked, disgruntled.

"I can't with him here," she said.

In the morning, while her visitors were still sleeping, Aglaya went to see her acquaintance at the motor base. He didn't have any spare wiper blades, but purely out of respect for Aglaya he gave her some taken from an official automobile.

They ate a silent and hasty breakfast. Marat hadn't slept enough and he was grouchy. He kept glancing into the room in amazement. During the night he'd thought Stalin had looked menacing and mysterious, but there was no menace now, just a little old man in cast iron, looking like a portrait of a doorkeeper by the Georgian painter Pirosmani, standing there with one hand raised absurdly. Perhaps that was what he'd been like—a little pockmarked nonentity—and people themselves had endowed him with superhuman qualities; their cowardly imagination had transformed him into an all-powerful ghoul so they had trembled in fear at the sight of him.

Marat and Zoya wanted to leave as soon as possible, and Aglaya wanted them to go. They were already in the corridor and ready to say their goodbyes when Aglaya said, "Just a moment," and went dashing into her study, then came back and handed her son an envelope with the address "L. I. Brezhnev, The Kremlin, Moscow."

"I want you to do something for me," she said, lowering her voice. "Take this to the Central Committee. There's an entrance on Old Square, number four or number six. They take in letters there."

"Oh, Mom!" Marat said, frowning. "When am I ever going to be there? It'll get there quicker by post."

"What's wrong with you? Don't you understand?" she asked in a whisper, and glanced toward the door.

He glanced in the same direction and looked at her.

"What don't I understand?"

"I'm being followed," she went on nervously. "Every step I take. They've gone soft on the enemies of the people, but they've put a communist and a partisan like me under close surveillance. They intercept my letters. But it's my duty. And the people at the top must know what the rank-and-file communists are thinking."

"Are you writing about that dummy?" asked Marat, jerking his head in the direction of the sitting room.

If only Marat had known the effect his words would have. Aglaya's heart began pounding furiously.

"What?" she asked in astonishment. "You said 'dummy'? Did you call Comrade Stalin a dummy?"

"Mom!" Marat exclaimed in fright.

"Aglaya Stepanovna," Zoya intervened. "He didn't mean Stalin. He meant the statue. It is a bit odd, after all—"

"Shut up!" Aglaya bellowed, the way she used to bellow when she was interrogating a *Polizei* or an embezzling collective farm chairman.

"Mom, what's wrong with you?" said Marat, trying to calm her down. He even held out his arms to give her a hug. "I'm not talking about Stalin himself, I mean that idiotic sculpture. It's not a man, it's an idol—"

"Ah, it's an idol!" Aglaya flared up. "How dare you! Take your hands off me! . . . How dare you say that about the man who means more to me than—"

"Mom!" Marat appealed to her one more time.

"I'm not your mom!" she yelled. "And you're no son of mine! Clear out the pair of you and don't let me ever see you again!"

"Mom," mumbled Marat. "I just don't get it, why are you so—"

"Get out!" said Aglaya, and pushed him in the chest.

Zoya stepped out onto the landing. Marat turned to follow her.

"Get out!" Aglaya repeated, and pushed him in the back. Then she slammed the door shut, turned the key in the lock and went into the sitting room, prepared to cry her eyes out. But glancing by chance at the statue, she froze. Stalin was gazing at her so expressively that she had no difficulty in reading complete approval of her courageous act in his eyes.

51

We simply cannot ignore one important event that occurred in Dolgov in the late summer of 1969. Georgii Zhukov and his wife, Elizaveta, having decided to celebrate their son Vanya's fifth birthday, bought a canister of Polish spirits from a conductor on a passing train and invited guests in. The spirit turned out to be methyl alcohol, both of the Zhukovs died, one of their guests followed their example and another three went blind.

The yard-keeper Valentina howled for a week over her beloved son and wanted to do away with herself, but then she realized she had no right, she had to carry on living for the sake of her little grandson Vanya.

Apart from that it was a good year.

An article entitled "Loyalty" appeared in the *Dolgov Pravda*. It had been written very much earlier. At the beginning of '65 a correspondent had come to see Aglaya and asked her a heap of questions. And he'd written the article soon afterward, but it hadn't seen the light of day at the time. From time to time in the newspaper office, they would take the material out of the editorial portfolio and prepare it for printing, but at the last moment they would decide the time hadn't come yet. Now, apparently, the time had come. It turned out to be a big article, covering two bottom half-pages. It gave Aglaya Revkina's heroic biography in full — in all honesty, embellished just a touch here and there. It spoke of the firmness of her convictions. Of the trials and tribulations through which she had maintained her devotion to her ideals, the Party, the Revolution and the state. It gave a highly detailed account of the most important achievement of her life: preserving the precious monument, a masterpiece of monumental propaganda. The hope was expressed that the day was not far off when this masterpiece would take its place on the pedestal that was waiting for it.

It can hardly be regarded as a coincidence that the day after the article appeared a courier came dashing over to Aglaya's place (on foot) with a brief note: "Dear Aglaya Stepanovna! Could you please call into the district committee urgently. Porosyaninov."

She would really have liked, through the courier, to send the sender of the message to hell or farther, but curiosity got the better of her.

As she prepared to go to the district committee offices, she wondered whether she ought to put on her military tunic with the medals, but decided that nowadays that would be going a bit too far. She dressed herself up in a dark blue suit and a blouse, displaying on the jacket the ribbons from her decorations and a university badge presented to her for taking some Party courses.

Her old office looked less modest than it had in her time. There was a new desk and cupboard of Karelian birch, a heavy bronze chandelier with cupids, a soft leather divan, two leather armchairs, a low table with the journals *Ogonyok* and *Woman Worker* and, above Porosyaninov's head, two portraits: Lenin and Brezhnev.

"Hello, Aglaya Stepanovna!" Porosyaninov greeted her joyfully. He came out from behind his desk, went toward her and even spread his arms wide, intending to embrace her, but he'd forgotten who he was dealing with. She mumbled a barely audible "Hello" and dodged his embrace. He caught on immediately and didn't insist, just directed her to one of the armchairs and took the other himself.

He said nothing for a while, as though he hadn't thought of the right way to approach the conversation, laughed and said, looking straight into her eyes: "Well now. Let's start by agreeing to let bygones be bygones. You suffered for sticking to your principles, that's clear enough, and it's been taken into account. The feeling is that it's time to put a few things straight, and so I can inform you that the decision to exclude you from the ranks of the Party has been annulled. Your period of membership remains continuous; for the time being you can register at your home address, and we'll sort things out later. Are there any questions on that point?"

"Yes," said Aglaya. "I demand an apology."

"What?" Porosyaninov was astonished.

"Well, you have to apologize to me."

"I see." Porosyaninov sighed, looked at her and said with feeling: "Aglaya Stepanovna! My dear Party colleague! You know very well that our Party acknowledges and corrects its mistakes, but it doesn't apologize."

"All right," Aglaya agreed. "Then the second question. When will you rehabilitate Stalin?"

Porosyaninov was embarrassed. He thought for a moment. "In the first place," he said, "since you, unlike Stalin, have been completely rehabilitated, you have the right to say 'we' instead of 'you.' So what is your question?"

"When will we rehabilitate Stalin?" she asked, switching the pronoun.

"I have a question to you in reply. What in hell's name do you want him for?" Porosyaninov asked, fixing Aglaya with an unblinking stare.

"What?" Aglaya was taken aback.

It was the same situation that had arisen with Marat. But Marat was her son, and this man . . .

"All right, let's move on," said Porosyaninov, switching into an official tone of voice. "In our party, Aglaya Stepanovna, we hold the opinion, which Stalin himself shared, that history is not made by individual heroes, but by the people under the leadership of the Communist Party. Headed at the present stage by the leading Leninist, Comrade Brezhnev. Now we've passed that station," he said, giving her no time to gather her wits, "and we'll switch trains. We, the Party leadership of the district, have applied for you to be transferred to a republican-level personal merit pension. And in addition, here is a travel warrant for a trip to Sochi, any ticket, train or air, will be paid for. Take some time to build up your health, steam for a while in the sauna, try the various treatments—massage, mud baths, the Charcot shower. It's very good, I've tried it myself. When you feel strong enough, come back and drop in to see us. If you want, we'll find you some worthwhile social work to do. If you don't, take it easy, read a few books, study the classics of Marxism-Leninism."

52

Divanich volunteered to see her off and lugged her suitcase to the station on foot.

Outside the station there were two police cars with blinking lights, a gray Volga and a military truck with soldiers under a tarpaulin.

There was a lot of noise on platform 1. A crowd of people Aglaya didn't
know were celebrating a wedding. The bride in a white dress and white
veil, the groom in a black suit with a white rose in the buttonhole. The
friends, girlfriends, parents and relatives of the bride and the groom. Lots
of people, all different sorts. A bayan player with gold teeth was stretching
open his bellows, a young man and woman were dancing, the woman
shrieking out rhyming ditties of distinctly ribald content. At first glance it
was a wedding like any other. Only there was something unusual about it.
There were some people acting too tensely and keeping a sharp lookout
on all sides. Aglaya recalled that later. But at the time, although she
sensed something, she was too preoccupied with her own problems. She
was afraid she might have been lured away with the travel warrant so that
they could remove the statue while she was gone.

"Oh no," Divanich reassured her. "That's not the way it looks. Quite
the opposite, full rehabilitation is what's expected now."

"Okay," she said, "but if anything happens, you run straight down to the
post office and send me a telegram. Not an open message, write: 'Granddad not well.' You understand?"

"And what if Granddad's fine?" Divanich joked.

"If everything's all right, don't write anything."

Carriage no. 4, the one Aglaya had a ticket for, stopped right in front of
her. First the conductress jumped out of the carriage with her curls peeping out from under her red peaked cap, then behind her Shubkin and
Antonina appeared at the top of the steps. "He's been to Moscow again!"
Aglaya thought furiously. He was surprised to see her and wondered what
she was doing there, but he smiled and said: "Good afternoon!" She didn't
reply, but she said hello to Antonina. He jumped down onto the platform
with a big, bulging briefcase and then helped his traveling companion
down the steps. Aglaya had already taken hold of the handrail when
Divanich tugged on her arm: "What's wrong?" she was about to ask, but
following the signs Divanich was making, she looked in the direction
Shubkin had taken and witnessed an extraordinary scene. Shubkin was
already nearing the station entrance when everyone involved in the wedding revels, including the bride, crowded around him and Antonina. Just
then the gray Volga came hurtling onto the platform out of nowhere, and
Aglaya heard first Antonina's cry: "Mark Semyonovich!" and then Mark
Semyonovich's own voice: "What's going on, Comrades? What is this? I
protest!" Then there was the sound of doors being slammed, and a second

later the Volga, its tires squealing, hurtled out of the crowd and raced along the platform with Antonina running along after it, her arms held wide open. Before it reached the warehouse, the car swung around the corner of the station and disappeared from sight. And Antonina stopped and stood there motionless with her hands held out stupidly in front of her, as though she was expecting somebody to put something in them. The crowd on the platform evaporated immediately and only then did Aglaya realize there hadn't been any wedding, it was a special operation.

"Yes!" said Divanich with a mysterious smile. "Neatly done! Now it'll be a long time, so to speak, till he sees freedom again."

53

I don't know about other people, but as I grow older, I find myself becoming less and less prepared to tolerate our Russian snows, blizzards and frosts, and even Pushkin's "frost and sunshine—glorious day" is, I fear, no longer for me. I become more and more fond of southern winters, with the gentle, muted sunshine, the warm showers, evenings that are not cold and faded blooms that are not frostbitten in the flowerbeds.

The sanatorium, named after some congress or other of the CPSU, was a place where the middle-level Soviet nomenklatura went to restore its health: deputy heads of Central Committee departments, deputy ministers, heads of industrial-sector central offices. According to the unwritten hierarchy (or perhaps it was written down somewhere), this class also included retired generals, certain leading industrial workers and certain members of the creative intelligentsia who were close to the top bosses—writers, artists and performers. This latter group was represented by People's Artist of the USSR Nikolai Kriuchkov, who walked with a rapid stride, smiled affably at everyone and ran down to the sea with a big towel in the mornings to bathe in the water that already had a wintry chill.

Aglaya had no interest in the sea, especially since she couldn't swim and didn't enjoy simply splashing about even in summer, although she did appreciate a steam bath, Russian-style, wet with a birch-twig besom. But she never actually went to the bathhouse. She was shy of being seen by people. Being such a well-known individual in Dolgov, she thought that they would scrutinize her in the bathhouse and then tell other people that they'd seen Revkina naked. And there had been a time when she was such an intimidating figure that not many people would have been able even to imagine her naked. There was no steam room here, but there was a sauna. Not quite the same thing, but better than nothing. What's more, she wasn't shy of the women here; they were from her own level, although they were pretty boring. They talked about nothing but their grandchildren, dieting, makeup and techniques of rejuvenation. By that time they were already excited about the silicone breasts and face-lifts that had become fashionable in the West.

After the three meals a day, the massage, mud bath, sauna and other corporeal pleasures and procedures, there was a lot of time left over, but Aglaya had left *The Foundations of Leninism* at home, she wasn't accustomed to sport and she simply didn't know how to occupy her time. She'd stopped reading the newspapers ages ago and was too lazy to watch television. What was there to watch anyway, apart from Brezhnev? Almost every evening he received some kind of award or gave one to someone else. They showed him so frequently and with such determination that the people christened the television program schedule "all about him and a bit about the weather."

The walls of the lobby were painted all over with pictures of happy Soviet life and the friendship of the peoples. Standing to the left of the entrance to the main building was a palm tree in a large tub, and beneath its spreading fronds people in flannel pajamas, blue tracksuits and slippers were playing dominoes. In the sleepy calm of the sanatorium the clattering of the dominoes sounded like gunfire. In collectives of simple folk the game of dominoes is usually accompanied by loud conversations on the most various subjects, funny stories, jokes and jibes. But when the nomenklatura gathers together, it behaves with greater caution, aware that before you make fun of anyone, you have to decipher the subtle lines of subordination. And you couldn't tell just any old joke here. So they played in silence, concentrating, with expressions that suggested they were occupied with something exceptionally important. But even here, someone might forget himself and suddenly declare with loud relish, "Fishtail!" Or "Double at both ends!"; "Double at both ends and done!" But then he would immediately fall silent and glance at the other players, concerned that he might have got too carried away for such august company. And he would modestly pull his head down into his shoulders just to be on the safe side

For lack of anything else to do Aglaya tried playing a bit, assuming it to be a simple business, but she saw that even here you had to take note of who had which pieces, guess your partner's intentions, pick up his hints and follow the general style of the game, and in these matters the public assembled here were such aces that she could never compete with them. She began walking a lot. Varying her route, she walked sometimes along the lower esplanade, sometimes through the upper park between the boat station and the Hotel Pearl, and as she walked, she thought about the strange way life turns out, not at all the way you imagined at the beginning. When he was still a young communist, her husband, Andrei, had once said that as they advanced toward communism people would become ideologically stronger, think more about society and less about themselves. And what was actually happening? People were bogged down in their daily round; they thought of nothing but their stomachs and how to make their own lives more comfortable. Many of them had fallen into the clutches of acquisitiveness, and far from combating this way of thinking, the Party itself was even more avidly devoted to money-grubbing.

In the dining hall she sat in the very farthest corner, and at first she sat on her own. But one morning she came down to breakfast, and sitting there wolfing down his semolina was an elderly man in a dark blue sweater with the inscription ADIDAS on the chest.

"Hello," she said.

"Good health to you!" The man raised his close-cropped head, and Aglaya glimpsed a swarthy face with high cheekbones and shaggy eyebrows. She caught her breath in astonishment.

"Is that you?"

The man, somewhat surprised at the question, looked himself over—shoulders and chest—and confessed: "It seems to be me all right."

"Major General Burdalakov?"

"Lieutenant general," Burdalakov corrected her, pleased to have been recognized. Although there was nothing surprising to Fyodor Fyodorovich Burdalakov about being recognized. Thanks to the television, cinema newsreels and newspaper photos, the general, a Hero of the Soviet Union and public figure, one of the founders of a major voluntary social movement, was known to practically everyone.

54

The movement For Yourself and the Other Guy had been born at the time when the people had grown a little weary of the all-inclusive building of communism and was hoping for some material incentive. But instead of giving the people money and a better life, new shining ideals were invented and tossed to it in the form of patriotic ideas. Ideologically armed with these, at the behest of the Party and the Komsomol, or under sentence by a court, the people felled the taiga forest, dug canals, plowed up virgin lands and laid the Baikal-Amur Mainline Railroad, all the time living in tents or barracks and eating unimaginable garbage. And so that the people would be more willing to expend its strength, calories and health, the Party rewarded it with various orders, medals, badges, certificates, pennants and challenge banners and set up these pseudopopular movements, pretending that they were the people's own idea. There were a lot of these movements. Their participants were invited to switch from the horse to the tractor, labor like shock workers, emulate leading workers, acquire a second profession, fulfill the five-year plan in four years, drive heavily loaded trains, pick cotton with both hands, tend twelve lathes each, save materials and produce additional output, overtake America, labor without laggards and work for the other guy. That is, for the guy who never came home from the Great Patriotic War.

Examined in the light of common sense, the appeal to work for the other guy was a little insulting. What did it mean to work for the other guy, and what was the point of working for him, if he didn't eat or drink and didn't require any other expenditure to support him? To be quite honest, this movement was a tactless rebuke to that same guy for lying where he had been dumped and forgotten and making no contribution to the building of communism. Nonetheless, the movement For Yourself and the Other Guy did exist, and one of its acknowledged initiators was Fyodor Fyodorovich Burdalakov, who had extensive personal experience in acquisition on behalf of "the other guy."

55

For Burdalakov "the other guy" was a concrete individual, and he was called Sergei Zhukov, or simply Seryoga. In '43, Fedya and Seryoga used to go out on reconnaissance together ahead of the front line. They were bold operators who collected valuable information and brought back prisoners for interrogation, and in times which were not too generous with awards, they had each been decorated for their work. They always went out together and came back together. But one day Fedya Burdalakov had come back alone. After successfully completing their latest mission he and Seryoga had been making their way home through the enemy rear lines when they were caught in an ambush, and in the brief combat Seryoga was wounded in the stomach. For some time Fedya had struggled honestly to carry him, draining his own last ounce of strength, but it was pointless and too dangerous. Seryoga was bleeding heavily, groaning and crying out; he would inevitably have been heard by the enemy. There wasn't the slightest chance of getting him through the line of the front at that point, and if Fedya had got him through, it would only have prolonged his agony. Seryoga himself had begged and pleaded to be spared pointless torment. And before he died, he himself had taken off his still-quite-new cowhide boots and given them to his comrade.

We would not wish to slander Fedya. Having dispatched many enemies to the next world, he was far from ready to dispatch his friends as well, even in such a nightmarish situation with almost no alternative. But what could he do? Leave Seryoga there and go? Stay with him and fall into the hands of the Germans? Not deliver to his unit the important information on which so much depended? No one who has never been in such a situation can judge anyone who has. Possibly in Fedya's place some pretender to the title of humanist would have done nothing, and that would have been very bad for Seryoga, for the humanist and in general. Fedya Burdalakov didn't think about whether he was a humanist or something else. After downing half a flask of vodka, he performed the act of ultimate compassion or, to use the modern term, euthanasia. And after performing it he wept for a long time.

Fedya abandoned his own down-at-the-heel boots with torn soles in the forest and on returning to his company reported that Seryoga had died heroically fighting against unequal odds, but omitted the details. What good would the details have done anyone anyway? People were being killed in such multitudes that one death more or less was of no interest to anyone. As was the custom, Fedya received three days' rations for Seryoga, including three-hundred-gram combat portions of vodka. And then, in an interview with a correspondent from the army newspaper, he promised to hammer the enemy for two: for himself and for his friend Seryoga. As a matter of fact, that was when he first got the idea about "the other guy."

As for Seryoga, even his posthumous story is a sad one. Burdalakov reported his death to the company commander, who was intending to pass on the information, but at that very time he was seized by enemy agents and carried off across the front for interrogation. The company commander went missing, dragging Seryoga after him into the lists of the missing. Which caused no end of difficulties for his wife, Valentina, the yard-keeper in Dolgov.

No two ways about it, Fyodor Burdalakov fought courageously. He didn't sit in staff HQs far from the front line, he didn't supervise rear-line supply structures. In the very fiercest engagements he hammered the enemy for himself and for Seryoga, demonstrating great valor, for which he was promoted and decorated. The closer the war came to its end, the more decorations were awarded. He finished the war as a Hero of the Soviet Union and a colonel, and he received two general's stars, the first for serving in the Central Political Administration of the Soviet Army and the second when he retired. But wherever he served and no matter what he did, Burdalakov never forgot about "the other guy," about Seryoga, the accordion player, joker and brave soldier. He spoke about him wherever he could, he gave speeches in his name and even now in peacetime he received numerous signs of favor, badges of distinction and banknotes, all of them for himself and for Seryoga, while Seryoga's family lived in wretched obscurity and abject poverty. Which Burdalakov probably simply knew nothing about.

When he retired at a relatively early age, Fyodor Fyodorovich was still strong enough to lift heavy objects, dig potatoes, drill wells and bore holes or, as a last resort, polish his pants sitting in some office, but now he spoke endlessly, without any unnecessary breaks, at gatherings and meetings, or sat in presidiums with a solemn expression on his face—that is, he engaged in the kind of activity that used to be called patriotic. And naturally, he called himself a patriot.

As a public lecturer for the Ministry of Defense, General Burdalakov devoted a lot of attention to the military and patriotic education of youth. He traveled around to all the cities of the Soviet Union. In military units and labor collectives he spoke about Seryoga and about his own experiences at the front line, about the taking of various cities, the storming of high ground and the forced crossing of rivers. But since he had performed his own feats of heroism which—let us emphasize once again—were genuine and not false, a lot of time had passed, some things had faded a bit in his memory, the forms of things had grown a bit vague under the moss and begun to get confused with things he had read somewhere, imagined or invented. Gradually, his reminiscences came to resemble the fictions of journalists in peacetime, whose idea of war came from movies shot by directors who had learned about war from reports by journalists.

Fyodor Fyodorovich traveled a lot around the sites of his own and others' glorious front-line feats, and now he was rewarded not for his prowess in combat but, as they used to say, for domestic services, with decorations, privileges, trips to good sanatoriums, treatment in the generals' polyclinic, improved housing conditions and the exchange of his old dacha for a new one, until eventually he was transformed into a genuine parasite, one of those who did nothing for entire decades except recall the heroic feats of the past, exhort, moralize and give instructions to artists, writers and scientists on how to paint pictures and write books and which areas to develop in science. And naturally, all the writers, artists and scientists who did not pay attention to the general's instructions were regarded as antipatriotic freeloaders sponging off the working people.

The reader should not think that the author has no respect for those who gave their lives for their homeland or were prepared to do so. The author honors all who fought courageously against the enemy, as well as those who fought without courage (they were more scared than the courageous ones). The author would even feel unmitigated respect for Fyodor Burdalakov if only he had not taken it upon himself to instruct people in matters about which he'd never learned anything himself. But he would teach anybody at all about anything at all, and if certain groups or individuals among the artists, writers, geneticists and cyberneticists failed to accord his precepts due respect, General Burdalakov personally sat down at his typewriter and rattled off like a machine gun: "We, the soldiers, the veterans of the Great Patriotic War, demand in the name of the fallen the severest punishment . . ." And the Soviet government could not always refuse such distinguished people.

For some time General Burdalakov had carried around with him as a visual aid a red battle standard in a specially sewn case. Not an ordinary standard this, but one riddled by bullets and shrapnel and perforated here and there with a kitchen knife, bearing the image of a Guards badge and the words TAKE BERLIN! Fyodor Fyodorovich had supposedly captured the enemy capital carrying this standard in 1945, and moreover, if you listened to him and forgot certain other well-known facts of history, you could easily believe that he had taken the enemy capital in the same way as he had dealt with the bear (he used to tell a story about a bear as well) — all on his own. We don't really know about Berlin, but Fyodor Fyodorovich had certainly conquered many Soviet cities with this standard. On all kinds of anniversaries — Soviet Army Day, Soviet Navy Day, Victory Day, the start of the Great Patriotic War, the defeat of the Germans at Moscow — and on dates when individual battles were fought, regions liberated, rivers forded, fortresses stormed, bridgeheads captured and capital cities taken, Fyodor Fyodorovich was an indispensable performer at the festivities, at which he arrived bearing his standard. And let us remind the reader yet again: he never forgot Seryoga, he always spoke on his behalf and on behalf of the fallen in general, he swore on their honor and cursed in their name. This without the slightest inkling or realization that having survived into old age, having received all of his honors, appointments, decorations and special rations for the war, it was shameful to speak in the name of those who had died leaving no trace behind them when still young, as the poet put it "without loving to the end or finishing their final cigarette."

56

Apart from all of this, Fyodor Fyodorovich turned out to be a sociable individual dedicated to healthy living. He easily struck up a friendship with Aglaya, began calling her Glasha, gave her a foreign book called

Running for Your Heart to read and persuaded her to go jogging along the seafront in the mornings. She didn't have the right clothes for this, but the general rang the secretary of the municipal Party committee, who rang the chairman of the municipal Soviet executive committee, who rang the director of the municipal trading trust, who rang the director of the sports shop, and two days later Aglaya turned out for her first run in a blue jersey tracksuit with the word "Dynamo" on the chest and sneakers, which were only just coming into fashion at the time. Burdalakov himself was in running shorts, an Adidas sweatshirt and Adidas sneakers.

Fyodor Fyodorovich, with his large, well-proportioned figure, graying slightly, but his face still suntanned and not yet old, was already waiting for Aglaya, warming up patiently by running on the spot.

On the first day she walked to begin with and he ran beside her at the same speed, but raising his knees high, pumping his arms like crankshafts and panting like a steam locomotive.

She liked the look of the general. He had a broad back like wrestlers have—slightly round-shouldered with mobile shoulder blades—and strong legs with well-muscled, suntanned calves that were sparsely covered with hair and gleamed as though they'd been waxed. Every day they made their way down the steep asphalt track that wound and twisted its way to the seafront like a paper streamer, on their way meeting the actor Kriuchkov with a towel around his neck, who was running up the hill, also puffing and panting.

On her first day Aglaya ran no more than fifty meters, but a week later she could easily manage the distance from the hotel to the boat station and back again, and she could easily have carried on running, but Fyodor Fyodorovich, who had become extremely cautious with age, advised her not to push herself too hard.

"Now," he would say as he ran alongside her, "if you would only give up smoking or at least cut down. If you could see your lungs from the inside, they'd look like a flue pipe. Coated in soot. If you could look inside yourself, you'd be horrified. I used to smoke too, like a trooper, and then I started having problems with my legs and the doctor warned me: 'You carry on smoking and you won't have any legs.' I told him 'Thank you,' walked out of the polyclinic, threw my cigarettes in a litter bin, and I haven't smoked a single one since."

They ran shoulder to shoulder, as though they were in harness. Sometimes the young Georgian Nukzar, a local good-for-nothing, would fall in with them and run alongside in football boots, always mumbling the same thing: "Hey, Dad, sell me the shoes! I'll give you a hundred rubles!"

"Clear off, young friend," Fyodor Fyodorovich said, waving him away, "don't pester me, can't you see I'm with a lady?"

"Sell me them, Pops," Nukzar persisted, and raised his price: 120 rubles, 130, 150.

This dialogue-on-the-run took place every day, but the young man's persistence was clearly pointless and therefore incomprehensible. Fyodor Fyodorovich explained to her the boredom of local life in winter.

"In summer he sells kebabs, but in winter there's nothing to do. It's boring running on his own, that's why he pesters us."

Usually, the general and Aglaya ran side by side, but sometimes he would warn her, "Excuse me, I'll just sprint a bit," and put on an abrupt spurt, running up to three hundred meters ahead of her and then coming back to meet her at a leisurely pace.

After the run she would slowly climb the hill, hot and sweaty, occasionally looking back over her shoulder at Burdalakov swimming in the cold sea.

She couldn't bring herself to bathe in the sea, but she did enjoy taking a contrasting shower—first hot water, then cold, then hot-cold, hot-cold several times.

They went down to breakfast together, sat down at the table on which there were already glasses of sour cream covered with napkins as well as plates of curd cheese and sour cream sprinkled with sugar, and immediately the waitress Ninulya would wheel over a trolley of other food, which she promoted in an affectionately cajoling singsong style: "Good morning," she would sing. "What are we going to have to eat? Lovely semolina, tasty porridge, scrumptious omelette, cheesy pancakes, rissoles, a little bit of potato?"

Fyodor Fyodorovich took the first meal of the day seriously, and for breakfast he ate the soft cheese with sour cream and a portion of semolina and a three-egg omelette and a piece of cheese. Aglaya had no appetite in the morning, she would just eat a cheese pancake and take a sip of tea, then reach for a cigarette.

"After your poison again," the general would comment.

"At least I'm not smoking on an empty stomach."

"You're just prevaricating," said the general, screwing his eyes up craftily. "Fooling yourself and trying to fool me. I used to be just the same.

Sometimes, I would wake up with my hands reaching out for a cigarette. And I'd be shaking all over, I wanted a drag so badly. In order not to smoke on an empty stomach, I'd take a bite of bread, or carrot, or a rissole. I'd swallow anything and then light up immediately, feeling pleased with myself. But in actual fact, Glasha, smokers should eat a particularly solid breakfast. Especially bearing in mind the wise old Chinese proverb: Eat your breakfast alone . . ."

"I know," Aglaya interrupted: "Share your lunch with your friend and give your supper to your enemy."

"Precisely," said Burdalakov, nodding keenly. "I have a friend named Vaska Serov, also a general, but as fond of jokes as a child and quite incrediblely simple. Gray-headed already and into his seventies, but he's always full of fun and games. 'Fedya,' he says, 'I live strictly according to the Chinese rules: I eat my breakfast alone, I'm prepared to share my lunch with you, and I give supper to my Ninka.' And he laughs at himself."

Of course, Burdalakov wasn't always lecturing Aglaya or trying to educate her. Often he simply related some story from his old days at the front, but once again these stories were in the genre of socialist realism and resembled short stories from the journals *Ogonyok* and *Soviet Soldier*.

More lively were his descriptions of various outstanding people of our times, and in his life he'd met a few good outstanding individuals. Members of the Central Committee of the CPSU, ministers and generals, and he remembered all of them, and called every one of them by his forename and patronymic: Leonid Ilich (Brezhnev), Nikolai Viktorovich (Podgorny), Mikhail Andreevich (Suslov), Anastas Ivanovich (Mikoyan) . . . he loved to describe top-flight receptions, especially in the Kremlin, and tell her who was there, what the tables and the chandeliers were like, what was served on what kind of china and what was poured into the glasses.

After breakfast they went their separate ways for treatments. Burdalakov went for a massage and sunbath in the quartz solarium and took a Charcot shower (he tried not to miss anything that they gave him for free), and Aglaya's timetable included electrophoresis and mud baths — just recently her knees and hands had been bothering her.

But there was enough time left over for walks. They went strolling together along the walks around the sanatorium before lunch and following the afternoon nap. The paths were laid out in circles on a level surface and some anonymous wits had nicknamed them the Lesser Infarction

Track and the Greater Infarction Track. It was a curious fact that Fyodor Fyodorovich looked different at different times of the day: the later it was, the older he looked. After lunch he walked along in a civilian raincoat and a knitted wool cap with his hands clasped behind his back, leaning slightly forward the way people with sick kidneys walk. Aglaya walked beside him, feeling as if her arms were somehow awkward and out of place, and whatever position she held them in—behind her back, crossed on her chest or simply lowered at her sides—it felt unnatural.

57

Their walks often led them to the spot where the steep descent to the sea began and there was a bench with a curved back made of wooden slats on a cast-iron frame that was usually empty. But there were times when it wasn't empty. Some couple would be sitting there, having sought solitude for purposes of tactile togetherness. The general and Aglaya would walk up, sit down and converse in low voices. And the young people usually felt embarrassed and annoyed, unglued themselves from each other and sat there with strained expressions, casting occasional glances at the newcomers, and once convinced that they had settled in for a long stay, they would get up and walk off without speaking in search of another secluded spot.

Burdalakov liked this situation; he enjoyed intimidating courting couples and he didn't do it only with people. In his young days he used to go around the village with a stick and prize dogs apart.

"You know," he said to Aglaya, "I see a beautiful young woman come to the resort. Her husband sees her off and meets her. Doesn't he realize that she's bound to take a lover here?"

"But not all of them," Aglaya objected.

"Every one," Fyodor Fyodorovich insisted. "Unless she's really very ugly. But if she's not bad-looking and, as they say, there's something to look at and something to grab hold of, then I assure you. I've spent a lot of time in resorts, but I've never seen any women who, given the opportunity, would never, no way, not with anyone. And by the way, the Germans have a custom that one day in the year husbands and wives can be unfaithful to each other, even spend the night apart, but then they don't mention it for the whole year—as though nothing had happened. That's more or less the way it is with our resorts. She's had her holiday, and what happened happened, and that's it until next summer."

"Not for everyone," said Aglaya. "Just recently I saw the movie *Lady with a Ginger Dog . . .*"

"With a ginger dog or a lapdog?" asked Burdalakov.

"Wait a moment." She thought about it and sighed. What a fool she was! *"Lady with a Lapdog*—there was a little dog in it. So they began at the resort and they couldn't stop. Although she had a husband, and a dog . . ."

"She did it with the dog too?" the general asked in horror.

"Oh, I don't remember. You know I watch these films with my eyes half-closed, I'm thinking about something else."

"I just don't understand," said the general, "what our inspectors can be thinking of. Sometimes they show such terrible, pardon the expression, garbage. The things people write in books! And it all gets passed. And they say we have censorship. What censorship, when we have ten thousand writers. Just imagine. Ten thousand! There were only half that number of soldiers in my division. I once raised the matter with Leonid Ilich. 'Leonid Ilich,' I said, 'why do we need so many writers? Pick five or ten, talented men, Party members, politically aware. Give them the subjects and let them work away.' "

"Do you mean to say you're personally acquainted with Brezhnev?" Aglaya asked.

"With Leonid Ilich?" Burdalakov returned. "Why, of course! It was in these parts that we got to know each other. If you take the ferry to the right here, first you come to Tuapse, then Novorossiisk, but before Novorossiisk there's a cape called Myskhako. We landed there in 'forty-three under the command of Major Tsezar Kunikov. He was a brave man, even if he was Jewish by nationality."

"And Brezhnev was there?"

"Well, let's say he was there some of the time. When the main forces arrived. He was head of the political department of the army. By the way, he presented me with the medal For Valor. And curiously enough, he remembers it to this day. When we meet somewhere at a veterans' rally, I ask him: 'Leonid Ilich, do you remember you presented me with a medal?' And he laughs and says: 'Why, Fedya, don't be silly—how could I not remember you?' Between you and me, he's a good guy. Well, he likes a drink, and he's not indifferent to the ladies, but if ever you ask him to do something, he always listens carefully, then he snaps his fingers and says to his executive assistant: 'Write that down and check to make sure it's done.' "

When Fyodor Fyodorovich met Aglaya, he was a recent widower; his wife had died six months earlier from lung cancer. "Yes," Fyodor Fyodorovich remarked to Aglaya, "she used to smoke just like you."

After losing his wife he lived in the country. He had a good general's flat in Moscow on Begovaya Street, but his elder daughter was there, forty years old and an old maid with a difficult character. His younger daughter, Asenka, beautiful and domineering, the kind that men like, had married a diplomat and now she had two children in India. His youngest son, Sergei, who had been named in honor of the general's front-line friend, had followed in his father's footsteps; he was a military man, a pilot and his squadron's deputy commander for political affairs.

"Do you have a dacha in the country?" Aglaya inquired.

"Of course. A big one. Half a hectare of land and eight rooms on two stories. Just imagine. Sometimes it upsets me so much I could cry."

"Why, what's the problem?" Aglaya asked anxiously.

"Other people have eight people to one room, and I have eight rooms for one person. And sometimes I sit in one room on my own and the other seven are empty. And if I go into another room, then the first one will be empty."

Despite his healthy lifestyle, Fyodor Fyodorovich often complained of headaches and insomnia.

"Last night," he would say, "there was a bird calling, then the wind was making a noise, then something else, I don't known what, but I simply couldn't sleep. There must have been some kind of atmospheric phenomenon taking place up there in the sky. When I was young, atmospheric phenomena never used to bother me. You couldn't wake me with a cannon, quite literally, but now somewhere up in the stratosphere two clouds have collided or the moon's in the wrong place, and here I am a man, the crown of creation, and I can't get to sleep. If I switch on the light and pick up a book, then I feel sleepy. If I put down the book and turn off the light, then the feeling's gone. You know, I went through the entire war without a single scratch, but it was still a tremendous strain on the nerves, and I'm feeling it now. It's like a time bomb."

After supper in the general hall they watched the news program *Time*, the ice hockey and the figure skating, or went to the movie hall if they were showing something old and familiar in black and white about the five-year plans, the war, bringing in the harvest, a Party membership card and spies.

58

To her delight, Aglaya discovered in Fyodor Fyodorovich a man who shared almost all her opinions. He shared her point of view on the October Revolution, the Civil War, electrification, industrialization, collectivization, the Rout of the Opposition, the Great Patriotic War, Stalin and Stalin's role in our achievements and victories. He also disliked Khrushchev, but he liked Brezhnev, which Aglaya was unable to say with certainty about herself.

Like Aglaya, Fyodor Fyodorovich detested revisionists—that is, people who took a negative attitude to the past, criticized the Party and Soviet power, and who preferred formalist trickery to realism in literature and painting.

"I was at an exhibition recently," he told her. "Such talented young artists, they told me. Call themselves modernists. Abstractionists. Well, I took a look. A load of messy daubs. You look at something and you can't tell what it is. A house, a forest, a river, a dog, you can't make out a thing. A line down here, some twirls over there. What they call 'God knows what tied up with a ribbon.' I went up to one of them and asked politely: 'What's your picture called?' He said: '*Wordlessness.*' I said to him: '*Brainlessness* is what you ought to call it.' I said to him: 'What do you paint pictures for, why do you waste the paint? A donkey could paint better than that with its tail.' And you know what a rude lout he was, he said: 'I can't even be bothered to talk to you on such a primitive level.' 'Why you,' I said to him, 'you vermin! I didn't spill my blood at the front so a parasite like you could sponge off the people and daub rubbish like this.' When I got home, I wrote to the newspaper. I got some of our lads together, veterans, they all signed it and the newspaper printed it. And the Union of Artists hit that lout with a reprimand for formalism, and I reckon they did right."

"No they didn't!" Aglaya protested sharply.

"Why didn't they?" Burdalakov asked in amazement. "You can't imagine what terrible daubs they were!"

"That's what I mean," she said, also growing agitated and clenching her fists. "They shouldn't reprimand them for that, they should shoot them!"

"What?" Burdalakov choked, as though a live fly had flown down his windpipe. "Oh you . . . Oh," he said, "you're a hot-tempered woman."

"What do you expect?" Aglaya went on. "It's not just harmless daubing, is it? It's not that simple. They're corrupting our youth. We lost twenty million Soviet people in the war. Didn't we? And what for?" Just at that moment she genuinely felt it was the abstractionists who were to blame for the death of those twenty million Soviet people. "No," she said, unable to see any reason for leniency, "only shooting will do."

"Yes," Burdalakov agreed, "I suppose you're right, at the front we used to . . ."

He was about to say that at the front they used to shoot artists like that, but when he thought about it, he couldn't remember any artists like that being at the front. There was a caricaturist who used to draw Hitler in the field news sheet, but there wasn't a single abstractionist.

"Well then!" The general seemed to wilt, and he yawned into his hand. "As far as the memory of Comrade Stalin is concerned, I think that in his case justice will be restored pretty soon. Perhaps even in a few days' time. A certain responsible comrade told me . . ." At this point Fyodor Fyodorovich glanced around, peered suspiciously into the bushes behind him and lowered his voice to a whisper. "They told me there's going to be a special decree. Mikhail Andreich Suslov is working on it specially . . ."

Before bed they called into the dining hall again, where there were already glasses of kefir standing on the tables, covered with napkins. Aglaya drank her portion there and then, but Fyodor Fyodorovich took his glass off to his room with him. Their rooms were next to each other — the second one after the stairs was his and the one after that was hers. Usually, they said goodbye at the door of his room and got together again in the morning for their run.

59

Sometimes when people heard that the famous general was in Sochi, they would invite him to one of the nearby sanatoriums or local towns to give a talk to the vacationers, the young people, soldiers, sailors or veterans. Then he put on his general's dress uniform with the gold shoulder straps, brocade belt, medals and Hero's star, and he looked important and unapproachable. But when he took up his signature flag wound up tightly in its case, the impression was tarnished and he looked more like Charlie Chaplin with his cane. He used to go away for the whole day, or even two. Left without his company, Aglaya was bored. In the mornings she went running on her own, but she cut down the distance, just as far as the boat station and back, then home.

One day the general was taken by helicopter to the town of Samtredia and flown back with numerous bags containing presents from "the workers of Sunny Georgia," that is, from the local Party bosses. One of the presents was a four-liter plastic container of the young wine Izabella.

Aglaya was invited to a tasting.

She accepted and entered Burdalakov's room with a certain restrained curiosity. So far, they had behaved like two pensioners, without even a hint at any other relations. But now it seemed to her that their relationship had arrived at some kind of threshold that required clarification. After all, he was a widower and she was a widow, both of them getting on a bit, but not so far gone that nothing was possible. In short, when she entered his room, she wasn't counting on anything specific, but she had a presentiment that some kind of declaration would be forthcoming.

His room was exactly the same as hers, square with two windows, a wooden bed, a divan, a low table for magazines, and two pictures on the walls. On one wall there were Shishkin's bears in the picture *Morning in a Pine Forest* and on another a picture by a local artist entitled *Storm Warning*—cliffs, a lighthouse and waves.

"Look at that," said Burdalakov, "he's an artist too, but you can understand it: these are rocks, these are waves, and that's a lighthouse. He might not be very talented, but everything's lifelike, it's not one of those 'gun smoke makes you choke and you can't make out a thing' pictures."

The aforementioned plastic container was standing on the table, together with a year-old number of *Ogonyok* with an unfinished crossword puzzle, two thin-walled tea glasses, a bowl of fruit (apples, mandarins and feijoa), a round flat loaf of bread, a large plate of suluguni cheese and some other strange food product that looked like a rubber sausage with nuts in it. Fyodor Fyodorovich said it wasn't made of rubber but of dried grape juice with walnuts and it was called churchkhella.

"Churchkhella?" Aglaya asked. "Isn't that what they call Kim Il Sung?"

"No," Fyodor Fyodorovich said seriously. "The Koreans call Comrade Kim Il Sung the Great Chuchkhe, but this is churchkhella. Not 'chuch,' but 'church,' like a house of worship in English. Your health, Glashenka."

Demonstrating his great knowledge of the art of consuming wine, he examined his glass against the light, then twirled it a little, turning it so that the wine inside swirled into a vortex, took a sip and looked up at Aglaya: "Well, how do you like it? A certain doctor of medical science, by the way, once explained to me that alcohol"—he emphasized the second o, French-style—"in moderate quantities is extremely good for the health. It's not like smoking. Smoking only does damage. But this . . . Shakespeare drank champagne all the time, and the German writer Goethe consumed a bottle of red every day. And Comrade Stalin was also fond of the Georgian red wine Khvanchkara. Although he wasn't averse to vodka too. I've clinked glasses with him myself."

"You?" Aglaya was amazed. "With Stalin? In person?"

"Naturally, in person," Fyodor Fyodorovich said with a smile. "How can you clink glasses any other way? If you've seen the old newsreel with the Victory Parade, you might have noticed me in it. I'm still young there and I have a mustache. I'm throwing a fascist banner into the general heap. Here, eat something, go on, this suluguni cheese is very good too— it's remarkably easy to digest and it contains calcium, which is absolutely essential for the female organism. Yes . . ." Fyodor Fyodorovich took a sip of wine, threw his head back, and his eyes grew misty. "Later, after the parade, there was a government reception in the Kremlin. I tell you, the supper was absolutely unique. You might say that I've been spoiled now, but back then it was the first time I'd eaten grouse or tried mushroom julienne. After supper we got up from the table to stretch our legs, and there we are, a group of officers, standing near the window and talking, when my friend Vaska Serov nudges me in the side with his elbow. I turn around and ask: 'Why are you shoving me?' I look, and blow me! Standing right there in front of me is Comrade Stalin in that, you know, dark gray uniform. And just a single Gold Star on his chest, nothing else. Standing as close to me as you are, or even closer. Holding a glass of vodka. And there beside him are Vyacheslav Mikhailovich Molotov, Georgii Maximilianovich Malenkov and Marshal Ivan Stepanovich Konev. And can you imagine, Comrade Stalin shifts the vodka from his right hand to his left, holds out his right hand to me and says: 'How do you do, I'm Stalin.' That's just what he said, 'I'm Stalin.' As though I might not know who he was. I was dumbstruck and just stood there with my mouth open. He says: 'And what's your name?' And you know, I tried to answer him, but my tongue just stuck in my throat, as they say. Comrade Stalin stood there, looking at me and waiting. But then, all right, Konev came to my rescue. 'Comrade Stalin,' he said, 'this is Colonel Burdalakov.'

"And then he asked: 'Burdalakov? Fyodor Burdalakov? Commander of the Hundred Fourteenth Motorized Infantry Guards Regiment? The former intelligence scout?'

"Well, at that I was totally stupefied. Can you imagine it, a generalissimo, the Supreme Commander—the number of divisions, people and intelligence officers he has, how can he possibly remember every one by name? And he said: 'Tell me, Comrade Burdalakov, are you a nondrinker then?' You can just imagine how scared I was, I didn't know what to say. If I say I do drink, he'll think I'm a drunk. But being a nondrinker's not so good either, somehow. I stand there and say nothing. And Comrade Stalin says to Konev again: 'Seems like you've got a dumb teetotaler here.' "

"Then Ivan Stepanovich helped me out again. 'Certainly not, Comrade Stalin,' he said, 'how could a front-line scout be a nondrinker?' 'That's what I thought,' said Stalin, 'there aren't any scouts who don't drink. A drinking man might not be a scout. A dumb man might be a scout, all he has to do is see and hear, but he can't be a nondrinker. A nondrinker could never be a scout.'

"Those were the very words he said to me, and I'll never forget them as long as I live." Holding up a piece of churchkhella in front of him, Fyodor Fyodorovich pondered in silence for a moment and then he brightened up again. "And just imagine, after that—after that he says to me: 'If you have no objections, Comrade Burdalakov, let's take a drink together.' Can you just imagine that? If I have no objections! And they talk about him being a megalomaniac. But what kind of mania has he got if he asks a colonel if he has no objections to taking a drink with him? If he'd told me: 'Burdalakov, drink a pailful of vodka,' or even kerosene, I'd have drunk it. I don't even remember how the glass of vodka ended up in my hand. 'Right,' he says, 'what are we drinking to?' I plucked up my courage, looked him straight in the eye and said: 'For Comrade Stalin.' And he smiled again and said: 'Why not, Comrade Stalin it is then—Comrade Stalin's no slouch, after all.' I held up my drink, we clinked glasses, he sipped a bit of his vodka and looked at me. And you know, back in the village before the war I'd learned to drink vodka without swallowing, straight down, just watch, the gravity takes it down into your gullet."

Fyodor Fyodorovich poured himself some more wine, got to his feet, threw his head back, opened his mouth wide, twirled his glass the way he had before tasting the wine and began tilting it over his mouth. The wine flowed into the general in a twisted stream, as if it were being poured from a funnel, and it gurgled like a mountain brook. But his Adam's apple didn't move.

"Yes!" said Aglaya admiringly. "You can do it all right!"

"Comrade Stalin was astonished. He watched me do it: 'Well, well,' he says, 'you're not Burdalakov, you're a vurdalak, a real ghoul. By the way,' he says, 'where does that name of yours come from?'

"What could I tell him? 'I couldn't say, Comrade Stalin,' I said. 'Of course you couldn't,' he says. 'Maybe your ancestors actually were some kind of ghouls. But of course, I'm only joking when I tell you that.' Then he laughed and moved on. And he started saying something to Konev, not about me, about something else. He forgot about me immediately, but it's something I'll remember for the rest of my life. I've seen lots of people you could call great, but after all, Stalin is Stalin!"

The general and his guest were silent for a moment—he excited by an experience relived and she by a story heard for the first time.

"They tell us now," she said, hoping to be contradicted, "that his face was pockmarked."

"Nonsense!" The general denied it immediately. "Pockmarked, him? Why would he be pockmarked? If anybody said that, I'd, well I don't know what I'd do to them. He had a fine, manly Russian face."

"But he was Georgian by nationality, after all." Aglaya felt she had to get that right.

"Well, yes," said the general, "of course he was. But his face was Russian."

They drank a bit more, and then Fyodor Fyodorovich began showing Aglaya albums of photographs, some of them faded. For the most part, they were ordinary snapshots, family photos. With his wife after their wedding. On a bicycle trip. On the beach. Their first son. Their son and their daughter. The three children. The children when they were little. The children when they were big. Fyodor Fyodorovich's patriotic endeavors were illustrated in a separate album. On the first page there was a recent full-length photograph of him in full military uniform, with his peaked cap, stripes on his trousers and decorations. Then there he was in uniform and in civilian dress, taking part in all sorts of ceremonies. An address to the graduates of the artillery college. A meeting of veterans on Mamaev Hill at Stalingrad. Fyodor Fyodorovich being presented with an award, a diploma, another award. With Marshal Chuikov, with Marshal Bagramian. A meeting of veterans on Victory Day, May 9, at the Bolshoi Theater. Something else at the Bolshoi Theater. Then suddenly—the general with Brezhnev. After the story about Stalin, Brezhnev didn't provoke any excitement, but it was interesting all the same.

"What's that you're handing him?" Aglaya asked.

"A diploma as the honorary chairman of our veterans' club. And look, this is me with this standard. Have you seen it unfurled? Hang on, I'll show you."

He took the standard out of its case, unfurled it and strode ceremonially back and forth in front of Aglaya, showing more or less the way he marched into Berlin with it. Aglaya tried, but she couldn't imagine how it was possible to march into a city like that in the thick of battle.

"But you were already a divisional commander," she reminded him. "You couldn't carry in the banner yourself . . ."

"That's nonsense!" Fyodor Fyodorovich protested passionately. "You can't even imagine the kind of man I was then. Young . . . Well, how young was I? When the war ended, I was thirty-six and I already commanded a division—the men used to call me Colonel Dad. But I was hotheaded, ai-ai-ai. Always trying to get out there in front. As for the standard . . . Of course . . . One day the standard-bearer was wounded in battle and he began to fall. And I thought: If he drops the standard, how's that going to affect the men? And then, you understand," he said, getting worked up again and starting to twitch, "I leapt to the front, grabbed up the standard and . . ." And he began describing to her a scene very similar to something Aglaya had seen very recently in some movie or other.

Aglaya looked at the clock. It was about midnight. She got up: "Time for me to be going."

"Wait." Burdalakov stopped her.

She gave him an inquiring look.

"I forgot to show you something," said Burdalakov, and he took a long object out of the drawer of the writing desk. It proved to be a dagger in a silver sheath. "Look. My front-line friend General Shaliko Kurashvili gave me that in Samtredia. Made in the early nineteenth century and presented to General Alexei Petrovich Yermolov. You remember, the one who conquered the Caucasus?"

The dagger was straight, with a groove along its center and a gold handle that terminated in a tiger's head with ruby eyes, and running along the blade was a nielloed inscription in Russian which Aglaya could just make out without her glasses if she screwed up her eyes.

KILLER OF ENEMIES' FRIENDS' SAVIOR, she read out in a loud voice, and looked at the general. "What does that mean?"

"I've been trying to think," said Fyodor Fyodorovich with a shrug, "but I can't understand it. And Shaliko doesn't know. It's a mystery, that's all there is to it. So I'll see you by the entrance as usual tomorrow morning?"

"All right," said Aglaya, feeling slightly disappointed. Fyodor Fyodorovich saw her to her door.

60

The next day they went running again, ate, went out walking, and in the evening he took her to his room to finish off the Izabella and showed her an album of newspaper materials, including several interviews with him, three large articles and a huge number of small clippings. One of the articles was entitled "The Peaceful Workdays of a War Hero," the second was titled "On the Approaches" and the third was "Nobody Is

Forgotten, Nothing Is Forgotten"—the general's reminiscences about his fallen comrades, including Seryoga Zhukov. But the clippings were mostly announcements of various different meetings, gatherings, receptions and other solemn ceremonies in which General Burdalakov had participated, where his name stood alongside others, some of them important and famous.

They sat and drank their wine, reminisced about the war, talked about their illnesses, about the disruption of the balance of nature, about the indecent way young people behaved: walking down the street with their arms around each other, in shorts and sleeveless sarafans, bathing on the beach in clothes so skimpy they might as well go completely naked.

"And abroad," said Fyodor Fyodorovich, "there are actually beaches where men and women go bathing in their birthday suits without feeling embarrassed of each other at all."

As he spoke about this, he frowned and spat.

And then at last came the moment to which the relationship between Aglaya and the general had been inescapably leading. As if by accident, the general put his hand on her knee and turned his face to look away. She shuddered, froze and turned her face to look in the opposite direction.

"And the weather nowadays," the general said, "keeps getting more and more unpredictable."

"Yes," she agreed monosyllabically.

"You should never eat mushrooms under any circumstances," he said, and suddenly, without the slightest transition, he threw himself on her with the same frenzied energy with which, perhaps, he had taken Berlin. He threw her down on her back, dived under her skirt and grabbed hold of the elastic of her panties. Not anticipating such an impetuous attack, she instinctively began to resist. She thrust both her hands against the prickly top of his head and pushed hard against it, and at that very moment, the way these things happen not only in the movies, but also in real life, there was a loud knock on the door. He took fright and instantly recoiled in panic. He looked at Aglaya, then at the table, with all the food and drink that hadn't been eaten or drunk yet. There was nothing unnatural or illegal in the situation, especially since they were both supposedly free people. But they weren't free people; they were Soviet people, raised from their childhood in the awareness that their every desire could be instantly discovered, discussed, condemned and punished. In this particular case their travel warrants might be taken away, they could be thrown out of the sanatorium, exposed in the satirical journal *Crocodile*, threatened with a personal hearing or excluded from the Party, which for him would be a catastrophe, and for her . . . Well actually, for her it wouldn't mean a thing, but she was scared too.

And so when someone began knocking on the door, the general began hurriedly putting the table in order, and she bounded away from him toward the opposite wall, hastily adjusted her skirt and began gazing out of the window, as though that was why she had come here, to admire the evening view from someone else's window. Finally, Fyodor Fyodorovich went to the door, half-opened it and saw the concierge Polina, a fashion-conscious little lady with big breasts tautly restrained by a jersey sweater. She was holding a piece of paper.

"Message for you," she said, and glanced into the room.

"Thank you," said the general, attempting to block her view with his body, spreading his arms as though he was trying to fly.

"Do you need me to tidy your room?" asked Polina, trying to get a glimpse of something, if only under his armpit.

"What are you waiting for?" he asked.

"Are you going to write an answer or not?"

"I don't know yet." Fyodor Fyodorovich suddenly remembered he wasn't a little boy, but a general, and a widower to boot; he was within his rights, he hadn't done anything reprehensible and it was nobody else's business what he was getting up to. "I'll read the note," he said sharply, "and if necessary I'll call you. And if there's no need . . ." He pondered and, unable to think of a better way to continue, concluded: "If there's no need, I won't call you."

He slammed the door in the concierge's face and went back to the little table, where his glasses were lying, muttering something under his breath. He picked up his glasses, read the note, and called to her: "Aglaya Stepanovna!"

She turned around and walked over to him, still confused and worried. He handed her the note without speaking.

"Can I use your glasses?" she asked, a little embarrassed that her eyesight also required support, then read, "Fedka, I'm in Novorossiisk, come immediately. L. Brezhnev."

"And will you go?" she asked.

He looked at her in amazement, and she realized that she'd asked a dumb question.

Less than a quarter of an hour later General Burdalakov, in full dress uniform complete with decorations, gold shoulder straps and brocade belt, with a long greatcoat thrown over everything else, a tall Caucasian hat on his head, his briefcase in one hand and his standard in the other—just in case—went downstairs to the government Seagull limousine that was waiting for him.

61

The reason for General Burdalakov's being summoned so urgently was that the general secretary of the Central Committee of the CPSU, L. I. Brezhnev, being in Novorossiisk, had decided to celebrate his sixty-third birthday in the company of his wartime comrades. Leonid Ilich was born on December 19, just two days short of Stalin's birthday.

Having received such an unexpected invitation, Burdalakov began wondering frantically what he could give the important birthday boy for his special day, remembered the dagger, picked it up and hesitated: Should he give him this or not? The inscription on the blade worried him a lot. But since the general had nothing more suitable with him (and how could you give anything unsuitable to a man like this?), he put the dagger in his briefcase anyway—and set off.

It was already late evening when the general's car passed through the green gates with red stars that had opened before it and drove into the grounds of the government dacha not far from Novorossiisk. Once inside the gates, the car halted immediately. A duty officer in a waterproof cape that concealed his shoulder straps approached the general and requested him to show his documents. A full moon hung above the grounds of the dacha, shining so brightly you could read a book by it. And in addition, there was a spotlight by the gates. But the officer also switched on his pocket flashlight, checked the photograph against the face and asked: "Was this taken a long time ago?"

"Why, do I look older?" Burdalakov asked coquettishly.

"Your I.D. needs renewing," the officer said, and asked his next question. "Are you carrying a weapon?"

"Of course not!" Burdalakov assured him. "Where would I get a weapon?"

"And what's in the briefcase?"

"Ah, in the briefcase!" Burdalakov began fussing with the locks, trying to open them. "There's nothing in the briefcase. What could there be in the briefcase? A change of underclothes, socks . . . Ah yes!" He remembered at the very moment when the briefcase came open. "There's that as well. You see, that . . . In there."

"Give it here!" The officer's hand dived into the briefcase and grabbed hold of the dagger. He stuck his flashlight in his pocket without turning it off and drew the dagger out of its sheath. He looked closely at Burdalakov. "You said you had no weapons."

"But that's not a weapon," Burdalakov objected. "What kind of weapon is that?"

"Then what is it?"

"This?" asked Burdalakov, the way he used to answer the teacher who asked him questions in class when he was a child. The teacher would point to the Kamchatka Peninsula on a big map and ask: "What's this?" And in reply the young Burdalakov would ask: "This?" Hoping that a hint would fall from the heavens. He asked the very same question now.

"Surely this is a weapon?" the officer asked.

"No, it isn't," said the general, becoming even more flustered, "it's not a weapon at all, it's a birthday present for Leonid Ilich."

Another officer came over, evidently with a higher rank, but that was also concealed under a waterproof cape. He asked what the problem was. The first officer explained. The second officer took the dagger, began inspecting it and asked curiously: "What does 'Killer of enemies' friends' savior' mean?"

"I don't know that myself," the general said ingratiatingly. "Maybe it's just a turn of phrase, or a Georgian folk saying. It's an old dagger."

"Yes, I can see it wasn't made today," said the soldier, and sighed for some reason. Then he thought a bit longer and said: "I tell you what, Comrade General, you leave this item with us, we'll look into things and get it back to you safe and sound."

"But no later than tomorrow morning," Burdalakov cautioned him.

"No later than that," the soldier agreed. "Perhaps even this evening."
And he saluted, allowing the car to proceed.

The main dacha was a separate structure of white stone with columns, standing on top of the bluff running down to the sea, and there were several more modest cottages scattered here and there around the grounds. As Burdalakov was getting out of the car, a maid—or a "nanny," as they called them here—came running over to him, a woman about fifty years old, wearing glasses, with a tall hairstyle, looking like some high-class lady from the movies about prerevolutionary Russia.

"My name's Aunty Pasha," she said, although she was better suited to be the general's niece. She took the briefcase from him and led him to a room on the second floor.

It was quite a good room, with a large wooden bed, a Record television and a washbasin.

"You'll have breakfast tomorrow in the main building, supper's already over, but I brought you that"—she pointed to the bedside table—"some goulash, cheese pancakes and kefir. There's tea in the corridor, in the big urn."

"And conveniences in the yard?" asked Burdalakov, not attempting to conceal his disappointment.

"Why no," Aunty Pasha reassured him. "On the first floor. As you go downstairs, it's the second door on the left. And the next door is the shower room."

And taking the three-ruble note he gave her, she left.

Feeling tired after his journey, the general didn't eat any supper; he opened up the bed, took off his uniform and put on his pajamas. He thought about going out to relieve himself but changed his mind. The washbasin was high and he had to hike himself up on tiptoe. Perhaps because a helicopter flew over the roof just at that moment, the general didn't hear the door creak, and when he heard someone clear his throat and looked around, he was overcome by such terrible embarrassment he wanted to disappear through the floor. Standing there in a civilian suit with a large number of decorations pinned to it, smiling with his hands held behind his back, was Leonid Ilich Brezhnev.

"Oh!" Burdalakov said, mortified, as he hastily concealed the offending weapon. "I'm sorry . . . I was just . . ."

"Don't worry about it," said Ilich. "Everybody does it. As the saying goes: 'Only a fink doesn't piss in the sink.'" He brought his hands out from behind his back, and Burdalakov saw his dagger in one of them. Brezhnev put the dagger on the table and clasped Burdalakov in his arms, slapping him at length on the back and mumbling about how glad he was to see him.

"I'm so glad, honestly I am, genuinely glad!"

"I'm very glad too," said Burdalakov.

"But of course you're glad, that's what your rank requires," Brezhnev joked, "but my gladness is worth more. And I'm glad to see you because I value front-line friendship. Here in Russia, when you occupy a high position, everyone seems to love you with an undying love and you can never tell who really loves you and who's just toadying. But our friendship's been tried in the fire, as the saying goes. I see you're not getting any fatter. Are you on a diet or something?"

"I go running, Leonid Ilich. And I advise you to try it. Every morning forty minutes of jogging till the second sweat, and you won't have any — begging your pardon — tummy at all."

"Tummy!" Brezhnev repeated. "That's not a tummy, it's a brute of a belly. A working man's callus, as the saying goes. Only when can I go running, eh? And another thing, if I start to run, an entire platoon of security guards will set off after me. What I came to see you about was this. My head of security brought it to me. He's been vigilant ever since last year's attack. 'Just to be on the safe side,' he said, 'we confiscated it from the general.' Well, I tore him off a strip or two. I told him: 'My friend brought me this, not Charlotte Corday.' I can guess what you brought it for."

"You're right," said Burdalakov. "Only I wanted it to be a surprise . . ."

"It can't be helped," said Brezhnev with a shrug. "We'll have to do without surprises. I had a good look at it already. It's a valuable piece."

Making no attempt to deny that it was valuable, Burdalakov told Brezhnev who it had belonged to before.

"Yermolov?" Brezhnev repeated respectfully. "Well I never!" Covetous of everything that glittered and never having assuaged this desire, he stroked the flat of the dagger's blade tenderly. "As we say back home in Ukraine: You can tell when you get your hands on the real thing. And just look at that tiger! Frightening! Rrrrrrr!" He growled at the tiger and laughed happily at his own joke.

Touched by his present, Leonid Ilich hugged the general, slapped him on the back and promised him the dagger would take its place on the wall of his dacha among the valuable exhibits of his weapon collection. At the same time his attention was caught by the strange inscription: KILLER OF ENEMIES' FRIENDS' SAVIOR. What's that? What does that mean? How are you supposed to understand that? Does it mean you have to kill the savior of your enemies' friends?"

"I've been puzzling my head over that, Leonid Ilich, but I simply can't figure it out."

"Perhaps it means that if you can kill the person who shelters your enemies' friends, then they'll turn against him . . . But no," the general secretary of the Central Committee of the CPSU contradicted himself, "no, I think this means something else. You know what, this is a Georgian dagger, isn't it? Let's take it over to my place and find the Georgian minister of the interior and ask him, he ought to know. Come in your pajamas. Just put your coat on and we'll go."

The moon hung overhead like an illumination flare; there was a pale light emanating from the neon streetlamps. The entire space that was open to view appeared to be absolutely deserted, but appearances were deceptive—there were secret service agents concealed behind almost every bush.

"A full moon again," said Brezhnev, disgruntled. "I used to love the full moon, but not anymore. Ever since the Americans landed on it, I can't bear the sight of it. I even think I can see them crawling around up there, like cockroaches."

"It bothers me a different way," said Burdalakov. "I remember the war. I have to go out on reconnaissance, but there's a moon. Galls me so at times, I want to shoot it down with an antiaircraft gun."

There was no need to look for the Georgian minister. He was in the foyer of the main building, playing chess with his adviser, a long-legged man with a mustache.

"Ah, Edward!" Brezhnev exclaimed happily. "You're just the man we need."

Brezhnev showed the minister the dagger, pointed out the inscription and asked him what it could mean. The minister turned the dagger over in his hands and passed it on to his adviser. He looked at it, ran his thumbnail along the sharp edge and commented that it was damask steel, then he looked at the name of the steel-smith.

"Oho!" he said. "It's a genuine Meladze."

"Who?" asked Brezhnev.

"Otar Meladze, a famous weapon-maker. In Georgia we used to call him the Stradivarius of the armory."

When he heard that, General Burdalakov began to think he might have been a little too hasty with his present. But he consoled himself with the calculation that for a present like that he might even receive a third star for his shoulder straps.

"Ha-ha," Brezhnev laughed, "I'm beginning to feel like Oistrakh."

"Why Oistrakh?" asked Edward the minister. "You're our Paganini."

"That's going too far," said the leader, lowering his eyes shamefacedly, but it was obvious that he was pleased by the comparison. "But what does this inscription mean?" he asked the adviser.

"Well, I think . . ." the adviser said, and began thinking hard. "I think there's an apostrophe instead of a comma here. It should say: 'Killer of enemies—comma—friends' savior.' Remember Pasternak's line: 'Victory—comma—defeat distinguish ye not.' "

"Aha!" said Brezhnev. "So it's really all very simple."

62

Leonid Ilich Brezhnev, a politician half-forgotten nowadays, loved all the varied delights that life afforded and was distinguished by a weakness for women, good food, expensive automobiles and all sorts of material tokens of respect: for decorations, weapons, gold, precious stones, for everything that glitters and tinkles, and he was very fond of eulogies. And what better excuse for fine words and presents could there possibly be than a birthday?

Sixty-three years may not be a round number, but the birthday boy and his guests celebrated it in style. Large volumes of beverages that were anything but weak were consumed; large amounts of hors d'oeuvres were eaten; a great many heartfelt and flowery toasts were proposed in praise of the innumerable virtues of the hero of the celebrations. Burdalakov got back to his bed at five in the morning, came around in the afternoon, read an address in the evening to the personnel of the cruiser *Perm* (the standard came in handy after all) and not until after lunch on December 21, the birthday of another great man, did he set off back to Sochi.

It should be acknowledged to the general's credit that although the time he spent in Novorossiisk had been passed in an unrelieved alcoholic haze, he had remembered Aglaya several times and thought . . . no, not about making her a part of his life forever, but he had not excluded the possibility of further developments in the situation. He'd taken a liking to her direct manner. She didn't flirt or make eyes, her opinions on everything were straightforward and definite, and at the same time she was feminine and still fairly attractive. And so before returning to Sochi the general made use of his customary method for obtaining goods in short supply: he rang the secretary of the Novorossiisk municipal Party committee, who rang the chairman of the municipal Soviet executive committee, who rang someone else, and the final link in the chain was the head man in the Novorossiisk department store, where Fyodor Fyodorovich acquired a Dawn woman's watch and the perfume Lights of Moscow, which the general's deceased wife had been very fond of.

He arrived back shortly before supper, stood his standard in the corner, took off his greatcoat and, clinking his medals as he went, set off with his presents to see his next-door neighbor. He knocked tactfully on the door. Nobody answered. He knocked again. The door opened to reveal Vyacheslav Mikhailovich Molotov, Stalin's comrade-in-arms for many years. And although Molotov had been deposed from the pinnacles of power long ago and his privileges had been reduced to those of the second-rank nomenklatura, Burdalakov, who had not forgotten that he used to be the most powerful man in the state after Stalin, became so confused that when he opened his mouth to speak no sounds came out, apart from "a," "o" and "u." Molotov gazed patiently and cautiously at Burdalakov through the lightly tinted lenses of his pince-nez, at his shoulder straps and decorations, perhaps anticipating some act of provocation or even arrest.

"Y," said Burdalakov.

"Y?" asked Molotov.

"Na-ah," protested Burdalakov.

"I don't understand what you want," said the former leader, beginning to lose his temper.

"But where's Aglaya Stepanovna?" Burdalakov eventually managed to force out.

"I don't know any Aglaya Stepanovna," said Molotov, and shut the door in Burdalakov's face.

Burdalakov went downstairs, where he met the matron, Kaleriya Frolovna, who told him that Aglaya Stepanovna had left the sanatorium that morning, a week before the term of her travel warrant expired. Kaleriya Frolovna didn't know why, how or what for, but Fyodor Fyodorovich had a pretty good idea.

63

What had happened was the following.

Fyodor Fyodorovich's sudden departure had upset Aglaya greatly. Not because she had been counting on anything serious (although their last meeting might have engendered certain hopes), but because it had happened unexpectedly, in haste, on the eve of a date that she would have liked to celebrate together with the general.

And then there was further unpleasantness.

On the morning of December 20 a letter arrived from Divanich, written in an ornate hand with whimsical curlicues and unusual style:

Hello, Aglaya Stepanovna! Good afternoon or evening!
     This letter comes to you from Com. D. I. Kashlyaev, retired c-nel. And he sends you his congratulations on the birthday of the Great Commander of our country and other peoples, Generalissimo Com. I. V. Stalin. And also permit me to wish you many years of good health and hap. life. There's nothing to write about us here, the weather is freezing cold. Deliveries of firewood and coal to the public are unreliable. Your ap-ment is in perfectly good order, as far as I can judge from the external appearance of the doors and windows and the testimony of the neighbors. Grandfather is well. That's all. I hope you are enjoying comp. rest and regul. meals, which is useful for the sake of health and well-being.
                    With that goodbye. Your fr-d.
                    Com. D. I. Kashlyaev, retired c-nel.

P.S. Also permit me to inform you that only yesterday your neigh-bour cit-n. M. S. Shubkin was rel-ed from custody due to the lack of any criminal offense and a shameless campaign by antiSov. cir-cles in certain Wn. Countries."

Aglaya was greatly displeased by Divanich's letter, or rather by the post-script to it, which aroused certain presentiments that would prove to be not entirely unfounded.

64

That evening she went to bed earlier than usual. Outside, the weather was clear and there was a full moon. Aglaya looked at the moon for a long time and attempted to find on it the features that Andrei Revkin had once tried to show her an entire lifetime ago, when he was not her husband but her comrade-in-arms. One twilight evening, in the company of a group of Komsomol members who spent the collectivization period attached to an NKVD unit, they had approached the rebellious village of Gryaznov and made their beds for the night in haystacks. She and Andrei had found themselves in the same haystack. It was a quiet, still, moonlit night. They had a view of the entire meadow with the dark haystacks standing on it and the separate trees that all seemed to be wandering off somewhere together, but each one on its own, retreating into the white mist that was rising from the river. Against the background of the mist the crookedly scattered huts of the village appeared absolutely black; it was sleepy and quiet over there, with only the cows occasionally lowing in their sleep and the dogs suddenly yelping and howling without rhyme or reason, or per-haps out of some premonition. First one would howl, then another would follow and they would all give voice in chorus, as though each of them were trying to howl louder than the rest, and the people, even those who were lying in the haystacks, felt a deep unease. But by the middle of the night the dogs had calmed down and total silence had set in. No sound at all but the rustling of the hay and the chirping of the crickets. Glowworms drifted in front of their eyes like tiny airplanes. Andrei had reached out for Aglaya and begun fondling her breasts, still young and firm then and quite untouched. At first he fondled them through her tunic and then, after unfastening a few buttons, he fondled them directly. She snuggled up to him, but before she gave herself to him, she asked him, as the senior comrade with the better grounding in theory, whether it was possible for two young Bolsheviks carrying out an important Party assignment to think of such secondary matters as those he was pestering her with. He told her that it was and cited Marx, who had said that nothing human was alien to him. And Comrade Lenin had written in a letter to Inessa Armand that as materialists and realists, Bolsheviks could not deny the objective laws of nature and a certain attraction might arise between Party comrades belonging to different sexes. Suppressing it was pointless, avoiding it was impossible and so comrades of one sex ought to meet comrades of the other sex halfway and satisfy their mutual desires, so that afterward they would not be distracted from carrying out the truly important assignments.

Revkin had convinced her, and Aglaya had given herself to him, having warned him beforehand, first, that she was a virgin, and second, that she didn't want any children. She was rather afraid when she allowed him to enter her, knowing from hearsay that the first time was painful. In order not to spoil her clothes, she took off everything she was wearing under her tunic. But while he was fussing with his own clothes, the passion that was about to overcome her had evaporated, leaving nothing but curiosity— curiosity and fear, which proved unfounded. To her surprise she felt no pain; she felt nothing at all, either pleasant or unpleasant. There was even one moment when she thought he must have missed the spot, and she had to reach her hand down to convince herself that she was wrong. With the job completed, in protecting her against the risk of pregnancy, he had spilled an entire puddle onto her belly. She dipped her finger in it and tried it on her tongue. He asked: "Is it good?" She said: "It's like raw egg." He hesitated for a moment, then asked: "But why did you tell me you were a virgin?" She said: "I told you I was a virgin because I was a virgin. I never lie and I don't intend to lie to you." "Then why wasn't there any blood?" he asked. "That surprises me too," she replied. A doctor had later explained to her that it was the way her anatomy was arranged: sexual activity had not disturbed anything, and she remained intact until the moment she gave birth. And so until that birth Aglaya was able to regard herself as perfectly virginal, and in a certain sense she remained virginal even afterward.

Later she and Andrei lay on their backs and looked at the moon. Andrei asked: "Do you see one brother stabbing another up there?" She asked: "Why, is there a class struggle up there too?" He laughed and said: "There can't be a class struggle up there because there aren't any classes." She didn't understand that either; she thought they'd built a classless society up in the sky. He laughed again and explained that there was no society up there because there was no life at all. Then which brother was stabbing which? He explained to her patiently: There weren't any brothers up there either, but if you looked at those spots they looked like people and one of them was stabbing the other. "Do you see? Do you see?" he asked her. "No," she answered. "I see the spots, but I don't see any people." Then he told her she had no imagination. It wasn't the first time she'd been told that. Once in his aggravation the teacher at school had told her she had no fantasy, sense of humor or feeling for beauty. In Aglaya's sister Natalya (a year younger than Aglaya, she had studied in the same class at school) the teacher had discovered fantasy and feeling, and this, that and the other thing (and then something else, when he slept with her in the school director's office), but in Aglaya—not a thing. But then none of this bothered her very much, because, along with the other feelings, she also lacked any sense that anything at all was lacking. She didn't always understand jokes, and she didn't know why poetry, ballet or opera existed. In real life people didn't speak in verse, they didn't dance when they were struck by an arrow and they didn't sing on their deathbed. Aglaya only tolerated the existence of these arts by way of an exception, when they glorified the heroes of the revolution or the war, bolstered the fighting spirit of Soviet soldiers or helped the workers to fulfil their pro-duction plans.

Now Aglaya lay in her room. The moon was shining in through the window and she could see the same spots on it, but once again they were simply spots and didn't look like brothers. She remembered Andrei's claim that if you looked at the moon long enough you would turn into a lunatic and go wandering around naked on the roofs at night. She felt frightened; she didn't want to go wandering naked across the roofs—at her age it would be dangerous and indecent. Aglaya turned away to face the wall and closed her eyes, and when she opened them, she saw that what she had tried to avoid had already happened: she was on the roof and she was naked. She was amazed that she'd turned into a lunatic so easily and so suddenly. She wasn't afraid in the least. It felt strangely interesting to be walking naked across the roof, and not even walking, more like gliding above it, only skimming the surface lightly from time to time with her feet. She hoped the roof would end soon and no one would notice her, but the roof turned out to be terribly long. At first it was pointed, but then it became flat and went on forever in all directions. Aglaya kept on running and running, and people began to appear, walking toward her, with rucksacks and suitcases, walking without stopping, a boundless crowd, but they were still looking at her, and she simply didn't know what to do; she had no clothes, and there was nothing to hide behind, no chimneys or other protuberances on the roof. Then she saw something in the distance and thought it must be a chimney, but it wasn't a chimney, it was a pedestal, and the inscription on the pedestal said I. V. STALIN, but L. I. Brezhnev was standing on it, alive and wearing the uniform of a generalissimo, with a standard that said TAKE BERLIN. She asked politely: "Did you take Berlin as well then?" He said: "But of course. Fedya Burdalakov and I took it together, the two of us." "I didn't know that," said Aglaya, "but where was Stalin?" "He was standing here." "And where is he now?" "Over there." She ran in the direction Brezhnev had pointed out to her. And she saw Stalin, or rather his back. He was walking along, lost in thought about something, without hurrying, and moving his feet as if he were kicking a ball along ahead of him. She knew there was danger lying in wait for him up ahead; she wanted to warn him, to avert it. She made a furious dash and suddenly slipped and fell to the ground, feeling quite amazed—hadn't she heard that lunatics never fell off roofs? First she felt amazed, then she felt frightened, and when she woke up, it was a long time before she realized where she was and what had happened to her.

It was still night outside and the moon was still shining, although it had slid a long way down toward the horizon. Aglaya switched on the bedside lamp, fumbled on the bedside locker to find her watch and looked at it. It was twenty minutes to six in the morning.

She no longer felt like sleeping, she could remember her dream very well and she began to wonder what a vision like that might mean. Then she remembered that today was December 21, the day of His birth, ninety years ago. Ninety years, she thought, that's a great age, but some people managed to reach it. Her aunt Elena Grigorievna had lived for ninety-six years, shallow and stupid, no good to anyone for anything. Why couldn't a man like him live to be at least a hundred? He would have had time to get so much more done.

She got dressed quickly and went downstairs to where the concierge Ekaterina Grigorievna, in thick wool tights lowered to her calves and felt slippers, was asleep on a narrow bench beside the desk with the telephone. Hearing a rustling on the stairs, the concierge instantly woke up, swung her feet down onto the floor and looked first of all at the tall clock standing by the entrance, then inquiringly at Aglaya.

"Good morning," said Aglaya.

"Morning," the concierge replied, abbreviating the phrase in accordance with the new fashion.

"Can you tell me when they bring the newspapers?" Aglaya asked.

Ekaterina Grigorievna looked at the clock again and stifled a yawn as she said: "They bring them about nine o'clock, why?"

"And does anyone," Aglaya asked, "have them earlier?"

"In the bo——" said the concierge, opening her mouth wide and covering it with her palm, " . . . sta——"—she shook her head—"ha . . . ll."

Aglaya was lucky. The kiosk at the boat station was already open, and the newspapers had just been brought in from the local printing works, where *Pravda* was printed from matrices delivered by plane. Aglaya bought a copy, which in addition to smelling of ink was still warm, as though it had come out of a baker's oven and not a printing press. Aglaya spotted an article on the bottom half of the front page, with a big headline, "On the 90th Anniversary of the Birth of I. V. Stalin," and immediately disliked something about it. Perhaps the fact that there was no portrait. Perhaps that it said "the Birth of I. V. Stalin" and not "of Comrade I. V. Stalin." She desperately wanted to read the article on the spot, but she realized that she'd forgotten her glasses, and without them her sight could only cope with big letters. She went running back to the hotel.

The concierge had already tidied away her bed and was sitting under the lamp by the phone.

"Did you get a newspaper?" she asked politely.

"Yes," Aglaya muttered, and climbed the stairs to her room, burning up with impatience.

What she read shook her perhaps even more than Baldie's speech at the Twentieth Congress. You could never have expected anything good from Baldie, but these people . . . They had started off so promisingly . . .

The article was no different from the ones printed in Baldie's time. Something for your side, something for ours. Certain services rendered were acknowledged, but from the very first lines they were clearly understated, and there were reservations: ". . . became actively involved in the revolutionary movement from the days of his youth . . . played an active part in setting up the newspapers *Zvezda* and *Pravda* . . . in directing the activity of the Bolsheviks, together with others, led the struggle against the Trotskyists and right opportunists . . ."

"Together with others," not "side by side with Lenin," not "one of the most important." And here in the second column was the shameless admission: "In its assessment of Stalin's activity the CPSU is guided by the decree of the Central Committee of the CPSU of June 30, 1956, 'On overcoming the cult of personality and its consequences.' "

After that it was one disappointment after another: "At the same time, Stalin committed theoretical and political mistakes which assumed an acute character in the final period of his life . . . Subsequently, he began gradually to deviate from Leninist principles . . . Cases of unjustified restrictions on democracy and gross violations of socialist legality, groundless repressions . . . he definitely miscalculated in assessing the likely timing of the attack . . . At its Twentieth Congress the Party exposed and condemned the personality cult. It has carried out an immense amount of work in order to restore . . ."

Aglaya was overwhelmed by a paroxysm of insane fury. She crumpled the newspaper, tore it into pieces, spat on them, flung the spittle-soaked paper onto the floor and trampled it underfoot. Then suddenly she froze, struck by a terrible thought: they had deliberately sent her here, lured her out of her own home especially in order to take Him away and fling Him out on the garbage heap, as they had all the other monuments to Him in all the other towns and cities of the Soviet Union. They had deliberately planted that general on her and he had entertained her and distracted her from her main goal.

"What a fool I am," she told herself, and repeating the word "fool, fool," she dashed to the telephone and asked the concierge to call her a taxi urgently.

It was still early, there wasn't much work and the car soon arrived. Aglaya carried her big suitcase downstairs, gave the concierge five rubles, said goodbye and set out for the station.

65

She was lucky enough to buy a ticket for a place in a sleeping compartment. At that time of year the train was almost empty, and she traveled from Sochi to Voronezh alone. Hers was the lower bunk, but she climbed onto the top one, hoping that no one would disturb her there. Although she lay there thinking all day long, she couldn't understand the current leadership. She even understood Baldie better. He'd wanted to make his career by denouncing the leader. He might even have been taking revenge on Stalin for old humiliations. He tried to win a cheap popularity with the people, attempted to please the West, but where were these people taking the cause? Why had they overthrown Khrushchev, promulgated ideological decrees, consolidated the regional Party committees, closed down the journals, repressed the dissidents . . .

At Voronezh an elderly man wearing the uniform of a railroad worker got into the compartment and traveled two stops down the line. He was replaced by two majors of the tank forces and a woman, the wife of one of them, who called her Doughnut. The officers immediately took out a bottle of vodka, and she took out a greasy roast chicken wrapped in newspaper. Doughnut's husband went down to see the conductor and brought back four tea glasses, and the other major looked up at Aglaya.

"I beg your pardon, lady, would you care to join us?"

"No thank you," said Aglaya, but then regretted it when she heard the glasses chinking and the chicken crunching as they broke it. From the soldiers' conversation she gathered that they were serving in Czechoslovakia and, sticking her head down from the bunk, she inquired what the counterrevolution was getting up to there.

"How do you mean?" asked Doughnut's husband.

"What I mean is, is there strong anti-Soviet feeling among the Czechs?"

"Yes, there is," said the major.

"About the same as here," his comrade added.

"Tell me," she said, getting agitated, "what's the general feeling about Comrade Stalin in army circles?"

Everybody below was silent for a moment, and then Doughnut's husband said: "You know, lady, we have a rule—when we're drinking, we don't talk about politics."

"And even less when we're sober," the other major put in.

"But in general," said Doughnut's husband, "we Soviet officers support the domestic and foreign policy of the Party absolutely and completely."

The officers were clearly afraid to say what they thought, and Aglaya reflected sorrowfully on the condition to which the people had been reduced by the present-day leadership. Even serving officers were afraid to express their opinion. And she thought that serving officers had never been afraid to express their opinion before.

At night she dreamed that some people were dragging Stalin out of her flat to his grave and that Porosyaninov and Mikoyan were directing the removal. The vision was so terrible and so distressing that she groaned and cried out, just like the previous night in the hotel.

"What's wrong?" Doughnut asked her anxiously. "Are you in some kind of pain?"

"No, no," she mumbled, and immediately cried out again when she dreamed of Him lying on the municipal dump, alive.

When she reached Dolgov, she waved down a dump truck at the station and rode home for a ruble. She ran up the stairs, almost knocking Shubkin off his feet as he made his way downstairs, whistling his beloved "Brigantine."

Her hand was shaking; the key wouldn't go into the keyhole. Eventually, she managed to turn the lock, pushed open the door, dropped her suitcase on the threshold and dashed into the sitting room . . .

He was standing in his place, with his shoulders slumped sadly and covered in dust, finally admitting his defeat.

"Comrade Stalin!" said Aglaya, falling on her knees before him.

She embraced his iron legs in her arms and pressed her wet cheek against them. Then she either fell asleep or her mind simply tuned into a different reality, but she saw a clear vision of that sunny day, October 29, 1941. It must have been the final fling of a long, lingering Indian summer. A day like that ought to have been quiet and peaceful, but it wasn't. Advance German units had moved right up to Dolgov, and the frequent rifle shots, bursts of machine-gun fire and occasional detonations of artillery shells could be heard only too clearly. Some of them had hit their mark. The railroad station and the grain elevator were burning, and the lacquer and paint factory was blazing furiously. The smoke from this flame, a mixture of unusual, poisonous colors—blue, green, yellow and crimson—first rose a little into the air, then twisted and stretched out into a long, vicious stripe above the eastern outskirts of the town. But the people Aglaya had seen as she walked along were behaving as though they hadn't seen or heard a thing. At the water standpipe there was a short queue of people with buckets and yokes for carrying them. In one of the yards a pregnant woman in a red blouse was hanging her washing out on the line and two teenagers were playing soccer in front of the gates, booting a tin can about for lack of a ball. Aglaya found the sight of all this strange, but she had no time for feeling surprised. She walked unhurriedly along Poperechno-Pochtamtskaya Street without really looking around her much, chewing on an extinguished a cigarette as she pushed a handcart with two bicycle wheels ahead of her like a child's perambulator. Laid out neatly on the trolley were about twenty bundles each about the size of a brick, wrapped in newspaper and tied up with string, a tractor engine battery, two field telephone sets, a reel of thin cable and another with cable a bit thicker.

As she was walking past the prison, Aglaya's attention was caught by a short citizen of indeterminate age who hadn't washed or shaved in a long time, wearing a tattered undershirt with nothing underneath it. The man was not alone—he had a piebald shorthorn cow with him, which he was leading on a long rope. The man seemed familiar to Aglaya, and when she looked closer, she recognized him as her own husband, Andrei Eremeevich Revkin, who had been arrested by the NKVD a few days before the war for getting politically immature ideas into his head. As though she weren't surprised to see him there, Aglaya didn't say hello; she asked: "What are you up to, have you escaped from jail?"

"Eh?" he asked, showing no surprise either and not understanding what was going on.

Aglaya repeated her question.

"No," he said. "The guards ran off and I just walked away."

"What's the cow for?"

"It was in the same cell as me."

"A cow?" This time Aglaya was surprised. "What was she in jail for?"

"For nothing," said Revkin. "Just for being a cow. The prison manager took her off someone and hid her in the jail to milk her."

"Okay," said Aglaya. "Dump her and come with me."

Revkin obeyed immediately. It was all the same to him where he went and what he did.

Now they pushed the handcart along together. Not knowing where it ought to go, the cow plodded along behind them, dragging its rope in the dust. Until a skinny old crone, who had evidently realized the cow didn't belong to anyone, came dashing out of her hut and dragged the cow back home with her. On the way Aglaya explained to Andrei Eremeevich that the regional committee, which had gone underground, had given orders for the Dolgov power station to be blown up immediately. The newspaper bundles were dynamite. The two mine layers sent with the explosive had run off, but before they went, they had explained to Aglaya how to assemble these pieces into an infernal device and how to detonate it.

A few minutes later Aglaya and Andrei trundled the handcart onto the grounds of the power station, which was not operating and was quite unguarded. They carried the battery into the checkpoint office and left one telephone there. Then they pushed the rest of their load to the main power unit, which contained the biggest generator.

"Stop!" said Aglaya. "Take some bundles and let's go. But be careful, it's dynamite."

It was quiet and cold in the generator hall, with a smell of damp and machine oil. Nothing was working and the hands of all the instruments stood at zero. While Revkin was bringing through the bundles, Aglaya carried in the second telephone and rolled in the drum with thick cable, immediately reeling out several meters. Then she took two bundles of dynamite and crawled in under the body of the main generator on all fours. As she was crawling out of there in the same position, her skirt snagged on a bolt and rode up, exposing her skinny backside in long, wrinkled lettuce-green pants. This sight proved too strong a temptation for Revkin to resist, and he gave her a hard kick, losing his shoe in the process.

Aglaya fell flat on her belly and immediately crawled out and fixed her husband with a stare of incomprehension. He picked up his shoe and stood there in front of her, smiling.

"What's wrong with you," she asked quietly. "Did you eat a daisy, or are you just plain crazy?"

He didn't reply, just smiled beatifically.

"Idiot," she said, scratching her buttock. "What kind of stupid joke is that? I'm carrying dynamite."

He seemed completely out of it, and she asked him if he understood where he was and if he could do what she was going to ask him to do. He nodded as though he understood, and she explained where to set the remaining charges, how to connect them with the thin wire and how to wind the thin wire onto the ends of the cable.

"I'll be waiting in the checkpoint office," she said. "When it's all finished, call me on this phone and then leave immediately. Exactly two minutes later"—she took a man's pocket watch out of her leather jacket— "I'll touch the ends together. We'll meet at Miliagi's grave on the Square of the Fallen Warriors. Do you understand?"

"Yes, yes, I understand," Revkin said with a nod.

"All right then." She put the watch in her pocket, gave her husband another curious glance and began rolling the drum in the direction of the checkpoint, unreeling cable as she went.

The office of the power station's head of security was a spacious room with windows on three sides, and the wall spaces between the windows were decorated with posters, diagrams and two portraits: Stalin lighting up his pipe and Lenin bending over the national electrification plan, GOELRO. The head of security's desk was empty except for a marble inkwell with dried-up ink and a small electric hot plate with a big kettle with some of its enamel chipped away. Aglaya set the battery down beside the hot plate and attached one end of the cable to the positive terminal, bending the other end as far as possible away from the negative terminal. The kettle contained water that wasn't showing any signs of turning stagnant yet. Aglaya remembered she had two stale honey cakes in her pocket (she'd picked them up on her way out of the house) and thought now would be just the right moment to have a drink, at least of hot water. She switched on the hot plate and began waiting for the spiral to heat up. But the spiral didn't heat up, and Aglaya, remembering that there was nothing to make it heat up, set about lighting the iron stove. Somewhere in the distance she heard the faint sounds of machine-gun and small-arms fire, but they mingled with the crackling of the firewood in the stove and didn't give her the slightest sense of any danger.

In the checkpoint office Aglaya found not only an iron drinking dipper, but even a packet of tea in the drawer of the desk and a piece of halva in gray, oil-stained paper. After she had arranged a tea party fit for a king, she looked out of the window at the dusty street, where there was a goat lying under a fence to which it was tethered and chickens were wandering about not concerned in the least about the distant gunfire. The idiotic thought came to her that those chickens probably couldn't care less who held power here—Soviets, Russians or Germans. Men would come from a different country, wearing a different uniform, introduce different ways of doing things, raise different flags, put up different portraits, erect gallows for the communists, and the chickens would carry on rummaging in the dirt, laying eggs and clucking idiotically. She was suddenly overcome by such a strong feeling of hate for those brainless chickens that if she'd had a machine gun she would have finished them all off there and then. But this feeling passed as abruptly as it had appeared: whatever faults Aglaya may have had, even she realized it was stupid and ridiculous to hate such innocent creatures.

Aglaya took the watch out of her pocket. Forty minutes had passed since she left her husband at the main generator, and he still hadn't given any signal.

The sounds of gunfire were less frequent now, but closer.

In former times Aglaya would never have doubted her husband for a second, but now she was rather worried: what was he doing over there, with his damaged mind, and was he doing anything at all? Aglaya twirled the handle of the telephone set. There was no answer. She began trying to make a roll-up and noticed that her hands were shaking badly, the makhorka was spilling and she couldn't put together a cigarette.

At the end of the street a cloud of dust rose into the air, gave out a chirring sound and began advancing rapidly toward the power station. The chickens scattered and ran, but the goat tethered to the fence didn't even stir, as though realizing its position was hopeless. As it drew close to the station, the cloud resolved itself into a column of heavy motorcycles driving two abreast, each carrying three motorcycle troops in dusty leather jackets and goggles, their faces blackened by dust, looking like some demonic force that nothing could ever stop.

As soon as they drove in through the wide-open gates, the motorcycle at the front on the right drove off to one side and stopped, and the two passengers who leapt out of it pointed their short submachine guns at the checkpoint, while the third soldier, a tall man, began waving with his arm to hurry on the rest as they rode into the station grounds.

And just then the telephone standing on the desk in front of Aglaya gave a tranquil, feeble tinkle, and Aglaya heard her husband's voice.

"I've done everything," said Andrei Eremeevich Revkin.

"Did you position the charges the way I told you?" In her right hand Aglaya was holding a half-eaten honey cake; with her left she picked up the end of the cable that was not yet connected to the battery.

"I set them all," Revkin confirmed.

The final motorcycle drove in through the gates and stopped with the others. The three members of its crew went up to the men who had arrived earlier and all six of them, their faces black with dust and soot, set off toward the checkpoint. The tall one, walking in front, took off his goggles and his peaked cap and turned out to be a bright straw blond. Aglaya spotted some little cubes and the letters SS drawn in two sinister zigzag lines on the tabs of his collar.

"And did you connect up the wires?" Aglaya continued with her questions, surprised herself that she felt no fear as the conclusion approached.

"Yes, I've done everything the way you said."

Clattering their heels, the Germans walked up onto the porch, and the tall blond man took hold of the door handle.

"The motherland will not forget you!" Aglaya shouted down the phone, and touched the end of the cable to the negative terminal.

At first everything was like a silent movie. The roof of the power station shattered and flew up into the air in pieces. On the crest of the column of flame that shot upward, above all the other objects, an empty metal barrel performed joyful somersaults as it soared up into the sky. The barrel had still not reached its highest point when an incredible force bent the trees over, tore one of the iron gates off its hinges and blasted the Germans off the porch that they had climbed onto.

Aglaya dived under the table just in time to protect herself from the shards of glass that flew into the room as if they'd been shot from a canon.

PART FOUR

SOMNAMBULISM

66

The following is an excerpt from the *Concise Medical Encyclopedia:*

"**Somnambulism** (from the Latin *somnus* — "sleep" and *ambulare* — to walk); also pop. *lunacy* or *sleepwalking:* a distinctive form of disturbance of sleep, during which those who suffer from this disorder involuntarily perform a number of sequential, frequently common, everyday actions without completely waking; they rearrange items that come to hand, move objects from place to place, clean and tidy a room, get dressed, wander about, etc. When they wake up, they have no memory of the actions they have carried out. This disorder arises in connection with a number of illnesses — psychopathy, epilepsy, trauma of the brain and severe nervous shock. Stories about the exceptional feats performed by lunatics (walking along the cornices of tall buildings and so forth) are apocryphal.

Somnambulism, or something like it. That was the condition in which Aglaya Stepanovna Revkina lived for about twenty years. After the sanatorium something snapped inside her, and she stopped taking any interest in events, people, herself or her lodger. She stopped running and started drinking. She never fully went to sleep and never fully woke up; she performed mechanical actions. She got up, smoked, washed (not always), drank tea, cleaned and tidied the room (rarely), went to the shop, bought a quarter-liter bottle and a bite to eat, came back, drank (not a lot) and ate (a bit). She completely stopped taking care of her lodger and carried on without paying any attention to him, as though he was an old man she had lived a lifetime with and there was nothing left to talk about, it had all been said many times over. She abandoned all hope of dancing on her street. She stopped studying *The Foundations of Leninism* and didn't read any other books. She switched the television on every now and again, but every time only made her even more convinced that there was nothing interesting to watch: nothing but Party congresses, ice-hockey matches, figure skating, parades on the Seventh of November and First of May and Brezhnev's birthday.

Soviet life was not distinguished by any great variety. Anybody who traveled around the country saw the same thing at all the stops along the railroad track: the words GLORY TO THE CPSU laid out in red stones. Or it might be PEACE TO THE WORLD. In the cities the main buildings were adorned with portraits of members of the Politburo of the Central Committee of the CPSU and banners all bearing the same words: THE PEOPLE AND THE PARTY ARE ONE. In absolutely every movie theater in the country, Lenin's words were written in white on a red banner hung above the screen: OF ALL THE ARTS FOR US CINEMA IS THE MOST IMPORTANT. And every post office in the Soviet Union was adorned with another quotation from Vladimir Ilich: SOCIALISM WITHOUT THE POST AND THE TELEGRAPH IS A TOTALLY EMPTY PHRASE, while not a single power station or electricity substation was lacking an aphorism from the same author: COMMUNISM IS SOVIET POWER PLUS THE ELECTRIFICATION OF THE WHOLE COUNTRY.

The life lived by Soviet people was boring in any case, but in those years it stood completely still. That was the way it was for many people, but for Aglaya it was particularly bad. She remembered the things that passed in front of her eyes in isolated patches, without any connection or chronology. A short summer, a long fall, a severe winter, and in winter all sorts of ailments due to lack of vitamins, old age and alcoholism.

In the department store an old woman was crushed to death in the queue for washing powder. Either before or after that there was a solar eclipse. Once a letter came from Marat in London. But when and what it was about she couldn't remember. There were two memories connected with Shubkin. Shubkin got baptized and Shubkin went to Israel. A description of the period from the early seventies till almost the mid-nineties based only on what Aglaya noticed and remembered would have fitted into a single page with plenty of space to spare. But we have the testimony of other people who were there during that period not far away from Aglaya, and the narrator himself also witnessed a thing or two.

67

Shubkin was christened at home by Aglaya's former neighbor, Father Yegor's son, himself a priest by the name of Father Dionisii, who had been known in his childhood as Deniska. Later, people couldn't get used to any other name, and they started calling him Father Deniska, and then Father Rediska, or Radish, an alias that was reinforced by the color, acquired over time, of the priest's nose. Father Radish was also regarded as a dissident in Dolgov after he committed an act of petty hooliganism. The local Party authorities closed down the city's only church, SS. Kozma and Damian, and Radish protested their action in an indecent fashion, namely: while under the baleful influence of alcohol and wearing his cassock, in broad daylight he urinated from the bell tower onto the Party's representative for religious affairs, Comrade Shikodanov, for which the local authorities jailed him for ten days and the clerical authorities defrocked him. The elders of the church accused him of paying scant attention to the official canons and arranging the liturgy, the order of service and his sermons to suit his own ideas, introducing far too much original material in the process.

Refusing to acknowledge the legality of his defrocking, the priest continued to provide his flock with unofficial spiritual nourishment, transgressing all the canons and working either in his own home or on call: he christened people, married them, gave them communion and buried them, and he blessed water, Easter cakes, property and real estate.

I happened by chance to be present at Shubkin's christening. It must have been some time in the mid-seventies. There was some book or other I had to return—I think it was Djilas—he'd given it to me to read, as always, for a single night. That morning I stuffed the book inside my jacket and set out for Shubkin's place. To tell the truth, I was feeling a little cowardly. I knew Shubkin's house was kept under close and not even very secret observation, and note was made of every person who went in and came out. You could even be stopped. What if they stopped me and found the book? What would I say then? That I just happened to find it somewhere on the street? That someone had planted it on me? Probably, I'd say I was just on my way to bring it in to you, to the KGB. In short, I was afraid, but I went anyway. I climbed up to the second floor and gave the special knock: *tap-tap* and then *tap-tap-tap* and then *tap* once again. Antonina opened the door wearing a bright flowery pinafore and holding a large mug in her left hand. When she saw me, she put a finger to her lips and whispered: "Mark Semyonovich is getting baptized."

"Then I'll come some other time," I said.

"My dear fellow, what are you whispering about out there?" I heard Shubkin's cheerful voice say. "Come here! Don't be afraid."

I went into the room.

At this point we really can't manage without at least a brief description of Shubkin's abode. During his period in residence the room had been transformed into an incredible spectacle. All four walls were covered from floor to ceiling with crudely cobbled together shelving, and the shelves were crammed with books. On top of the books standing vertically there were books lying flat. Papers, manuscripts, letters and yellowed newspapers were also dumped in the same space. But not everything fitted onto the shelves, so there were also piles, mounds and drifts of books, old newspapers and other papers heaped up on the floor under the shelves. Books and papers covered half of the room's only window. Mention should also be made of the photographs: a great number of snapshots of Shubkin himself, Antonina, their friends and acquaintances. Shubkin had so many friends and acquaintances that of course I couldn't know them all, but they included the Admiral and Raspadov and Sveta Zhurkina, and even me in several different versions. But the most interesting part of this permanent exhibition of photography was the section of idols, the contents of which had changed radically since I first got to know Shubkin. It had changed earlier too, but slowly. I remember Shubkin's portrait collection including Lenin, Marx, Dzerzhinsky, Pushkin, Tolstoy, Gorky and Mayakovsky. Then Gorky was replaced by Hemingway and Mayakovsky by Pasternak. At one time the exhibition had been graced by the presence of Ho Chi Minh, Fidel Castro and Che Guevara. Now all of the above had disappeared and their places on the shelves had been taken by cheap icons and portraits of Sakharov, Solzhenitsyn, Father Pavel Florensky and Father Ioann Kronstadtsky.

On entering Shubkin's room I discovered Shubkin himself looking very strange. The only clothes he had on were a pair of long drawers with the legs rolled up, held in place by a soldier's belt with a brass buckle-badge. He was standing barefoot in a large enameled basin of water and bustling about beside him was Father Radish, still quite young at the time, but already slovenly and unwashed, his matted beard containing a cockroach that had dried into it forever. The cockroach might possibly be a trick of the memory; it's hard to imagine that, even if the cockroach were not combed out, it would not have simply fallen off at some time. But the way I remember things, it was an ever-present feature of Father Radish's beard.

As I describe Father Radish, I can just anticipate the accusations of hostility, even blasphemy. I know people will say that I hold nothing sacred, that I am ridiculing faith and the church and portraying all clergymen in the image of Father Radish. Let me say immediately that this is not so. I am not in the habit of mocking faith and the church; in general, I regard clergymen with respect and in the image of Father Radish I am portraying no one but Father Radish—him personally, alone and unique of his kind. I have met many other priests, and they were all distinguished by their exceptional cleanliness. They washed, brushed their teeth and combed their beards every day, and they changed their clothes, washed them and had them dry-cleaned. But Father Radish was precisely as he is here, so what can I do about it?

And so I entered the room at the very beginning of the ceremony. Shubkin was standing in the basin of water facing the door. Radish was there beside him. I said hello to both of them and loitered in the doorway, slightly embarrassed and feeling that perhaps I was intruding on a private secret.

"Come in, dear fellow," said Shubkin in a loud, cheerful voice. "Don't be embarrassed. I'm not embarrassed. I'm ashamed of the way I used to be, but now I believe that I'm on the right road. Isn't that right, Father?"

"God only knows," the priest said absentmindedly. Then he surveyed me dubiously and asked: "Do you want to be the godfather?"

"Yes," I said.

"Then stand at the right hand of the baptizee."

"Only I'm not baptized," I warned him.

"Not baptized?" the priest echoed. "Then why are you so keen to be the godfather?"

"I'm not that keen. You asked if I wanted to and I said I did. But if it's not possible, then . . ."

"But of course it's not possible. I'm a Reformed Church man myself, I don't stick blindly to the canons, but having a godfather who hasn't been baptized, that's just . . . Perhaps we could do it like this: first we'll baptize you, and then you . . . But then—" He cut himself off short. "Okay. Do you have a compass?"

"A compass?" I asked in surprise. "On me? Here? What for? I'm in a town, not in the forest or out at sea."

"Yes, yes, I understand," the priest sighed. "The problem is that we have to stand the baptizee facing to the east, and we can't work out which way it is."

"Just a moment, Father," said the baptizee, "what do you mean 'we can't work out which way it is'? At nights here the Great Bear is visible in that corner of the window. The polestar's over there, so east is here . . ."

And with those words he turned to face the right-hand corner, from which precise spot the red spines of a multivolume edition of Lenin's works gazed out at him.

"All right," said the priest. "Now lower your hands and bow your head, you must appear meek."

He went up to Shubkin, removed his belt and flung it into the corner. Then he puckered up his lips and began blowing into his face. I don't know how Shubkin managed to stay on his feet, I was standing behind him and the smell of raw vodka made me feel queasy.

"Let us pray to the Lord!" the priest proclaimed, first crossing himself and then making the sign of the cross three times over the baptizee and beginning to sing in a thin, high-pitched voice: "In Thy name, O God of Truth and the name of Thine only begotten Son and Thy Holy Spirit, I lay my hand on Thy servant Mark, who has turned to Thy holy name and seeks refuge beneath the shelter of Thy wings. Antonina," said the priest, interrupting himself again, "why are you just standing there?"

"What should I do?" she asked.

"Pour water on his head."

"Just a moment," she said, and went dashing toward the door.

"Where are you going?" the priest shouted.

"For the water."

"Stupid woman!" the priest said angrily. "You have to take the water from the basin. Take it from his feet and pour it on his head. Everything returns to the place from whence it came. We come from dust and to dust we return. Water comes from water and returns to water. In this lies the secret meaning of our existence. Take some water, take it. Pour it in a thin stream."

And he began singing again: "Rid Mark of his former delusions, fill him with hope, faith and love, and let him comprehend that Thou art the only True God and with Thee Thine only begotten Son, our Lord Jesus Christ and Thy Holy Spirit."

Shubkin stood there in the water, quiet and submissive, with his hair and beard wet, in wet long drawers, shivering rapidly from the cold. Antonina took another mugful.

"That's enough for now," Radish said to Antonina, and turning toward Shubkin, he began speaking in a voice that was almost a bass: "Baptizee Servant of God Mark, do you acknowledge the erroneous nature of all your former faiths?"

"I do so acknowledge, Father," the baptizee confessed meekly.

"Do you renounce your illusions?"

"I do so renounce them."

"Then," said the priest, and suddenly his right hand was extended toward the shelves with the volumes of Lenin, and his voice rang out: "Behold the teaching of the devil which you did worship. Do you curse it?"

"I do curse it!" the baptizee replied resolutely.

"Blow on it and spit on it thrice."

Shubkin promptly jumped out of the basin and ran across to the collected works, leaving a wet trail on the floor, and began spitting at the books in the red binding, pulling them out and throwing them onto the floor, growling like a dog as he did so. The priest ran over to Shubkin and also began throwing books on the floor, intoning: "O thou Satan, O devil, enemy of our Lord Jesus Christ, our true God, I adjure thee, brazen spirit, foul, unclean, loathsome and alien evil one, by the power of Jesus Christ I adjure thee: come out of this man, now, immediately and forever, and enter into him no more."

At this point a portrait of Lenin that Shubkin had obviously hidden away earlier flew out from somewhere behind the books and fell on the floor faceup. It was in a wooden frame and covered with glass but, strangely enough, the glass didn't break. Vladimir Ilich Lenin with a red ribbon in his buttonhole squinted out from under a hand raised to the peak of his cap, peering with a benign smile at Shubkin and all the rest of us involved in such strange goings-on.

At the first sight of that face Father Radish was dumbfounded and bewildered, but he immediately recovered his wits, reached out a hand with the index finger extended toward the portrait and began shouting hysterically: "Behold the Antichrist, repulsive, most loathsome and most putrid!" He stepped on the portrait and began stamping on it in a frenzy, spitting and intoning: "Be gone, spawn of darkness, cunning fisher for erring souls!" The priest was wearing tarpaulin boots that evidently had metal tips. The glass crunched and shattered under his soles. "Why are you just standing there?" he snarled at Shubkin. "Spit on him, trample him!"

"I'm afraid, Father. I'm barefoot."

"Fear not!" shouted the priest. "Since you have believed, remember: not a hair shall fall from your head but by the will of God. Spit on him, trample him—and you shall come to no harm. Well?"

Shubkin, not as yet firmly established in his faith, stepped gingerly onto the portrait with his bare feet and, bending up his toes, began walking carefully across the glass, but seeing that it really didn't cut his feet and that his safety was guaranteed by Divine Power, he went wild and began jumping up and down and trampling the image that only recently had been so dear to him and spitting with even greater fury than Radish.

Meanwhile the priest ran in circles around the baptizee and shouted at the vanquished devil: "Get thee hence, paltry, squint-eyed demon, know the vanity of thy strength, that has no power even over swine. Remember the One Who set thy abode in a herd of swine and cast thee in the abyss together with them. I adjure thee by the saving agony of Jesus Christ, our Lord, and His terrible coming, for He shall come without delay to judge all the earth, and shall punish you and your attendant hosts in the fires of hell, and cast you out into the outer darkness, for the power and the glory are with Christ, our God, with the Father and the Holy Ghost, now and for ever, world without end. Amen."

After these words the priest sighed and calmed down for a moment. Shubkin stood beside him, tired after all the work he had done, but unharmed. Lenin's face, distorted under the shards of glass, now really did look like a satanic mask.

"Stand in the water again!" the priest said wearily.

Shubkin obeyed.

"Get out!"

Shubkin got out.

"Get in again. Repeat after me: 'I believe in the one God, the Almighty Father, Creator of heaven and earth and all things visible and invisible, and in Jesus Christ, the only begotten Son of God, born of the true God, of one essence with the Father and by Him was all created. He it was Who for the sake of mankind, in saving us, did come down from heaven as a man—born of the Holy Ghost and the Virgin Mary, He was made flesh and for us He was crucified. He suffered, was buried and rose again and now, ascended to heaven, He does sit at the right hand of the Father and shall come again in glory to judge the quick and the dead and His kingdom is for ever. And in the Holy Ghost, the Life-giving Lord emanating from the Father—together with the Father and the Son we bow down also before Him and glorify Him, Who did speak through the mouths of the prophets.' Say after me: 'I believe in the catholic apostolic Church, holy and unique, I acknowledge only one baptism for the forgiveness of sins and the resurrection of the dead, and I do long and hope for life in the hereafter. Amen.' "

The rite continued for a long time, concluding with the priest hanging a cross around the newly baptized believer's neck and dressing him in dry clothes. Then Antonina wiped the floor, rang out the wet drawers and put them on the radiator and carried the water out. After that we sat down at the table to celebrate the event. We drank some vodka, accompanied with fried potatoes and rissoles. Then we drank some more.

As we ate, the priest asked me if I would like to be baptized after all.

"All right," I replied evasively, "perhaps, someday."

"Look here, dear fellow," said my newly baptized host, "leave it too late and it'll be the worse for you. The devils will roast you in a frying pan. Won't they father?"

"They will," the priest confirmed.

"I don't think so," I said. "Of course, I'm up to my eyes in sin, but the devils ought to like that. They'll roast the ones they hate. The righteous."

68

Aglaya could remember almost nothing of that time. Shubkin's baptism took place without her being aware of it, but her memory did retain something of his departure. He knocked on her door, holding a bottle of some foreign beverage. She was amazed.

"You've come to see me?"

"That's right," said Shubkin, "I want to say goodbye. I'm going away."

She thought for a moment, then stepped aside and said in the familiar fashion she had once used to address him: "Come on in!"

She led him through to the kitchen and sat him down opposite her. He stood the bottle on the table and said: "It's calvados, apple vodka."

The only food she had to go with it were potatoes baked in their skins.

"Where to?" she asked. "America?"

"Israel."

"Yes?" she asked in surprise. "But how are you going to live there? They've got Arabs there. You must be afraid."

"That's one thing I didn't expect to hear from you—talk about being afraid," said Shubkin. "You're a partisan and a heroine."

"Ah!" said Aglaya with a wave of her hand. "I used to be a heroine. Out of stupidity. But I was fighting for the homeland. For the homeland and for Stalin . . ."

"Well, I'm doing the same," Shubkin joked. "For my historical homeland and Menachem Begin."

"A-ah!" said Aglaya. "If that's it, then of course. And I can see there are brave people among your nation too."

"Yes, there are a few," Shubkin agreed.

"Yes, yes," she said, nodding. "But everyone's always saying, 'The Jews, the Jews.' Why do they think like that? Maybe you need to think up a different name?"

"Okay then," said Shubkin, getting up. "I'll be going."

"Okay." As she saw Shubkin to the door, she suddenly said in amazement: "It seems odd even to me, but I've got used to you. I used to listen to that BBC of yours with you."

"Just a moment," he said.

He went out and came back with a Speedola radio and a book. He held the radio out to her.

"There. Take it."

"Oh no!" She was startled. "It's such an expensive thing."

"Never mind. And by the way, the radio's been adapted. It has other frequencies as well as the basic shortwaves. Sixteen and nineteen meters. You can listen to the BBC, Radio Liberty, Voice of America and Deutsche Welle. And this is my novel, *The Timber Camp.*"

She started reading it that very evening, but she didn't get beyond the Bolshevik who wheezed something about Lenin.

That evening there was a farewell party in Shubkin's room. The members of the Brigantine Literary Club and the Meyerhold Drama Club came, and with them Father Radish. They had a drink, held a prayer service and sang, "The Brigantine hoists its sails."

In the morning, when Shubkin and Antonina were piling themselves and their luggage into the taxi they had called, Aglaya came running down to them in her slippers. She gave Shubkin's hand a firm shake and surprised even herself by hugging Antonina and kissing her on the cheek.

When she saw that, Shurochka the Idiot thought she was imagining things.

69

Everyone who listened to the "voices of the enemy" that year knew that Shubkin's departure was the result of an ultimatum issued to him by our "organs." The Western radio stations interpreted this event as yet another success for the KGB in the struggle against dissent. They broadcast the details: who saw Shubkin off to Moscow's Sheremetievo-2 Airport and who met him at the airport in Vienna. But there wasn't a single word in the Soviet mass media. This was the new tactic—to keep mum about the dissidents, not kick up any fuss about them, not give them any free publicity. Naturally, our district press didn't print a word about Shubkin either. Then suddenly, about two or even three months later, when many people really had begun to forget Mark Semyonovich, the *Dolgov Pravda* unexpectedly came out with a swinging article entitled "Any Old Rags," in which Shubkin's entire biography was deliberately misrepresented. Supposedly born into a prosperous Jewish family (in actual fact Shubkin's father was a poor tailor), he was imbued with the ideas of Zionism from childhood. He joined the Party in order to undermine it from within. He committed a number of crimes against Soviet power but had eventually been magnanimously forgiven. He was offered the chance to reconsider his views and mend his ways, but, compelled by a morbid vanity, Shubkin had begun to court cheap fame beyond the bounds of the country that had raised him: He had written and published the libelous and worthless work *The Timber Camp* and attempted to sell it for as much money as possible. He had supplied the special services of the West with libelous material about the Soviet Union, for which his masters had paid him less in money than in secondhand clothes, things the Americans throw out with the garbage. Then came the finale, the event that the entire logic of his preceding life had been building up to. His shifting ideals led him to the betrayal of his homeland. And he himself had been tossed out onto the garbage dump like worn-out goods that were no longer of use. In the final analysis there was nothing unusual about the appearance of such an article. From time to time slanders against dissidents were printed in many of our newspapers and the *Dolgov Pravda* was no exception. No, it was not the appearance of the article that was surprising, but the name of the author—Vlad Raspadov. The same Raspadov whom Mark Semyonovich Shubkin had considered his best pupil. And who, by the way, had maintained relations with his teacher right up until his departure and helped to see him off. The entire Brigantine literary circle had said goodbye to Shubkin at the railroad station, and Raspadov had been there with the others.

Of course, the article evoked a strong response from the members of the Brigantine and the general public. Many people stopped saying hello to the author, and Sveta Zhurkina, whom Vlad had been courting, threw his book of poetry—*Touch*—back in his face. But there were others who didn't rush to break off relations with him, on the assumption that the article was the result of pressure applied to him by the organs. They said he had been summoned to Where He Needed to Go and threatened with a jail sentence for distributing anti-Soviet literature, specifically the novel

The Timber Camp. Then an even spicier rumor started doing the rounds: that Raspadov was actually gay and he had not only been Shubkin's pupil, but his lover as well. Shubkin himself, according to this account, was bisexual. Then one of the reasons for what Raspadov had done could have been that he was jealous of Shubkin's relationship with Antonina. If all this was true, then Raspadov could be absolved of blame, at least in part. You can imagine what a difficult situation he found himself in, what unpleasant consequences he was threatened with if he refused to speak out against Shubkin. And Shubkin himself was no longer under any kind of threat. He had already settled into life in a country where the authorities didn't read the *Dolgov Pravda*, and it almost certainly didn't even reach him.

Of course, we lived in difficult times back then. When civic passions boiled over, nobody forgave anybody, apart from themselves, for even the slightest weakness. But nonetheless, when I met Raspadov in the street, I didn't dash over to the other side and I didn't refuse to shake the hand held out to me. I didn't even ask him about anything, but he began talking aggressively, running Shubkin down, saying he'd acted with calculated cunning from the very beginning. He'd written his *Timber Camp*, created a sensation abroad and cleared off to his historical homeland, essentially betraying those of us who were left behind. In other words, Raspadov had redirected his conflict with Shubkin into a different channel. I realized that when he read me his poem "You and We," of which I can only remember the end:

> You could not care where you set up your home,
> Whose hand you feed from, you could not be bothered.
> You have a handy reserve aerodrome —
> Our reserve is the graveyard of our fathers.

He recited his opus, then asked what I thought of it.

"Well now," I said to him, "it's professional verse. It has regular meter and it rhymes in the right places."

He said: "You know I'm not asking you about that, but about the content."

"Well, the content is absolutely vile," I said. "You can feel any way you like about Shubkin, I'm no great admirer of him myself, but it's not all the same to him what food he eats, and his father's graveyard is in the same place as yours."

"What?" Raspadov shouted. "My parents, grandparents and great-grandparents are buried in Russia."

"And where are his grandparents and great-grandparents buried?" I asked.

"His?" Raspadov thought about it. "Then why do they [he didn't say who "they" were] leave?"

"They get a bellyful of poems like that and they go. And by the way, on the subject of food," I said to Vlad, "I don't know who eats what delicacies from whose hands, but I don't think we need to wonder any longer whose hand throws you your chaff to chew."

He never could forgive me for that phrase.

70

Man embarks upon old age unprepared. For as long as childhood, adolescence, youth and maturity last, man dwells on this earth with his own generation, with those who are a little older and a little younger than he is, as if they are all traveling together in one company. At school, at work, in the street, in a meeting, in a shop, in the bathhouse and the movie theater, by and large he always meets the same people — some he knows well, some he knows to say hello to and some he has simply seen somewhere at some time or other. And some are older than he is, some are younger, and yet others are just like him. A man can be imagined as walking along in the middle of a long column: there are still plenty of people ahead of him and people keep joining in behind. The man walks on and on, and suddenly he realizes that he has reached the front and there is no one left ahead of him. There are no more people who are twenty years older, ten years older, five years older, and even most of his contemporaries have died. And no matter which way he turns, everywhere he is the oldest. He looks back over his shoulder and there are many people who are younger, but they have grown up after the man glancing back had already stopped working; he has never associated with them and he doesn't know them.

And so it turns out that an old man, although he still has other people around him, is alone. Surrounded by the buzz of other people's lives. Other people's ways, passions, interests. And he doesn't even completely understand the way they speak. And the old man begins to feel as if he has been transported to a foreign country even though he has stayed put in the same place all his life.

Aglaya had lived in Dolgov all her life. The town had not changed especially fast, but gradually and inevitably it had become strange and unfamiliar to her. The people she could remember had disappeared. Shaleiko died of a stroke. Nechaev was killed in an automobile crash. Muravyova died in an insane asylum. Botviniev choked to death on a bone. The former public prosecutor, Strogii, was killed by convicts in a prison camp. Nechitailo died of lung cancer.

One old acquaintance she did happen to meet in the street one rainy day in fall, but didn't recognize immediately, was Porosyaninov. He had long hair and a fluffy gray beard, and he was dressed unusually for those parts—his body robed in a black cassock, white gym shoes on his feet, a ginger fur cap with earflaps on his head, and above his head an orange umbrella. He was clutching the umbrella in his right hand and holding up the hem of his cassock as he picked his way through the puddles.

"Have you joined the priesthood then?" she asked, amazed at such an unexpected metamorphosis.

"I serve as a deacon in the church," Pyotr Klimovich informed her.

"Been there long?"

"It'll be three years soon. Why, don't you go to church?"

"Not me," she said. "I'm an atheist. A nonbeliever."

"You are a believer," Porosyaninov objected. "You believe that God doesn't exist."

"And you believe that he does?" she asked mockingly.

"I believe," he said, failing to notice the mockery, "that it's not possible to live without faith in something. You're probably baptized, aren't you?"

"I should think so," she said. "Before the revolution my father was a churchwarden."

"Then come to church. Repent of your sins before God, and He'll take you back again."

"Leave me alone! I have my own God," she said, and walked away.

"What you've got is not God, it's the devil!" he shouted after her.

Aglaya would run through various names in her head, and no matter who she thought of, they were either no longer among the living or she'd completely lost track of them.

The grannies—Old Nadya and Greta the Greek—had died, but two other women neighbors had turned into old grannies and taken their place on the bench in front of the house, and there was no obvious difference between them and the previous ones. But there was no din generated by new generations echoing around the house, because the building was gradually emptying.

In the course of its existence it had grown extremely dilapidated and been declared unfit for human habitation, so no one new was moved in anymore. Those who had left had left. The others were ignored; they could live out the rest of their lives here. But there were no more housewarmings celebrated here. Eventually, of all the former residents the only ones left were Aglaya, the two old grannies already mentioned, Shurochka the Idiot with all her eternal cats and Valentina Zhukova and her grandson Vanka. By this time Valentina was already Granny Valya to many people and her grandson abbreviated this name, calling her Gravalya.

71

Everybody called Vanka Zhukov Vanka Zhukov. It was his real name and at the same time a nickname. Had it not been for Chekhov's famous story "The Letter," Vanka would simply have been called Vanka. Or simply Ivan. Or simply Zhukov. Or simply Zhuk. But since Chekhov had a story about a Vanka Zhukov, and a very well-known story at that, and since Vanka Zhukov lived in a society in which people still read books and remembered them, and actually studied Chekhov in school, that was what Vanka Zhukov was called by many people—Vanka Zhukov. And nothing else.

Gravalya doted on Vanka. She had never paid her own son half as much attention. Because when she had a little son, she was still young and stupid. And she wanted to have a bit of fun herself. Go to the movies. Or an amateur concert. Or have a gossip with a neighbor. Or pass the time with a man. Perhaps that was why Georgii had grown up such a good-for-nothing. But she watched over Vanka with bated breath and was constantly amazed.

"I can't imagine," Gravalya used to say to Aglaya, "who it is he takes after. I was a good-for-nothing, my son was a wastrel, my son's wife was an alcoholic, but look at him . . . Thirteen years old and he still doesn't drink or smoke, and he's a star pupil in school."

Even at that stage Vanka was most interested in the exact sciences—mathematics, physics and chemistry—and he attended meetings of the model-airplane hobby group and the Young Chemist Club. With his own hands he made models of airplanes, ships and locomotives; he built a radio receiver and a tape deck. He engrossed himself in articles about the possibility of melting the Arctic and Antarctic ice caps and reversing the direction of major rivers by means of controlled explosions.

Of course, in his history and sociology classes in school, they tried to beat something into his head about socialism, communism, the CPSU and the struggle for peace, and they forced him to study Brezhnev's biography, but that all made no impression on him at all.

Vanka didn't hang around with hooligans, but they had begun to pay attention to him. He was small and weak, exactly the kind that made a safe and easy target. One day the hooligans met him in the waste lot when he was coming home from school. There were ten or twelve of them; their leader was a lanky kid by the name of Igor, and his surname was Krysha, meaning "Roof." It was no nickname, but strangely enough it suited him very well. With his short-cropped hair, sloping crown and low forehead he did have a certain resemblance to a single-pitch roof. Roof was distinguished from his peers and gang comrades by the fact that he wore a good suit and a tie and from a distance he looked like a cultured young man. Roof and his gang were fairly well known in town, where they were regarded as genuine bandits, and so Vanka was not afraid of them, believing he was too insignificant a person to be of any great interest to bandits. But he was not entirely right. He was not of any great interest to the bandits, but they never passed up anything that was even slightly interesting.

So on this day they met him in the waste lot and began pushing him about, but Roof immediately stopped them and asked Vanka a question.

"Where are you headed, sonny?" he asked, being no more than six years Vanka's senior himself.

"I'm going home," said Vanka, not suspecting a thing.

"Where from?"

"From school."

"Aha," said Roof thoughtfully. "Now you're going home from school, and tomorrow you'll go to school from home. Right?"

"Right," Vanka agreed.

"Have you ever been in America?" asked Roof.

Vanka confessed that he hadn't.

"Well now, over in America," Roof explained to him, "you have to pay to use all the roads. We ought to introduce the same system here. Have you got any money?"

Vanka said he hadn't. Roof announced that now there would be a customs inspection. They hemmed Vanka in, turned out his pockets and found a three-ruble note, as well as about a ruble in change.

"That's not good," said the Roof, counting the money again. "That's already fraud and attempted importation of currency without payment of customs duty. So this is subject to confiscation." And he put the money in his pocket. "And now," he said, "we'll check what you have in there." He pointed at the briefcase. "Open it please."

Vanka did as he was told. There was nothing in the briefcase that interested Roof, apart from a Parker ballpoint pen in a mother-of-pearl case. Gravalya had bought the pen at a flea market and given it to Vanka for his thirteenth birthday. Roof tried the pen on his own wrist to see how it wrote and declared that it was confiscated as foreign goods illegally imported into the country. After that Roof and his hoodlums began meeting Vanka regularly and relieving him of the ruble Gravalya had given him for exercise books, or the scarf she had knitted him for New Year, or the cap—genuine lambskin—that had belonged to his father. Vanka tried changing his route, but the bandits commanded by Roof trailed him, intercepted him and once beat him very badly. Gravalya noticed Vanka had a black eye and asked him what it meant. Vanka said he'd been running down the corridor at school when he tripped and bumped into something metal. Gravalya inquired where his pen, scarf, cap and a few other things had gone to. Vanka gave her some unintelligible answer, but of course he didn't tell her the truth. And she didn't actually press him too hard. She was the yard-keeper and she knew what went on in the neighborhood. And she knew Roof. One day Gravalya spotted Roof down by the delicatessen, and he was wearing Vanka's cap and scarf. Roof was standing there, surrounded by his little runts and lanky brutes—his thugs, as people called both groups. Everyone was afraid of them and gave them a wide berth.

Gravalya strode briskly toward the crowd of them. When two blocked her way, she tossed them roughly aside. She grabbed hold of Roof's scarf.

"Where did you get that?"

"You flipped your lid or something, Granny?" Roof asked in surprise, and the gang began closing in around the old woman.

"Take your hands off, Granny," said Roof. "I respect old people, but even so—"

He didn't finish. Gravalya let go of the scarf, grabbed hold of both of Roof's ears, pulled down hard and put her knee in the way of his face.

"Boys!" the Roof roared, streaming blood.

The boys immediately moved in and, of course, the first was Roof's closest friend Tolik, nicknamed the Ax. He'd already reached out his hand and spread his fingers to grab the old woman's face when he received a blow to the solar plexus that doubled him over and dropped him to the ground, gasping for air like a fish. The gang leader's second-best friend Valya Dolin, nicknamed Validol, advanced on the old woman from the other side. She turned to face him in time and he retreated, setting a good example to the others. Having increased the distance between themselves and the granny, the others stood in a semicircle, not knowing what to do. But the granny grabbed the back of Roof's neck with her left hand, squeezed it in her powerful, crooked fingers, clenched her right hand into a fist and raised it to his nose. Reciting as she did so a tirade consisting of lexical items not all of which were even in Roof's vocabulary. If the old woman's speech were translated into literary language and the gist isolated, one could say that it contained a warning to the effect that the person of Ivan Zhukov was inviolable, and anyone who chose to disregard this would face irrevocable and severe retribution. Following which Vanka went to school in his own cap, in his own scarf, with his own pen and without paying any customs fees, annexations, contributions or reparations. If Roof happened to encounter Vanka, he was the first to acknowledge him with a wave of the hand and the respectful greeting: "Hi there, Vanka lad!"

And when Vanka became friends with his classmate Sanka Zherdyk, the guarantee of personal inviolability was extended to him too. Although before the friendship, anybody who happened to feel like it used to beat Sanka Zherdyk hard and often.

72

We introduce Sanka Zherdyk into the narrative at this point since he has also been allotted a role of some significance in our story. Sanka Zherdyk and Vanka Zhukov became friends quickly and easily, because children in general make friends easily, particularly if they study in the same class and especially if they sit at the same desk. But by nature they were very different people from the very beginning. In contrast with Vanka, Zherdyk was suited by character for the humanities. It was as if there were two people living inside him. The first sought fulfillment in art. He sang in a choir and wanted to be an opera singer. He knew a lot of arias, but there was one he could sing better than any other: the Duke's song from the opera *Rigoletto*, that well-known and popular piece "La donna è mobile." Maybe he suffered from some kind of mania, but in any case, beginning from his schooldays he would sing this song all the time, everywhere. At amateur concerts, at parties and for no reason, just for himself. He also dreamed of being a poet, and when he was still in school, he composed quite tolerable verse with a bias toward the romantic. In his poems he dreamed of love, believed in the affinity of souls, appealed to people not to close their hearts, not to lock their doors at night, not to build walls, not to hoard money in money boxes and not to hoard it at all, not to concern themselves with material things, not to resign themselves to evil, not to cherish their own lives, but hand out free flowers and love to all and sundry. But in life Zherdyk would have no truck with romanticism of any kind and harbored the worst possible suspicions of everybody.

Maybe the origins of this contradictory character lay in his biography. At one time, like everybody else, he had a father and mother. And of course, like most normal children, he had thought the world of his parents. Then they had separated. But his father didn't simply leave his mother, the way it often happens; he fled to the north, switched addresses and dodged out of paying alimony—that is, he refused to support his son. His mother and he both struggled along on her miserable salary as a book-keeper in some office. Sanka had loved his father and believed in him more than in anybody else, and the realization that his father had betrayed him was the initial cause of his disenchantment with adults. The second blow he suffered was struck by his mother. No, she didn't betray him. But left without a husband, she started bringing lovers home. They lived in a single room in a communal apartment, and at the age of nine Sanka already knew what grown-ups get into bed for and what they do to each other in there. The conclusion he drew was that grown-ups were villains, bigots, hypocrites and lechers. The only thing they were interested in was "that," and nothing but "that." In the daytime they worked, spent time with each other, talked about something intelligent, but in reality all they were thinking about was "that," waiting impatiently for the hour when evening would come and the children would fall asleep. At first Sanka was so badly shaken by this discovery that he even contemplated suicide, but he settled for regarding grown-ups with contempt and derision. In school, when the teacher called him to the front of the class or the headmistress summoned him to the teachers' room and they put him through the mill, he laughed as he gazed at his tormentors and thought: I know how you're put together, what it is you're really looking for and what you do at night.

In their serious talks about life Sanka tried to convince Vanka that man is a base creature, venal, egotistical and hypocritical, motivated only by his own personal interests, or at most by his family's interests. And all the words spoken about goodness, love for one's neighbor and one's country, for truth and justice—that was just for public consumption.

Vanka and Sanka graduated from school together, Vanka with a gold medal and Zherdyk with a certificate full of basic passing grades. Vanka went on, without taking any entrance exams, to study at the Moscow Chemical and Technological Institute, but Zherdyk's start in life proved less auspicious. He tried to get into the Moscow Conservatory. At the entrance examination he sang the aria "La donna è mobile." The examiners liked the aria. They asked him to sing something else. But his something else didn't turn out quite so well, and they didn't give him a place. He didn't get through the competitive examination for the Literary Institute either. He entered the school of journalism. But although Vanka and Sanka were students in different colleges and lived at opposite ends of Moscow, that didn't put an end to their friendship.

73

In Moscow, Vanka found lodgings not far from his institute. He rented a room of six and a half square meters from Varvara Ilinichna, a thin old woman who reeked of tobacco smoke. She smoked savage cigarettes called Whiff, three packs a day, several times a day she drank strong tea with caramels, and from morning till night she typed something on her old Erika typewriter.

She turned out to be typing samizdat literature, which Vanka had heard about vaguely at some time or other, but he didn't know what it was. Now he found out that samizdat was texts, usually rather pale, typed out on tracing paper and distributed from hand to hand.

From time to time, modestly dressed, cultured-looking people would gather at the old woman's apartment and discuss human rights, articles of the Criminal Code, prisons, banishment, transit prisons, food supplies and BBC broadcasts. And also their acquaintances, who were either serving sentences in the camps or had been released, or had been released and emigrated. After some time Vanka realized that Varvara Ilinichna's guests and she herself were those very dissidents he'd read things about in the newspapers, always bad things, but had never been able to imagine that he would ever see them with his own eyes.

He used to think that dissidents were secret conspirators who always wore dark glasses and carried guns, actually hid underground in cellars or catacombs and used some device like a hectograph to print flyers with appeals to overthrow Soviet power. But now he'd seen for himself that they didn't hide from anyone, went about their business openly and gave the authorities every opportunity to catch them and put them in prison without any excessive difficulty or risk.

Sometimes in the evening the dissidents would organize a party, and someone would bring a bottle of vodka, someone else a piece of salami or a fancy cake, and the fare would be as unsophisticated as they were themselves. They argued about the fate of Russia, discussed various open letters, recited poems (usually bad, bombastic ones) on civic themes. Sometimes foreign correspondents showed up; they brought wine, whiskey or gin and tonic (that was when Vanka first got to know the taste of these foreign drinks) and took interviews for their agencies and newspapers. The dissidents answered the questions they were asked directly without trying to be cunning, talked about the situation in the country—acts of repression against dissidents, the suppression of national self-awareness, the oppression of the workers, the collective farms in which the peasants were kept by force and made to work without pay, the tyranny of the authorities and the police—in other words, about everything that was bad in the country and not about anything good, because in their opinion there wasn't anything good. And while they did this they ate, smoked and told jokes. The ones who were a bit younger made up to each other and hugged and kissed in the corridor; in fact, they seemed to live a normal life. But from time to time, one of them would be arrested again, put on trial, sent to a camp or a crazy farm, and the ones who remained at liberty would protest outside the court buildings, go to visit the exiles, collect money, clothes and food to support the families of the ones who were in prison.

From the very beginning of their acquaintance Varvara Ilinichna made no real attempt to hide what she was doing from Vanka, and almost immediately she began to give him her own retyped copies of works by Sakharov, Solzhenitsyn, Djilas and Avtorkhanov, as well as the regular numbers of the *Chronicle of Current Events*.

After he read all these things, Vanka began thinking for the first time about politics, about what Soviet power was, how many nations it had ruined and the goal it had done it for. Being of a technical turn of mind, Vanka decided to assist the development of samizdat in a concrete way. With a bit of thought and a bit of physical effort, he invented and manufactured the item that was later referred to in the case materials as the instrument of crime—a photocopying machine. A machine that was every bit as good as the similar machines of the famous firm Xerox. Perhaps even better. A light construction of stainless steel with winking lights of various colors, it rustled quietly as it printed off samizdat on ordinary paper in any quantity desired. It reduced or increased the size of text and if necessary sharpened its definition. And the samizdat writers no longer came to Varvara Ilinichna with their own texts and those of others; they came to Vanka Zhukov.

Whenever he met Zherdyk, Vanka used to tell his friend about the dissidents and his meetings with them. He supplied him with samizdat. Sanka read the samizdat eagerly and listened to Vanka's stories with interest, but he didn't share his enthusiasm for the dissidents, believing that most of them were merely promoting their own interests, making a name and a career for themselves. But even so, whenever he came to see Vanka, he used to ask if he had "anything else anti-Soviet."

And of course Vanka did. Because his machine was working away full speed ahead and producing samizdat a hundred or more copies at a time instead of five.

I hardly need to say there was no way Vanka's activity could have gone unnoticed. He was eventually arrested for what was called the manufacture and distribution of anti-Soviet literature in especially dangerous quantities. In Soviet times, of course, any quantity, even a quantity of only one copy, was dangerous. And Vanka had virtually an entire printing house.

Vanka was arrested. He spent two months in Moscow's Lefortovo jail, where the investigators promised him seven years of strict regime exile under Article 70 of the Criminal Code. But the organs received a letter from a group of professors and students. The authors requested mitigation of the imminent sentence in view of the fact that Ivan Zhukov came from a simple working family, had been raised without any father or mother, was a gold medal–winner in school, possessed substantial knowledge in the field of the exact sciences as well as exceptional abilities as an inventor, and could still be of great service to our society. A famous electronics specialist and academician also wrote a plea in his own name, pointing out that Zhukov's copying machine was highly advanced and its performance parameters exceeded those of Western industrial models. In view of all these circumstances, Vanka was first reclassified from Article 70 to the less harsh Article 190 and then, going even further, it was decided to limit his punishment to exclusion from the Komsomol, expulsion from the institute and deprivation of his Moscow residence permit.

74

It would have been better if they'd jailed him.

As soon as Vanka arrived back in Dolgov, he was drafted into the army and sent off to a place where the return address was "Field Post" and letters bore the stamp "Inspected by the Military Censor." Vanka's first letter to Gravalya began with the words "Greetings from Afghanistan." The word "Greetings" and the word "from" had been left, but the third word had been thoroughly bleached out. But since the military censors were Soviet censors, which meant they were not exactly overzealous in performing their professional duties, the censor's inspection overlooked Vanka's account in the middle of the letter about how he was helping Afghani peasants to build roads and bring in the harvest. In actual fact, of course, Vanka was involved in work of a quite different nature. Bearing in mind his special education and interests, the army authorities posted him to a special unit that was effectively a small factory for producing explosive devices required for subversive activities.

Gravalya was unaware of these details, but rumors of the zinc coffins coming back from Afghanistan did reach her and she lived in a constant state of fearful anticipation. The sight of the postman made her clutch at her heart. She was right to be worried. The war was apparently already over and the last general had already crossed the bridge from Afghan to Soviet territory when a notification arrived stating that Ivan Zhukov had died the death of the brave while carrying out his international duty. Gravalya wept twice. The first time when the notification arrived and the second when they brought the zinc coffin.

But after she'd wept a bit, she demanded that the coffin be opened. She said she could feel in her heart that Vanka wasn't inside. They dismissed that out of hand, but they did explain patiently that the coffin could not be opened for fear of severe psychological trauma. The body was supposedly in such terrible condition that a single glance at it might trigger a heart attack or a nervous breakdown. Gravalya insisted, but they ignored her requests. Without the coffin being opened, the dead man was interred on the Avenue of Glory with music and full military honors, including a farewell salute of rattling machine-gun fire.

By the way, Sanka Zherdyk came down from Moscow for the funeral. He had already graduated from the school of journalism, but he was making his career in a different area—as the head of a department in some Komsomol district committee. He delivered a long speech over the coffin and spoke so touchingly about what a pure-hearted, honest and talented man his friend Vanka Zhukov was that everyone sobbed.

Into the ground above the grave they stuck a temporary sheet of plywood, on which it stated that here lay Ivan Zhukov, born 1964, who perished heroically in the course of a military mission.

But the people who had refused to allow Gravalya to open the coffin hadn't realized who they were dealing with. She dug the grave up herself at night and found the badly decomposed corpse of an elderly Eastern gentleman in a turban with a long beard down to his waist. Gravalya carried the coffin under her arm to the district committee of the CPSU and set it down on the porch. There was a lot of fuss about the case in the town. Some people regarded the old woman's actions as sacrilegious and demanded that she be punished in exemplary fashion. Others, in contrast, called her a heroic defender of human rights and even compared her with Mary Magdalene and Marfa Posadnitsa. Some people were encouraged by what had happened to hope that perhaps someone else had been buried by mistake instead of their children, and an epidemic of nocturnal grave digging swept through the district.

At this very time a letter arrived from Tashkent from Vanka Zhukov himself, although not written by his own hand, saying that he was alive but he had been blown up by a mine of his own construction and lost both legs, one arm and one eye, as well as all hearing in one ear, but might be able to hear with the other using a hearing aid.

Gravalya leapt up and down for joy. They told her: "Are you crazy? He's a total cripple now!" The old granny wouldn't listen: better a cripple than a corpse. But when Vanka arrived home (after spending more than a year lying in hospital) and she saw him on his improvised buggy with no legs, one arm and one eye, with a face turned blue all over by the gunpowder that had eaten its way into his skin and steel teeth set random and crooked in his mouth, Gravalya couldn't even cry; she simply fainted and didn't come around for several days. When she eventually did, she gazed at her grandson with bright, lucid eyes and said to him: "Never mind, Vanka, we'll get them for this."

If only someone had taken his granny's words seriously then.

75

Aglaya continued her somnambulistic existence: she lost track of the passage of time, she didn't know what had happened yesterday, what had happened five years ago and what was happening around her today. She only noticed specific, individual symptoms of global changes: vodka was sold starting from eleven o'clock, then from two o'clock, then from five o'clock, and then around the clock.

From time to time when she switched on the television, she would see the funeral of someone important on Red Square. One was being buried and another one was giving a speech. She closed her eyes and opened them again: now the one who had just been speaking was being buried and the one who was speaking was being supported under the arms. She closed her eyes, opened them and heard the words *perestroika* and *glasnost*. The screen showed meetings, banners, posters, the people chanting: "Boris! Boris!" Boris threw his Party card down on the table, fired a tank gun at the White House and market relations came into being. The postwoman arrived and brought her pension—three hundred thousand rubles. Aglaya thought: that's not bad! She was afraid to go out on the street with the big notes, so she collected together three rubles and sixty-two kopecks in small change, dashed to the shop for a bottle and they said to her: "Hey, Ma, are you in your right mind or what? Why? I'll tell you why! Vodka doesn't cost three rubles sixty-two kopecks, it costs twenty-five thousand rubles. Brought back down to reality, she felt scared. She bought vodka every day and she was used to shifting prices, but this time it was like her memory had totally misplaced several years. She ran home to get the money she needed, and on her way to the shop she called in to the district Party committee to find out when all this disorder was going to end. But at the spot where she expected to find the district committee, she found the Wheel of Fortune casino with the erotic show "Night Flight." She stopped a boy riding past on a bicycle and asked if he knew where the district committee of the CPSU had moved to. He asked her what corporation she meant, and when he couldn't understand her question a second time, he rode off. Then she met Gravalya in the street, who explained to her that in the last few years there had been a total restoration of capitalism. The CPSU had been disbanded. Lenin would soon be removed from the Mausoleum and the tsar's family would be buried with full honors in St. Petersburg. In Leningrad, Aglaya corrected her. But it turned out there was no more Leningrad; it was St. Petersburg.

Aglaya went out in the street, exchanged a privatization voucher for a bottle of vodka and withdrew into hibernation again.

76

In the middle of the nineties the company Fireworks Inc. was registered in Dolgov to manufacture Bengal fire, firecrackers, jumping crackers, skyrockets and other, similar goods.

The company was located in a semibasement apartment in house number 1-a on Komsomol Cul-de-Sac, and its personnel consisted of two people: Ivan Zhukov, the president, and Valentina Zhukova, the vice president and executive director.

Responsibilities were divided in a natural manner between the partners in the company. The president handled the creative side of the work and the vice president did everything else. Gravalya obtained the necessary materials and helped her grandson assemble all these things that they produced, while not neglecting her responsibilities as a nurse, which were considerable. In good weather she carried him outside "for an airing" and sat him, muffled in a rug, on the bench between the two old women. At home she washed him and in the early days put him on his potty. With time he learned to use the toilet, the washbasin and most things else for himself, and that was very important—now Gravalya could leave him on his own. And sometimes she had to leave him for a long time: to get some of the components for the products manufactured by the company, his granny had to "go riding," as she put it, as far as Moscow. She proved to be a very competent materials supply manager and fairly soon she built up an entire network of basic suppliers. She got some stuff from the blasters in the local stone quarry, something else from a sergeant she knew in the forces of the Ministry of the Interior who was in charge of a munitions depot, and she even bought some things at the pharmacy on Vanka's instructions.

When they set up their business, our entrepreneurs weren't counting on any great success; they expected the demand for their goods would be limited to the period between celebrations for the New Year according to the new and the old calendars. And at first that's how it was. But soon bigger customers appeared, customers for all seasons. Municipal authorities and then various organizations, large and small, began taking an interest in special effects for inclusion in their festive functions. Some "New Russians" wanted to mark their own birthdays and family events with multicolored fire and deafening thunder. And so Fireworks Inc. did pretty good business from the very beginning.

The living conditions of the partners also improved.

Until just recently Gravalya and Vanka had lived in a single semibasement room, but their neighbor had died, and the Zhukovs had been given permission to occupy the entire apartment. At long last. Before that, all the grandmother's efforts to improve their living conditions had come to nothing, which had only fed her thirst for vengeance. First she had been put on a waiting list that moved far too slowly. Then they told her that the quota for state apartments had expired along with Soviet power. Now, they said, we have capitalism and you can buy anything with money, even an apartment. Gravalya had tried to make the manager feel ashamed. She reminded him that Vanka was a Group One war invalid who lived on his pension. To which the manager replied: "It wasn't I who sent your grandson to Afghanistan." Next, she said that if she had a grenade at that moment she would set it off right there in that office without a second thought. And when she got home, she repeated the threat she had uttered once before: "Never mind, Vanka, we'll get them for this." And she said the same thing again when she rejected the one-room fourth-floor apartment they were offered without any elevator or balcony. But now, thank God, life was a bit easier. Now they at least had a separate apartment, even if it was in the semibasement. It was still a bit cramped, of course. Because everything was in there together: living space, workshop, materials store and product store. It was cramped, but life was manageable. Especially with the telephone that Vanka was actually given as a disabled war veteran. Which made his life richer and more varied. Especially after he acquired a computer and got hooked on the Internet.

77

Gravalya did everything for Vanka. She nursed him, washed him, washed his clothes, took him outside for his "airings" and even brought him home girls for money so he wouldn't miss out at least on that joy of life. At first Vanka felt ashamed of Gravalya's procurement activities, but later it stopped bothering him and one day he told her after supper: "I'm lucky I have you, Gravalya. With you I feel almost like a human being."

She nodded and sighed: "But you've still got to learn how to get along without me somehow. I'm going to die soon. How are you going to live without me?"

"There's no way I can," Vanka said, unconcerned. "When you die, I'll follow you. There's nothing to keep me here in this world on my own."

"Perish the thought!" said Gravalya with a sweep of her arm. "You're still young yet, you've got to live out your time."

"What for?" Vanka asked.

"Because," she said angrily. "If you've been given a life, then whatever state you're in, you've got to carry it through to the end."

"Who says I've got to?" he sighed.

"He does!" She pointed up at the ceiling.

"He does?" Vanka queried, growing angry himself. "Then tell me, why did he make my life like this? Why did he turn me into a helpless cripple? What did I ever do to him? Print samizdat?"

"Don't tempt God's mercy," Gravalya said in fright. "It was done to you by bad people, and we'll get them for it yet. God had nothing to do with it. God is merciful."

"No, Granny, I don't believe it. He's cruel. I remember when the spooks pounded us to pieces down in the Kandahar ravine and there were wounded men with their arms and legs torn off lying all around, men with their stomachs ripped open and their eyes smashed out, and the screaming in the air was more frightening than when they were bombarding us with their rockets. I thought then: Here's the Earth flying through space with our voices wailing so loud that if God exists and he is like a man and he can hear us but he can't put an end to our suffering, then it would be better if he destroyed the entire planet and all of us along with it."

Gravalya's reply was interrupted by a gentle knock at the door. Before either the granny or her grandson had time to respond, the door opened and a middle-aged man of average height with a massive neck appeared in the doorway, wearing a black coat and looking like either a bandit or a deputy to the State Duma.

After inquiring whether this was Fireworks Inc., the visitor expressed a desire to have a word with someone from the management.

"We're both top management," said Vanka, struggling to shake himself out of the state he'd been in during the conversation with Gravalya. "I'm the president and Valentina Petrovna is the vice president and executive director."

The visitor scrutinized Vanka, his granny and the surroundings with a dubious expression.

"So you manufacture all sorts of fireworks right here?"

"Firecrackers, jumping crackers, skyrockets, cherry bombs," said Gravalya. "What is it you need?"

"What I need is something like a cherry bomb," said the visitor.

"How many?" asked Granny Valya.

"One," said the visitor.

"We don't take orders for individual items," Vanka interjected.

"One big one."

"How do you mean?" Vanka asked again.

"I mean a big one," the visitor said with a smile. "Big enough, for instance, to blow an armored Mercedes to pieces. Preferably, tiny little pieces."

"A terrorist attack?" Vanka asked cautiously.

"Is the armor thick?" Gravalya inquired.

"We don't do that kind of work," Vanka cautioned her.

"About four millimeters," said the visitor. "Maybe five."

"A thousand a millimeter," Gravalya quoted. "Five thousand altogether."

"Rubles?" the visitor inquired.

"Baubles," the granny responded. "Books."

"Not books, but bucks," Vanka corrected her.

"Ah come on, guys," said the client, trying to haggle. "Five grand in bucks—that's too much. All I need in TNT equivalent is about two hundred grams, maybe three hundred—"

"If it doesn't suit, that's okay," Gravalya said with a shrug. "Go to someone else. There's a blaster called Vaska works down in the stone quarry. He'll sell you a saucepan full of dynamite for a thousand rubles. Only it'll be the kind that doesn't go off when it ought to or explodes in your hands. But we provide a guarantee. This is a sound firm. That's not a head there on his shoulders," she said, pointing to Vanka, "it's an entire Federal Council."

The visitor carried on sighing and haggling for a long time, and eventually they settled on four thousand, half paid in advance.

When the visitor left, Vanka asked: "Gravalya, have you decided to become a terrorist now?"

"Not a terrorist, an avenging angel," said Gravalya. "I told you we'd get them for it."

"Get who?" asked Vanka. "Do you know who he is, this guy in the Mercedes? Maybe he's a good man."

"The good people ride in buses, Vanka—we won't touch them."

In this way the Zhukovs, granny and grandson, took their first step along the path of terror, and soon the fame of Fireworks Inc. spread far and wide. Very many people knew about it. Everyone, in fact, who had any interest in their kind of products. With the possible exception of the public prosecutor's office, the police and the security services.

78

Every person who is not dead possesses the peculiar quality that the very fact of his existence is irksome to someone else who is still alive. Even some bum out on the street, collecting bottles from garbage dumps, irks another collector like himself. But a dead man is irksome to no one. Unless, that is, he happens to be lying in a mausoleum.

Of course, Aglaya too had always irked someone. In the past she had irked people so badly that they made attempts to dispose of her by radical means. In 1930 one dekulakized peasant had attempted to hack her to death with a mattock, which left its mark on her temple and her shoulder. When she was with the partisans, the Germans had offered more money for her head than for a cow. And when she was secretary of the district Party committee, someone had once lobbed a cobblestone through her window. But now, after being away from work for so long, how could she possibly irk anybody? But she did.

One day the *Dolgov Herald* happened to carry a small article by a local hydrologist about the fact that the town was apparently built over an underground spring—no, not oil, merely mineral water. But very good water. Saturated with all sorts of salts and other healthy substances. Good for drinking and for taking baths that facilitated the rejuvenation of the organism. This article caught the attention of a certain Valentin Yurievich Dolin, a New Russian businessman, but not one of those who wear thick gold chains around their necks and ride around in Mercedes 600s. No, he wore a relatively thin chain, rode around in a Mercedes 300 (although admittedly, he had already ordered himself a 600) and all in all was an educated man, who in Soviet times had graduated from the school of philosophy at Moscow State University and had almost got as far as defending a doctoral dissertation on the topic "Problems of Reinforcing Discipline in Production Work and Mutual Support in the Labor Collective in the Period of Advanced Socialism in the Light of Instructions by General Secretary of the Central Committee of the CPSU Comrade Konstantin Ustinovich Chernenko." While he was preparing to defend his dissertation, Comrade Chernenko's instructions had suddenly ceased to be of any philosophical value; a new and different life had begun and our doctoral candidate had abandoned scholarship and moved into the activity that was referred to as business consultancy. That is, for big money he provided a "roof" to foreigners who wanted to make a killing in the new Russian bazaar and provided them with consultation on how, in the incomprehensible local conditions, they could avoid taxes, pay bribes, launder their money and take it out of the country. In a short while he scraped together quite a respectable fortune—he had two casinos, three restaurants, one movie theater, a real estate company called Housewarmer and a tourist agency called the World in Your Hand.

I have always admired businessmen and criminals. How cleverly they react to all sorts of discoveries or events and turn them to their own advantage! Even an eclipse of the sun. When we simple folk hear that one's coming up soon, we just act dumb and talk about it without seeking any material advantage for ourselves, saying how interesting astronomical phenomena are and how we really ought to watch them. A businessman, though, realizes that people will want to watch the eclipse but they won't want to go blind in the process. That means they'll need special glasses, and plenty of them. The businessman gets to work on the glasses, but meanwhile the criminal is already figuring it will be dark during the eclipse, and while the people are gazing up into the sky, they're sure to lower their guard and forget to keep an eye on their pockets. Or else, let's say, they'll go dashing out into the street to observe the eclipse without closing the door to their apartment.

Being in every respect a man of business, Valya Dolin, known in criminal circles by the nickname of Validol, having read the notice in the *Dolgov Herald*, immediately discerned that a fluid so beneficial to the people's health shouldn't simply be going to waste lying under the ground. He immediately imagined the sequence of actions that had to be taken: build a glass factory, make masses of bottles, drill a well, pump out the water, bottle it and sell it for a fair price. And if there was a lot of water, he could build a hydropathic clinic. And if there was an awful lot of it, there was a chance of transforming Dolgov into a balneological resort that would make him rich and famous.

Validol engaged in some of that activity known as market research. He found out which way the water flowed, how deep it was under the ground, where was the best place to drill and locate the first hydropathic clinic. And it turned out there was not and could not be any place better than house no. 1-a on Komsomol Cul-de-Sac.

After carrying out a second piece of market research, Validol calculated how much money he needed to acquire this house and resettle the remaining residents somewhere else. In the process it transpired that one of the residents, Aglaya Stepanovna Revkina, would not agree to the move at any price, due to the impossibility of taking with her the monument that stood in her apartment. On account of the ceilings in the new apartments being too low for the monument. This circumstance greatly complicated his problem, but Validol was a resourceful man, he didn't believe in problems that couldn't be solved, and Aglaya Stepanovna was suddenly in very serious danger.

79

As the Admiral once remarked, Russia is a country where they talk a lot about repentance, but it's a rare event for anyone actually to say "I'm sorry." His words always come to mind when I remember Mark Semyonovich Shubkin's return to Dolgov. Or rather, his attempted return. Following the auspicious changes that took place in our country, many émigrés, especially people from the world of the arts, began coming back to their homeland. Shubkin decided to return too. And not to Moscow, like the others, but to Dolgov. Because, as he used to say (and quite correctly), Moscow is not Russia. And his praiseworthy intention was precisely to go back to Russia. The reader can imagine what an event this was. Maybe in Moscow it would have been nothing out of the ordinary, but for a district-level town it was really big. While Shubkin was still packing his suitcase in Jerusalem, the whole town of Dolgov was already buzzing. An entire delegation was put together to meet the returning émigré, and it was headed, of course, by Vlad Raspadov. Although in his time he had written some unpleasant things about Shubkin, time had gone by, the old memories had dimmed and Shubkin himself had very probably never read that article. In any case, who could have met Shubkin if not Raspadov? After all, by that time he was the most important and authoritative literary figure in the district in question. On the eve of the event he was apparently spoken to in person by the mayor of Dolgov, Korotyshkin. The same Korotyshkin who once used to work in the KGB. But with the passing years many people had revised their former views, and Korotyshkin had become a thoroughgoing democrat, a resolute anticommunist and a God-fearing parishioner of the local church. He might even have turned out himself to meet the famous writer, the author of that celebrated novel *The Timber Camp*, but there were new elections coming up, the communists were making a bid for power and it was essential for them to be rebuffed. Basically, Korotyshkin didn't have the time. And as he told Raspadov, to arrange an official reception for Shubkin would be going too far. If, he said, we were to arrange personal receptions for everyone who went away, we'd be spending all our time welcoming these departees home. That, at least, was what he told Raspadov, apparently apprehensive that departees would descend on this godforsaken backwater in hordes, whereas in fact there had only ever been two departees from Dolgov: Shubkin himself and Antonina. But even though a full-scale official reception was not expected, a certain number of people did turn up at the station. I happened to be in Dolgov at the time, and I also went along to welcome home the illustrious foreigner. There were many people gathered on the platform: local intellectuals, the teaching staff of the children's home and some of its former wards. The *Dolgov Herald* sent its own correspondent, and a reporter and cameraman from the regional television company tagged along. It was a clear, sunny day. The starlings were warbling in the trees, there was a smell of hot diesel fuel and boiled potatoes with dill. The local grannies had come to meet the train with their customary goods: potatoes, pies, dried fish and pickled cucumbers.

The train was a bit late. So everyone started getting nervous. And I remembered that time when Shubkin had been arrested right there on the platform. "He must be savoring the contrast," I thought. Finally, someone shouted out: "It's coming!" Everyone tensed and froze. The train approached. Not as picturesquely as it used to. What an occasion it used to be! The locomotive Iosif Stalin tearing into the station, enveloped in clouds of steam! Huffing and puffing so loud! Gleaming so bright! But now? A pathetic-looking, grubby little electric locomotive whistled in a thin falsetto and pulled sixteen carriages into the station as easily as if they were toys on a string. And everyone saw Shubkin standing above the steps of carriage no. 4. Only they didn't recognize him immediately. With his big gray beard he no longer resembled Lenin; he looked more like Karl Marx or one of the biblical prophets. He was holding on to the handrail with one hand and waving to the waiting crowd with the other. And peeping out from behind him with a big smile was Antonina, her head tightly bound with a silk scarf. This scarf seemed somehow out of place, and it was only later that I discovered its significance. It turned out that in Israel Antonina had converted to Judaism, and she adhered strictly to the tenets of her new faith, completely shaving her head and covering it with a scarf. But Mark Semyonovich had remained in the Orthodox Church. So their family had become sort of ecumenical. And there they were, waving their hands as they rode in, and the people there to meet them were waving too and shouting something, and several women were even pressing handkerchiefs to their eyes.

Shubkin stepped down onto the platform and Antonina followed him with two suitcases. People immediately surrounded them, embraced them, kissed them, presented them with flowers. The critic Raspadov also stepped up to the returnee with a bouquet of three scarlet carnations. But he didn't present the flowers immediately; he transferred them from his right hand to his left and raised his right hand as a sign for everyone to be quiet. And he then delivered a speech that could be called historical.

Shunted off to one side by the eager crowd, I was standing a long way from the orator and the wind carried his words off into the air, but I was able to make out a bit here and there and I marveled at our critic's ability to direct his flow of thought first in one direction and then in its opposite. First Vlad extended hearty greetings to the returnee, calling him an outstanding writer whom we (who? he himself perhaps?) had missed all these years. "We," he said, "are pleased to greet all of our compatriots whose return has become possible because of our perestroika and, let us say it, avoiding false modesty, thanks to us, its rank-and-file engineers. Our labors have created the appropriate conditions for their return, and it is good that Mark Semyonovich is now with us. It must be admitted that at the time not everyone regarded his departure with understanding—some of us even condemned him in harsh terms . . ." At this point, I thought, there ought logically to follow an apology. Or an expression of regret. Or something of the sort. But Raspadov came out with something different. Some of us, he went on, had condemned him in harsh terms, even, perhaps, unjustly, but we should not go to the opposite extreme of praising Mark Semyonovich excessively and making him into a hero. The man left—it had been to his advantage to do so. Over there they live well; they eat kosher. Here we were eating Chernobyl potatoes and tomatoes full of nitrates. But after all, someone had to stay here to protect our culture, our monuments, our graves . . .

I repeat, I was standing a long way off, and I couldn't see everything. And then a train going in the opposite direction pulled in at platform 2. So my view was obstructed and I could hear almost nothing. But people who were a bit closer told me that when he got to the subject of our graves— apparently, indeed, as a result of some powerful excitation associated with graves—Vlad Raspadov suddenly lost control of himself. The picture painted by his own words seemed to be that while he'd been here sitting on the gravestones, Shubkin had been living it up and wolfing down kosher meatballs in the Garden of Gethsemane. And though his arms were already spread wide to embrace Shubkin, instead he spat in his face. Shubkin, who had been listening with a bewildered smile, froze, still smiling. But a sigh of surprise ran through the crowd "Aagh-aagh-aagh!" For his part, after this gaffe, Raspadov himself was aghast at what he'd done and stood there for a long time in a defenseless pose, as though expecting his opponent to take adequate satisfaction. But when it didn't happen, he said: "And in general, welcome back to your homeland!"

And he tried to hand Shubkin his carnations. But Shubkin turned out to be touchy! He grabbed the suitcases and with a cry of "Antonina, follow me!" he leapt onto the train going back the opposite way, and that was the last we saw of him. He went back. As someone wrote about him later in the newspaper, he was fonder of his matzos than he was of his homeland.

Of course, in the eyes of many, Mark Semyonovich Shubkin was and remains a comical figure: all those ideals and beliefs of his, the way he arrived at them and the way he abandoned them and, most importantly, all the grimacing and gesturing involved looked funny, but at the same time there was something touching about him—his actions were driven by noble impulses and elements of the recklessness that is so highly esteemed in our society. You could pass as many ironic comments as you liked on all of this, but it wasn't right to spit in his face.

Nonetheless, Raspadov's gob of spittle was soon forgotten, and people recalled Shubkin with incomprehension, resentment and bitter irony. He just came, stuck his nose up in the air and went away again. There was no orchestra to greet him, you see. And the only explanation they could find for the way Shubkin acted was that he'd got too used to the good life and the good food in the Promised Land. And to this day certain people in Dolgov regret the sincere feelings they invested in the attempt to welcome Shubkin back with open arms.

80

You know, it's an interesting condition, complete freedom. You can write or read what you like, listen to the foreign radio, tell political jokes, insult the president, travel abroad, make love to a partner of either sex, in a group or on your own, grow your hair long, wear rings in your ears and rings in your nose and generally transfix yourself with anything you fancy. Of course, many people were annoyed by all this. Especially since public-sector workers' wages were delayed and pensioners weren't being paid their pensions at all. Both groups were occasionally paid in locally pro-duced goods. There was one time they began paying everybody for every-thing in the output of the local poultry farm, i.e., in chicks. Dolgov was swamped by an unprecedented number of chickens. They filled all the yards, swarmed over the kitchen gardens, wandered along the roads and got under your feet; there were so many of them it was hard to drive through town in an automobile without running over at least one. The chickens were all the same breed—Dolgov Dutch Whites—and in an attempt to distinguish their own chickens from other people's, the women marked the birds with ink of various colors: red, green, blue, black. Aglaya didn't take any chickens, not having any idea how to deal with them. She'd lived her entire life in a rural district, and she didn't even know how to milk a cow, let alone kill a chicken. Aglaya refused the chickens and ran out of money, and she had absolutely no idea what to do, but it's no accident that even atheists use the old saying "Don't worry, God won't let the pig eat you."

On the warm morning of March 8, International Women's Day, a young couple knocked on Aglaya's door, tall and smiling, dressed well but modestly with carefully styled hair—she had little earrings in her ears, but he had no rings in his ears or his nose. He was carrying flowers and a hard briefcase, and she had two plastic carrier bags. They asked if they could come in. When they were asked who they were and what their busi-ness was, the young man held out a business card: "Valentin Yurievich Dolin, President of the International Charitable Organization 'Age with Dignity.' "

"And I'm Gala," the woman said with a friendly smile.

Aglaya thought they'd come to ask for money, but it turned out to be just the opposite . . .

When they were allowed in, the visitors removed their shoes and were left in just their socks. Stepping softly, as though they were afraid of waking someone up, they walked through into the sitting room. They stood for a moment in silence in front of the monument, with their heads bowed and their hands lowered. Valentin Yurievich confessed that although it was very unfashionable now, Stalin was his favorite historical figure. Then he got straight down to business.

"First of all, Aglaya Stepanovna, allow me to congratulate you on International Women's Day and present you with . . ." Valentin Yurievich turned to his female companion and she began extracting items from a plastic bag and setting them on the table: a bottle of "Soviet Champagne," a bottle of Finlandia vodka, a thick piece of dietary sausage, a carton of Rossisky cheese, a box of Red October chocolate candies and a block of Marlboro cigarettes. Aglaya looked at all of this in great amazement, as though a magic tablecloth from a fairy tale had been spread out before her.

"What's all this?" she asked.

"It's for you," Valentin Yurievich said quietly.

"Me? What for?" she asked.

"For your quintessential femininity," Gala declared.

"Nonsense!" interrupted Valentin Yurievich. "Certainly Aglaya Stepanovna is feminine, but we intend to help her not only because of that, but for everything that she has done for our homeland and for future generations, for us."

And he ran through the program of the Age with Dignity foundation. The foundation had been established by young people, patriots who had decided to help old people who had fought selflessly to build communism in our country. To free them from poverty and protect them against the tyranny of an antipopular regime. For a start they had come to find out what Aglaya Stepanovna was particularly in need of (food? clothes? medicines?) and then to provide all the help they could. The foundation's council had adopted a resolution to provide her with a supplementary personal pension of sixty conventional units a month from its own funds.

"Sixty what?" Aglaya asked.

"Greenbacks," said Gala.

"What's that? Dollars?" asked Aglaya. "I don't want dollars."

"You've misunderstood us," said Valentin Yurievich with a smile. "It's not dollars, but conventional units. Rubles tied to the dollar."

She took that to mean the rubles would be given to her literally tied to dollars with something—rope, thread, string—and it cost the young people an effort to explain that the connection would be conceptual and in actual fact the number of real rubles would increase with inflation, but the number of conventional units would remain the same.

"And apart from that," said Gala, "we're going to help you with food. Once a week you will receive a food parcel."

When asked what she'd done to deserve such good fortune, they started talking across each other in their haste to explain: It was for her outstanding services. For having been an uncompromising communist. And a partisan. And an educator of the young. And in general a worker.

"But all the same," said Aglaya, still unable to make sense of it all, "what do I owe you?"

"Oh God!" exclaimed Gala, throwing her arms in the air and rolling her eyes up to the ceiling.

"Aglaya Stepanovna!" sighed Valentin Yurievich. "What are you talking about? You owe us? That's ridiculous. We owe you. When you think about it, you did so much for us, the members of later generations. It will be a great honor for us if you will accept at least the little help and support that we are able to offer you today."

"And you don't want anything at all from me?"

Gala mimed total dismay once again.

"Well perhaps," said Valentin Yurievich, "if you should wish in turn to help our foundation . . ."

"So that it can grow and develop," Gala explained.

"In that case," Valentin Yurievich continued, "if you . . . how should I put it . . ."

"None of us live for ever," Gala sighed.

"Yes!" Valentin Yurievich glanced reproachfully at Gala for being so tactless, but he continued on the same subject and his words included the phrase "a will."

His speech was rather flowery, but even so Aglaya gathered from his words that her visitors were not exactly insisting, but they felt that if she bequeathed her apartment to the Age with Dignity foundation, together with all her property and this work of art—a gesture of the hand in the direction of the statue—then, God grant her, of course, good health and long life . . . but afterward it would be a good thing if her property fell into honest hands. It would still be able to do some good for people, help other pensioners who had been robbed by the antipopular regime . . .

When Aglaya realized what they wanted from her and what they would give in exchange, she didn't hesitate for a moment. She was a genuine atheist and she wasn't concerned about what would happen after death. Of course, it would have been natural to leave the apartment to her son, but where was he? She hadn't heard a word from him for years now. And she knew for certain he was alive and well. He was an ambassador in one of the Western countries; every now and then they even showed him on the television, turned flabby and bald. He praised the changes and said he had always been a convinced anticommunist . . . Oh no, he wasn't going to get a thing. And anyway, what good to him was an apartment in a dump like this?

"Yes," said Aglaya, suddenly remembering, "what about him?" She nodded toward Stalin. "When I die, is he for the garbage dump?"

"Aglaya Stepanovna," said Dolin, rolling his eyes. "How can you! For me and for Gala, Comrade Stalin is . . ."

"Like Jesus Christ," said Gala.

"On the word of a communist," Valentin Yurievich went on, "we will preserve this holy relic until the time comes when it will proudly resume its rightful place. And believe me, it will happen."

"It will definitely happen," Gala confirmed. "We'll make it happen. Because Stalin is our idol."

"Oh, all right then," said Aglaya with a wave of her hand.

81

Alexei Mikhailovich Makarov, alias the Admiral, used to divide up our post–October Revolution history into the eras of Cellar Terrorism (under Lenin, when they shot people in the cellars of the Extraordinary Commission, or Cheka), the Great Terror (under Stalin), Terror Within the Limits of Leninist Norms (under Khrushchev), Selective Terror (under

Brezhnev), Transitional Terror (under Andropov, Chernenko and Gorbachev) and Terror Unlimited (the present time).

The latter phase of terror is distinguished from the preceding phases by the fact that it is not perpetrated in the name of SCOSWO, is no longer centralized and has been simplified. Anybody at all can sentence anybody else at all to death for anything at all. People eliminate each other by every possible means: by stabbing with knives, shooting with shotguns, pellet guns, rifles, pistols, submachine guns, machine guns and grenade launchers, by using poisons, chemical fumes, radioactivity and explosive devices. All with a high level of efficiency and a zero solution rate. We always find out who's been killed, but who killed them remains forever a secret. Everywhere in the cities, both large and (in some cases) small, criminal gangs, known to everyone, are active, with leaders whose names are also known, underworld bosses who hide from no one and ride around in armor-plated limousines with bodyguards, conduct international business and bank their money offshore. They are known as bankers, oligarchs, mayors, governors, ministers, industrialists, and the owners of newspapers, shipping lines, oil wells and television channels. The life they live is good, but it is often short and overshadowed by fear. They are not afraid of the police, but of each other, and with good reason. Their laws are not recorded in writing, but they are strict. Capital punishment is the routine sentence. And so there is a constantly rising demand among these people for all sorts of firearms or items that explode and which can be used to take out a colleague. These items have to be manufactured by somebody and Vanka Zhukov became one of these manufacturers, with a growing reputation among his potential clients. Everybody knew that if a cracker was made by Zhukov it wouldn't let you down. Fireworks Inc. had a constantly expanding customer base, the clients who drove around to see Vanka on their foreign sets of wheels treated him with deference, spoke to him respectfully, calling him Ivan Georgievich, and didn't haggle over the price. They allowed him total creative freedom, which was important to him, because he was a creative artist in his own line of work. He always tried to do something distinctive and original, but with limited impact. Let us not overromanticize the image of our people's avenger. The work he did was reprehensible, but even so he was distinguished from other craftsmen in the same business by a certain fastidiousness, always calculating precisely the power and direction of the explosion and attempting to avoid unnecessary casualties.

The detonators of Vanka's crackers were all of original construction: mechanical, chemical, acoustic, bimetallic, electrical and electronic. They reacted to the most varied of signals and impulses, to the touch of fingers with specific prints, to smell, to color, to light, to a tone of voice — in other words, every time the goal was redefined in every respect with regard to the specific case in hand. Vanka's first large cracker was installed in an automobile and was supposed to go off when it reached a speed of 120 kilometers an hour. Vanka didn't think it was possible to drive through the streets of the town at that kind of speed.

82

Aglaya Stepanovna had never lived so well and with so few worries. One pension had not been enough, but with two there was no need to deny herself anything. Especially since apart from the money she also received a comprehensive food delivery. Every Thursday, vivacious and smiling, Gala turned up at her place with two string shopping bags, her fine figure sporting denim jeans and a stylish denim jacket. She came through into the kitchen and laid everything out, chattering away in a manner reminiscent of one of the waitresses in the sanatorium in Sochi: "Look, I've brought you some bread and a nice bit of butter, some beautiful eggs and some sausage, lovely cucumbers, fine tomatoes and this too." And she narrowed her eyes as she took out a bottle of Finlandia vodka. "It's fine vodka, this, pure stuff, not like ours. I quite like getting a bit of a high on, as they say, myself, but we mustn't overdo it, you and me. My brother's a doctor; he says, just you remember, Gala, the female organism is more susceptible to alcohol than the male."

Gala would ask her not to hurry with the drinks. First she would tidy the sitting room and make dinner. Then she would take off her jacket, roll up the sleeves of her white blouse and the legs of her jeans and set to work. When she leaned forward, her little gold cross would tumble out and dangle on its chain. She shoved it back inside her blouse. She set soup and buckwheat or potatoes to cook on the stove, and while the flames were doing their work, she plugged in the vacuum cleaner and cleaned the carpets. She wiped down the statue with a damp cloth. She watered the plants on the windowsill. And she did all of this quickly and easily, flitting around the apartment and repeating to herself: "Oh, what a lot of dust you have! Where can it all come from? I wiped everything last time, and here it is again. It's terrible! I really think something must be happening to the environment."

Sometimes she would ask about Stalin: Why did people love him so much? Was he kind?

"How can I put it?" said Aglaya, pondering. "He showed his enemies no mercy, he exterminated them ruthlessly, but that way he did a lot of good for the working class."

Aglaya had never been sentimental, but now some sort of shift took place inside her. She noticed herself waiting for her benefactress, feeling happy when she arrived, and sometimes she even called her Galochka. And she liked it when Gala addressed her as "Mama Glaya."

Gala cooked, spread the tablecloth, set the table tastefully, took out two spirits glasses and two glasses for apple juice, and then they ate together, sometimes talking on late into the evening.

Gala was happy to talk about her parents. Both of them were communists. They worked in the metallurgical combine in Norilsk. They'd wanted to save up some money and leave it to their daughter. "But then these you know, whatever they were called, pardon the expression, came to power, and all of my parents' savings were just wiped out. The shock of it killed my dad. In fact, yesterday was his anniversary—I went to church and lit a candle. Sent mum some money. She gets a miserable little pension. Even less than yours. I help her, of course, she's my mother. Imagine it, she's been slaving away all her life, and now she can't even feed herself. I wouldn't be able to, either, if not for Seryozhka . . . You know, Mama Glaya, my Seryozhka's really kindhearted. When he sees some old person with their hand held out begging, he really suffers! He'd be just perfect if he wasn't so jealous! Oh, Mama, how jealous he is! Did you see the bruise I had last time I was here? Maybe you didn't notice, I powdered over it, but look, you can still see."

"And has he anything to be jealous of?" Aglaya asked.

"Well, Mama Glaya, to tell the truth, he has. He's always working, working, working. He comes home tired and sometimes a bit tight as well, lies down and just turns to face the wall. But I'm a lively young woman, Mama Glaya, I'm twenty-six years old . . . I expect you were the same when you were twenty-six . . . ?"

"At twenty-six I was in command of a partisan unit." Aglaya tried to make the announcement proudly, but it came out as though she were apologizing for a misspent youth, when she had wasted her time on foolishness.

But Gala was embarrassed too: "Oi, Mama, I'm sorry, I feel ashamed. Oi, what incredible people you were. So high-minded and brave. And who are we? I could never be a partisan, I'm so terribly afraid of blood. Even when someone I don't know at all cuts their finger, I feel faint. You really did work for us and fight for us. And we . . . I feel so ashamed . . . Seryozhka says we're young communists, but actually we haven't got any ideals at all. Our heads are just full of nothing but having fun, clothes, food and sex. Sometimes I do get a yearning for something above all that, but my thoughts drag me down. I'm what they call an easy lay. Do you know what Seryozhka calls me?"

"What?"

Gala sighed and said nothing for a moment, as though wondering whether she should say or not, and giggled in embarrassment: "Giveaway Galka."

"So he has good reason to belt you?"

"Of course he does. I wouldn't stand for it otherwise. It upsets me too, Mama Glaya, you can't imagine how much. I wonder myself why it is I'm such a whore, pardon the expression. But a man only has to touch me and I just melt like butter. I can't say no, and that's all."

"Tell me . . ." Aglaya began, then stopped in sudden embarrassment.

"What?" asked Gala.

"Oh, nothing . . . Anyway you know . . . at your age I had different morals, we were all for the motherland, for Stalin, for the Party, we fulfilled the five-year plans and we didn't think much about ourselves. Don't laugh now, but now in my old age all I hear is 'orgasm, orgasm.' But what is an orgasm? Are you going to laugh?"

"What a question, Mama Glaya!" Gala opened her eyes wide and her voice dropped to a whisper. "You really don't know? Oi! What are you saying? Well, basically, it's—I don't even know what it's like. When I'm doing it . . . first I feel as though something inside me is being pumped up, bigger and bigger, like a balloon, you know, one of those huge great balloons, and I'm flying away somewhere, flying away when suddenly—bang!—it bursts. It just bursts all over on every side and spills out, like a puddle, like a lake, like a sea. And at that moment I'm completely gone, I'm dying, there's music in my ears, how can I put it . . . it's like . . . Michael Jackson." Gala looked at Aglaya and thought for a moment, then asked, as though she wasn't sure what the answer would be: "Mama Glaya, you were young too once, weren't you?"

"What do you think?" Aglaya asked.

"I don't know," said Gala. "I know you must have been, only somehow I can't imagine it."

83

A certain citizen of the state of Nebraska (USA), rummaging around in the nooks and crannies of the Internet, noticed a World Wide Web user who was evidently interested in the latest advances in the area of explosives technology—substances, components, reagents, catalysts, reaction accelerators and retardants. This unknown individual was also studying the latest means of remote signal transmission and the details of various sensor devices. He had in addition evinced obvious curiosity concerning the life of disabled war veterans in America, how many of them there were, their pensions, daily lives, social-aid programs and technology for improving their lives.

The inhabitant of Nebraska decided to contact this searcher, worked out his ICQ and sent him the following message: "Hi, I'm Jim Bardington. Who are you?"

Vanka (whose English was quite good) was surprised. He thought for a moment and gave his name. The next question was "Are you disabled?"

Vanka asked: "How did you guess?"

"You are very intelligent."

"Thank you. And what about you?"

"Me too."

"Intelligent or disabled?"

"Both. Vietnam War veteran. Are you Russian?"

"Yes."

"I hate the USA too!"

Before Vanka had time to think how to express his surprise, there was a coded knock at the door. Vanka apologized to the American and exited from the Internet.

Gravalya let in a short man with a leather cap pulled forward over his eyes. Once inside the room, the caller bent up the peak of his cap and took a good look at the surroundings. There was no general lighting in the room, but there was an orange silk lampshade with a 150-watt lightbulb hanging low over the worktable. By the light of this bulb the visitor surveyed his host in his wheelchair—a stump of a man with a mutilated face and only one eye and one arm. His right leg—a plastic prosthesis clad in a canvas trouser leg with a shoe on the foot—was standing on the low footboard. The trouser leg of the pink-colored left prosthesis was turned up, and the prosthesis itself was lying across the knee of the right leg, without any shoe but wearing a sock. Even though he had a computer, Vanka often used this limb as a notepad. He wrote on it in pencil, recording orders, working out chemical formulae or simply adding up figures, and he rubbed out his old notes with an eraser. At this stage the room was a genuine chemical laboratory, reasonably well equipped. On the table there was a computer, a chemical balance, two soldering irons, microcircuits and chips, a reel of copper wire and a copy of the journal *Chemistry and Life*. The shelves around the table held flasks of various liquids, jars with labels reading AMMONIUM NITRATE, MERCURY, POWDERED CARBON, GELATIN, SULPHUR, BLUE VITRIOL, GLYCERINE and NITROGLYCERINE. Standing and lying on and under crudely assembled racks, were canisters, buckets, cans, two antipersonnel mines, four antitank grenades and all sorts of other deadly bits and pieces.

"And you keep all this out in the open?" the visitor asked in amazement.

"Sit down," said Vanka, indicating an old brown armchair with sagging springs to the left of the table. "Will you tell me your name?"

"Yes. Ivan Ivanich. Will that do?"

"Yes," agreed Vanka. "So what do you want?"

For some reason Ivan Ivanich suddenly became embarrassed.

"There's a certain person here," he began uncertainly.

"Where here?" Vanka asked sternly.

"In Moscow." Ivan Ivanich was obviously feeling a bit bashful. "Well, basically he's from around here, but his bank's in Moscow. And he has to be . . ."

"I can guess what he has to be, but who is he?" asked Vanka.

"Do you need the name?"

"I need details. What he does, where he goes, who he associates with, how he spends his free time, his weaknesses and habits."

"I have all that," said the visitor. He took a wallet bulging with numerous credit cards stuffed into special slots out of his side pocket. From it he extracted a sheet of paper on which the necessary items of information were listed in computer type. President of a bank, age twenty-nine, divorced, one child, takes his work seriously, arrives earlier than anyone else and leaves later, has two bodyguards, lives in a well-guarded building, is having an affair with the wife of the owner of the Golden Goose restaurant, meets her in a specially rented apartment; this building is not guarded, nor is its entrance, the apartment has an alarm system, but it can be switched off by someone in the police.

"Our suggestion," said Ivan Ivanich, "is to plant a bomb under the bed and rely on the pressure. While only the mistress is in the bed, the bomb just lies there. When there's two of them, it explodes. Very simple."

Vanka held the paper in his hand, read through it again and thrust out his torn lower lip in a gesture of disdain.

"Simple and stupid," was his assessment.

"Why," the visitor asked, surprised and a bit offended.

"Because, if he's lying on top of her, she'll shield him. She'll be torn apart, but he'll survive."

"How about a bit more explosive? We'll pay for everything."

"You'll pay all right. But there must be other apartments there. Downstairs, upstairs. Families, children . . ."

"What of it? Are you some kind of humanist then?" the visitor asked.

"I'll ask you to be a bit more civil," Vanka growled, his mind on something else. "I'm not a humanist, I'm a specialist. I don't like primitive solutions. What other habits does he have?"

It turned out that the future victim had a bar in his office and drank whiskey and tonic several times a day.

"Whiskey and tonic?" Vanka repeated in amazement. He took a pencil from the table and began writing something on the plastic leg. "Does anybody really drink whiskey and tonic?"

"Why not?" asked the client with a shrug. "I drink whiskey and tonic too."

"Well, well," Vanka shrugged his shoulders. From his time at Varvara Ilinichna's place in Moscow, he remembered the Western journalists regaling the dissidents with the foreign drinks they drank themselves, but they drank gin with tonic, not whiskey. "Okay," he muttered. "I suppose it's a matter of taste."

In the course of the question-and-answer session that followed, Vanka established how the banker spent the beginning of his working day. He went into his office and straight across to the bar, poured himself a whiskey and tonic, and mulled over this drink for at least half an hour. After that he opened the safe, took out his business papers and got down to work. As it happened, the client knew the combination.

"Okay," said Vanka, and he made another note on his leg. "Come back in a week."

"It's a deal." As he was leaving, the client nodded at Vanka's leg. "That's a handy notepad you have."

"Very handy," Vanka agreed. "Always to hand, in fact."

When their visitor had gone, Gravalya locked the door and Vanka went back to the computer and asked his new acquaintance why he hated America.

84

Nowadays, nobody but an extreme skeptic has any chance of being a sage or a prophet. The further things go, the worse people treat each other, and as for morality . . . People talk about it endlessly in Russia, rolling their eyes sensitively all the while. Oh, morality, morality . . . But morality here is in such a poor state it's best not to talk about it at all. The bigger villain a man is, the more he talks about morality, patriotism and love for mankind. In actual fact the continuing historical process merely renders man increasingly callous.

How can we even imagine that a mere hundred years or so ago there was only one executioner for the whole of Russia? They couldn't find a second person who was willing to execute people. Sometimes people ripped each other open with knives or beat each other to death with stakes, but that was the result of drinking or foolishness, acts committed in a state of excitation, as they used to say back then, and sometimes, of course, for money, but not as part of the routine responsibilities of a job. Not out of ideological considerations. Not out of sexual motivation. Not as a matter of scientific research. And not in such great numbers.

How many murderers of various calibers have paraded in front of our eyes: Lenin, Stalin, Hitler, Himmler, Dr. Mengele, Pol Pot, Chikatilo . . .

And note that not a single writer has managed to re-create the character of any of them in an authentic, convincing portrait. Because in describing this or that character you have to put yourself in his place and imagine that you are him. This imagining you are somebody else is what a writer does every day. He can imagine he is Flaubert's Emma Bovary, Tolstoy's Pierre Bezukhov, Gogol's Chichikov and Korobochka, even a horse called Yardstick or a dog called Chestnut. Even a horse and a dog have feelings and impulses that are accessible to our understanding, but I don't know a single writer who has managed to feel his way into the character of Lenin, Stalin, Hitler or even Chikatilo. Lenin, Stalin and Hitler killed millions of people through the hands of their agents. Chikatilo cut out little girls' wombs with his own hands and ate them raw. He killed, raped and partially ate about fifty people, but his record didn't stand for long. In Russia a certain Kolya did away with a hundred women, but the only part he consumed fresh was their blood. The flesh he boiled, roasted, dried, smoked and made into sausage, eating it himself and feeding it to his guests. Kolya was followed by other murderers who surpassed him, and the competition is still continuing. And the longer it goes on, the more sadists, ghouls, butchers and processors of human flesh are spawned. Little children are abducted so that their internal organs can be taken. And as for the professional craftsmen of the killing business, their work inflames the imaginations of schoolboys, and hot-blooded youths with fire in their eyes dream not of being poets or explorers or cosmonauts, but hit men. It's an alluring and romantic prospect—to pick out your victim and shadow him, to wait in the dark entrance, lurking under the stairs, to fire at point-blank range, then step over the corpse and stroll away after delivering the coup de grâce to the head.

Validol had never been either a romantic or a sadist. He only killed people if he could see some profit in killing them. And he didn't touch anybody else. He derived no pleasure from killing, but he didn't experience any discomfort either. Business is business—that was the way he thought about it. Killing a man was like splitting a log. With the sole difference that killing meant risking your own life. You might get killed. And the trouble with killing people was that afterward you had to cover your tracks, dismember corpses, destroy clues, figure out alibis. And so if Validol had been able to earn good bread, as he put it, without killing anyone, then he wouldn't have killed anyone. In fact, he was already toying with the idea that when he'd accumulated his start-up capital he could drop all the dirty work and go into legitimate business. But before he could do that, he had to finish what had already been started and that meant . . . As he thought about it, Valentin Yurievich mentally shrugged—unfortunately, he still needed to take someone's life, but afterward . . . afterward . . .

Anyway, after sleeping he didn't feel much like thinking. He really felt like sleeping a bit longer, but the early spring sunlight that seemed to be sparkling with dew was shining straight into his eyes, forcing him to squint. He turned away from the sun and toward the woman he loved, the one he called Galchonka when he was in a good mood. She was sleeping with her back to him and her shoulder, tanned in February on the isle of Bali, was exposed. The shoulder was dark with a white stripe from her bikini strap. Validol put his hand on her shoulder and stroked it tentatively. He was in an excellent mood. So far, all his business affairs had gone well and he'd achieved many things he could never even have dreamed of before, although he'd known the feeling of big money rustling in his pocket for a long time now. But just recently, what had he been able to spend it on? Sure, he'd done the rounds of the restaurants, he'd pampered himself in Sochi, steamed himself in the sauna, bathed a few girls in Abrau Dursot champagne and drunk himself into a swinish stupor with that same champagne and vodka. But he'd paid dearly for all of that. He'd been inside twice, and he would have gone down a third time if not for perestroika, the reforms and all the rest of it.

But now he had the casino, the restaurants, the movie theater, his company Housewarmer and his travel agency, The World in Your Hand. Recently, he'd bought a gas station as well, and a few days ago he'd finally given in to temptation and bought a Mercedes 600, although he used to laugh at other people who owned that model, those New Russians from all the jokes. The handsome beast was standing in his garage. Armorplated, with tinted windows, gilded door handles and fully loaded, it had alarms and automatic controls, heated seats, a computer, a thermometer and a navigation system (which was actually quite useless in this part of the world). The owner hadn't been stingy; he'd insured his new wheels for their full value. Against theft, accident, natural disasters and all the rest. To be on the safe side, he had also augmented his insurance with Divine Power through the agency of a priest who had sprinkled water on his purchase in the name of the Father, the Son and the Holy Ghost and intoned a prayer for the safekeeping of this carriage and the servants of God who would ride in it.

So far then, things had been going well. And they could be expected to go even better. Just a few more jobs to push through, one of them being to polish off that drunk old dame. A perfectly simple killing with almost no risk. He'd thought everything through. He'd already helped four similar ancient dipsomaniacs to shuffle off this mortal coil. It was simple. First you had to have a drink with the old dame, and then have a lot more, and then say to her, "Drink up now, Granny," and if she started getting awkward, open her mouth and pour it in until she choked on it. It was disagreeable work, but he could live with that. And it would definitely be one of the last jobs like that he ever did. Soon he'd build his hydropathic clinic and his factory for bottling mineral water and give his water the name invented by his best friend Mosol—Valya's Valley. And he'd run an honest, legitimate business, or almost honest—honest enough to be able to buy off public prosecutors and the tax police. He was already living half-legally, conducting business openly and sharing his earnings. He'd fixed all the local bosses, and he'd supported the Church of SS. Kozma and Damian, and set up the Age with Dignity foundation. He had the respect of the town's mayor, the chief of police, the chief of the security services. There would be new elections soon and he would be running. With his money and contacts success ought to be assured. And that meant guaranteed immunity and a career for the future, and eventually he could see himself sitting in the mayor's chair, with everyone answering to him: the bank, the police, the public prosecutor's office and the court. In short, he woke up feeling good and turned toward the woman he loved, who was sleeping with her face buried in her pillow. He stroked her shoulder. She woke up: Eh? How? What? Then she realized what and how and reached out for him . . .

Afterward, they drank freshly brewed coffee with cream on the balcony, with hot rolls and cheese. The sun was shining, it was warm, the air was scented by the jasmine blossoming profusely at the same height as the balcony.

"Wonderful!" Validol exclaimed suddenly.

"What?" Gala asked in fright.

"What do you mean, what?"

"Nothing," she said, embarrassed. "I just didn't think you could actually feel anything."

"You fool!" he said. "You're the one who doesn't understand and never will understand how beautiful life is!"

"Why?" she asked, offended. "Do you think you're more sensitive than I am?"

"No. But in order to really feel how lucky you are to be living like this, you need to have been through the mill. Spend some time in the camps, for instance."

"You told me you used to live pretty well in there too."

"Pretty well. I lived better than the others in there. I was leader of the pack in there. I had the best places on the bunks, I didn't do any work, I drank chifir and the lags carried out my every wish."

"Just like I said."

"Like you said!" he retorted, almost angry. "Can't you understand, that was still slavery! Chifir instead of coffee, smelly foot-rags instead of the jasmine that's blossoming now, and being surrounded all the time by those brute-ugly louts. No, I don't want to go back there again."

"Why should you go back? What for? You're legit, aren't you?"

"Me?" He gave her a mocking look. "You're asking me? What about you?"

"Me-ee?" she said in astonishment. "Are you trying to say that I . . . ?"

Tears sprang to her eyes. "You think I'm not legit?" She was all set to have hysterics on the spot.

"No," he told her hastily. "I'm not saying anything like that. But don't you go getting too laid back and forgetting we've got to take care of the old woman today."

"Why are you telling me that?" she shouted. "I've never refused to do a job, I've always helped you with everything."

"Okay, cool it!" He moved closer and took her head under his arm. "Don't you worry, everything's going to be fine. We'll bump off the old woman, just one, the last one, and then we'll go absolutely straight all the way. We'll do business, earn money, take trips to the islands . . ."

Shortly afterward, they went outside. Validol opened the garage with the remote control. The flexible door creaked as it crept upward. The sunlight gleamed on the bumper and the radiator of the four-wheeled beauty. Two kids passing by stopped to gape at the limousine of the twenty-first century.

Valentin Yurievich drove out of the garage. The door came down. Gala settled down on the leather seat to the right of the man she loved. He shifted the lever to the DRIVE position and stepped smoothly on the gas, pulled out onto Monastery Street and accelerated from a standing start to a crazy speed for these narrow, bumpy, neglected streets.

"Valya! What's the rush?" said Gala, clutching at her safety belt and squinting at the speedometer. The hand raced around the dial and hit the 120 mark . . .

At that moment Aglaya Stepanovna Revkina was walking home from the shop at a speed of about two and a half kilometers an hour. In a plastic bag she was carrying two hundred grams of Odessa sausage, a chicken, a kilogram of potatoes, a tin of marrow paste and a head of cabbage. She remembered that Gala was coming today, and she'd be bringing vodka and some groceries. And perhaps (Gala had said) Valentin Yurievich might drop in too. Aglaya had decided to make some appetizers herself. She was just about to turn off Monastery Street into her own Komsomol Cul-de-Sac when a Mercedes emerged from around the corner, picked up speed, hurtled past her and was suddenly transformed by some strange metamorphosis into a flying ball of flame. Almost simultaneously, there was a thunderous bang, she felt a sharp pressure against her eyes and her eardrums, and chunks of metal and glass went flying in every direction. A torn-off wheel first shot up into the sky like a rocket, then fell onto the roof of a passing bus, bounced off and went hurtling along the precise center of the street, then swung to one side, knocking over a dog that was running past, and crashed into a cobbler's kiosk and knocked that over, complete with the cobbler sitting inside it.

Since our narrative does not belong to the genre of crime fiction, being no more than a truthful reflection of our criminal social reality, we shall avoid keeping the reader in a state of pointless suspense and say immediately that the reason Aglaya Stepanovna Revkina had been spared the fate intended for her by the Age with Dignity foundation was that Validol had a powerful rival—the financier Andrei Ignatievich Mosolov, nicknamed Mosol, who could have been a very faithful friend to Validol if only he didn't have ideas of his own for the mineral-water spring and the forthcoming elections.

The reader will no doubt recall that Validol had had his Mercedes insured and blessed. It might therefore seem strange that Valentin Yurievich's buggy exploded despite enjoying divine protection. It would seem strange, if we didn't happen to know that the infernal device located under the Mercedes had also been blessed. Mosol had taken it to the church specially, and he'd been more generous than Validol. And in addition, the device really had been put together very well.

Vanka Zhukov had calculated everything precisely. He just hadn't thought that Validol could drive through the streets of the town at that kind of speed.

85

"Can you explain to me why you hate America?" Vanka asked his new friend.

"Not just America," Jim replied. "I hate the whole world and all mankind. Man thinks he's the crown of creation. In actual fact, he's the most base and deceitful of all the animals—he can't ever be trusted—and the most irrational. Most people spend their time producing weapons and killing their own kind or preparing to kill them. How can beings claim to be rational if they can't even come to terms with each other and live in peace without causing each other suffering? Even the fiercest predator kills its victim to satisfy its own hunger. It's only people who kill each other and subject each other to incredible torment for the sheer pleasure of it. But most of all I hate people who are fit and well. One way or another, they were the ones who sacrificed us, and now they don't feel ashamed to walk and run and jump and play basketball and hug each other and wave their arms about. And when they see me or you, they turn their faces away, because we make them feel uncomfortable. The only people I have any time for are invalids like you and me, and I'd like everyone to be in our place for a month or a couple of weeks at least."

"But maybe the whole point is," wrote Vanka, "that people are more unhappy than animals. Unlike all the other creatures, they know that they're going to die."

"Yes," Jim agreed, "they are unhappy. But then they should all pity each other, not just themselves."

"But you don't pity them."

"That's precisely why I don't pity them. I used to, while I was a fit, healthy young man who studied in college and loved a beautiful girl and played basketball. Now I've earned the right not to pity anybody or love anybody. Apart from people like you and me. I drink to you."

"What are you drinking?"

"I always drink whiskey."

"With tonic?" Vanka asked.

"What?" asked Jim. "Whiskey with tonic? Do you seriously think it's possible to drink whiskey with tonic?"

"Why not?"

"Stop right there, my friend. If you drink whiskey with tonic, you'll go way down in my estimation."

"Why?"

"Because drinking whiskey with tonic is very bad taste. Something they only do in California. Nobody anywhere else ever drinks whiskey with tonic. They drink gin, vodka, vermouth, Campari and anything you like with it, but not whiskey. Whiskey is a noble drink, it's drunk with ice, with soda, with mineral water, with tap water and straight, like I take it. But with tonic . . ."

The next day he sent Gravalya to the supermarket, she brought back whiskey and tonic, and Vanka started drinking,

He drank for an entire week. Mixing whiskey with tonic in various proportions, drinking it, breathing it on to scent-detectors that he'd made himself and making various adjustments that only he understood. A week later the new device was finished and handed over to the client.

86

Vanka didn't watch television very often. But sometimes he took a very keen interest in the news. Usually, a few days after he completed another one of his products, there would be reports from Moscow or St. Petersburg or, more rarely, from other cities about an apartment, automobile or office that had been blown up and somebody or other important who had been killed. That was the way he found out just who he rid mankind of each time. But when it was reported that an explosion had occurred in a bus, a trolley-bus or a railway station, Vanka knew for certain that was someone else's sloppy handiwork.

A week and a half had gone by since he said goodbye to Ivan Ivanich, but nowhere—not even on the radio or in the newspapers—had there been a single report that fitted. Vanka was mystified, until one rainy afternoon a Land Rover jeep came tearing into the yard and Ivan Ivanich tumbled out almost before it had stopped moving, together with a blond guy who looked like some kind of soccer star. Gravalya was away dealing with the supply end of things and Vanka was sitting home with the door unlocked. They burst into the room without knocking and Ivan Ivanich, forgetting his manners, raised his voice from the doorway: "You bastard . . ." and noticed straightaway that something in the corner began rumbling menacingly.

Vanka warned him calmly: "Be careful, there are sensitive devices here. They react very acutely to rudeness and especially to firearms."

Ivan Ivanich immediately came to his senses and stopped the blond hulk, who was already pulling a metal object out of his pocket.

"So what exactly is the problem?" Vanka asked when his visitors had calmed down.

"As if you didn't know, jerk," said Ivan Ivanich.

"Less of the familiarity, if you don't mind," Vanka warned him again. "What happened?"

"That's just it, nothing happened," said the blond hulk, with a grim, searching look at Vanka. "We planted the bundle behind the safe, connected up the detector. Nothing happens."

"Mm," said Vanka thoughtfully. "He hasn't given up drinking by any chance?"

"Aw, come on!" Ivan Ivanich protested heatedly, almost as if he were offended for his boss, then immediately mended his manners. "I mean, of course not. First thing, the moment he arrives, he goes straight to the bar."

"Ugh." Vanka scratched his head. "Maybe he's switched to gin? Or vodka?"

"No, definitely not," Ivan Ivanich protested irritably. "He drinks the same way he always did, whiskey and tonic. And it's always the same brand—Jack Daniel's."

"Jack Daniel's?" Vanka repeated in amazement. "Why didn't you tell me that before? I thought it was Scotch whiskey, but if it's Jack Daniel's, that's bourbon. If he even drinks that with tonic . . ."

"And why not?" asked the blond thug.

"If our bankers drink garbage like that first thing in the morning, what confidence can anyone have in that kind of bank, and what kind of economy can we have? Okay, bring me a bottle of this Jack, we don't have it around here . . ."

"I've got one in the car," said Ivan Ivanich. "I'll just go and get it."

87

A few days later at half past nine in the morning, as always, Andrei Ignatievich Mosolov rode up in his emerald-green Jaguar to the side entrance of the Orion Bank, which, in his capacity as president, he used to launder his modest personal savings. The chauffeur immediately drove the car off to the guarded parking lot, and the president's two personal bodyguards entered the building but stayed downstairs. The president walked up to the second floor alone. He walked past the secretary and into his office. Hung his coat, hat and white muffler on the coat rack. Switched on the computer, opened the bar, tossed four ice cubes into a chunky glass, poured Jack Daniel's over them and added tonic. He'd learned to drink this barbarous concoction when he was living in America and studying at Stanford University. While he mixed his drink, the computer booted up and Mosol went online. He began reading the market reports and became rather concerned. While he was asleep, the equities in which his bank had invested the bulk of its capital had fallen sharply on the Tokyo exchange. Switching to another site, he discovered that the rights to the development of a mineral-water spring in the area of the town of Dolgov had been granted to his competitor Felix Bulkin, whom Andrei Ignatievich knew under the pseudonym of Chuma, or "Plague," from the days when they ran a scam together on the railroad and earned their first profit from selling fake Royal Polish pure spirits. Although his education was limited to two years in a textile-industry technical college, Plague had proved bright enough to break into big business and compete successfully even with a high-flying economist like Andrei Ignatievich Mosolov. Plague made up for his lack of education with his innately brazen character and his ability to worm or—as he put it—to slip and slide his way in absolutely anywhere.

"Why, you rotten slag!" Andrei Ignatievich exclaimed furiously, addressing his brazen rival. After delivering himself of a few more expressions that he learned in places far away from the London School of Economics, Mosolov dashed over to the safe to take a look at some compromising materials he had on Plague: a few documents, extracts from old court proceedings, videotapes.

Mosol opened the safe, and with the words "I'll show you what for, scumbag," he stuck his head inside.

The explosion wasn't powerful. The secretary thought it was just a loud pop. But when she glanced into the president's office, all she could see at first was smoke. And then through the smoke she made out the president's head smoldering like a dying firebrand where it had rolled away from his body. The secretary fainted, and afterward she took several months of hypnotherapy for a stammer.

PART FIVE

DANCING ON OUR STREET

88

Times were hard once again for Aglaya, living off a pension that was nowhere near enough. Not even enough to mend the window in her bedroom that was broken by boys playing soccer. She pasted it over with newspaper, but the newspaper tore and the bedroom was cold and drafty. She moved into the sitting room and slept on the sofa bed, leaving it unfolded all the time. The bed was hard, consisting of two convex halves like the twin humps of a camel. During the night Aglaya slipped down into the hollow in the middle and even though she had a warm blanket, she got chilled because there was a wide crack between the two halves of the sofa that let a cold draft through. She began getting headaches that prevented her from sleeping. And when she finally did get to sleep, little creatures—cockroaches, mice and bats—came to visit her, laughing and grinning. Sometimes the beasts looked like members of the Politburo. Sometimes she dreamed of members of the Politburo who looked like the beasts. When they disappeared, she would resurface into a state of wakefulness or semiwakefulness, chilled to the bone whatever the weather, her body covered in goose pimples and coated with cold, sticky sweat.

In the spring she started getting pains under the right side of her ribs. When she could bear it no longer, she called in the doctor. The local general practitioner arrived, aging and melancholy with a sea-skipper's beard branching sideways into two large clumps and wearing a white coat over his old overcoat. He examined her, listened to her chest, took her blood pressure, asked how her appetite was, did she have any nausea, vomiting or belching?

"I don't have any appetite," she said, "but I've got all the rest."

"Can you show me your hands?" He turned her palms toward the light and kneaded them with his soft fingers. "Pink palms. Your liver's switched on its cirrhosis alarm signal."

"What does that mean?" Aglaya asked.

"It means you have to stop drinking immediately and go on a diet: nothing fried or roasted, less salt and fat, more vitamins. If you stick to all that, then you'll live a while longer."

When the doctor left, she thought for a while, but unable to think of a reason for living any longer, she went out to the shop for some vodka.

89

In the shop she met Divanich wearing a filthy old civilian jacket. He'd grown his hair long like a priest's and woven it into a braid at the back. He was yellow and skinny as a rake, with the jacket dangling loosely on it, and there was not a single tooth in his head. She couldn't remember whether the last time she'd seen him was last year or yesterday, but for some reason she'd thought he was dead.

"I very nearly did die," Divanich mumbled through his gums. "I was in the hospital. They found growths in my rectum, and if, they told me, you don't have them out, they might turn malignant. Last time when they fixed my hernia the surgeon there was Semyon Zalmanovich Kantselson, an absolutely marvelous doctor. Hands worth their weight in gold. I never used to go to our Russian doctors, always tried to see the Jewish ones. Because a Jewish doctor works like a jeweler. He'll cut off what needs to go, but he won't touch anything else. This time when I get there, the doctor's Ivan Trofimovich Bogdanov. Two meters tall, shoulders way out here, hands all covered in ginger hair and freckles. I thought, He's been demoted from the meat-processing combine. I ask him, 'Where's Semyon Zalmanovich?' 'Him,' he says, 'he's gone to Israel.' 'What about Raisa Moiseevna?' 'Raisa Moiseevna went to America, to Chicago. And,' he says, 'what with our conditions and our pay, I wouldn't mind going to

Israel myself, but who'd let me in with a mug like this.' But he did me the operation well enough all the same."

"For money?" Aglaya asked.

"Where would I get money, Aglastepna? The number of times the government's abandoned us. First they give us Black Tuesday, then they come up with Black Friday. It's what they call a survival test. They want to get rid of all the country's dead weight. It costs the state too much to keep us pensioners, so they want to wipe us all out."

"Who are they?" Aglaya asked.

"Who else could they be?" said Divanich. "The Yids. They're everywhere. In the government, in the Duma—they're all Yids. Don't you think?"

"Aha," said Aglaya and nodded, although she had no opinion of her own.

Divanich had come without any money, but with his own glass, which he leased out. The dipsos who were a bit better off would ask for it to drink their bottle, and they'd pour him out a mouthful too. A mouthful here and a mouthful there was all he needed—his system was weak, it didn't require very much. Aglaya gave him a splash too and then trudged off home.

In the yard she skirted automatically around the foreign jeep on tall wheels with its number plates plastered over with mud. For quite a while now there had always been jeeps, Mercedes, Volvos and other foreign makes of automobile belonging to clients of Fireworks Inc. standing in the yard. There was a hulking brute behind the wheel of the automobile that Aglaya saw. As Aglaya walked past, he covered his face with the newspaper *Izvestiya* so that his repulsive features couldn't be seen, just his ears sticking out in opposite directions from behind the edges of the newspaper. But he needn't have bothered. It was a long time since Aglaya had noticed anything she didn't need to see, and what she did notice she immediately forgot.

She walked into the entrance hall and at that moment Vanka Zhukov's door opened. Aglaya caught the smell of nitroglycerine, which she knew from the time when she was a partisan and used to sabotage the railroads. Now the smell merely aroused a vague memory that failed to condense into any distinct image.

Two men came up the stairs from the semibasement, both thin and wiry, wearing long leather coats and peaked leather caps. Between them, each holding one handle, they were carrying a traveling bag, obviously very heavy, that bore the legend COPENHAGEN. As they climbed up, one of them looked Aglaya over closely, and the other gave her a look too, probably wondering whether it was worth bumping off the old dame as a potential witness. But his next thought was that the old dame was blind and deaf and probably wouldn't understand a thing, let alone remember anything. And instead of committing the crime he simply pulled the peak of his cap over his eyes and turned his face away slightly.

Aglaya walked on to her own apartment. First she carried her shopping bag through to the kitchen, but it was dirty and unwelcoming in there, so she decided to eat in the dining room. She spread out the *Dolgov Herald* on the low side table. Then she set out her bottle, a glass, some black bread on a carving board, two hardboiled eggs she'd prepared that morning, some onion and salt. She made herself comfortable and poured herself a third of a glass tumbler of vodka. Looked over at Stalin, smothered in dust and cobwebs. Thought he was looking at her reproachfully. "You stay where you are," she said, waving her hand at him. The newspaper was lying open in front of her, with the first and fourth pages of text upward. On the first page was news from Moscow: The president had met with the minister of justice and discussed problems of political extremism. The mayor of Moscow had decided to build the tallest skyscraper in the world in the Russian capital. An explosive device had been discovered in a kindergarten, with a mixture of nitrates and TNT. The local reports included one on the preparations for the district administration elections. The power involved wasn't that great, only within the limits of the local district, but just look at the number of people who were desperate to wield it! Aglaya's eyes were dazzled by the sheer number of political parties: communists, socialists, monarchists, liberals, democrats, constitutional democrats, social democrats, liberal democrats, members of the Unions for the Struggle for Freedom, of the Patriotic Forces, gays, whites, greens and all sorts of other tendencies, shades and hues.

Aglaya was not the only one afflicted with this kind of color blindness. The Admiral, confirmed as he grew older in his skeptical view of everything he observed taking place in the world around him, said that all our politicians came from the same incubator: they'd been marked with different-colored inks, but essentially there was no difference.

The final page held the sports news, the astrological forecast and the small ads, over which Aglaya's gaze slid indifferently: "Windows white-washed and wallpaper hung." "Opel Kadet auto for sale with spare set of tires." "The Indian sorcerer Benjamin Ivanov—supreme magic." "Instant binding and enchantment of your loved one by voodoo zombification. Free your husband completely of mistresses and bring him back home. 100% guaranteed." "Inexpensive. Dog coats cut, plucked and trimmed." "I bless apartments and offices, houses, lots, furniture and autos. Father Dionisii, priest." And in verse: "Doctor Fyodor Pleshakov cures alcoholics. Esperal, implants and programming for you. No more drinking the whole year through."

Aglaya wondered whether she ought to pay Dr. Pleshakov a visit. But not to drink for a whole year—was that possible? She dropped the idea and carried on reading about a sale of fur and sheepskin coats, getting windows glazed, getting wells drilled, having teeth removed painlessly, having floors sanded down and having your virginity restored (reliable, cheap, confidential).

90

Sitting there on the sofa, she fell into a doze and was visited once again by those little cockroaches or mice or something halfway between the two. They made faces at her, grinning and laughing, and when Aglaya asked them who they were, a little Divanich appeared and said: "Yids." And the cockmice's laughter became really insolent then, and Divanich banged his glass on the table and sang "La donna è mobile . . ."

The mouseroaches disappeared and Divanich evaporated into thin air, but the knocking continued. Aglaya tiptoed up to the door and asked in a quiet voice: "Who's there?"

The answer came back: "The Yids."

"Who?" she asked in amazement.

"The Yids," a male voice repeated. Aglaya took the chain off and saw a young man standing there in a long, thick woolen coat, holding a velour hat in his hand.

She glanced over his shoulder and asked: "Where are the others?"

"Who?" asked the visitor, puzzled.

"You said you were . . ." she said, and faltered to a halt, unwilling to pronounce a word which she avoided using.

"Zherdyk," said the visitor, introducing himself. "Alexander Petrovich Zherdyk, secretary of the district Party committee."

"Which party?" Aglaya inquired cautiously.

"The Communist Party, naturally, Aglaya Stepanovna," Zherdyk said impressively.

"Does the Communist Party still exist?" she asked.

"Of course it does," Zherdyk assured her. "It's growing stronger by the day. May I come in?"

She went through into the sitting room and he followed her. She felt embarrassed about the mess.

At the sight of Stalin her visitor didn't freeze and gape as others had done. He inspected the statue respectfully, bowed briefly toward it, turned around and bowed to Aglaya.

"Thank you," he said quietly but with feeling. "Thank you. Soon we shall restore Comrade Stalin to his rightful place."

Even these words failed to make any impression on her. He sat down on the stuffed arm of the sofa and, stretching his hat over his knee, began in an embarrassed voice: "Aglaya Stepanovna, we know all about you."

She didn't react to that either.

"We know all about your heroic past, your commitment to principle, your incorruptibility."

"Aha," she said, nodding.

"We may be at a bit of a low ebb right now, but you are not to blame for that," Zherdyk said passionately. "It's the times we live in. The uncertainty is enough to undermine anyone and bring them down. Elements alien to Russia have seized power. Snatched out of our hands what you devoted your life to fighting for. And what are we going to do about it?"

"What are we going to do about it?" Aglaya echoed.

"There is something we can do, Aglaya Stepanovna," Zherdyk said with conviction. "There certainly is something we can do about it. Just think. When we were in power, people didn't like us. But now they compare and they see how things were under the communists and how they are today. Poverty, prostitution, unemployment, a ruined army, striking miners, hungry teachers. Stealing, corruption, armed conflicts and terrorism. The people are coming back to us, Aglaya Stepanovna."

"Good," she responded indifferently.

"But we need your help."

"Mine?" she said in feeble surprise.

"Yours, Aglaya Stepanovna! Your help. Your immense experience of life and politics, your indomitable energy."

"Energy?" she protested. "What energy? I'm an old woman. Very old, weak." She looked her visitor in the eye, thought for a moment and confessed: "A drunk."

Zherdyk nodded sadly. "Yes. I've heard. You overdo it a bit. But we'll cure you. Of course, it will take determination to succeed from your side." Zherdyk jumped to his feet and ran across to Stalin, as though enlisting him as an ally: "Aglaya Stepanovna, remember who you are. Shake off this lethargy and join our ranks. The motherland and the Party are waiting for you!"

"Oh, don't do that," she said with a wave of her hand. "Don't say such things."

"I have to!" Zherdyk protested resolutely. "Aglaya Stepanovna, there's a war going on in the world. The forces of good have entered upon the final battle with evil. The struggle is taking place absolutely everywhere. Including our own district. And we have a very good chance of being victorious. But to win the victory we have to gather all of our forces. Aglaya Stepanovna, our organization, the Party and the people are begging you to rejoin the ranks. Join us and we will win, this time forever."

"And what am I supposed to do?" she asked disinterestedly.

"Address workers' collectives, take part in meetings and demonstrations . . . We'll send you to Moscow to take part in All-Russian events, in picket lines and street marches. Do you agree?"

"I don't know," said Aglaya, hesitating. "It's a bit unexpected. But won't they . . . won't they put us in jail for that?"

"What?" Zherdyk responded in amazement. "Aglaya Stepanovna, you're a partisan! A fearless warrior! What are you talking about? Jail a distinguished individual of your, I beg your pardon, age . . . What for? We have democracy now, after all."

"Democracy?" she looked at him doubtfully. "And you say they don't put anyone in jail?"

"Aglaya Stepanovna," said Zherdyk with a smile, "it's a corrupt democracy."

91

On April 16, 1995, Dr. Pleshakov made the following entry in his register of patients: "Aglaya Stepanovna Revkina, 80 years of age, referred with a case of chronic alcoholism. Complains of general weakness, debility, headaches and pains in the region of the liver, as well as a sour taste in her mouth, lack of appetite, hallucinations and loss of interest in life. In view of her advanced age it was decided to employ psychotherapeutic methods of treatment. A false blocking procedure was carried out with an intravenous infusion of physiological saline. The patient has been warned that for the next year the intake of even an insignificant amount of alcohol could result in fatal consequences."

The outcome of Aglaya's visit to Dr. Pleshakov was that she gave up drinking. And smoking too. She gave up both completely and was amazed herself at how easily she did it. And after only a few days she had already noticed that a sober life had a lot to recommend it. She was more aware. She no longer received visits from cockroaches, mice and little members of the Politburo. She began to find her bearings in time and space. She began to feel that life had some meaning and she wanted to do something; she felt once again that she was needed by the Party, the homeland and the people. And she loved Stalin with a new strength and hated those she had hated before with renewed vigor.

Delighted with her new condition, she made an effort to eat regularly, went walking for half an hour before breakfast and after lunch and took cool showers. And she made arrangements to travel to Moscow at the Party's bidding and expense, to take part in meetings, demonstrations and picket lines, where Stalin's portrait was always on show. Not the one that hung in her room. A color portrait. With Stalin in a forage cap and a military tunic with shoulder straps and decorations.

You might say that she had been reborn.

92

Evening was drawing in as a gentleman imperceptible against the twilight in his mouse-colored coat and fur cap (natural reindeer, article 4/6) approached the building at 1-a Komsomol Cul-de-Sac, carrying a smart briefcase with two number-coded locks.

"Tell me, Grannies, is this where Ivan Georgievich Zhukov lives?"

"Ivan Georgievich?" one of the old women queried. "You mean Vanka the bomb maker, do you?"

"The bomb maker?" The gentleman raised his eyebrows. "Does everyone know that he's a bomb maker then?"

"How could they not?" said the old woman. "We all live together here, neighbors, aren't we? Know all there is to know about each other."

"Yes?" he said in surprise. "You know, Grannies, what you know could be very useful to some people."

"You what?" said the second old woman, putting her crooked hand to her deaf ear.

"I was asking," the stranger said, raising his voice, "where he lives, this bomb maker of yours."

The old grannies immediately began talking across each other in their haste to explain to the stranger that Vanka lived in the semibasement, turn right as soon as you got downstairs, managing in the process to narrate to the stranger the entire story of Vanka's life. When and in what circumstances he was born and who his parents were, what a handsome boy he was before the army and how ugly he'd become afterward. And they told the stranger about Vanka's parents, and about his granny, who looked after him: cooked for him, did his laundry and was always going off somewhere on his business with great big bags and bringing him back things that they called spares.

"You mean his granny's there with him too?" asked the stranger.

"His granny's not there," said the first old woman. "She went to Moscow for spares. It's three days now since she left and she's still not back."

"So there's nobody looking after him right now then?" said the stranger.

"Oh yes there is," the same old woman answered. "We're looking after him. We go to the shop and do his washing and he pays for it all."

"Is he rich?" asked the stranger.

"Well he's certainly not poor. He does well out of those bombs of his. His customers come calling in those whatchamacallits . . ."

"Serdemesses," put in the second old woman.

"Not serdemesses, merdesesses."

"Six of one, half a dozen of the other," responded the second old woman.

"And in jeans and scallywags too," added the first old woman, meaning jeeps and Cadillacs, so putting the second old woman in her place.

The stranger thanked the old grannies for the detailed information and walked on. The steps down to the semibasement were crooked and slippery, the lightbulb was missing and the stranger walked down carefully, pressing one hand against the damp, rough wall.

When he got down, he groped till he located the torn felt upholstery of the door, but before knocking he transferred the briefcase from his right hand to his left and, holding on his cap with his right hand, pressed his eye to the keyhole. In fact, he spied nothing of any great interest, apart from a damp, narrow room with tattered wallpaper, a table illuminated by a low-hanging lightbulb with an orange shade, a hunched back in a gray sweater and a head of gray hair.

Without removing his eye from the keyhole, the gentleman knocked twice, then three times, then once again, and on seeing the man sitting at the table turn around and start moving toward him in his wheelchair, he jumped back from the door.

When he had a clear view of Vanka's condition, the stranger experienced a desire to back away, but he had been taught to control himself no matter what the circumstances, so he controlled himself.

Zhukov aimed the plastic leg at his visitor and his one eye glinted with a glint expressive of doubt. "Are you from Ivan Ivanich?"

"No, no," said the stranger, "let's just say I'm here on my own account. May I come in?"

"Then who sent you to me?"

"What makes you think somebody had to send me to you? Surely I can come on my own account?"

"But you found out from somebody what the secret knock is."

"Well, you know, that's one secret that's not hard to figure out. All amateur conspirators invent exactly the same formula for the knock. First *tap-tap*, then *tap-tap-tap* and then *tap* again. Always the same. No variety at all. Do you mind if I come in?"

After a moment's thought Vanka wheeled backward to the table and only then said: "Come in. Put the latch on the door. Stand where you are. Who are you?"

"I'll tell you in a moment." The unexpected visitor took off his cap, revealing a bald head with a sloping crown that was sunburnt and cracked like old tiles. "Only don't be scared and don't do anything hasty. I'm the official agent, or to put it more simply, the boss of the local branch of the FSB—a KGB man in your terms."

"Have you come to arrest me?" Vanka asked in a quiet voice.

"Oh come now!" said the stranger with a smile. "If this were an arrest, I would hardly have come alone. Especially to this place. We have your laboratory listed as 'Little Hiroshima.' How do you like that for a name? Anyway, I have no sinister intentions concerning you at all, quite the opposite, in fact . . ."

"You want me to tell you about my clients?"

"I can't pretend it wouldn't be interesting. But in this particular case I'd like to tell you about our clients. Or at least about one of them. As you know, we recently had local elections in our district. And united in a single expression of will, so to speak, our public elected a young, energetic—"

"You mean Sanka?"

"Well, you have the right to call our civic head Sanka because you're old friends, but for me he is now Alexander Petrovich, although in the distant years of our youth I also had the honor of his acquaintance. But this is all nonsense. I simply wanted to ask you how well you remember the time you used to rent a room from an old dissident woman in Moscow and Zherdyk used to come to see you there?"

"You want me to rat on him?" Vanka asked ironically.

"What a horrible expression! But it's taken root, I suppose. Well then, what I want to do is rat on someone to you. Would you really mind if I came a little closer?"

"Okay then," Vanka agreed. "But just bear in mind—"

"I already am . . ." his visitor was quick to reassure him.

Having moved closer, he looked around for a chair, and not finding one, he sat down on a green crate like an ammunition box, put his hat on the table, his briefcase on his knees, took out a red cardboard file, untied its silk ribbons, took another file—yellow this time—out of the red one and handed it to Vanka with the words "I think you'll find this interesting." It was a photocopy of some old handwritten texts. The reports, from an agent with the alias of La Donna, or LD in the abbreviated form, read approximately as follows:

> . . . he gave me Orwell's book 1984 to read. When I gave him back the book, he asked how I liked it. I said it was a powerful book, but the horrors in it seemed far-fetched and implausible to me. He asked me if I didn't think that life in the Soviet Union was like the life described in Orwell's book. I said that I didn't, that there wasn't such total control over each individual here and there couldn't be. It could happen in Germany or England, but not here, where thanks to the character of the people there had always been and would be the kind of disorder that was the most effective form of unintentional sabotage. He agreed with that opinion, but insisted that Orwell's prophecy was a work of genius. He gave me *The Gulag Archipelago* to read and asked my opinion about that as well. I said that it was a remarkable book as a documentary work, but some of the facts seemed dubious to me. He began arguing with me, saying that it was a book of exceptional artistic power, that perhaps in the entire literature of the world there was nothing to equal its power. I asked him if it was even better than *War and Peace*. He said yes, it was better than *War and Peace*. I said that was going too far; he said if that was going too far he wouldn't give me anything else to read. But only half an hour later he offered me a book to read by the Yugoslavian author Milovan Djilas, saying that it was an extremely powerful book, even more powerful than *The Gulag Archipelago*.

Vanka read the report, unable to believe his one and only eye, read about how he had listened to the BBC and Deutsche Welle, called Brezhnev a senile vegetable, believed that Brezhnev could not really have written his books for himself, been indignant when Brezhnev was awarded the Lenin Prize for literature and the Order of Victory, agreed with Reagan that the USSR was an evil empire, praised Levi Strauss jeans, expressed negative opinions about the collective farm system, claimed that Lenin had died of syphilis, asserted that Stalin was the illegitimate son of General Przhevalsky and joked that Stalin was a hybrid between Przhevalsky and Przhevalsky's horse and he looked like both of them.

Vanka went on to read about how he'd told jokes about the Civil War hero Chapaev, shown people photographs of Academician Sakharov, with whom he was supposedly in personal contact, had been pleased when the Canadians beat our national ice-hockey team and, most importantly of all, had built a photocopying machine on which he duplicated the *Chronicle of Current Events*.

Vanka read holding his gray head low and twisting it around as his one-eyed gaze crept from the beginning of a line to the end and back again. He stopped reading halfway through, turned his face away from the manuscript and froze motionless for a while, closing his eye and even seeming to go to sleep.

The visitor waited patiently. Vanka opened his eye and turned it toward the visitor.

"Why did you bring me this?" he asked.

"I wanted to open your eyes to your friend's real character," said the stranger, and suddenly felt an unexpected embarrassment at the thought that you couldn't open the eyes of a man who only had one.

"And that's all?" Vanka asked.

"Not entirely. Now you know that Zherdyk is a very bad man, but he is much worse than you know. A terrible man," the visitor said with feeling. "He ratted on you. He ratted on everybody he could. It was because of him that you ended up in the war, because of him that you became a cripple. This is a man with no principles, no honor, no conscience. In 'ninety-one he burned his Party card in public. And then in 'ninety-four he rejoined the Communist Party, rose to high positions in our district and now he's aiming higher. I tell you as a democrat—"

"You're a democrat?" Vanka asked in disbelief.

"Yes," his visitor said with dignity. "Basically, I'm a democrat. But I don't believe that democracy can be introduced and maintained with weak hands. The commies are willing to use any methods at all against us, and if we fight them wearing kid gloves, we'll lose. In other words, Vanya, I'm begging you to help—"

"I seem to have seen you somewhere before," said Vanka.

"You have," said his visitor with a nod and a smile. "You certainly have. And more than once. Roof is my name. Igor Sergeevich Roof."

The room went quiet. Vanka was silent, struck dumb by the sudden revelation.

"But . . ." he said. "Then why did you . . . you say you're from the KGB, that is, from the—"

"I'm telling the truth," said Roof. "Here, take a look."

He held out his open identity card. Looking out at Vanka from the photograph was the same Roof, only he was wearing a uniform with a major's shoulder straps.

"Well, well, what a career!" said Vanka with a shake of his head.

"We live in a time when many things are possible," said Roof with a laugh. "Bandits become secret policemen, secret policemen become bodyguards, Komsomol leaders become bankers, regional Party committee secretaries become governors, and Zherdyk becomes mayor. And hopes for greater things."

"And does he still sing 'La donna è mobile' like before?"

"Yes. When he's feeling happy about something."

"And does he often feel happy?"

"More often than I would like. He won the elections and he's planning to put Stalin's monument back up . . ."

"When?"

"I don't know. Most likely on December twenty-first, the tyrant's birthday."

"Okay," said Vanka after a moment's thought, and turned his eye toward the visitor. "Generally speaking, I take a large fee for my work, but I'll carry out this commission for nothing. All I need is for you to tape him singing 'La donna è mobile.' Can you do that?"

"What do you want it for?"

"A souvenir."

"We'll do it," promised Roof.

93

For the October holidays the communists in Moscow were planning a massive street demonstration. They were gathering together their adherents from all over the country who had nothing else to do, and one of them was Aglaya. She went, despite the fact that the holidays coincided with the local elections. As the elections approached, all the polls had put the communists in first place, and she naturally wanted to witness their victory.

But she couldn't miss the demonstration either.

"Go," Zherdyk told her. "You go, and we'll wage the struggle for you down here as well."

He gave her the money for an open-compartment ticket.

The train was packed with refugees, Russians from the Caucasian republics. They were not a very attractive crowd; they smelled bad and aroused as much disgust as pity. They were carrying with them everything that was left after the pillaging and extortion, and they had heaped up their suitcases, bundles, cardboard boxes and plastic bags tied around with sticky tape on all the upper bunks and on the floor between the bunks and the corridor.

Aglaya's bunk was the top one along the wall of the carriage, and the soldier who was traveling below her refused to swap for anything. For a long time he gave no reply to her attempts to appeal to his conscience, and then he explained to Aglaya in a whisper, but without any great embarrassment, that he was going into hospital for the treatment of incontinence.

"If anything happens during the night, Granny, it'll be the worse for you."

He helped her to clamber up onto the bunk, and she settled herself, lying on her back, but she fought against sleep, afraid of falling off the bunk in the night.

Despite the soldier's apprehensions, everything passed off without any embarrassing incidents, but she spent a restless night. It was hot in the open-plan carriage, but there were wandering drafts. The window in the next section didn't close. They'd covered it with plywood, but not tightly enough to keep the wind out, and it was especially strong when anyone opened the door to the vestibule on their way to the toilet or the next carriage. And apart from that, it was noisy. Children crying, old men snoring, someone groaning and a little distance away four men playing a furious game of cards and swearing venomously at each other for any bad leads.

After midnight the carriage became quiet, but at about two o'clock there was a sudden commotion: someone had been robbed in the first-class sleeping carriage. The victim had earlier noticed two Caucasians standing beside his compartment, and now the captain of the train, a policeman and the victim himself were waking up men who were sleeping, turning them over and shining a flashlight in their faces, and the captain of the train kept asking the victim: "This one? This one?" The roused men grumbled and muttered, asking why on earth they were being woken up, but as people without any rights, they expressed their indignation timidly and uncertainly. Naturally, the thieves were not discovered, because they were being sought in the wrong place. Divanich had once told Aglaya that thieves in railway carriages always worked in collusion with the conductors and the captain of the train was in on it too, so if there was a scandal he deliberately organized a raid where nothing would be found.

94

At Savyolovskya Station she was met by a man in a thick padded coat, a peaked leather cap and tall boots. He was at least fifty years old, but he introduced himself familiarly as Mitya. Aglaya had the idea that she'd seen him somewhere before. Mitya led her off on foot to somewhere close by—he said they were going to the Marina Roshcha district. It was cold and windy and there was a fine drizzle falling, running down people's cheeks and turning to ice on the asphalt. Aglaya's knees were hurting, her head was full of cotton wool and her throat was feeling sore. Her feet slid apart on the wet pavement, and she was afraid of falling. She couldn't keep up with her guide, and every now and then she stopped and Mitya hopped from one foot to the other as he waited patiently, smoking and wiping his face with a coarse palm.

Eventually, they reached a three-story brick building and a green metal door bearing the modest notice KNIGHT INC. BOOK DEPOT. They walked up jagged brick steps to a landing, then walked down more of the same kind of steps into a semibasement, across a floor of crookedly laid bricks to another door, also metal, beyond which they found a large open space generously illuminated by daylight lamps. There were no indications of any book depot; it looked more like a canteen or perhaps a lecture hall: several rows of long green tables with synthetic tops and plastic garden chairs. On the wall opposite the entrance there was a blackboard with a list of names written on it in chalk. There was also a large sheet of paper with a picture of a target pinned to the board.

Standing on the table to the right of the entrance in front of a red-headed girl wearing jeans and a crimson jumper was a folded piece of card with the words DELEGATE REGISTRATION. Mitya gave Aglaya's name and initials as a new arrival, the girl noted it all down in a register and asked what organization she was from. "From Zherdyk in Dolgov," Mitya answered. Beside the redhead a blond man of the same age wearing a baseball jacket was selling books. The most prominent spot was occupied by a book by the Party's leader, Alfred Glukhov, entitled simply and modestly *Marching Together*, an expensive edition in a colorful binding with numerous color photographs, each protected by tracing paper. Everything here was jumbled up together: *Das Kapital* by Karl Marx, *Report with a Noose Around My Neck* by the long-forgotten Julius Fuchik, two tattered volumes of Lenin, the stories of Victoria Tokareva, dictionaries, the manual *Windows 95 for Dummies*, a brochure called *Learn Sharpshooting*, detective novels and books about sport. And then Aglaya spotted Mark Shubkin's book *The Timber Camp*. She turned the book over in her hands, noticed that it was a new edition amended by the author and decided to buy it.

Beside the counter two young artists were crawling around on a sheet of Whatman paper laid out on the floor, drawing caricatures of the president in a dunce's cap sitting on a throne with an idiotic expression on his face. On each side of the president an obsequiously bowed, hook-nosed oligarch was whispering something in his ear, and the oligarchs were being prompted in turn by the prime minister of Israel and the president of the United States. There were several people standing over the artists and looking at their work, laughing and exchanging spiteful comments.

There were already quite a lot of people in the hall who had arrived before Aglaya. Most of them were elderly people from out of town, with suitcases, kit bags and bundles at their feet. Many of them were drinking tea, to which they helped themselves from a nickel-plated electric samovar. Two Cossacks in long cavalry greatcoats with shoulder straps bearing insignia unfamiliar to Aglaya, wearing tall fur hats and with sabers at their sides, were dozing sitting face-to-face. One of the Cossacks was wearing decorations of some order that Aglaya didn't recognize pinned on the front of his greatcoat—crosses that looked as though they'd been cut out of tin cans or cast from tin in a village stove.

In the corner, under a copy of the painting *Stalin at the Demonstration in Baku*, sat a man whom Aglaya had recently seen on the television. He was a famous writer who had come from abroad, and until recently he'd been regarded as a rabid anti-Communist. Now he had repented. Being of a very high opinion of his own works, he was sure that they were the only reason the Soviet regime had collapsed. But one look at the forces that had now assumed power had been enough to make him feel ashamed of his former books, statements and actions, regret that he had destroyed the Soviet regime, and promise in his penitence to set the old order back on its feet with his new writings.

The writer was not sitting alone; he was with an old man wearing an unbuttoned general's greatcoat, with three stars on his shoulder straps. Aglaya recognized him as Fyodor Fyodorovich Burdalakov, the same man with whom she had once had a brief holiday romance. How could she fail to recognize him, when he had been shown so many times on television as one of the main instigators of various communist events? But how he had changed! That winter when they used to run along the seashore in Sochi, he was still a robust man with a broad, strong back and muscular legs, but what she saw now was a decrepit, feeble grandfather with sparse, disheveled gray hair protruding untidily in all directions and a short-trimmed gray mustache. Gleaming brightly under Fyodor Fyodorovich's open greatcoat were two golden stars of a Hero of the Soviet Union (he had been awarded the second for length of service). He had his medal ribbons on the left side of his chest and two orders on the right side. There was something that looked like an umbrella in a silk case leaning up against the table beside the general. Aglaya recognized the stick and the case.

"Hello, Fyodor Fyodorovich," she said, approaching the general.

He lifted his head to look at her, mumbled a brisk " 'lo" and turned back to the writer. But then he immediately swung back and asked uncertainly: "Aglaya Stepanovna? Glasha?" He jumped to his feet, at the same time clutching at his waist. "Well I never! Look at that! Fancy seeing you! You haven't changed a bit."

"Oh haven't I!" said Aglaya, rejecting the compliment. "I'm an old woman."

"Oh no, don't say that!" said Fyodor Fyodorovich, refusing to concede. "The gray hair ages you a little, of course, but with a touch of color . . ."

Fyodor Fyodorovich apologized to the writer and switched all of his attention to Aglaya, and the writer immediately began to sulk and pulled a sour face. He always took offense at anyone who didn't regard him as the center of attention. He sat there beside them for a while feeling bored, then went off to find someone he could tell about his historical guilt before the Soviet people and the means for making restitution.

Aglaya and Fyodor Fyodorovich talked about this and that, reminisced about Sochi. Fyodor Fyodorovich asked why she had gone away so suddenly that time. She said: "I just did."

"And can you imagine," said Fyodor Fyodorovich, "there I was just back . . . And not empty-handed either, by the way. I bought you a watch"—he hesitated for a moment—"a gold one. And perfume"—he exaggerated again—"French it was. So there I am knocking at the door, the door opens and who do you think is standing there in person? Vyacheslav Mikhailovich Molotov. Just imagine it . . . Molotov himself . . ."

They spoke of their age and their ailments. Aglaya told the general what an uncomfortable journey she'd had in the heat and the draft, and now it felt like she'd caught a cold—her throat was sore, her chest was clogged up and her back was aching. Fyodor Fyodorovich promptly set about trying to cure her with hot tea with sugar and lemon. Over tea they began swapping recipes for mixtures and infusions from folk healers, but before they got on to the liniments and rubs, there was a slight commotion in the hall. The door opened, and a number of powerfully built young men with expressionless faces, all wearing identically distended jackets, entered in menacing silence and immediately took up positions around the walls. Following them, appearing out of nowhere, came a stout man of about fifty with a gray, lumpy face and two warts on his nose. Aglaya, of course, immediately recognized him as the leader of the Party, Alfred Glukhov—how could she fail to, when she saw him every day on every TV channel? The leader's appearance was greeted with disorderly uproar: people began clattering their chairs on the floor, banging on chair backs and clapping their hands. Fyodor Fyodorovich rose to his feet with the others, but the leader immediately ran over to him and pushed him back down onto his chair with both hands, saying: "Please, please, Fyodor Fyodorovich, no need for that. Anyway, my rank doesn't merit it; you're a general and I'm only a senior lieutenant." To which Fyodor Fyodorovich replied humbly, with no small hint of flattery: "Today a senior lieutenant, tomorrow the Supreme Commander-in-Chief."

"Well, perhaps," the leader replied modestly, but without attempting to reject the prospective assignment. "If we have to, we'll take power. Certainly we will. The bottom line is that we have a historical responsibility, and no one has relieved us of it. Are you also a member of the Party?" he asked, turning to Aglaya.

"Yes, and what a member she is!" Fyodor Fyodorovich responded enthusiastically.

And he immediately informed the leader that Aglaya Stepanovna Revkina, a communist since before the war, had been a district Party committee secretary and commanded a partisan unit . . .

"Oho!" the leader interrupted him. "Very pleased to meet you."

She had expected to feel a firm comradely handshake, but the leader's hand proved to be as flabby and soft as a sponge, and it was sweaty as well, which made an unpleasant impression on Aglaya. From socialist-realist works of literature she knew sweaty hands and shifty eyes were signs of a very bad person who was not one of us. Our people looked you straight in the eye and shook your hand firmly with a dry palm. But it was no more than a fleeting feeling that disappeared almost as soon as it appeared. Especially when the leader noticed Aglaya's feverish eyes and asked whether she had a cold. Which endeared him to her greatly. A man like that, who had taken on such a weight of responsibility, who had dealings with so many people, and he still had time to notice that she looked unwell. Aglaya was about to say, "Never mind, it's nothing serious," but at that precise moment she began sneezing and coughing painfully. Fyodor Fyodorovich took the opportunity to tell the leader he'd like a quick word with him about something.

"What's the *problème?*" the leader asked quickly.

"The problem is," Fyodor Fyodorovich explained, "that here we have an old woman who had to travel on the side bunk in a carriage with a broken window."

The leader listened with a frown.

"There," he said, "see to what a state an antipopular administration and a drunken president have reduced the country. A distinguished veteran, a war hero, a woman, and she has to travel in conditions like that.

"Don't you worry," he said to Aglaya, "just endure it a little while longer and you'll travel back in comfort, I promise you."

With these words he clapped his hands and said quietly: "Mitya!"

Mitya promptly popped up like a genie out of a bottle.

"Here, Mitya, deal with this," said the leader in a low voice. "A ticket home for Aglaya Stepanovna Revkina in a first-class sleeping compartment. Understand? Not an open carriage and not second class, but a first-class sleeping compartment." And as he slowly moved away, he repeated it so that other people noticed, "Don't forget! First-class car, not second class."

After he left Aglaya, he began moving rapidly around the hall in a seemingly haphazard pattern, but actually zigzagging his way toward the exit, squeezing people's hands, asking what the *problème* was, swapping phrases, slogans, jokes and interjections. And he wriggled his way out as imperceptibly as he had entered . . .

95

Immediately, a crackling loudspeaker announced that it was time to board the bus.

"Allow me," said Fyodor Fyodorovich gallantly, and took Aglaya by the elbow, either to support her or to support himself against her. He limped quite noticeably, and in an extremely interesting manner, setting his left foot down gently, but smacking his right foot down hard, as though he were driving home a nail. "Old wounds," he explained to Aglaya, although he'd never been wounded in his life. He went right through the war without a scratch; the only thing wrong with his legs was old age.

At the door of the book depot the redheaded girl and the young man were now handing out what they called agitational accessories to everyone who wanted them. These were portraits of Lenin and Stalin, but mostly of Stalin (no one took Lenin), and for those who were a bit younger and stronger, banners with communist and revolutionary slogans such as GLORY TO LABOR! or COMMUNISM IS INEVITABLE! or negative oppositional slogans such as NO TO THE ANTIPOPULAR REGIME! or ZIONISTS OUT OF THE GOVERNMENT! and something else about wages and pensions. Fyodor Fyodorovich didn't need anything. He always had his own banner with him, but Aglaya had forgotten to bring her own portrait and had to use one of the cheap official ones. It showed Stalin in uniform with all his orders in place and wearing a peaked cap, but somehow the image completely lacked majesty. The subject looked less like a glorious generalissimo than a local policeman due for retirement.

96

Waiting outside in readiness were four big Hungarian Icarus buses with Yaroslavl license plates, but the passengers easily fitted into one. Aglaya and Fyodor Fyodorovich found themselves on the front seat. He sat with his banner clutched as usual between his knees, telling Aglaya how that time back in Sochi he'd been courting her with absolutely serious intentions, since he was a widower and he needed a companion in his campaigns. And since on that occasion his romance with Aglaya had come to an end unexpectedly, he had been obliged to seek another candidate. And just then his front-line comrade General Vasya Serov had died. So Fyodor Fyodorovich had married the general's widow.

On Sushchevsky Embankment Street they got stuck in a hopeless traffic jam, and Fyodor Fyodorovich explained to Aglaya that jams like this appeared every time the president drove through Moscow.

"So he's just driven by somewhere near here?"

"Not necessarily," replied Fyodor Fyodorovich. "No matter where he drives, the traffic is backed up all over Moscow. He drives down this street, so they close all the connecting streets. Those streets are closed, so there are jams on the others. Those create more problems, and the whole of Moscow is paralyzed. It's like a coronary thrombosis."

"That's our people's president for you," commented the Cossack with the crosses, who was sitting behind them. "I served in Brezhnev's bodyguards — we used to stop the traffic too. But only as he drove along the route, not in advance."

"But they have to stop the traffic," said Fyodor Fyodorovich. "He doesn't travel alone. There's the lead car in front, then the bodyguards, then him, then the escorting cars, then the reanimation unit. He's a very old man," the general reflected, forgetting that the "very old man" was twenty-something years younger than he was.

The bus stopped outside the left wing of the movie theater Russia. The doors opened and the passengers began jumping out and opening their umbrellas at the same time, so that all in all they looked like paratroopers on a raid. The cold, thin, sticky rain was still falling, and Aglaya had no umbrella.

A marshal in a cloth coat swollen by the damp, with a gleaming-wet bald patch and a nose the same red color as his armband, asked the new arrivals to walk across to the statue of Pushkin.

There were two crowds at the monument: the participants in the meeting, and policemen. The latter were standing in their wet, baggy greatcoats on the corner close to the offices of the newspaper *Izvestiya*, smoking and glancing at the demonstrators every now and then without any particular curiosity. As though they'd just turned up here to stand around in the rain.

Aglaya looked around curiously. Although she had often been in Moscow recently, she kept on being surprised. Everywhere there were signs of a life that wasn't ours. The McDonald's restaurant, the advertisement for Renault automobiles, a poster for a foreign film described as an erotic comedy and one with a portrait of a sad old woman with the plea PLEASE, PAY YOUR TAXES. The slanting rain inundated the poster, turning the tears running down the old woman's face into a living stream.

The meeting didn't start for a long time—they were waiting for Glukhov. A marshal made a call on his cell phone, putting his hand over the top to protect it from the rain. He got an answer; he told them Comrade Glukhov was stuck in a traffic jam, but he was getting close. Finally, the leader appeared in his Mercedes with a flashing blue light and four bodyguards. One of the bodyguards leapt out while the car was still moving and opened the rear door, as though Comrade Glukhov were an invalid or a woman. Several other members of the core leadership emerged from the two Volga automobiles that followed the Mercedes, also with their bodyguards, which bulked up the crowd significantly. Glukhov, accompanied by a man with an umbrella advertising Coca-Cola, squeezed his way into the middle of the crowd, but still the meeting didn't start. After a while a Mitsubishi minibus drove up, and members of the Workers' Shield movement, who didn't actually work anywhere, tumbled out of it with their red banners. Their leader, Syropov, a thick-set man with a damaged lip, pushed his way through to Glukhov, trying to speak to him and grabbing hold of his elbow in a passionate attempt to persuade him of something. Glukhov kept turning away and pulling his arm free, until his bodyguards managed to push Syropov aside.

Fyodor Fyodorovich asked a marshal what they were waiting for. The marshal explained that they were waiting for the journalists. Two television channels had promised to send teams to cover the event. They waited for at least an hour, but no journalists arrived apart from Maxim Milkin, who rolled up in an armored jeep with security men of his own. Since he had had his face beaten in twice, Milkin rode around inside armor-plating, accompanied by bodyguards, just like Glukhov. On seeing before them such an illustrious representative of the fourth estate, the men surrounding Glukhov made way for him and Milkin stepped up to Glukhov, holding his Dictaphone.

"Tell me, Mr. Glukhov, what are you trying to prove with today's demonstration?"

"We," Glukhov replied with dignity, "don't have to prove anything; life itself provides our proofs. The ideals of the revolution and communism live on in the people's aspirations, and the people honor the memory of our glorious past. As you can see, despite the opposition of the antipopular regime, despite the bad weather, thousands of people have come to the square today."

"Well, I'd say hundreds," Milkin corrected him cynically. "Or even tens. But tell me, I see your supporters are carrying portraits of Stalin. Don't you think your loyalty to that butcher drives away people who might share your ideals?"

"You know, as a historian, I take an unbiased view of the figure of Stalin. Under Stalin's leadership great mistakes were made. Mistakes, well anybody can make mistakes, but viewed against the course of the historical process, they naturally don't appear so significant. Especially, well, you know they say Stalin killed so many millions. But we're realists. We realize that if he hadn't, sooner or later those millions would have died anyway."

"A final question. Do you intend to run for president?"

"In our Party we don't put the question like that. Our candidates at all levels, including for president, are nominated by the Party. But I won't indulge in false modesty. As you yourself know, I occupy an important position in the Party, and it is quite possible that the communists will nominate me."

"But how do you feel?" Milkin persisted. "Would you like to be president?"

"Your question is posed incorrectly. We communists don't regard power as a way to get rich or fulfill our personal ambitions, but as a historical duty. Some of our politicians allow their heads to be turned by the desire to achieve supreme power, but I take a cool view of power. If I have to be president, I'll be working full tilt all the time, not just between the booze, the bathhouse and the intensive care unit," he confided, with a dig at the current president.

At this point people standing nearby laughed and applauded loudly. Milkin made a note of the answers and drove away, leaving the crowd a bit thinner.

Then came another pause. Eventually, a team of four people arrived: a cameraman, a director, a sound engineer and a producer. They asked Glukhov to step aside with them for negotiations. He went across to them, only not alone, but with the umbrella-bearer. The talks were brief but furious. Aglaya couldn't hear all the conversation, but she heard Glukhov say several times: "I don't understand what the *problème* is. I repeat, we have a specific agreement, and you're breaking it. I'll be talking to your management, which is attempting to deprive the people of its right to be heard on the orders of a criminal regime."

Without waiting for him to finish, the television men got into their Latvian RAF minibus and drove off. Glukhov looked embarrassed and disappointed. And in response to Fyodor Fyodorovich's glance of inquiry, he explained that the television men had demanded ten thousand dollars for a ten-minute slot and refused even to discuss half of that amount.

"Never mind though," said Glukhov, "we have our own cameraman. He can shoot it with an amateur camera, and then we'll copy it to VHS."

So saying, Glukhov once again mounted the steps at Pushkin's feet and addressed the people gathered there with a speech about how today our entire people was celebrating the holiday that the workers still regarded as the most important one in their calendar. Confused by the pseudodemocrats, a president who had dissolved his brain in drink, his criminal family and the oligarchs, the people had deviated slightly from the ideals of socialism, but the further it deviated, the more eagerly it returned to them, as our action today testified, with participation from the broad masses of the workers.

They applauded politely at "broad masses" and heard that they were once again girding themselves to struggle for what their grandfathers had once won.

"People," Glukhov continued, "are flocking to our banners, and with great joy we are organizing communist cells for them right across the former Soviet Union . . ."

"Former and future!" came a shout from the crowd.

"And future," Glukhov agreed.

"Including the Crimea and Sebastopol," added Syropov, who had appeared beside him.

"Naturally, including them too," Glukhov agreed. And he concluded his speech with the standard incantations: "Marx's teaching is all-powerful because it is true. Communism is inevitable because it is unavoidable."

With these words he stepped down onto the ground and his place was taken by a marshal, who announced through a megaphone: "Demonstrators, form up into a column six wide. Standard-bearers walk at the front. We walk calmly without hurrying, ignoring any provocations. Comrades, I warn you especially, we will not give way to provocation either from the left or from the right. We walk as far as Vladimir Ilich Lenin's Mausoleum, lay a wreath and then move on to the tomb of the unknown soldier, lay a wreath and after a brief final meeting we disperse peacefully. Comrades, I especially want to say this: There are many policemen here at the moment. By agreement with the mayor's office they are keeping order. But of course, they may resort to the use of violence. We ask all participants to behave in an organized and peaceful manner. Maintain discipline."

97

Everything was going well. Even nature had decided to smile on the demonstrators. The rain stopped, gaps appeared in the clouds and rays of sunlight poked out through them like bundles of straw. Pushkin's wet bronze head gleamed in the sun's rays, the big yellow M of "McDonald's glowed, the running neon slogan of the Renault advertisement dimmed a little and only the old woman asking people to pay their taxes remained sad, her drying tears a reminder to her fellow-citizens that the sun might have come out, but the taxes had still not been paid.

Somewhere someone shouted something. Aglaya couldn't make out what, but from the general movement of the assembly she realized a command had been given and in response people were moving out into the middle of Tverskaya Street, which was closed to traffic.

"Comrades," the organizer with the gleaming bald patch called, running back and forth, "let's form into a column six wide. At least one step between the rows. Plenty of space between the lines. Lady with the portrait," he said, turning to Aglaya, "don't be so timid! Stand over here. No, not in the middle, at the edge, so the people standing on the pavement can see your portrait."

Aglaya stood where she was shown, but she was immediately spotted by Fyodor Fyodorovich, who came across to her, limping heavily.

"Come on, Glashenka, this isn't the place for you. Come with me, come on."

The column gradually took shape and evened out. The front was taken by two heavyweights carrying an unfurled banner with an inscription in white on red: "The people are with us, we are with the people." Then came Alfred Glukhov and other Party leaders with red bows of ribbon on the lapels of their coats, and in the next row Fyodor Fyodorovich, Aglaya and assorted veterans. Fyodor Fyodorovich took the place in the very center, immediately behind Glukhov, putting Aglaya to his right, and to his left he put another old woman, also with a portrait of Stalin. Afterward, incidentally, some sharp-eyed journalist spotted that there were about ten portraits of Stalin in the column, but not one of Lenin.

"Right then," muttered Fyodor Fyodorovich, pulling the tarpaulin cover off his standard, "even the weather appears to be significantly, so to speak, favoring us."

There was a wind, not a strong one, but enough for Burdalakov. The general unfurled the standard, raised it above his head, it fluttered in the wind and the words TAKE BERLIN! shimmered and danced like a running advertising slogan. And at that very moment Glukhov quietly gave the command to the heavyweights. "Okay, let's go!" They hoisted their proud banner still higher and set off, with the whole column following them.

Meanwhile, the weather improved even more, the sun shone for all it was worth and steam rose from their wet clothing. From the very first steps Aglaya felt more cheerful and warmer and actually quite well. They didn't walk fast, but the way they walked made it clear that although these people might be old they were accustomed to marching in strict formation. Fyodor Fyodorovich dragged his left foot slightly and smacked the asphalt hard with his right foot, but he kept up, gripping his martial standard firmly, his hatband, chest and mouth gleaming brightly with assorted metalware.

At first they walked in silence. Aglaya unintentionally overheard the conversation taking place behind her between a Cossack and an old man in a dark raincoat and hat. The Cossack was saying that he lived in Tuapse and had got rich by simply taking a riverboat that had been standing idle and ownerless, repairing it and ferrying shuttle-traders to Turkey and back, then he'd bought a big diesel-electric ship and started taking tourists all over Europe.

"Now I've got two diesel-electric ships, three pleasure cruisers and five launches."

"So how come you've joined up with us?" the old man asked curiously. "All of us here have been screwed by the authorities, we're lumpens, but you've got a fortune."

"That's right, a huge material fortune. But what good is it to me? I get no satisfaction out of it. I wanted to get married, but then I thought, No. As long as I'm rich, I'll never be able to tell whether she married me for love or for money. I used to be an engineer in the construction mechanization office, so Liudka wouldn't marry me, because I only earned a hundred and fifty a month. She took the director of a shop, who earned a hundred and stole a thousand. But now she says she's realized what her real feelings are. Now she's realized. I reckon it's my diesel-electric ships that have helped her make up her mind."

The column moved slowly toward the former Soviet Square.

Suddenly, Glukhov turned around and said: "Why are we walking along as if it was a funeral? Let's sing something revolutionary. Aglaya Stepanovna, you probably remember some revolutionary songs."

Aglaya Stepanovna was embarrassed, but after a moment's thought she said that she didn't remember the songs because at the time of the October Revolution she was only two years old and the granny who rocked her in the cradle had not sung "Hostile Winds Circling Above Us," but something like "Bye baby bunting, daddy's gone a-hunting."

"Oh really?" said Glukhov, unable to imagine that this old woman had ever been a child, but then he realized this was nonsense and felt embarrassed himself. "Yes," he said profoundly. "The distant, irretrievable time of childhood. It seems so long ago—I can hardly believe myself that I was once a little boy chasing barefoot after the pigeons and singing pioneer songs round the campfire . . ."

He made up his past out of his head on the spot, assuming that a childhood like that—proletarian and barefoot with pigeons—must be compulsory for a leader of the people. In actual fact, as the son of a Party boss, he had never gone barefoot and never chased pigeons and in general had been a well-nourished, plump, sluggish and rather stupid boy. It is possible, however, that he did some sitting around a campfire.

Once launched on his reminiscences, he couldn't stop himself: "Those were good times. Romantic. And the way people treated each other then! Such noble, joyful relationships. Everyone prepared to sacrifice his own life for his comrade! But life was hard, Aglaya Stepanovna. Sometimes there wasn't even a crust of bread in the house," he lied again, and then said sadly, "But never mind all that. Let's sing something revolutionary anyway."

"I can try something," responded the owner of the diesel-electric ship from behind Aglaya, and launched straight into a song in a hoarse bass:

> *Exhausted by oppression and unfreedom,*
> *In death you won fame and renown.*
> *You fought for the cause of the people*
> *And honestly laid your weary head down.*

There had been times when Aglaya, thinking about the revolution, had regretted being born just a bit too late and missing the romantic period of the Party's struggle with the old tsarist social order—when young communists had turned out for meetings and demonstrations and walked along singing under the whips of the Cossacks and the bullets of the police. Of course, she had also lived in fascinating and eventful times, but she'd missed out on that revolutionary romanticism. But now . . . Even though, of course, many bad things had happened and the enemies of communism had seized power . . . Now she had been given the chance in her old age to experience the conditions under which the revolutionaries of former times had lived. She recalled the picture she had seen earlier that day, *Stalin at the Demonstration in Baku*. Soso Djugashvili walking at the head of a detachment of Bolsheviks in close ranks, wearing a Russian-style shirt with the collar unbuttoned, young and dark-haired, with his eyes open wide as they gazed ahead into the future. History repeats itself. Now she, Aglaya Stepanovna Revkina, was striding along in the ranks of her comrades, proudly carrying the portrait of their beloved leader.

Glancing back, she couldn't see how far the column extended. In actual fact, it couldn't extend very far because there wasn't very much of it, but it seemed to Aglaya that she was striding along at the head of a procession of the people. As she walked, she saw people on the sidewalks along the edges of the roadway watching the column go past and imagined they were admiring onlookers. In fact, they were only casual passersby who were so well used to spectacles like this that they didn't even display any particular curiosity. Several of them actually felt uncomfortable and pitied these stupid, malicious, helpless and ridiculous old people. As people of the new generations, they thought they were quite different and could never become like them. But that is not the way things really are. The generations are no better or worse than each other; their beliefs, mistakes and behavior depend on the historical and personal circumstances in which they grow up. It doesn't take a prophet to predict that people will be blinded again, and more than once, by false teachings, will yield to the temptation of endowing certain individuals with superhuman qualities and glorify them, raise them up on a pedestal and then cast them back down again. Later generations will say that they were fools, and yet they will be exactly the same.

98

On Tverskaya Square opposite the former Moscow City Soviet Building, a unit of mounted police was waiting, and the equestrian statue of the city's founder, Yury Dolgoruky, towered up in the midst of these horsemen like their commander.

Suddenly, someone said: "Look, look!"

Aglaya glanced ahead, and where Tverskaya Street ran into Hunter's Row, she saw a cordon of men in green helmets with Plexiglas shields and truncheons. They stood there in a menacing, unassailable wall, their faces tensed as if they were facing the advance of 180 crack enemy divisions, not just a bunch of old people. Some of the demonstrators felt a bit frightened and slowed their stride despite themselves. But Aglaya broke off the song they were singing and took up the Soviet national anthem:

> Unshakable union of free republics
> Forever united by Russia the great . . .

Her voice was decrepit, hoarse and low, but Fyodor Fyodorovich joined in and supported her in his creaky tones:

> Created as one by the will of the peoples,
> Soviet Union, united and strong . . .

They were supported in turn by the owner of the diesel-electric ships, and everybody picked up the refrain:

> Glory, our Fatherland . . .

They approached the OMON Special Police to the strains of the anthem, halted face-to-face with them and marked time as they continued singing.

The sun of our freedom shone through the dark storm,

sang Aglaya, remembering the beginning of the second verse.

And our mighty Lenin illumined our way,

continued General Burdalakov, smacking his right foot against the cobblestones.

Raised up by Stalin,

Aglaya joined in joyfully . . .

"Comrades," called a marshal, running along the column, "please, all of you, maintain formation. Do not break formation."

But despite this the column gradually folded into itself, its ranks spreading out along the cordon, and Aglaya found herself standing face-to-face with a policeman, a young country boy of about twenty, with little slanting eyes set in a round face. The demonstrators carried on singing their song and Aglaya sang with them, looking the policeman straight in the eye. He gazed at her in unblinking amazement. Aglaya looked around at the other policemen; they were standing firm too, but they were exchanging glances and laughing. Aglaya's feelings were absolutely divided. On the one hand, these seemed like our very own Soviet, Russian lads, the same kind she'd gone into the attack with against a detested enemy, but on the other hand they were the detested enemy, prepared to join battle with her when the order came.

Meanwhile, a police sergeant, also wearing a helmet but without a shield, approached Glukhov and tried to tell him something, but Glukhov wouldn't let him speak, he carried on singing and only gave him his attention when the song was finished.

"What is it, Colonel? What's the *problème?*"

"Mr. Glukhov," the sergeant said in a quiet voice, "I have been instructed to inform you that your demonstration terminates at this point. Please inform your people and have them disperse."

"Why should we?" asked Glukhov. "We had a firm agreement with the mayor."

"I don't know what agreement you had with anyone, but I have been ordered—"

"Ordered by whom? Who gave the order?"

"It doesn't matter who, but the order has been given to clear the road and restore the movement of traffic. And I shall carry out that order."

"You can carry it out, but first we'll go through to the Mausoleum and lay our wreaths . . ."

"One at a time, by all means, but not in a column."

"No," said Glukhov firmly, "we're going through in a column."

"Mr. Glukhov," the sergeant said wearily, "I have no wish to squabble with you, but your demonstration is terminated. If you do not do as you are told, force will be used against you."

"What? Force?" cried Fyodor Fyodorovich, suddenly leaping forward with his standard. "Do you know whom you're talking to? And what way is that to stand in front of me? You're standing in front of a general. Attention!"

"Comrade General, please restrain yourself. I am carrying out the order of the government of Moscow here, and for me you are not a general, but an individual disrupting social order."

"I'm disrupting social order!" Fyodor Fyodorovich was outraged. "Why you sniveling brat! You scum! I took Berlin! I spilled my blood for you! I'll strip you of your epaulettes!"

He even reached out for the sergeant's epaulettes, but Glukhov grabbed his arm.

"Fyodor Fyodorovich! Control yourself! We are an organized force and we do not allow ourselves to be provoked."

The general was still twitching, but he let himself be restrained.

The rows of demonstrators were nervous. They huddled together into a tight bunch, and some of the participants began making their way to the edge to get out of harm's way; but others did the opposite and pressed forward.

Glukhov attempted to calm the crowd down, waving his hands above his head and shouting out: "Comrades! Keep calm and maintain order! Take your places in the column!"

Suddenly, Syropov was there beside him again. He began pushing Glukhov in the chest, spitting at him and yelling: "Comrades! Friends! Brothers-in-arms! Don't listen to renegades! We're all Russians, aren't we? We're the heirs of Lenin, Stalin, Minin and Pozharsky! Forward to the Kremlin! Forward to the Kremlin!"

Out of nowhere a group of young men with wild, staring eyes

had appeared beside him. They began howling in chorus: "Stalin! Beria! Gulag!"

The other group carried on chanting: "To the Kremlin! To the Kremlin!"

Someone pushed Aglaya in the back, forcing her right up against the special policeman with the wooden face, but he still didn't react and carried on staring at Aglaya without blinking.

But she suddenly felt like a bold young fighter again, and forgetting when all this was taking place, she shouted: "For the motherland, for Stalin—forward!"

"Take Berlin!" Burdalakov squealed beside her, and turning the staff of his standard around like a pike, he lunged with it, seriously intending to thrust it through the colonel standing in front of him. The colonel dodged, and the general, misjudging his balance, fell to the ground and began twitching.

"They've killed him! They've killed him!" someone shouted.

"They've killed the general!" shouted someone farther off.

"Comrades, maintain order!" called Alfred Glukhov's voice, faint and lost, but no one listened to him. The demonstrators, transformed into an unmanageable crowd, fell on the special policemen, pushing them in the chest, but the police deftly protected themselves with their shields. Aglaya transferred the portrait of Stalin to her left hand and began shoving her policeman with her right hand. He repelled her lazily with his shield. Aglaya became even more furious, and, leaning around the shield, she struck his helmet with the portrait. Nothing happened to the helmet, but the portrait came to pieces. The frame fell apart and the paper tore. That drove Aglaya into an even greater frenzy, and, putting her head down like a young bull, she dashed at the policeman intending to butt him, but he put his shield in the way again and she smashed her unprotected head into it as if it were a concrete wall.

If she had been forty or less, perhaps it wouldn't have mattered much, but for an old woman of eighty the blow was too strong. She felt no pain, but suddenly she wanted to sit down, and she slumped onto the wet asphalt. The jostling, squealing and shouting continued all around her, and someone was groaning and swearing obscenely. Unfamiliar faces—young, handsome and wet—bent down over her, she laughed, they asked what she was laughing at and someone answered for her that she was delirious.

Then she finally lost consciousness and came to in a room on a canvas camp bed. A woman in a white coat and glasses was sitting at a table and writing something. Another woman in a white coat was standing beside her and speaking on the phone in some language Aglaya didn't know:

"Pizza Hut. Groovy menu. Lobsters, roast beef, fricassee. Prawns, pudding. Chianti—sixty bucks . . . Okay! Dump it on the pager. Or fax it over. No e-mail yet, the provider's changed . . ."

Leaning against the wall by the door with his arms crossed on his chest was the imperturbable Mitya.

"Where am I?" she asked.

"The first-aid station," said Mitya.

"But what country?" Aglaya asked.

Mitya glanced in surprise at the woman sitting at the table. She explained: "Typical amnesia." She turned to face Aglaya. "You're in Moscow. You've got a concussion. You have to lie down for a while, and then we'll send you home."

Aglaya closed her eyes. Opened them again. And again she saw Mitya and suddenly remembered the district movie theater in Dolgov, the film with Stalin and the young man who had called her a fool. It was the same Mitya. Mitya Lyamikhov, the eternal dissident and opponent of all forms of authority in existence at any particular time.

"Get up now," said Mitya. "Get up, it's time for you to go."

He took her to the railroad station and put her in a first-class sleeping compartment as she'd been promised.

99

She couldn't sleep during the journey after all the agitation she'd been through; her head was throbbing and her heart ached. She looked in her bag for some Validol and came across a book. She took it and read the title—*The Timber Camp*—and only then remembered where she'd bought it. She tried reading it to take her mind off things and make the time pass more quickly.

"Have you ever seen a spar pine fall, sawn off at the root?" She read the first phrase and started thinking. She could reply in the affirmative to the question posed. In '35 in response to the Party's appeal, she had worked for three months in the logging camps, and she had seen a thing or two. The people working there were enemies of the people, intellectuals who had never held anything heavier than a pencil in their hands and who therefore suffered very badly from the intense cold and the work that was too heavy for them. Pretty much the way it was in this book. Aglaya had tried reading this novel sometime earlier, but as she recalled, the beginning had been a little different. That is, there was the same Khanty-Mansiisk taiga, with the bitter cold, snow, convicts, armed guards and fallen pine. Only as Aglaya remembered it, the man under the tree had been some Bolshevik called Alexei, and now it was Father Alexii, a priest who had suffered for his faith. Crushed by the pine, he wheezed to the narrator who had gone running across to him: "Read the Holy Gospel. Read our Lord Jesus Christ. Go forth and spread the word of God. And you shall be re——"

Strangely enough, Aglaya became engrossed in the novel. So engrossed that she almost missed her station.

There was no one on the platform with its light dusting of snow apart from the duty guard Pukhov, an elderly, unsober man in a cloth coat with the elbows frayed into holes. The train stood for the two minutes allotted to it, Pukhov blew on his whistle, held out his yellow flag and waved it without looking at the departing carriages. He gestured with his free hand to ask Aglaya to wait. She waited. Seeing Aglaya get off the train, he gestured for her to wait. She waited. Pukhov came up to her, stuck the flag under his arm and held out his hand: "Congratulations."

"On what?"

"Haven't you heard?" he asked, and wiped his nose on his sleeve.

"No," she said irritably. "I haven't. Tell me."

"Okay, okay, I am telling you." He jumped up and down and blew on his frozen hands. "Yesterday the district duma . . . your communists . . . voted by an overwhelming majority . . . In the interests of the restoration of historical justice and the preservation of valuable cultural artifacts . . . to put your idol, your tyrant, back where he used to be . . ."

Having uttered these words, Pukhov took a small step backward and froze in anticipation of a violent response, and we could quite legitimately have anticipated something of the sort. For indeed, if Aglaya had been young and in good health, her body would quite certainly have responded to the news in the appropriate fashion—and the amount of adrenaline that suffused her ardent blood, the triumphant chords of the melody that sounded in her ears, would have been beyond our powers to imagine. But her body was old, it functioned listlessly and sporadically, and the news failed to produce the impression it ought to have.

"What are you so pleased about?" she asked. "What's it to you? Are you so fond of Stalin?"

"I'm not fond of him at all," Pukhov confessed. "But I have my aesthetic considerations. That pedestal standing there smack in the middle of the square like it's lost its way home, it spoils the whole town. Makes you ashamed in front of visitors. It's about time they got around to putting someone on it."

"Yes, it is," she agreed indifferently and set off toward the exit, leaving the guard frozen in a pose of bewilderment.

100

In the square in front of the station, a drunken bum with a sparse beard sprinkled with snow sat on the bench under the monument to Lenin, wearing a filthy, leathery sheepskin coat and a knitted woolly hat. He'd been dozing with a bottle in his hand, but the sound of steps woke him and he beckoned Aglaya with his finger, as though inviting her to conspire with him.

"What?" she asked as she got closer.

The bum twisted his head left and right as if he was making sure there were no unwanted eyes or ears around.

"I'm here," he informed her in a whisper, winking and pointed upward, "purging myself under Lenin in order to journey further into the revolution. Unnerstan'?"

"I understand," said Aglaya. "And it would be a good idea to give yourself a wash as well."

She liked the joke she'd made and that made her feel better. She lengthened her stride.

There was no wind, and a fine wet snow was falling.

Aglaya's route lay a little to one side of the Avenue of Glory, but she decided to take a look to see what was going on. The Wheel of Fortune casino had recently been repaired and painted, and it looked festive, not like in the past, when it was the district Party committee building.

"Look at that," Aglaya thought reproachfully, thinking of the owners of the casino. "All that money they've spent on repairs! But they wouldn't go spending money like that on the district committee."

And she was right. Not for anything would these people have spent as much money on the district Party committee, the regional Party committee or even on the Central Committee of the CPSU, as they spent on their casinos, restaurants, delicatessens, nightclubs and other establishments.

Strangely enough, the space in front of the casino had so far remained almost unaltered, although the wind of change had snagged a couple of things here too. The district Board of Honor was still standing there, but the oval frames in which the portraits of industrial shock workers had once been displayed as in a columbarium were now empty or contained notices about the sale or purchase of apartments, pedigree puppies and super fat-burners. And on the Avenue of Glory the graves of heroes of the new era had been added to those of heroes of the Revolution, the Civil War and the Great Patriotic War. In the seventies they had buried the director of the delicatessen here, in the early eighties two Afghan war veterans, including the fictitious Vanka Zhukov, and just recently they had been joined by the president of the Age with Dignity foundation, known to the criminal world as Validol, and the bank president Mosol. Validol had been blown up by Mosol. Who had got rid of Mosol remained a mystery to the organs, but people who weren't in the organs knew for sure that Felix Bulkin, also known as Plague, a prosperous businessman and politician, was responsible. Both underworld bosses had been buried with full church rites and in grand style. The local hoodlum fraternity had been there, as well as representatives of business circles and the creative intelligentsia. Several colleagues had come down from Moscow in jeeps and Mercedes, but Plague had arrived in a ZIL-114—they said it was the same one Brezhnev used to ride around in. On Validol's grave they placed a marble slab with a Mercedes radiator set into it, and above Mosol's they erected a bronze Prometheus with an eagle welded to his liver.

The other graves—Commissar Rosenblum, Captain Miliagi and Andrei Revkin—had fallen into a state of neglect, but right now they were sprinkled with snow and didn't look too bad.

Aglaya could see from a distance that there was a crowd jostling on the square. The vision called to mind memories from fifty years earlier, when they unveiled the monument. But what could be going on there now?

She approached the crowd. People were standing in several rows in a semicircle. The ones at the back were standing on tiptoe as they tried to see what was happening up at the front. Aglaya touched the rounded shoulders of the woman muffled up in a shawl who was standing in front of her and asked her what was going on.

"The devil's marrying a pig," said the woman, turning to face her. It was Shurochka the Idiot.

"Don't talk rubbish," whispered the man standing beside Shurochka, and he explained that the pedestal was being blessed on the eve of the statue being returned to its rightful place. Aglaya pushed her way farther forward and saw Father Radish clad in full vestments walking around the pedestal with a cross in his left hand and something that looked like a house-painter's brush in his right. Shuffling along beside the priest with a tin bucket was the ancient deacon Father Pyotr Porosyaninov. The priest dipped his brush in the bucket, splashed water onto the pedestal and intoned: "In the name of the Father and the Son and the Holy Ghost is this blessing made of the pedestal for the image of the Servant of God Joseph, which shall stand here henceforth, always and forever more. Amen!"

The ceremony was attended by the head of the district administration, Zherdyk, the chairman of the municipal duma, the heads of the district offices of the police, the FSB (Federal Security Service) and the public prosecutor's office, the chairman of the district court, the commanding officer of the local garrison, the president of the agricultural bank, Plague and two other professional criminals, and a man in a threadbare coat, very thin with a yellowish-green face, big eyes and long, matted gray hair that hung down from under a battered hat. Aglaya had the feeling that she'd seen this man somewhere before, perhaps in some former life. The congregation listened to the priest patiently, with the same resignation with which they had once listened to Party reports about the fulfillment of plans and the imminent advent of communism. With the single difference that then they had applauded after every figure cited, but now at the appropriate points they jerked their heads down and crossed themselves rapidly and clumsily. The yellowish-green old man did this more fervently and more frequently than the others.

When he had finished the rite, the priest put the brush in the bucket, handed the cross to Porosyaninov and addressed the congregation with an informal sermon, in which he gave a brief account of Stalin's life.

"It was," he said, "the complicated life of a complicated man. In his youth he decided to dedicate himself to God and entered a seminary, but afterward, tempted by the devil, he was seduced by a false satanic creed and turned his back on God. But we can say that the devil was not able to master him completely. As you remember, during the war, when our motherland was in great danger, it was Stalin who gave orders for the church to be allowed greater freedom. God moves in mysterious ways, and the paths that bring man to God are unpredictable. And we cannot tell what point this undoubtedly sinful man would have reached if his life had only been longer."

The priest also remarked that the installation of the monument and even its blessing did not constitute forgiveness of the sins of the man to whom it was dedicated.

"The blessing of the statue does not signify its transformation into a holy shrine, but it is a historical relic, and the church facilitates its standing secure here for a long time. So that there should be no more of the blasphemy to which we have all been witnesses."

In conclusion, the priest made the sign of the cross over the pedestal once again and everybody crossed themselves, following which he gathered up the skirts of his cassock and he and Porosyaninov set off toward his four-wheel drive Niva. Zherdyk came over to ask Aglaya how things had gone in Moscow, and then said with pride:

"Now you see, Aglaya Stepanovna, you see, but you didn't believe that there would ever be dancing on our street again. But there will. Tomorrow. And there's nobody and nothing that can stop it," Zherdyk assured her, and as he walked away, he began singing gently under his breath: "La donna è mobile . . ."

101

While Zherdyk was speaking, the old man with the yellowish-green face had been standing behind him waiting his turn.

"Don't you recognize me?" he asked. "I'm Max Ogorodov, the sculptor."

And then he launched into some string of gibberish out of which it gradually emerged that he had been seriously ill and it had cost him a great effort to come here, driven by the urgent need to say farewell to his finest creation and the passionate desire to approach it and touch it before he died.

"Why not?" said Aglaya. "We'll be putting it up tomorrow, you can touch it then."

"No," protested the sculptor, "not tomorrow, tomorrow he'll be standing way up there. What I'd like is . . . before he's up on the pedestal, while I can still embrace him."

Aglaya didn't much like the idea of what Ogorodov intended to do. Why would he want to embrace him? What would happen if everybody got it into their heads that they wanted to embrace him?"

"But it's my creation," Ogorodov reminded her.

"All right then," she agreed, "let's go." And he plodded obediently after her.

Getting up the stairs to the second floor was hard work for both of them. Aglaya set her bag down two steps ahead, stepped up, moved the bag on and so eventually reached her landing.

"I didn't have time to tidy the place," she warned him, feeling guilty, and observing to herself that when she was drinking it didn't matter to her whether the place was tidy or not, or what anybody thought about it. But now it did.

The sculptor made no reply, panting rapidly, like a dog that wants to drink.

Her hands were shaking too and the key kept missing the keyhole. She walked in through the door so slowly that in his impatience Ogorodov even pushed her aside rudely, darted through into the sitting room and went down on his knees in front of the statue.

"Well, hello," he said, holding his arms out wide, as if he were expecting something to fall into them from above. Aglaya set her bag down at her feet and leaned against the lintel. Ogorodov moved closer to the statue, put his arms around it and began crying quietly.

Aglaya did not like people who cried. But she disliked men who cried most of all. And never felt sorry for them. Despised them. But old age must have made her weak, and she gave way to a feeling unworthy of a Bolshevik.

"There's no point in crying over it," she said in her rough manner. "All of us are only here for a while. Even him"—she pointed to the statue—"what a man he was, and he still died. But us . . . Look how many people there are in the world. If we don't die, then how many of us would there be? There'd be no space left anywhere on the planet."

Ogorodov moved away to the wall, wiped away his perspiration with his sleeve and, looking at the statue, he said: "You don't think I'm crying for my life? I've completely vindicated my life. I had a vision. That all I had to do was touch him, and my illness would leave me immediately. He absolutely must save me . . ." Ogorodov suddenly began wheezing and coughing, he shuddered and clutched at his chest. Black foam began bubbling out of the corner of his mouth.

"Hey, don't do that, stop!" she cried in alarm, and began fussing around him. "Wait a bit. Don't die here. This isn't the right place. I'll call a doctor right away."

She was weak herself, but she managed to shove him across to the sofa. He collapsed backward onto it and froze there with his eyes bulging out of his head. He lay there for several seconds with his head thrown back and didn't even seem to be breathing. Which frightened Aglaya even more. Luckily, the fit passed and her visitor recovered his senses, even to the extent that he was invited into the kitchen and given tea to drink from the mug with the inscription WPRA—20 YEARS.

Aglaya watched him purse up his lips, blow into the mug and then drink the tea without any apparent desire.

"So what do you do now?" Aglaya inquired.

"Now? Nothing. Before that I used to sculpt leaders. Khrushchev, Brezhnev, Andropov, Chernenko . . . I kept thinking about your pedestal. How it wasn't good for it to be standing empty."

"It was good," Aglaya objected. "It was waiting for its master. The old saying still holds good: 'There'll be dancing on our street again.' "

"Yes, it still holds good," her visitor agreed, and then once again he was racked by coughing and clutched at his chest.

"If you don't mind my asking, what illness is it you've got?" asked Aglaya, reverting to a more formal tone of voice. "Something like cancer, is it?"

"Worse," he coughed out.

"What could be worse?"

"Apparently, there is something." He smiled strangely and looked her straight in the eye. "I've got AIDS. Have you heard about it?"

"AIDS?" she queried, perplexed. "How can you have AIDS. You can only get AIDS if you're one of those . . . Aha," she guessed, "so you're one of them too?"

"Yes, I'm a homosexual," Ogorodov said defiantly. "And I'm proud of it. Nowadays the entire civilized world knows that it's nothing to be ashamed of. Especially since I'm an artist. A creative individual. All artists are the same."

"All of them?" she said disbelievingly. "All artists give it to each other up the backside, do they? Repin and Shishkin and our satirists the Kukriniksy too?"

"Why, don't you know about Tchaikovsky?" he asked. "Everybody knows that gays are the most talented people. All the rest are worthless mediocrities. All the rest are just—pah!" He spat. True, not in Aglaya's direction, off to the side, but she was alarmed all the same.

"What are you doing?" she shouted. "What do you mean spitting in someone else's house? Especially since you're infectious. Give me that!" She grabbed the mug out of his hand, swilled out the remaining tea, already cold, and said in a feeble but decisive voice, "Get out of here."

"What's wrong?" Ogorodov asked, puzzled. "You can't catch AIDS from a cup."

"Get out, I told you. It makes me sick to look at you. You miserable homo! Go away. Get out!"

She shoved him into the hallway, stuck his hat and coat in his hands and scarcely even gave him enough time to put them on, and then afterward, as he was already making his way down the dark stairs, clinging to the handrail, she shouted after him: "Rotten queer!"

And then, as though in reply, she heard: "La donna è mobile . . ." It was Zherdyk's voice.

Aglaya leaned over the banister, hoping to catch sight of the singer, but there was no one on the stairs and Zherdyk's voice seemed to be coming from the basement, where Vanka Zhukov lived. Only it sounded odd somehow. Zherdyk wasn't singing the whole song, he kept repeating "La donna è mobile . . . La donna è mobile . . ." over and over again, endlessly.

"What stupid nonsense," thought Aglaya.

But it wasn't nonsense. It was Vanka Zhukov running a tape loop with a recording of Zherdyk's voice and tuning a device that would respond only to that voice, only to that melody, and only to the words "La donna è mobile . . ."

102

What is life like for an individual transformed from a handsome young man full of energy into a hideous stump and robbed even of the ability to cater to his own needs? Healthy, happy people can't even imagine it. A cripple like that has different feelings and different joys; his view of the world is not the same as ours and life doesn't seem such a very precious gift to him.

Ivan Georgievich Zhukov was watching an old movie comedy on TV, starring the actors Mironov and Nikulin. Vanka was relaxing and he had a right to. In his efforts to solve a highly complex task, he had finally achieved what he wanted. It had not been easy to make a thing like that. It would respond unfailingly to certain words and a certain melody sung by only one man and no one else. It might happen tomorrow, December 21, the birthday of Stalin, or Uncle Joe, as Jim called him. Tomorrow the statue of the cast-iron uncle would be set in its old place. And after that certain people would want to celebrate the event. They would drive to the Golden Spring restaurant. They would have a drink. And they would want to sing something soulful . . .

The film was followed by advertisements for a washing powder that washed everything clean and didn't spoil anything, an antidandruff lotion and a chocolate bar which, according to the gibberish of the jingle "had the right to share your success." After the chocolate came the chronicle of crime. A stern-looking policewoman told everyone what had happened over the last twenty-four hours in Moscow. There had been an explosion at one of the markets. A bomb with a timing mechanism had been hidden in a sack of potatoes. Nine people had been killed and thirteen wounded. "Not one of mine," remarked Vanka. A nineteen-year-old girl student, assisted by a male classmate, had strangled her mother with a washing line in order to get her hands on an old icon. A three-year-old boy had fallen from a sixth-floor window and lived. There had been a fire in a hotel. An Audi 6 automobile driven by a drunken driver had veered into the opposite lane and crashed into a tiny Tavria. The driver of the Tavria and his wife had been killed instantly; the driver of the Audi had been saved by his air bag. Then suddenly Vanka saw Gravalya. They showed her seated, evidently in a police station. The newscaster said: "An elderly woman has been detained at the Belorussian Railroad Station. During a search her suitcase was found to contain about two kilograms of hexogen, four hundred grams of TNT and two antitank grenades. The suspect claims that the explosives do not belong to her, but cannot explain how they got into her suitcase. When arrested, the woman was not carrying any identification, and she refuses to give her name. We ask anyone who knows this person to call us on—"

"Oh no!" Vanka said to himself, then switched off the television and started thinking. Although there was no point in thinking at this stage. They'd picked up his granny, and there wasn't much chance they'd let her go. Which meant they would soon turn up here. What was to be done? From his chair he gazed around through a full 360 degrees, surveying his equipment and stocks of explosives, and realized there was nothing that he, an invalid, could do. Except wait for them to come for him. Ah, but when they came . . .

His laboratory was well equipped with everything necessary to transform it into a thundering, flashing hell for anybody who came there. Vanka laughed. He'd often thought about how his life would end, and he'd been intending to go out in spectacular style. But how exactly? He'd dreamed about it so often. Blinding flame billowing up in brilliant colors, and people flying through the flame like birds . . .

Vanka turned on the computer and contacted Jim via the Internet.

"Hi," he sent to him.

"Hi," Jim answered. "How's it going?"

"Getting close to the end," Vanka told him.

"Can you be a bit more precise?"

Vanka explained.

"Okay," Jim responded. "I won't try to talk you out of it, even though I'll miss you."

Vanka didn't respond.

"Don't you want to answer me?" Jim asked.

"I don't know what to say to you," wrote Vanka, and at that moment someone knocked at the door.

"Who's there?" asked Vanka without moving. And he heard singing: "La donna è mobile . . ."

Vanka froze. He'd thought there was nothing left that could excite him anymore, but now his heart was pounding so fast he was amazed. His hand trembled as he drew back the bolt. When he opened the door, Vanka saw a man in a long unbuttoned coat and a red scarf, clutching a bottle of something foreign in his hand and already clearly tipsy.

"You?" Vanka asked.

"In person," Zherdyk laughed loudly and started singing again: "La donna—"

"Stop!" Vanka shouted at him. But as yet, he hadn't put the batteries into the device he'd created, and the bomb was still safe.

"What?" asked Zherdyk, unable to understand why Vanka was so agitated. "Don't you like my singing?"

"Yes, I like it," said Vanka. "But sing a bit later, if you don't mind."

"Sing not, my beauty, unto me and sing not unto others," said Zherdyk merrily. "Ah, you, my old bosom buddy!" He moved toward Vanka, intending either to embrace him or slap him on the back, but stopped short, realizing that it wouldn't be easy to do either. "I only just learned today that you're alive. I was at your funeral, wasn't I? You were given full honors, by the way. Buried as a hero. But you scoundrel, you fooled us all, you sly dog."

Zherdyk clowned in lively and merry style, and if he had had any feeling for words, he would have realized that he was striking a false note. But he had no such feeling, and he put his foot in it again by asking Vanka if he'd recognized him right away.

"And did you recognize me?"

"Did I? Recognize you?" said Zherdyk, attempting to express amazement or indignation. What kind of question was that? How could he fail to recognize his friend from the old days? But he did at least realize that would be a bit too unlikely. "Yes. I'm sorry," he said. "But I really did recognize you. I always would. You know there are people who are nothing but an external shell, and then there are personalities. And a personality, Vanka, always finds some way to express itself. It radiates its own special light or . . . I don't know what to call it . . . Vanka, my friend, you can't imagine how glad I am!"

"Come in," said Vanka, rolling backward toward the computer. "Take a chair, sit down, I'll just log off the Internet."

"Sorry," he typed to Jim. "An old friend has dropped in."

"Okay," Jim replied. "Do I know him?"

"Yes," typed Vanka. "It's La Donna."

"O!" typed Jim, concerned. "What has he come to see you for?"

"He wants to have a drink."

"And will you drink with him?"

"Maybe," replied Vanka.

"O.K.," wrote Jim, and Vanka sensed the doubt expressed in those two letters. "But will we still be in touch or . . ."

"Or," replied Vanka.

He logged off and turned to face his visitor. Zherdyk was sitting on the chair, holding the bottle on his knee.

"You're something, you know that! I bet you're the only one in our town who's really mastered the Internet."

"Not the only one, but I was the first," said Vanka.

"Yeah? Maybe. I'm on the Internet too, of course. But . . ." he waved his hand dismissively. "Vanka, what are we talking about this garbage for? That's not what's important here. What's important is that you're alive. You're living, breathing, creating. Yeah, you've got a whole laboratory here! Have you got a name for it?"

"Yes, I've got a name," Vanka confirmed. "I call it Little Hiroshima. Haven't you heard it?"

"Yeah, I have," Zherdyk confessed. "Our district FSB man informed me. Know who he is? You don't and you'd never guess. But I'll tell you. Later. Meanwhile, why don't you show me your Hiroshima?"

"You won't sell me out?" asked Vanka.

"Me?" Zherdyk was flabbergasted. "You?" He puffed himself up and turned bright red, not from shame, but from the insult. "Listen, Vanka, if that's a joke . . ."

"It is," said Vanka.

"It's a pretty stupid one."

"Okay, don't get angry," said Vanka. "Look at this. See this powder? It's mostly powdered sugar. But if you mix this powder with this coal dust, tip it into a tin can and seal it in with gelatin, then bang on it with a hammer . . . Would you like to see what happens then? You wouldn't? Pushkin was right: we are lazy and stupid, how does it go? . . ."

"Uninquisitive," Zherdyk corrected him.

"That's it. Uninquisitive. And here we have the stock of finished articles. Do you remember I used to have a photocopying machine?"

"Sure I do!" said Zherdyk. "Of course."

"Well then. Everything here is just as technologically advanced. This thing here. Put it in an automobile. It goes off at a specific speed. I made it for one idiot's Merc, so it would go off at a hundred and twenty kilometers an hour. I thought he'd pick up speed somewhere out of town. But he did it right here, on our ruts and potholes . . ."

He showed his childhood friend cunning devices hidden, according to the purpose they were intended for, in a tin can, a saucepan, a violin case, or an engine cylinder. They were triggered by various means: a radio signal, the touch of fingers with unique fingerprints, the smell of rosin, the pressure at a certain height or the pronunciation of a specific password. Vanka showed and Zherdyk admired. And in reply he told Vanka about the career he'd made for himself and why.

"Remember we used to talk about the dissidents. I thought then that what they were doing was wrong. And I still think I was right. Back then they were already depriving people of faith in a better future with their disclosures, destroying—how can I put it?—their spiritual infrastructure. And what happened? The total collapse of all life and all moral principles. But even so, people have a need to believe in something good."

"In communism?" Vanka asked.

"Communism is only a name. But it is possible after all to build a more or less just society. The people running things now don't think about people, but we do. And we're going to do something for them. Little deeds are more important than stupendous achievements. And we're starting with the little things. Now we've won the election, we'll start doing something concrete for people. For instance, we've already decided to buy you a wheelchair with an electric motor. We'll give you a specially equipped apartment. As far as possible, we'll try to give you a normal life. And in general, there's a lot we could do, if only people didn't interfere."

"Who's interfering?"

"Plenty of people. Yesterday one of the oligarchs was speaking on TV. Frightening the people by saying that if they started redistributing property again there'd be a civil war?"

"Well, won't there?"

"Who against who? Millions of people believe they've been robbed by an oligarch, and they want to take back what he stole. Who's against that? No one but the oligarch. So who's going to fight on his side? His bodyguards? They'll be the first to turn him in."

"So your main enemies are the oligarchs?"

"Not only. All kinds of bastards are our enemies. All sorts of fascists. We have one really hideous specimen around here too. An old acquaintance of yours, as it happens . . ."

This hideous specimen, as you've probably guessed, was Roof.

"He was a bandit and he still is. Only now he's a bandit with an idea. Have you heard of the White Hawk?"

"No."

"It's a fascist organization. Clear-cut ideology, iron discipline. Local organizations right across the country."

"So is Roof a member of this Hawk?"

"Not a member—he runs it."

"From Dolgov?"

"The headquarters is in Moscow. But it's handier to run it from here. Not so high-profile."

"And what are the FSB and the MVD and the public prosecutor's office doing about it?"

"You really are a naïve man, Vanka. What are they doing? He's one of them. A really hideous specimen!" Zherdyk repeated. "If he's not stopped . . ."

"We'll stop him," Vanka reassured him.

103

Just at that moment there was a coded knock at the door and the subject of the conversation himself appeared in the doorway holding a bottle of vodka. As a well-trained operative, Roof said hello to Zherdyk without showing the slightest sign of embarrassment and only glanced at Vanka in an attempt to guess what had brought the victor in the elections here and whether Vanka had revealed certain schemes to him. Zherdyk in turn probed Roof with a searching glance, realizing that this was obviously not the first time he'd been here. But while neither of them revealed his suspicions to the other in any way, both of them began suspecting Vanka of playing a double game. At the same time, all three of them behaved in a friendly fashion, and after a little while they sat around the shaky little table standing at one side of the room. They drank and ate, and the more they drank, the more tender the feelings they expressed for each other became. An hour or so later they were recalling all sorts of incidents from their former life, proposing toasts to friendship, paying each other all sorts of compliments, and from the outside it would have been hard to tell that these men were enemies. But then in Russia the path from friendship to hate is always a short one. One minute we're drinking and embracing, you respect me and I respect you, and the next minute we're reaching for a knife or an ax or some kind of firearm.

Outside the window, the night was calm and frosty, the full moon was shining, the cats were screeching on the roof and the strains of songs rendered by a discordant male trio came drifting up out of the basement: "On the Wild Shores of the Irtysh," "On the Wild Steppes of Baikal" . . .

"Guys! My friends!" Zherdyk exclaimed in an excess of convivial feelings. "How beautiful life is after all! And how good it is to feel that in this life you are a man, a being born—"

"Born for what?" asked Vanka.

"For something good. Korolenko said: 'Man is born for happiness, as a bird is born for flight.' "

"Mind if I rephrase that a bit?" Roof asked good-naturedly. "I take a simpler view of things. Man is a permanently operational factory for transforming the products of nature into shit."

104

Meanwhile, from the west, or perhaps from the east, or from some other direction—we won't be too precise in order not to subject the reader to the temptation of any double interpretation of text and subtext—anyway, approaching Dolgov from one of many possible directions was a cloud, which was by no means wintry in appearance, but charged with thunder and an ominous beauty. Probably few people had even seen it as yet, but Vanka could sense its approach from every side of his multilaterally truncated body. Let us immediately note here—although in the interests of the plot it should have been highlighted earlier—that any electrical storm reduced Vanka to a state of feral agitation, perhaps because almost all of his nerves had been severed so that they protruded at the surface and were more sensitive than any barometer at detecting even the most obscure of atmospheric disturbances. During meteorological cataclysms Vanka sometimes went insane, and the most terrible thoughts illuminated the inside of his externally mutilated head.

Looking up at the sky that evening, it was possible to observe that one side of it was a deep lilac-black while the opposite side, in contrast, was virginally clear. The black side slowly advanced on the clear side and the clear side advanced on the black side until finally they fell into each other's embraces directly above the center of the city of Dolgov. Afterward, they said that two atmospheric fronts had collided. One of the fronts was a very warm, damp cyclone, and the other was a dry, cold anticyclone. They collided, and suddenly the air was filled with howling and whistling. The lilac cloud was swirled into a vortex and transformed into a shaggy, dirty-black whirlwind, a spinning column with its lower end reaching down to the ground and its upper end extending out toward space. An incredible force spun this black slurry around, tearing dark tufts out of it and then drawing them back into the center again. And whirling and seething around this column were clouds of smoke, mist, steam, dirt and God knows what else, in the most loathsome shades of all the colors of the rainbow. The whirlwind didn't stand still in one spot and it didn't move in a straight line; it circled around the center of the city, as though it wanted to annihilate this particular spot totally. It bent down to the ground and broke trees, tore the roofs off houses, overturned automobiles, rolled empty barrels along the streets, dragged billboards around, smashed kiosks to smithereens and lifted up a horse and cart, carrying them away like a hot-air balloon, with the horse jerking its legs about helplessly. Everything was whistling, howling and roaring. The city was bombarded from the sky with rain, snow, hailstones the size of a man's fist and every other form of precipitation that can possibly be imagined, in volumes quite impossible to imagine. Zigzag lances of lightning flashed blindingly and thrust themselves into the earth with an appalling crash.

All the people woke up and looked out of their windows in terror, stopped up their ears and prayed to anybody or anything they could. Nobody had ever seen a storm like it in that season, or in any other, and they would rather not have seen it at all. And some even began to think it wasn't a storm at all, but a war—not just an ordinary one, but thermonuclear. Or plain ordinary doomsday. The last judgment, when the earth shall gape, all graves shall be opened and hordes of corpses will come clambering out with their teeth chattering. Everything was flashing and rumbling. Vanka started to get excited, and he was seized by the feeling that he himself was a part of this elemental chaos. Although to look at him no one would have thought it.

As we know, his room was located in the semibasement. The lower section of the window was set in a concrete recess about half a meter below the level of the pavement, and the upper section rose about a meter above that level. A stream of water came flying straight at the window as if it was blasted from a large-diameter pipe. The concrete recess immediately filled up, and the water began pressing against the glass and seeping dangerously into the room. A lightning bolt struck directly into the recess and the water immediately began to boil, but the windowpanes didn't burst. Another bolt evidently struck the roof, and it felt as though a large bomb had fallen on the building. The three friends were still sitting around the table, casting glances in the direction of the window. Vanka recalled once again the battle in Kandahar, when their battalion had been caught practically defenseless in the gorge and the Mujahadeen had pounded it with every weapon they had. Roof also recalled his Aghanistan experience and the storming of President Amin's palace.

Zherdyk had nothing of the sort to recall and he crawled under the table.

"What's wrong?" Vanka shouted at him, lifting up the flap of the oilcloth.

"I'm afraid," Zherdyk shouted from under the table.

"Everyone's afraid," Roof said to him, "but why go crawling under the table? Come out of there." He grabbed hold of Zherdyk by the scruff of the neck and began pulling him out, but he resisted, crying and shouting.

"Don't, guys! Don't. Leave me here! I'm afraid. You're not afraid, you're heroes, but I'm afraid."

"Don't be. This is nothing to be afraid of," said Vanka, apparently perfectly calm.

"Not for you it isn't!" yelled Zherdyk. "Because you're just a sawn-off stump. You've got nothing to live for, but I'm still full of life."

It was hard to tell what the expression on Vanka's face meant.

"Out you come, Sanya!" he said to Zherdyk, almost tenderly. "Calm down. Haven't you ever seen a storm before? Come out and we'll have a chat."

Strangely enough, these words worked on Zherdyk, and, pushing aside Roof's hand, he crawled out and shook himself off in embarrassment.

"That's right," said Vanka. "That's better. Have another drink and calm down."

Zherdyk took the glass that was proffered to him and sipped at it with his teeth rattling against the side, spilling vodka onto his chest.

"You know," Vanka said to him, "when you're really afraid, you should think about something to distract you. When they were pounding us to bits in that gorge, I began remembering poems that I'd read somewhere and had memorized for some reason." Vanka closed his eyes and began reciting in a singsong voice:

> "Recently I was in a nearby Somewhere,
> A ghetto district, cramped and overcrowded.
> The climate's harsh—all winter and no summer . . .
> And heat and light are never there when needed.
> The day and night cannot be told apart
> And people grope their slow way through the dark,
> And though they cannot see each other's faces

All they feel for each other is pure hatred.
The only pastimes that these people know
Are squabbles, fights and rumor-mongering.
The only time their hearts feel a warm glow
Is when they know their next-door neighbor's suffering,
He's ricked his neck or else broken his leg,
Or had his wallet stolen in the subway,
Or had misfortune of some other kind.
That always really makes his neighbors' day.
So life is spent in ignorance and spite,
With soul and body starved for entertainment.
But if somebody does somebody in,
Of course, that makes the whole thing very different."

As he recited, things outside the window got a bit calmer, and as Zherdyk recovered his senses, he asked who wrote the poem.

"I don't know," said Vanka with a shrug. "Some dissident or other."

"Sounds like it," remarked Roof. "What does 'in a nearby somewhere' mean? Does it mean in Russia?"

"Of course it does," said Zherdyk, casting a nervous glance at the window. "Where else would you find people who hate their own country?"

"Everywhere," Vanka muttered, remembering Jim. "There are people everywhere who—"

"But that poem," said Zherdyk, "it isn't art, it's something else . . ."

"It's depressing," suggested Roof.

"That's it, depressing," Zherdyk agreed. "Art should be bright and happy. Its purpose is to exalt man, inspire him with faith in himself, in people, in friends."

"That's right," Vanka put in with unexpected enthusiasm. "How would you like to exalt us all a bit? Sing us 'La donna è mobile.' "

"What, now?" Zherdyk asked in astonishment, and shuddered as the lightning flashed again outside the window.

"Sure, why not?" said Vanka. "Come on."

There were two bright flashes of lightning, one hard on the heels of the other. Zherdyk was about to say something and he opened his mouth, but there was a flash and a thunderclap, as though an entire battery of jet-propelled rocket-launchers had turned all their firepower against this one house. Zherdyk clutched his head and climbed back under the table. The next bolt of lightning hit the concrete. This time the glass broke and boiling water came pouring into the room. Clouds of steam concealed everything from sight.

"I'm dying!" Zherdyk shouted from under the table.

"You'll die now all right!" Vanka confirmed. "With a song." And he reached out toward the tape deck.

Roof immediately realized what that meant, but he couldn't see Vanka anymore.

"Stop," he shouted, and made a dash at Vanka through the steam. He pounced like a jaguar. With his hands stretched out in front of him, he flew on an intercept course, rather like an air-launched torpedo. And when it came, it caught him in full flight.

Vanka pressed the key and Zherdyk's pure tenor poured out of the speaker: "La donna è mobile . . ."

And then there was a blinding flash, not from outside, but inside, and Roof didn't fall onto Vanka; instead, he went soaring upward and continued his flight on into infinity.

105

Shortly before the storm Aglaya Stepanovna Revkina was sitting at the table drinking tea with vanilla rusks and occasionally glancing out of the window. It was calm and clear outside. Absolutely no portents of any kind.

Aglaya was remembering her journey to Moscow, the meeting with General Burdalakov, the fight with the police, the row with the sculptor Ogorodov. What a nerve! Turning up to say goodbye with a disease like that. And now it was time for her to say her farewells to her lodger. Thirty years he'd lived here.

"You see," she said, going over to him with her cup, "we got there after all. Tomorrow they'll put you back in your rightful place, and no one will ever move you from it again."

She looked at him, but neither in his face nor his stance could she discern any sign of what he thought about the forthcoming event. Then a sudden thought struck her: What if he doesn't want to go? It's cold and damp out there, all those pigeons, and there could be all sorts of vicious plots. They'd already blown up a monument to Nicholas II in one town somewhere. They could blow up this one too. And she also thought: If I give him to them, then who will I be left with?

Alone in an empty apartment . . . Just as she used to do before, in her musings she lost sight of the fact that he wasn't really alive. And the thought flitted through her head: What if I don't give him back at all? These people repudiated him, she thought—forgetting that she was living in different times now, not in the age of the repudiators—so what right did they have to him?

After tea she began getting ready for the night. She made up the bed and switched on the television. The local channel was summarizing the results of the election. The communists had won an impressive victory. A woman journalist was interviewing the mayor of Dolgov, Alexander Zherdyk.

"I think our victory is only natural. People are sick of living in poverty and uncertainty. Now they can see for themselves that only the communists can provide them with a life of peace and dignity. And as far as I personally am concerned," he added with a sorrowful expression, "I don't regard my new position as a source of any kind of privileges or advantages or anything of that kind. For me it means a hard daily grind of thankless work, but if we love our people and our homeland, then we have no right to shirk even the most difficult and tedious of jobs."

After a break for advertisements there was a film from the series *Our Old Movies*. It was a genuinely old film about the war, in black and white, with Vanin, Zharov and Astangov acting in it. A naïve sort of movie, of course, but ideologically correct. They knew how to make them in those days! A thriller with good actors and consistent ideology. Perhaps Zherdyk was right. Everything was going back to normal. Young people were watching these films and something must be reaching their hearts. Eventually, they would start to realize that the previous generation had lived by its ideals, not like these New Russians whose ideals were measured by the weight of the gold chains around their thick necks.

It was warm, even hot, in the room, but she was feeling a bit shivery, and she pulled the padded blanket up tight around her.

Outside the window the moon was shining, shining quietly and calmly and brightly enough to read a book by. Aglaya had warmed up now and she was feeling good. She watched TV, glancing occasionally at the moon, and now she could see it quite clearly: one brother stabbing the other. On the TV the village elder who had worked for the Germans and been captured by the partisans began shouting: "I'm Russian," but the secretary of the district Party committee told him: "You're a traitor and for us you're three times as bad as any German, you snake." Aglaya tried to follow the plot, but she was distracted by her thoughts. She didn't even notice when the film ended and another program began. One in which they were showing Valentina Zhukova and asking people to identify her. What did they need to identify her for, when everybody knew her anyway? Aglaya didn't understand it, she switched to a different channel and wound up with a quite different kind of program. They were showing a hall full of people who didn't look anything at all like partisans, and a young woman was walking around between them with a microphone, asking questions: "Tell me, you say you broke up with your husband because he didn't satisfy you sexually. What does that mean, 'he didn't satisfy you'? Was he impotent? Couldn't he get an erection?"

"No," replied the interviewee, "physically he was quite normal. But he simply refused to understand that there could be certain elements of fantasy, he wouldn't accept any deviations from what he regarded as the norm."

"For instance?"

"Well, for instance he was against anal sex, and when I told him I wanted to sleep with his friend, he kicked up a terrible row and even went as far as to hit me. Eventually, I left him and married someone else."

"And this someone else helps you realize your fantasies?"

"Yes, of course."

"And he doesn't forbid you to sleep with his friend?"

"No, he doesn't forbid it, he actively encourages it. We often engage in group sex."

"And do you like group sex?"

"Very much."

"And what exactly is it that you like about group sex?"

"What I like best of all is double fellatio."

"Double fellatio?" The presenter raised her eyebrows. "What's that?"

"Two pricks in your mouth."

"Oh, I see! Yes, that must be really exciting. And have you ever tried triple fellatio?"

Spurred into action, Aglaya sprang up off the bed, ran to the television and began spitting on the screen and shouting: "Stupid fool! Two pricks in your mouth! People like that should be shot, shot!"

She was trembling in indignation and she'd covered the entire screen in spittle. She turned off the TV, and lay down, but it was a long time before she could calm down. What was going on? Had she and her generation really sacrificed their health and their lives for these parasites? She turned the TV back on and switched to a different channel. Thank God they were showing something old and familiar. A repeat from the *Blue Lamp* New Year series with cosmonauts, leading industrial workers, famous writers and actors. The poet Robert Rozhdestvensky, still alive then, read his poem "about the other guy." Ludmila Zykina pressed her hands to her bosom and sang her song "Out of the distance slow, See the great Volga flow."

Aglaya had once sailed down the Volga on a passenger boat. It was a floating interregional Party conference. The people on the boat were regional and district Party secretaries and Party activists, with two members of the Politburo—Kaganovich and Voroshilov. The journey had not left much of a trace in her memory: endless hilly, forested riverbanks; songs from the movie *Volga-Volga*; lavish meals in the passengers' lounge; sailors bobbing up and down dancing the Little Apple and Voroshilov puking over the side—with two KGB men holding him by the elbows so he wouldn't fall overboard. One of them had spotted Aglaya on the deck and given her a very hostile look, and she had immediately made herself scarce. Remembering Voroshilov, she began thinking about Stalin, Stalin, Stal . . . and then she saw him. He was coming toward her down the steep opposite bank, a pair of long drawers tied around his head like a turban, with the tapes fluttering in the breeze. She wanted to tell Stalin: Careful, it's steep here, but she saw that the steep incline posed no threat at all to Stalin—as he leapt from one rock to another, he hovered in the air for a few seconds, seeming to soar like a bird, and then came down on the next rock. At first Aglaya was amazed at the way he did it, then she tried it herself and discovered that she could soar too. She didn't rise very high, perhaps only about five centimeters above the ground, but, holding herself at this level by a slight effort of will, she began moving toward Stalin, and when she came close, she said happily: "Comrade Stalin, yesterday in our shop they were selling groats." Stalin smiled tenderly in response and said: "When I was little, I loved to ride on the locomotive Iosif Stalin." Then he immediately climbed up onto the step of the locomotive, took hold of the handrail with his right hand, flung out his left arm and began singing in a beautiful voice: "La donna è mobile . . ."

Aglaya was a bit surprised at Comrade Stalin singing such a strange, non-Caucasian song, and her surprise woke her up.

There was no more moon outside the window. In fact, it was absolutely dark. And very quiet. Very calm. Too calm. Like before a sudden attack by the enemy. But she immediately asked herself what could possibly happen. She told herself nothing could happen. And she closed her eyes again.

. . . It was a bright summer day, the sun was at its zenith and Aglaya was standing in the tall grass of a clearing in a pine forest. The forest flowers were in bloom, there were butterflies and dragonflies in the air and Comrade Stalin was standing in a big tin basin, covered from head to toe in thick, soapy suds. She began rubbing him down with a bast scrubber and rinsing him off with water from a big enamel mug. And he was so small, like a five-year-old child, but with a mustache, and it wasn't clear if he was cast-iron or alive and in his uniform or without it. Aglaya kept on pouring the water out of the jug, but all the time there were more and more suds; they surrounded him like light, fluffy lace. Stalin kept disappearing in it and then reappearing. Aglaya wanted to ask someone what she should do about all these suds, and she saw Vladimir Ilich Lenin. Lenin was sitting with his jacket thrown over his shoulders on a tree stump by his forest shelter and rapidly writing his April theses in the middle of June, with a fuzzy ginger bumble bee circling over his head. She went up to him to ask what she should do about all the suds enveloping Comrade Stalin, but the leader didn't hear her; he carried on writing and wagging his beard, she touched his shoulder, he lifted his head and she saw it wasn't Lenin, it was Shubkin. Shubkin immediately covered his scribble with his hand, but she realized he was writing a report denouncing Stalin. "No, it's not a report," Shubkin told her, "it's a satire. It's a fairy tale about three little pigs and its called *The Timber Camp.*" "All the same," Aglaya said to him, "what do you want with a Timber Camp in Israel? There aren't any forests there." She went back to Stalin. But he wasn't there anymore, neither was the big basin. General Burdalakov was standing there with his standard, which had unfurled even though there was absolutely no wind, and she could see the Guards badge on it and the inscription TAKE THE CHURCHKHELLA. And there were no holes. Aglaya went up to the general, said "Hello" and asked: "Have you already taken Berlin, or are you just getting ready for it?" "Church is the English word for a house of worship," Burdalakov replied, "concerning which I have personally informed Leonid Ilich Brezhnev." "And why not Comrade Stalin?" she asked strictly. "Comrade Stalin doesn't live here any longer, he's taken some leave and gone to Sochi." Aglaya was delighted, recalling that she had to go to Sochi too, because she hadn't bought any kefir yet today. After saying "Thank you" she set off across the steppe, and beside the road she saw an abandoned cart with its two shafts resting on the ground. There was an armful of straw in the cart, with a naked child lying on it. It was Marat. He was two and he was dead; one of his eyes was closed and the other was missing altogether. She couldn't believe that he'd died completely and couldn't be brought back to life. She looked to see if there was anybody there, and again she saw Stalin. Now he was wearing a white coat with a stethoscope slung around his neck. "Comrade Stalin," she said, "see how I suffer! My son has died and my husband perished heroically for the motherland." "I'll help you," said Stalin, and, setting his stethoscope against her chest, he began to sing: "La donna è mobile . . ." And the moment he began to sing, her husband, Andrei Revkin, touched the wires together and the dive-bombers came roaring out of the black clouds toward the ground. Bombs rained down and began exploding with a blinding brilliance and a terrible cracking noise, like canvas tearing.

Aglaya realized that this was all a dream; she only had to wake up and it would all go away. By a monstrous effort of will she forced her eyes open and saw that reality was even more terrible than her dream. There was flashing, rumbling, whistling and crackling outside the window. The oil depot was blazing, a tall pine tree burned as it fell, and a power-line pole did the same. The wires gave off showers of colored sparks as they touched, the television screen was lit up and the television was on fire. The glass from all the windows came hurtling into the apartment and spread itself across the floor in a glittering kaleidoscope, and Stalin—not the live one, the iron one—stood there amid the elemental chaos, rocking from side to side and singing "La donna è mobile." He was trembling as he swayed; she could see he was desperate to move but he couldn't— some force was holding him back. He couldn't break free of the force, and he was hoping to overpower it with his song "La donna è mobile." "La donna è mobile," he sang yet again, and his efforts seemed to produce a response. There was a sudden rumbling and crashing, the light flashed in her eyes more brightly than before and the house began swaying. Stalin began to move, heading straight toward Aglaya, together with the metal sheet to which he was welded. He came waddling toward her, trampling the glass shards so that they crunched and jangled, sending showers of white crystal spray flying in every direction. And he kept advancing stubbornly, menacingly, implacably. Suddenly realizing that he was coming to her to take her as a woman, Aglaya was inflamed by an insane reciprocal passion. She raised herself up on her pillow, opened her skinny arms and legs wide and said quietly but passionately: "Come to me! Come quickly, come, come to me!" And he was coming to her, swaying and shuddering in an insatiable fever fed by some demonic force raging within him. He kept coming. Pieces of glass flew into his face, the light dazzled his eyes and they spouted streams of fire as though he were trying to see Aglaya with them. "Come to me, my darling! Come to me, my little boy!" she entreated him. At the edge of her bed he stopped, as if struck by doubts. He even swayed so far backward that he almost fell flat. The back of his iron head almost touched the floor, but some mysterious force halted him, lifted him, set him upright, tossed him up toward the ceiling and dropped him on his feet. He began trembling again, and with a cry of "La donna è mobil-e!" he collapsed onto Aglaya, and she received him with every inch of her spread-eagled body.

The song went on, explosions thundered, glass jangled and broke, the floor beams were warping, breaking and rattling against each other and there was a crunching sound inside Aglaya. She didn't realize it was her own bones shattering.

"A-agh!" she howled as she experienced that incomparable, tempestuous feeling more acutely than anyone had ever experienced it before.

And a flame shot out of her chest.

106

They say the locals had never seen a storm like it during the winter. They'd never seen one like it in any other season either. The lightning strikes, gusts of wind and the tornado smashed, burned, demolished, crushed and tore to shreds everything in their path. The power station, oil-

depot and motor depot were destroyed by fire. The flour-milling combine simply fell to pieces. But witnesses who saw the house where Aglaya
lived burn and explode could find no words to describe the spectacle.
Some of them who tried began like this: "Well, it was, you know, it was,
you know . . ." and then lapsed into a silence expressing wonderment and
awe. Of course, it was clear to everyone that this was not just a fire, and
not just an explosion, and not just several explosions, but something
much bigger.

After the explosion all sorts of experts came to Dolgov from the
regional center and from Moscow; they collected fragments and scraps in
polyethylene bags and took them away. All sorts of explanations were put
forward. Some of them really wild. Even including the idea that there had
been an earthquake. In our part of the world, which is so seismically sta-
ble! Then they started looking for clues to a Chechen connection. It was
only after they'd run through all the most unlikely conjectures that they
remembered about Fireworks Inc. and finally decided that the most plau-
sible explanation of the initial explosion was a lightning discharge. The
strike had been interpreted by one of Vanka's devices as a remote control
radio signal. The first device had exploded, triggering a chain reaction:
bombs, mines, grenades, slabs of TNT, sacks of nitrate, boxes of dynamite,
the gas-collector cylinders. The semibasement had been aptly named Little Hiroshima.

To give them their due, the firemen arrived in good time. And they
unrolled their hoses just like they're supposed to. But at the last second
it was discovered that the water in the tank had frozen (water in fire-
engine tanks has a habit of freezing in temperatures above the freezing
point), that in some places the hoses were frayed and punctured and the
pump wasn't working anyway. And so the firemen simply ran around the
flames, which were reflected in their shiny helmets, and used gaffs to drag
out charred chunks of anything that tumbled out of the fire. Beams, rafters,
parts of doors, tables and chairs. Along with all these objects another
charred, elongated item came flying out, looking something like a log.
The firemen pulled it clear with their gaffs and only then discovered that
it wasn't a log but a body, still alive, with the vestiges of arms and legs.
And then of course, the entire emergency ambulance team went dashing
to this living cinder, which was gurgling as though it was still saying something even as it burned. Doctor Sinelnikov put his ear to the hole that was

once a mouth and through the gurgling he made out the words: "He was right: he said there'd be dancing on our street ag—"

And with a final shudder the charred body fell silent.

Everything else organic that had been in the house was burned away, and the iron melted. The statue, melted on every side, was transformed into a fused, shapeless ingot. There was nothing at all left of any living beings, including Shurochka the Idiot, apart from the smell of burning flesh and fur. Many people, of course, recalled Shurochka the Idiot and her various predictions, including the one that iron birds would fly and a dead person would fall on a living one. In hindsight many even endowed Shurochka with exceptional prophetic powers, but she didn't possess any powers; she simply spoke whatever nonsense entered her fevered mind, like the celebrated Nostradamus. And naturally, there were some individuals inclined toward mysticism who reinterpreted Shurochka's ravings, threw out what they couldn't use and then embellished what they could and adapted it to real events as if they were the very ones that their prophetess had been thinking of.

Of course, nothing was left of Vanka Zhukov or his guests, apart from the charred remains of a plastic leg with leather fastenings that was discovered two blocks away from the scene. The surface of this remnant was covered all over with letters of the Western alphabet, chemical formulas, e-mail addresses, numerals and the phrase, written in large Russian letters: "Revenge for Afghanistan!"

EPILOGUE

It was early summer by the time I arrived in Dolgov. And I could see immediately how much here had changed for the better and how much had remained the same as it was before. The old women on the platform were still offering their goods to the passengers, but now they had a wider range. Not only were there boiled potatoes and pickled cucumbers, but also meat pasties, beer and Coca-Cola. And in addition to the edible products there were printed goods, mostly of one particular orientation, such as the magazines *Playboy* and *Penthouse* and a brochure—*Sex Technique for the Middle-Aged*—with various recommendations, tables and diagrams.

On the platform, which was very clean, there were several kiosks trading in ice cream, chewing gum, hamburgers, cheeseburgers, hot dogs, Snickers and sneakers, matryoshka dolls with the faces of eminent politicians, army-uniform peaked caps, belts, badges and military insignia, house slippers, spectacles, mohair wool and every sort of trifle imaginable. During my absence the town had clearly been integrated into global civilization, as testified, for instance, by the notice in English for foreigners passing through: THE PAY TOILET IS BEHIND A CORNER. THE PRICE IS UPON AN AGREEMENT—meaning it had to be defined by contract. And across the other side, in the little square in front of the monument to Lenin (Vladimir Ilich is still sitting there, covered in thick mold, to this very day), I also came upon the following warning notice: DO NOT TEAR FLOWERS OUT! DO NOT WALK ON THE GRASS!

Although I had been a close witness and a participant in everything that had taken place over the previous fifteen years in Russia, Dolgov seemed a rather strange town even to me. An unnatural mixture of features from the old life and the new. The same old twisting streets with the same names: Lenin Street, Soviet Street, Marxist Street, Alexei Stakhanov Street, 22nd CPSU Congress Street, and in among them Crooked Street, Transversal Post Office Street, Monastery Street, Cathedral Street. I found Komsomol Cul-de-Sac easily, and the spot where Aglaya's house had stood. The neighboring houses had clearly also been demolished, and several buildings that were too grand for a simple district-level town had sprung up in their place. Six-story blocks faced with granite, with big windows and blue spruces at the central entrance to what had to be the main building, with its four columns. The entire lot was fenced off by tall metal railings with gold tips, gates that closed automatically and guards. A sign hanging on the gates read DOLGOV MINERAL WATERS BALNEOLOGICAL COMPLEX. There was a whole collection of expensive foreign cars standing in the parking lot inside. I asked the gatekeeper what kind of complex it was. He told me it was a private hydropathic clinic for very rich people.

"For New Russians?" I asked.

"For foreigners too," he said. "Turns out the chemical composition of our water's no worse than at Karlsbad, and the treatment may be expensive, but it's still cheaper than it is there. And we sell water for drinking. Right across Russia. Even in Moscow."

And who does all this belong to?" I asked.

"Who else?" he said. "Felix Filippovich Bulkin.

"Bulkin?" I asked. "You mean he built all this?"

"And not only this. He founded a new church too. He bought the nightclub and the casino, opened two restaurants and two supermarkets. He's a rich man. See that children's playground over there? He gave that to the city. He supports the home for the aged with his own money."

"So he's the local oligarch then?" I said.

"Something of the sort," the guard agreed.

The children's playground was no different from millions of others, except perhaps for the poster with a black witch who looked like she was from the Caucasus stuffing a fair-haired child into a sack and the appeal: PARENTS! BEWARE OF KIDNAPPING! Beyond it began a long, high concrete wall, and beyond that I glimpsed an architectural miracle—a red-brick palace with four towers. A bit like the Petrovsky Castle in Moscow.

I asked a middle-aged woman walking by with a cat whose castle it was.

"Plague's," she said.

"What, does he live here?"

"No, but he comes here. He lives in Moscow."

After that I saw the cement works and the gas station and a few other things, and, according to the local residents, all of it belonged to Plague. Some of them spoke about him with indifference, others with respect and still others with great dislike.

The Avenue of Glory reminded me of Moscow's New Maiden Convent Cemetery in miniature. Among the graves of former times, overgrown with tall weeds, and the luxurious monuments to the new criminal bosses, it took me a while to spot the modest grave with the granite slab which had evidently replaced the stone that had previously lain there. Traced out on it in gold were the dates and the names of Andrei Eremeevich Revkin, perished heroically, and his widow Aglaya Stepanovna, perished tragically. A little lower were the words: TO MY PARENTS, NEVER TO BE FORGOTTEN, FROM THEIR SON MARAT.

I stood for a moment immersed in thoughts of the impermanence of life and then walked on. A lot had changed in Dolgov, but the pedestal in the middle of Victory Square was still in the same place, as if they were keeping it in case it might be needed. Not just as if, in fact. They really hadn't destroyed it because, as I discovered later, local minds were constantly generating ever-new projects for installing on the pedestal, if not actually Stalin, then someone whom they wished to bring closer to the people, or rather, someone to whom they wished to bring the people closer. In various years the individuals envisaged for this role included Marshal Zhukov, the academician Sakharov, the writer Solzhenitsyn, Pyotr Stolypin and Nicholas II. And Felix Bulkin even had the brass balls to hope that for really big money he could see himself immortalized here as a symbol of the new age, when the world was not ruled by political leaders and military commanders, but by businessmen. The district legislators had enough wit and courage to summon up a majority (of one vote) and reject Bulkin's proposal, but nonetheless the people had no doubt that pretty soon somebody was bound to be hoisted up there. But who? No answer was forthcoming to that question, but the plot of ground around the pedestal was tended and planted with marguerites and the low openwork fence was freshly painted.

After standing there for a while thinking senseless thoughts about nothing much in particular, I looked at my watch, decided it was time for lunch and set out for the hotel restaurant. But along the way I was destined to meet someone I thought I would never see alive again. As I was walking past a two-story building behind a green wooden fence, first I noticed the sign that said OLD FOLK SCARE HOME in which the shifting of the "s" to transform "care" into "scare" seemed to me somehow symbolic. And then I spotted this old man—fleshy, a big head with the fluffy remnants of gray hair protruding in all directions, sitting in a wheelchair wrapped up in a woolen rug and holding his glasses in his left hand as he read a book. I recognized him immediately and went running over.

"Admiral!" I exclaimed in joy. "Is that really you?"

"Ah, it's you!" he quavered affirmatively, not interrogatively. "Surprised I'm still alive? Don't be. Sickly organisms live a long time. Because they don't burn up, they just smolder."

Not only, it seemed, was he alive, he was perfectly lucid and he remembered everything. He asked me not to be surprised at that either.

"I've been a thinking reed all my life. People fall into dotage because their brains stagnate. But I've been thinking about something, and that's kept the blood flowing to the brain cells.

We recalled old times, spoke about Aglaya, about Shubkin . . .

"Yes, by the way," I asked, "do you happen to know where he's living? I got a letter from him last year, saying he'd arrived at the true faith—the faith of his ancestors—and he was intending to rework *The Timber Camp* to correspond with his new convictions.

"Unfortunately," the Admiral said with a sigh, "he won't be able to do that now." In response to my look of inquiry he said: "He died of blood poisoning after his circumcision."

We both sighed and felt sad, but what was there to be done? We agreed that Shubkin had lived a long and complicated life and been happier than many, because he had always believed fervently in something.

"What about you?" I asked the Admiral. "Have you taken up religion, or are you still an atheist?"

"I haven't taken anything up and I haven't dropped anything. I don't believe that God exists and I don't believe that he doesn't."

"How's that?" I asked in surprise. "If you don't believe in one then you have to believe in the other."

"I don't have to do anything," he said stubbornly. "I simply don't see any proofs of the existence of God and I don't see any proofs of his nonexistence. But I do believe in something. I believe in the ineffability of our existence."

"You don't mean that!" I protested. "The way science is developing now, it's inevitable that we'll be able to understand—"

"The more science reveals to us," said the Admiral, interrupting me, "the clearer it becomes that it will never grasp the most important thing of all."

I agreed with a few of the things he said, but I suggested coming back down to earth and asked what he thought of the way people lived in Dolgov nowadays.

"They live the same way they always did," said the Admiral. "If there's something someone can steal, he steals. If there's nothing for someone to steal, then he works. He who works does not eat."

"What about you?" I asked.

"Well, I don't work. Which means someone feeds me. In my case it's our benefactor Mr. Bulkin. He feeds me and he feeds others and he feeds the whole town, and the people joke that if it weren't for the Plague we'd all have died out ages ago."

"Then tell me this, Admiral. Until just recently we lived under a terrible totalitarian regime. We had no freedom. We couldn't read the books we wanted to read, they prevented us from believing in God, they forbade us to criticize the government, tell jokes, listen to foreign radio stations, talk about death, about sex, engage in trade or travel abroad. We voted for candidates from a list of one and everybody dreamed of freedom. And now it's arrived, but we don't like it. And there are many people who want to go back to the old ways and even dream of Stalin. What's the real problem here?"

"I can answer you this way," said the Admiral. "Until recently we were living in a zoo. We all had our own cages. The predators had theirs and the herbivores had theirs. Naturally, all the inmates of the zoo dreamed of freedom and were desperate to escape from their cages. Now they've opened up our cages. We've got our freedom and we've seen that you can pay with your life for the pleasure of running around on the grass. The only ones who are unconditionally better off are the predators, who are now free to eat the rest of us in absolutely unlimited quantities. And now that we've seen this freedom and experienced this fear, we're wondering if it might be better to go back to our cages and put the predators back in theirs as well. They'll still feed them on us, but in regulated amounts. And so we're looking around for . . ."

"For whom?" I asked.

"Well, let's say, a director for the zoo, who'll restore order and put everyone back in their cages, but give us hay and cabbage and, sometimes if we behave ourselves, give us a treat of a carrot or two."

"By the 'director' you mean Stalin?"

"Someone of the kind."

"Will he be a communist?"

"I expect he'll use some other name. But the Scuswu he'll invent for us won't be very much different from the previous one, because there really aren't that many variations. Its basis will be the dream of equal happiness for all. The recipe for how to achieve it is well known: confiscate from the rich, distribute to the poor, chastize the bureaucrats, exterminate your enemies."

"But everybody already knows that's an impossible dream, because—"

"Yes, we all know why. Every individual human being knows it. But individual human beings, when gathered together, are transformed into the people. And the people is a naïve creature, willing to be deceived a thousand times over and then believe again for the thousand and first time."

"But you have to believe not just in something but in someone."

"Good thinking," laughed the Admiral. "But that someone is already on the way. He's already rehearsing his gestures in front of the mirror."

"You even know what he looks like?"

"But of course I do," said the Admiral. "He's modestly dressed. In something semimilitary. Unpretentious in his daily life. Indifferent to objects of material value. Even more so to items of luxury. Not very tall, but stocky, about the same build as you."

"Then perhaps we've already found our man," I said, inspired.

"No," said the Admiral, "you can't play this role. You doubt yourself too much, you speak fast and wave your arms around too much. This man behaves enigmatically, he speaks slowly and softly, but always confidently. His gestures are sparse, but expressive. With a single glance he reduces men to terror and women to a different state, but he's impotent."

"He has to be impotent?"

"Yes, he has to. The man who becomes a genuine idol of the people cannot suffer from any passions and temptations, except for unlimited power over people's bodies and hearts."

"That's some character portrait you draw!"

"The standard portrait," said the Admiral. "The standard portrait of a tyrant. There's not a lot of variety among people of that type."

I hardly slept at all during my last night at the hotel. Or rather, I fell asleep right away. But then I immediately started dreaming about the individual the Admiral had described. He was standing on a pedestal, waving to me and grinning. Grinning to greet me, but his grin filled me with horror and I woke up. After that I was afraid to go to sleep. I tossed and turned, switched the light on. Tried to read something. As I read, I lapsed into a reverie and again he appeared, grinning at me from his pedestal. And when morning was already near, he appeared to me in a form so real that the materialization of this apparition seemed perfectly possible. As I was leaving Dolgov in the morning, my taxi cut straight across Victory Square. There was a thick, swirling fog, and the houses, trees, telephone poles and other large objects concealed within it hove into sight as if they were surfacing from some abyss. The pedestal surfaced in the same way. It was empty, of course. It had to be empty, if only because the time had not yet come for whoever it might be to appear on it. The pedestal was empty, and I, as a realist devoid of the slightest inclination whatever toward any kind of mysticism, was not the one to doubt that it was empty.

Laughing at myself and my nocturnal ravings, I glanced back with the stupid intention of confirming yet again that everything looked the way it should. The pedestal was still visible. Its lower section was wreathed in mist, so that the top appeared to be separated from the ground and floating above it. And then above the pedestal, fashioned out of the foggy vapor and my no-doubt-fevered imagination, a figure took shape. Something human in form. It watched me as I drove away, grinning and waving with its raised right hand.

Vladimir Voinovich is the author of *Pretender to the Throne: The Further Adventures of Private Chonkin*, *The Fur Hat*, *Moscow 2042*, *The Anti-Soviet Soviet Union*, *The Ivankiad* and *In Plain Russian: Stories*. He lives in Munich.

Andrew Bromfield studied Russian at Sussex University and has taught it at university level. He has lived in Russia for long periods, where he cofounded (with Natasha Perova) the journal *Gla*. He is best known for his acclaimed translations of Victor Pelevin and Boris Akunin and now lives in Surrey, England.

A NOTE ON THE TYPE

The text of this book was set in Electra, a typeface designed by
W. A. Dwiggins (1880–1956). This face cannot be classified as
either modern or old style. It is not based on any historical model,
nor does it echo any particular period or style. It avoids the extreme
contrasts between thick and thin elements that mark most modern
faces, and it attempts to give a feeling of fluidity, power, and speed.

Composed by Creative Graphics, Allentown, Pennsylvania
Printed and bound by Berryville Graphics, Berryville, Virginia
Designed by Virginia Tan